Praise for *Th*

"A trilogy like the kind that made me fall in love with fantasy in the first place." —*SF Site*

"An entertaining, old-fashioned adventure." —*Locus*

"Fantastical adventure tales involving witches, warlocks, and dark mysteries in the tradition of Anne McCaffrey and Marion Zimmer Bradley." —*News-Mail Bundaberg* (Australia)

"Stirring epic fantasy . . . harrowing, exciting, and sometimes humorous adventures in a land far, far away . . . a worthy first novel from a writer with a sound streak of both imagination and talent." —*dB Magazine* (Australia)

"Superb . . . a rich, vividly described world peopled with such complex characters . . . twists and turns in unexpected ways." —*Australian SF News*

"Enthralling." —*The Daily Telegraph* (Australia)

"A well-written book with magic, dragons, strange, mystical creatures, and death. An enjoyable read." —*Newcastle Herald* (Australia)

"An excellent read for anyone who enjoys fantasy." —*Hobart Mercury* (Australia)

"A rich fantasy novel with a great cast of characters." —*New Englander-Armidale* (Australia)

"A remarkable fantasy debut." —*The West Australian*

ALSO BY KATE FORSYTH

THE TOWER OF RAVENS

BOOK ONE OF RHIANNON'S RIDE

Kate Forsyth

A ROC BOOK

ROC

Published by New American Library, a division of
Penguin Group (USA) Inc., 375 Hudson Street,
New York, New York 10014, USA
Penguin Group (Canada), 10 Alcorn Avenue, Toronto,
Ontario, M4V 3B2, Canada (a division of Pearson Penguin Canada Inc.)
Penguin Books Ltd., 80 Strand, London WC2R 0RL, England
Penguin Ireland, 25 St. Stephen's Green, Dublin 2,
Ireland (a division of Penguin Books Ltd.)
Penguin Group (Australia), 250 Camberwell Road, Camberwell, Victoria 3124,
Australia (a division of Pearson Australia Group Pty. Ltd.)
Penguin Books India Pvt. Ltd., 11 Community Centre, Panchsheel Park,
New Delhi - 110 017, India
Penguin Group (NZ), cnr Airborne and Rosedale Roads, Albany,
Auckland 1310, New Zealand (a division of Pearson New Zealand Ltd.)
Penguin Books (South Africa) (Pty.) Ltd., 24 Sturdee Avenue,
Rosebank, Johannesburg 2196, South Africa

Penguin Books Ltd., Registered Offices:
80 Strand, London WC2R 0RL, England

First published by Roc, an imprint of New American Library,
a division of Penguin Group (USA) Inc.

First Printing, June 2005
10 9 8 7 6 5 4 3 2 1

Copyright © Kate Forsyth, 2005
All rights reserved

Cover art by Keith Birdsong

 REGISTERED TRADEMARK—MARCA REGISTRADA

Printed in the United States of America

To my three beautiful children,
Benjamin, Timothy, and Eleanor

"[Necromancy] has its name because it works on the bodies of the dead, and gives answers by the ghosts and apparitions of the dead, and subterraneous spirits, alluring them into the carcasses of the dead by certain hellish charms, and infernal invocations, and by deadly sacrifices and wicked oblations."

Francis Barrett,
The Magus, 1801

"Through the Necromancer's magic words, the dust in the decayed coffin takes shape again and rises from a long forgotten past."

Emile Grillot de Givry,
Witchcraft, Magic and Alchemy, 1931

A HORSE OF AIR

"With a heart of furious fancies
wherefore I am commander
With a burning spear
And a horse of air
To the wilderness I wander."

TOM O' BEDLAM,
traditional folksong

Barbreck-by-the-Bridge

The girl crouched on the stone ledge, hugging her cloak of furs and skins close against the bite of the night. Far to the east, where the towering peaks of the mountains broke and fell away, the moons were rising. First the little moon, blue as a bruise, then the big blood-moon, glowing as orange as the leaping flames on the far side of the lake behind her.

She could hear the distant sound of voices and laughter across the ice as the wind shifted, carrying with it a shower of bright sparks. The pale circle of her face sank a little deeper into the dark huddle of her skins. She set her gaze resolutely to the east, where the snow-swollen river ran headlong towards the unknown future, towards freedom and the sea.

Tonight the inexpressible yearning was fierce in her. She could smell the bitter green coming of spring in the air, hear it in the clink of ice upon stone as the lake began to flex and test itself against the chains of winter, feel it all around her in the surge of sap and blood. These first few weeks of the green months were the cruellest of all, for they sang of joy to some-one who had no understanding of the word. She could only sense it, like a deaf child hearing bells ringing all around her as a thrum of air against her skin. She did not know what she yearned for. She did not know why she sat here in the dark loneliness with a hot ache in her throat. She only knew that she could not bear to be with the herd tonight as they gloated over the spoils of their latest hunt, swaggering and boasting and wrestling about the fire while their new captive sat bound and bloodied, trying not to show his fear.

The girl was not driven away from her herd's carousing by any sense of compassion for the prisoner. She had no time to feel or wonder for anyone else. All her pity and terror were saved for herself. She sat on the ledge of stone and set her face to the east, wondering only if she should take the chance to creep away tonight, while the herd was busy carousing. If she ran all night, hiding her scent in the tumult of white water, running on stones so she would leave no footprints, if she ran till her heart was bursting, could she win her way free? The desire to escape was so fierce in her that she could only keep herself still by clenching her fingers so hard she cut purple crescents into her tough, calloused palms. For no matter how fast she ran, no matter how well she hid her tracks, the herd would find her in the end, and they would kill her for wanting to be free.

Below her, something moved. She tensed and looked down at once, for there were many wild and dangerous creatures in these mountains. At first she saw only darkness, but as her eyes adjusted from the brightness of the luminous moons, she began to see a dark shape emerging from the shadows. There was a round rump, the deep curve of a back, the long line of a graceful neck lowered to drink from the river. Beyond she saw the vague shape of more horses, a whole herd of them, moving slowly along the stony bank of the river.

Behind her there was a burst of raucous laughter. The horses flung up their heads. One whickered. Moonlight glinted on the two long, scrolled horns that sprang from each forehead. She caught her breath in surprise. These were no wild ponies, but creatures out of myth and folklore. Whether it was the sound of her gasp, or a sudden shift in the wind that took her scent to the horses' quivering nostrils, she could not know, but suddenly the herd all flung out great shadowy wings and, with a rattle of hooves and a soft defiant whinny, took flight. For a moment she saw their soaring shapes outlined sharply against the red moon, the sound of their wings filling her ears. Then the herd of winged horses was gone, lost in the darkness.

The girl was on her feet, filled with exultation as sharp as thorns. *If I could only catch one,* she thought. *If I could only tame one. Then I could escape. They would never be able to stop me if I flew away on the back of a creature like that.*

She would not even admit the impossibility of such a plan. That she should see the fabled black winged horses on the very night that her need to escape had grown so urgent could hardly be coincidence. Those of her kind were ruled by superstition and omen. They did not believe in coincidences. The girl's brain boiled with ideas. Maybe if she tracked the winged horses to their lair, tried to tame one, make friends with it. She had tamed many a mountain pony that way.

Winged horses were notoriously wild, however, and she knew she did not have much time. The herd was growing tired of waiting for her horns to bud. Many younger girls had the buds of their horns swelling strongly, and had been bleeding at the rise of the full moons for months. Her first blood had come only that day, filling her with sick fear. She had scrubbed away the stain on her clothes with stones and icy water, and stuffed herself with a wad of crushed pine needles and sap so they could not smell her womb-blood and guess her secret.

She did not know how long she could hide the coming of her womanhood. Certainly no longer than a month. Today they had all been distracted by the man who had ridden into their territory and had given them such a splendid chase. Next month she may not be so lucky. The herd had always viewed her with suspicion and disdain, for she had feet instead of hooves, and only two breasts instead of six. If she had grown a proud, strong horn like her mother, or even ten short, stubby ones like her cousin, the other deformities could have been ignored. A satyricorn without a horn was a freak, though, an embarrassment to the entire herd. They would scorn her and challenge her and, in the end, kill her for her lack. Four times already she had seen a hornless one hunted to their death. She knew there would be no mercy.

The girl put her hands up to her head and felt her smooth forehead, running her fingertips back into her hair. Not even the faintest suggestion of a horn. She gave an involuntary sigh, and turned reluctantly to head back to the camp. She had been away too long already. Soon someone would notice she was gone, and snuff the air for her scent. She wanted no-one to notice her tonight, with her skirts still damp from their scrubbing and the womb-blood seeping its way past the plug of pine needles.

She made her way silently round the lake, taking care to leap from stone to stone so as to leave no print in the mud, and then

emerged casually from the bushes as if she had just visited the
latrine and was now seeking her bed again.

The herd's camp was set in a wide clearing on the shore of
the lake, sheltered to the west by a tall bluff. In the centre of the
clearing the bonfire gnawed sullenly at the great log cast down
across its ashes. A charred carcass was impaled upon a spit
above it, its equine shape still recognisable despite the havoc
the herd's knives had made upon its flesh. The sight grieved
her. She had always loved horses and often used to leap onto
the back of one of the wild mountain ponies, galloping it over
the high meadows until at last it stopped trying to throw her off
and submitted to her will. When she was twelve she had taught
one of the shaggy little ponies to come to her whistle. On its
broad back, she had explored all the hills around. It had been
her one great pleasure, galloping along the sweeping green
meadows, as swift as the wind, leaping over fallen logs and
brooks, swimming with it in the lake. In those days she had not
yet dreamt of escape. She had ridden the horse only for pleasure and for the satisfaction of at last being faster than the other
girls in the herd. One-Horn had not approved, however. The
herd had hunted down her friendly, shaggy pony, killed it and
eaten it. She had never forgiven them.

Now, most of the herd was sleeping, worn out from the chase
and too much *tia-tio,* the dark pungent ale they brewed from
pine cones and honey. They lay where they had fallen, some
still clutching their curved cups of bone.

Lying close to the fire, snoring loudly, were four horned men.
Their hairy paunches were huge, and they had a sleek, well-fed
air about them that the lean, muscular women did not share.
Their brows were blunt and heavy, their noses flat and wide
with flaring nostrils. Most had only two small curved horns,
just peeking through their matted curls. One, though, had two
much longer horns that curved up and out of his head in a perfect crescent. He was also the largest, with burly shoulders, a
thick neck and heavy features. As First-Male, he was richly
dressed, wearing a brown woollen kilt, a filthy jerkin, and many
necklaces of bone and semi-precious stones. A golden brooch
in the shape of a running horse was pinned to the jerkin. The
girl knew the clothes and brooch had once belonged to her fa-

ther, a human who had been captured by the herd many years ago. He had died in captivity when she had been only five.

In a stony corner, surrounded on two sides by the high walls of the bluff, lay two men without horns. One was dressed in a rough loincloth and cloak of hide, with very long, grey, matted hair and a straggly beard. He was so thin his ribs stood out against the wrinkled brown skin. He was tied to a stake with a long leash, his ankles hobbled for the night.

The other prisoner was young and fair, with thick curly hair the colour of summer grass. He was dressed in a dishevelled blue jacket over a white shirt and breeches, all much stained with mud and blood. His head slumped forward onto his chest, and congealing blood obscured most of one side of his face. His hands were tied tightly behind his back, and leather straps wrapped his arms and body from shoulder to waist.

Stepping quietly through the sleeping bodies, the girl saw his belongings scattered across the ground. There were the long, black boots, thrown away in disgust when no-one was able to make them fit over their hooves. The pretty painted box that magically played music when opened lay in the ashes, still tinkling away, while the silver goblet with the crystal set in its stem had fallen from One-Horn's hand as she snored by the fired. The blue cockaded hat was still on the head of Seven-Horns, though she slept with her face pressed into the dirt. Hanging around the neck of First-Male was the little golden medal with its intriguing design of a hand radiating rays of light like the sun, while pinned to the fur cloak of Three-Horns was the silver badge cunningly forged in the shape of a charging stag.

The girl noticed all this with perturbation, for it showed who had won the squabbles. It was not a good sign that One-Horn had lost the hat and the brooch, for such spoils of war were marks of power and prestige. Since One-Horn was her mother and had offered her some protection from the scorn of the other women, it was just one more sign to the girl that she must make her escape quickly if she was to survive. Battles for supremacy were to the death, and One-Horn was beginning to lose her speed and aggression. There were many other women eager to take her place as leader of the herd.

The girl's sleeping furs were close to the prisoners, for she was nearly as low in prestige as they were, and not permitted to sleep near the fire. As she stepped past them to reach her bed, she was dismayed when a thin hand suddenly reached out and seized her ankle. She did not make any sound, but she paused and bent as if to pull a thorn from her foot.

"Lassie, this man they've caught, he's a Yeoman o' the Guard," a reedy voice said urgently. "It's treason to waylay him so. Any that lays a hand on the Rìgh's own bodyguard will feel the tug o' the hangman's noose. Ye must let him go!"

"Me no fool," the girl said softly and pulled her ankle out of his grasp, beginning to straighten up. She met the prisoner's eyes. He had lifted his head and was staring at her pleadingly. His eyes were the colour of the lake in summer. He opened his swollen, blood-caked lips and managed to croak, "Please!"

She looked away, shaking her head infinitesimally.

"But he's the Rìgh's own guard! He says he has news he must take to the court—the Rìgh is in dreadful danger."

"So? What that to me?"

"Please!"

She shrugged a shoulder as if shaking away a mosquito and moved on to her bed, curling up with her back to the prisoners, pretending an indifference she did not feel. She could only hope no-one had heard Reamon speaking to her. Few of the herd had ever bothered to learn to speak his strange, lilting language, but One-Horn's daughter had always been an oddity with her soft feet and mobile toes, and her smooth torso. Because she looked so much like a human child, Reamon had looked to her first and sought to make her understand him. It was he who had taught her about the world outside and, once she began to dream of escape, she had learnt hungrily.

"Lassie!"

One-Horn's daughter heard his anguished whisper but drew her smelly furs closer about her, curling up like some small animal, instinctively trying to protect the deep, hidden parts of her body that had betrayed her so bitterly.

She slept badly. Her dreams were stained with blood and shadowed with dark wings. Her mind kept trying to come up with ways to capture a winged horse even while her exhausted body craved unconsciousness. *Nets,* she kept thinking. *Ropes.*

Though I must not injure it . . . they were so beautiful, so free . . .

She came awake at some point in the hours before dawn, suddenly thinking of the saddle and bridle the herd had torn off the horse before cutting its throat. Surely if the prisoner had used such devices to ride his steed, they would help in retaining control of a winged horse? If she could just hide them before anyone woke, the herd might never realise they were gone. The satyricorn were in general rather self-absorbed, and paid little attention to anything outside their immediate concerns of hunting, eating, sleeping and fighting.

At once the girl rolled out of her skins and looked about her. All was quiet and dark. Mist hung across the steep, green hills. It was light enough for her to see the shape of her hands but dark enough that none were stirring. Cautiously she stood up. She saw the saddle lying in the dust to one side of the clearing, near the limp, discarded boots, but there was no sign of the bridle.

Swiftly she bent and picked the saddle up, settling it on her arm. It had a long, dangling girth and two small saddlebags hanging on either side. Many of the prisoner's belongings lay spilled out from the bags, as the herd had only taken those things they perceived to be of value. She stuffed everything back into the saddlebags, managing to work out how to fasten the buckles so they would not spill out again. There was a blue saddlecloth nearby, embroidered with gold. She picked that up as well, and then seized the boots on impulse. She knew well how much harder it was for her to run with her soft-fleshed feet. The boots could be of use.

As she hurried into the shelter of the forest, she cast a quick glance behind to make sure no-one was watching. The sight of the prisoner's intent blue gaze was like a lash across her nerves. It drove her forward, stumbling, hoping she was not betraying herself to danger.

She hid the saddle and boots in a fallen log she knew, and hurried back to the clearing, her pulse hammering with fear. Still no-one stirred, all satiated by the feast of horse meat and pine-cone ale the night before. Only the prisoner was awake, and he was busy sawing the leather that bound his hands against a sharp-edged rock he had somehow managed to prop upright behind him. She watched him for a while from the shelter of the trees. There was quiet desperation in every move he made. She wondered how he thought he could possibly escape, with his horse rounding the bellies of the herd, and blood still leaking from the wound on his temple. He would be better, she knew, to accept his fate and make the best of it, as Reamon had done ten years earlier. Yet she could not help a stirring of empathy. She too was desperate to escape.

Slowly the mist melted away and the sky grew lighter, while she stood there and hesitated, wondering if she should call the alarm. Then she realised the leather straps wrapping his arms were the reins of his bridle. He could never cut himself free in time, yet he could damage the reins given long enough and she did not want that to happen. The bridle could be of use to her.

Quickly she came up behind him. He heard her step and went quiet, every muscle tense. She bent over him, quickly unknotting the leather and unwinding his arms, whispering fiercely, "Quiet, else I cut your throat."

Once he understood that she was freeing him, he said hoarsely, "The Rìgh will be grateful, he'll reward ye . . ."

"What use he to me?" she asked.

"I'll tell him what ye did . . ."

"If ye no' get catched again."

"They will no' catch me!"

"They'd better no'," she said and stood back from him, holding the metal bits of the bridle so they would not betray her by jangling. She did not dare take the time to hide the bridle in the hollow log, thrusting it instead in the bushes and covering it with old leaves. Then she returned hurriedly to her skins, covering her head and trying to control the pounding of her heart. If anyone had seen, or if they guessed! She knew the prisoner had run stumbling towards the lake and had begun to make his faltering way across the thin, uneven ice. She was disappointed in him, if relieved. A drowned man could tell no tales. She heard the crack of ice and a splash a few minutes later and was surprised at how sorry she was.

The sound must have penetrated the drunken mists of some of those that slumbered nearby, for she heard a slow stirring and groaning, and a bad-tempered grumble as someone rolled over and tried to get comfortable again. Under the shelter of her skins the girl held her breath and waited for the sounds to die away. Instead, she heard someone get up and begin to lurch towards the latrine. For a minute or two there was silence and then came the inevitable cry of alarm.

Immediately the camp was in uproar. No matter how bad the hangover, a satyricorn would never allow a handsome young man to escape. Boys were rarely born to satyricorns and so were very highly prized. Once their horns grew, showing they were old enough to mate, their favours had to be shared among the many women of the herd, which led to many quarrels. It also, in time, led to the birth of weak and deformed babies. The satyricorns were therefore always eager to mate with males not of blood-kin.

Once, when there had been many herds of satyricorns in the mountains and forests, boy children had been exchanged between the herds. With few satyricorns left now, the males of the species were more respected and esteemed than ever. There were only a few of them, though, and the herd needed to raise children that were not too closely related to each other if they were to survive. Consequently, the women were always looking for men of other races with which to mate. There were few contenders for this honour. Ogres sufficed at times, though they were so ugly there was no pleasure to be had in the act, and the birthing of a half-ogre child was always painful and difficult due to their enormous size. Occasionally a seelie or Celestine was seized in a raid into the forest, but they never thrived in captivity. The herd would be lucky if they sired a child or two before they wasted away.

Most sought after of all were the horned men of the snowy heights, for they were lusty and strong and their children rarely failed to grow horns as they reached maturity. But the Children of the White Gods were fierce warriors, and it was very difficult to capture them or to keep them once they were caught, and so the satyricorn women would only seek to seize one in desperate circumstances.

A human male, however, was considered a fine prize. They often lived in captivity for many years and fathered many children, and usually they brought forged metal weapons and tools with them which the herd found very useful. Once it had been easy to catch a human male, but now they rarely rode alone into satyricorn territory. To have a young, strong, comely man come galloping through their valley had been the best thing that had happened to the herd in many years and no-one would allow him to escape easily.

One-Horn's daughter was dragged out of her skins by the hair, her mother screaming, "Why you not hear? Where he gone?"

"Me sleep," she responded, in the harsh, gutteral language of the satyricorns. "Me hear nothing. No-one hear nothing."

Her mother dropped her and ran down the beach, her nostrils flaring wide as she snuffed the air, her eyes darting over the ground. "Here! And here! He run here! In water."

Everyone howled in dismay. Satyricorns hated water. It confused their senses and none of the herd could swim.

Beyond the lake, the river ran fast over sharp rocks. A shout went up as the man's head broke through the foam. He had flung one arm over a branch and was being swept along at breakneck speed.

One-Horn shrieked: "Hunt!"

Quickly the women of the herd seized their weapons and began to run, circling round either side of the lake. Most had rough clubs of stone lashed to wood; one or two had metal-forged daggers which had once belonged to Reamon or other past prisoners. One-Horn's daughter hesitated for only a moment. She bent and picked up the curved bow that was her only legacy of her unknown father. He had not lived long enough to teach his daughter how to use the bow, but Reamon had had some knowledge of the weapon, enough to teach her the rudimentary skills. The rest she had taught herself, in the lonely meadows and forests around the lake, hewing herself arrows with the steel blade she had won gambling. Most of the girl's few possessions had been won gambling, for in feats of strength and speed she would always be the loser.

Fast as deer, the satyricorns leapt through the trees, howling and shouting with excitement. There were fourteen of them, led by the woman with the rapier horn, and they all carried crude weapons—clubs and stone axes and slingshots. Not one of the satyricorns was the same. Some had antlers like a stag, others thin twisting horns. One had ten stumpy horns like a goat's all over her head; another had two long, outward curving horns above her ears and two small, curving horns above her eyebrows; yet another had three sets of down-curving tusks framing her face.

They had all discarded their long hide cloaks, some running naked, some wearing short skirts of animal skins. All of them were tall and muscular, with a ridge of coarse, wiry hair running down their backs and ending in a long, tufted tail. Necklaces of bones and teeth bounced on their six bare breasts. Their hooves rattled on the rocks and their bloodcurdling shrieks echoed round the valley. The girl ran after them, though the sharp stones cut her bare feet. She dared not fall too far behind, for that would draw attention to her, and might make them suspect she felt sympathy for the escaped prisoner. It was hard to keep up, though, for the satyricorn women were long-legged and swift.

The river began to force its way down the hill in a series of gushing rapids. They saw the man's head go under again and again, but he clung valiantly to his branch, fending himself off the rocks with his free arm. The branch spun round and round and at times was completely submerged. The river was swollen with melting snow, and running so fast the satyricorn were unable to keep up. They howled with rage and frustration, some coming to a halt on the ridge so they could shake their weapons. The girl came up behind them, panting, holding her side, her feet bruised and cut. For a moment she thought the prisoner was actually going to make it.

Then One-Horn took a dramatic flying leap down the ridge, landing on all fours on the pebbly shore below. With that one leap, she had cut across the curve of the river and got ahead of the man. She seized the end of a fallen log and heaved it into the water with one of the spectacular feats of strength that had won her the leadership of the herd. The effort obviously cost her. She rested her arms on her knees, her head hanging.

The man in the water tried desperately to swim round the obstacle, but the momentum of the river was too strong. It swept him up hard against the fallen log and pinned him there. One-

Horn drew her dagger and walked out along the log, bending down to seize the man's hair and twist his face up towards her. One-Horn's daughter could only watch, struggling to catch her breath. She felt an odd mixture of regret and relief. At least knowledge of her treachery would die with him.

But One-Horn only menaced the escaped prisoner with her knife, before dragging the sodden, exhausted man out of the water. He was too valuable to kill. The girl's heart sank. Her mother would find out how he had escaped. The prisoner may not mean to betray her, but in the end, he would. Even a guilty glance at her would fire her mother's suspicions. She gripped her bow with shaking fingers and wondered if she dared kill him, to keep her secret safe. She dared not. One-Horn would kill her for snatching away her prey. They would suspect . . .

One-Horn was hauling the man along the log to the beach. Suddenly he spun and kicked out with one foot, sending her dagger flying out of her hand and into the river. Then he slammed his foot into the back of her knee, sending One-Horn to the ground. Before anyone had time to react, he was kneeling on her back, his arm about her throat, bending her spine to breaking point.

Time seemed to slow. The satyricorn were leaping up and down on the ridge, howling and throwing rocks and spears, all of which clattered harmlessly on the stones below. One-Horn was fighting for breath, trying desperately to wrench the man's arm away from her throat. He was too strong. Any moment now he would snap her spine and she would be dead.

The girl fitted an arrow to her bow and lifted it. It seemed she gazed along the line of her arrow forever, its point aimed directly at the prisoner's straining back. For a moment she teetered on that moment of decision, seeing with a strange anguish all the possible ramifications of letting the arrow fly. The prisoner would be dead but her mother would be alive and perhaps even grateful. Her own prestige among the herd would be immeasurably enhanced. She would be able to add the prisoner's teeth and fingerbone to the necklace that hung down between her breasts, and she could claim with impunity whatever of his belongings she cared for. Secretly she would be sorry, though. He was young and fair and he had fought well for his freedom.

She let the string go. With a twang that caused her nerves to jolt, the arrow leapt free. She watched its pure and perfect arc, flying out from her taut bowstring, down, down, down through the clear morning air and deep into the back of the prisoner. He jerked upright, crying aloud, and then he fell. The girl stepped back, feeling sudden inexplicable nausea rising in her throat. Beside her, the satyricorns howled with blood-lust and the pleasure of the kill. On the beach below, One-Horn thrust the man's dead body away from her and leapt to her feet, her face twisted in a snarl of fury. She kicked the fallen body and then turned and looked up at her daughter. Begrudgingly she lifted one fist in acknowledgement.

One-Horn's daughter had to clench her hands together to hide their shaking. The herd was slapping her on the back, congratulating her for a fine shot, teasing her for stealing such a fine prize from her mother. They all bounded down along the curve of the ridge and onto the beach, where they hailed One-Horn with malicious glee.

"Why kill him?" One-Horn demanded furiously. "No use dead. Can't mate a dead man. I would have thrown him off."

"He too strong, he got you good," Five-Horns chortled. "You dead but for daughter. You owe daughter blood-debt. Kiss her feet."

"No kiss anyone's feet," One-Horn snarled. She cast her daughter a look of seething dislike and kicked the young man over so he lay on his back with his arms askew, staring blankly at the sky. The arrow protruded through his breast, clotted with blood. One-Horn's daughter averted her gaze.

But then Five-Horns began to rip off the man's clothes, and One-Horn angrily seized his other arm, shouting, "Get off, he's mine!" The girl saw that she would lose everything if she was not careful. She wanted his clothes. They were beautiful, blue as the sky and white and soft as clouds. They would be warmer than her rough uncured skins, and would not smell so bad. Besides, if she followed the river east as she planned she would no doubt come in contact with other men and it would be best if she did not draw too much attention to herself. The man's clothes would be camouflage. So she lifted her dagger and leapt between One-Horn and Five-Horns, saying angrily, "Get off! Me kill him, he mine."

The two horned women looked at her in rage and surprise. One-Horn made a move as if to strike her daughter but the girl thrust her away, staring up into her mother's yellow eyes.

"Blood-right," Seven-Horns said. "She kill him, he hers."

Five-Horns began to laugh. She stepped back mockingly. "All yours, No-Horn."

The name was an insult, but One-Horn's daughter could do nothing about it. Like a child, she had no horns and so the name was warranted. Besides, she had no desire to challenge Five-Horns to a duel, for the other woman was almost a foot taller and very strong. She swallowed the insult and bent to strip the man, trying not to let her fingers touch his clammy skin. She could not understand her revulsion and hoped no-one else would notice it. She had killed before, but never a creature that walked on two legs as she did, and spoke to her in a language she could understand. It seemed to make a difference.

It took a while to strip him naked, for he was heavy and his clothes were drenched. Then she had to cut off his finger and hack out his teeth, a task which made her feel utterly sick and wretched. By the time she had finished, the rest of the herd had lost interest and had headed back to the camp. She did not know what to do with the body. It seemed wrong to leave him lying on the stones for the wolves and eagles to feast upon, so after a moment of indecision and anxiety she heaved him up and slid his body into the river. Then, she toiled back up the hillside to the camp.

There One-Horn's daughter arrogantly demanded the return of all the dead man's belongings: the blue hat, the stag brooch and silver goblet, the golden medal, the music-box, the silver dagger he wore at his belt and the little black dagger he had worn inside his boot, and the warm hooded cloak, blue on one side, grey on the other. Angrily they were relinquished to her, for she had the blood-right and this was one law sacred to the satyricorn. She washed the white shirt and did her clumsy best to sew up the jagged rent, front and back, where her arrow had torn through the material. She sponged the blood and mud from the coat and breeches, then discarded her own smelly hides to dress herself in the dead man's clothes. Everything fitted her well, for she was as tall as the prisoner had been. She enjoyed the feel of the soft clothes against her skin.

She dusted off the soles of her filthy feet and pulled on the stockings and boots, slipped the double-edged black knife into its sheath inside the left boot, and twisted the tangled mass of her hair into a knot at the base of her neck. Then she pulled the cockaded blue hat onto her head, and strapped the silver dagger to her belt, feeling stronger and prouder than she had ever felt before. She wished she could look at herself. Was she as handsome as he had been, the young man whose clothes she wore with such satisfaction?

The rest of the day was spent carefully filing holes in his teeth so she could hang them on a thin leather thong around her neck. She already had a fair collection of teeth and bones—mainly those of birds and small mammals, but a few sharp yellow goblin fangs as well. She stripped his finger-bone of skin and flesh and scrubbed it well, then hung it in the centre with the goblin teeth on either side, then the other bones and teeth from the largest to the smallest, finishing with the dead man's twenty small, white teeth. All the while she worked she was aware of Reamon's distress and revulsion but would not let it bother her.

The necklace looked good when she had finished, very full and heavy. She hung it around her neck, conscious of its weight against her skin. It rattled when she moved. She tried to keep her movements smooth, knowing she had aroused a lot of jealousy with her newfound glory. She told herself she would have aroused contempt and scorn instead of jealousy if she had not claimed the clothes and teeth, but the truth was she was enjoying the new respect in the eyes of the other satyricorns. Soon she would be gone. She did not need to fear their envy.

The Black Mare

Many stories of the fabled flying horses were told around the campfire. It was said they could not be tamed, and that any who dared try would be thrown from a great height and killed.

Yet Reamon had once told her that some men of his race had succeeded in taming the golden winged horses of the west, and these men became great princes and warriors. The only way to tame a flying horse, he said, was to stay on its back for a year and a day, without dismounting once. If a rider managed this feat of skill and determination, then the respect of the flying horse was won and it would submit to its rider's will. Few ever succeeded, however, and many died trying.

One-Horn's daughter thought to herself that if a man like Reamon could stay on a winged horse's back for a year and a day, surely she could do it for a mere day or two. Just long enough to escape.

It was her plan to tie herself so firmly to the flying horse it could not throw her off. She thought the horse's response would be to soar as high into the sky as it could. Eventually it must tire and come down to earth, and then she would cut herself free, letting the horse go. She did not care where she found herself, as long as it was many miles away from the herd.

Her big problem was how to capture the winged horse and keep it still and quiet long enough to saddle and bridle it, and to tie herself to the saddle. She had thought of rigging up a trap with a net but was afraid she might break the horse's leg or wings. She knew it was no use leaping from a tree trunk onto its back, because satyricorns had tried that in the past and had only been thrown off.

From the moment she had seen the horse, an idea had been brewing in her brain, but while the herd was still looking at her sideways and keeping track of her movements, she dared not see if the idea might bear fruit. She waited two full weeks, long enough for the herd to begin to forget. During that time she kept up her usual solitary habits, practising her archery in the high meadows, bringing in the occasional fish or bird, sleeping well away from the fire. Eventually the other women stopped spying on her, being too busy with the normal squabbles over the men and the food.

At last One-Horn's daughter felt free to return to her cache in the forest. She chose a chilly, misty evening when the herd was tired after a long day spent hunting, and filled with roast bear and *tia-tio*. Busy with their wrestling and boasting and gambling, they would not notice she had gone. Or so she hoped.

Going by a torturous, labyrinthine route, and taking care to leave no trail, One-Horn's daughter came at last to the hollow log where she had hidden the saddle and saddlebags. She paused there for a long moment, listening, before daring to drag out her prizes. She had brought with her a hot coal wrapped in a pouch of fur. She used it to kindle a fat-dipped reed which she stuck in a knothole, and then she quickly rummaged through the saddlebags.

On the day the herd had hunted down the rider and his horse, he had somehow managed to knock out three of his pursuers before the herd had dragged him down. He had done so from horseback, at a full gallop, and without apparently drawing a weapon. None of the herd had thought to wonder how he had done it, except for One-Horn's daughter. As usual she had been lagging behind the rest of the herd, not having their speed or stamina, and so she had seen the three women fall. While the others had raced on after the horse and rider, One-Horn's daughter had stopped and examined the three fallen women. All three had had a sharp-pronged black thorn sticking out of their skin. She had pulled the thorns out and thrown them away, and all three women had woken some time later, red-eyed and grumpy and complaining of headaches. One-Horn's daughter thought the rider must have had some way of throwing or spit-

ting out the thorn, since he had hit the women at quite a long
distance and with amazing accuracy.

With satisfaction, she found a pouch of black barbs tucked in
the front flap of one of the saddlebags. With them were two
small bottles, one red and one green, and a long blowpipe. Over
the next few days, she was able to establish that barbs anointed
with liquid from the green bottle only knocked their target unconscious, while those doused in the liquid from the red bottle
killed. The girl's plans crystallised.

She began to spend as much time as she dared searching for
the herd of flying horses. Whenever she had a chance, she in-
terrogated Reamon for all he knew about horses in general and
winged horses in particular, although she feared him guessing
her plans. She practised buckling and unbuckling the saddle
and bridle, and whittled herself a quiver full of new arrows. She
kept the blowpipe and pouch of barbs in her pocket, dousing the
tips with the soporific liquid first. Whenever she could, she
practiced using the blowpipe, until she began to have a fair
measure of accuracy.

Having a plan to work towards steadied her and made it easier to deal with the petty unkindness of the other women,
though at times she found it hard to hide her excitement, which
thrilled her blood like pine-cone ale.

One clear fine evening, she was hunting high in the alpine
meadows when she heard the distant neigh of a horse. Her heart
leapt so sharply in her breast that it pained her. She looked
about quickly and saw the herd of black horses galloping along
a far ridge. There were more than a dozen of them, led by a tall,
deep-chested stallion with horns as long as swords springing
from his brow. The mares that followed him were smaller and
daintier, and their horns were not so long, but they were still far
bigger than the wild ponies she was used to.

The girl gazed up at the herd for a long moment, enthralled
by their beauty, but then, as they cantered out of sight behind
the ridge, she dropped the brace of coneys she held and began
to run after them.

She ran till her breath tore in her chest, clutching at the stitch in
her side, bounding over boulders and between trees, tearing her
flesh on brambles and bruising her feet. Her anxiety was acute.

Two and a half weeks had passed since the last time she saw the winged horses, and she dared not lose her chance. As she came leaping and stumbling over the stony edge of the ridge, tears were beginning to blur her vision. She did not think she would be able to bear it if the horses had flown out of sight. She would just keep running, she swore to herself, and take her chances.

The horses were standing together in the meadow, heads bent to graze the sweet new grass. The stallion flung up his head and stared at her, his ears laid flat against his skull, his eyes ringed with white. Then he trumpeted a warning, rearing up on his hind legs before galloping about the herd, biting one mare on the flank when she was too slow to react. Black wings snapped open and the herd leapt up into the air, neighing in alarm. The stallion leapt with them, his wings so vast they blotted out the sun.

The girl flung up one pleading hand, calling silently, *No, wait . . .*

One of the mares turned to look at her, even as it launched itself into the air, tucking its legs up under its chest and belly. The stallion had soared over the ridge and the sky was again full of light, so the girl could see the mare clearly. She was very tall but delicately made, with slender limbs and a small, proud head. The long, scrolled horns were opalescent blue, and more blue flashed at the tip of her sable wings.

The girl dragged out the blowpipe and the pouch of barbs, her fingers shaking so much she sent a spray of thorns cascading out as she fumbled to fit one into the pipe. She lifted the blowpipe to her mouth, struggling to drag oxygen into her lungs. The mare rose into the golden air, black and uncanny as a raven, and the girl expelled the barb with a great rush of air. It sang out into the sunset wind. Then there was no sound but the strong beat of wings. She let her hand drop. Tears rushed down her face. Her chest heaved in a great sob.

Then the surging movement of wing faltered. The mare dropped back down to the ground, the wings furling again along her side, her legs folding beneath her. She turned and collapsed to one side, her finely sculpted head drooping down to the ground. One-Horn's daughter stood there for a moment, frozen between triumphant joy and dread, then ran over and flung herself down beside the mare. She ran her hands along the

drooping neck, down the long slender legs with their feathery
fetlocks, back to the mare's soft velvety nose. The black skin
was warm and silky; breath gusted out of the mare's large, sensitive nostrils and her eye quivered behind the closed lid. Relief
weakened the girl's limbs so she could not move. She bent over
the mare and laid her cheek against its soft skin. The horse's
breath was warm and smelt of grass.

The girl did not linger long. Excitement filled her with new
energy. She did not know how long the soporific would work.
She covered the sleeping horse with her cloak, left her bow and
quiver of arrows on the ground, and began to run back towards
the valley. She did not need to go back to the camp. It was the
saddlebags in the hollow log she wanted, packed with everything she thought she might need. Over the past two weeks she
had prepared carefully, winning a new water-pouch, a whetting-
stone and some tinder and flint in a gambling game. She had
even challenged First-Male to a game of chance and for once
had not allowed him to win, so that she could claim the brooch
of the running horse that had belonged to her father. First-Male
had been very affronted, for no-one ever let him lose, but One-
Horn's daughter had not cared.

It did not take long to retrieve the saddle, bridle and bulging
saddlebags but carrying them back through the forest, up the
steep hills and over the ridge was an exhausting struggle. The
boots were chafing her heels unbearably and her arms began to
ache.

Much to her relief, the winged mare still slept. It was fully
dark now, and the arch of night sky was freshly dusted with
stars. A new anxiety constricted her breathing. Soon the herd
would notice she was gone. Would they wait till morning before they began to hunt, or would they start looking for her
straightaway? Surely she had a few more hours before they
began to track her? Would the horse wake before then, or would
she sleep on till dawn?

One-Horn's daughter began to make ready. It was incredibly
difficult to strap on the saddle in the dark, with the mare lying
down, but at last she managed to push the girth under the
mare's belly with a stick, dragging it through and buckling it
with stiff and unsure fingers. The bridle was no easier. It

seemed to have far too many straps than necessary, and she could not work out how to make the horse open its mouth for the bit. At last she wrenched the mare's jaw open, and the horse stirred and hurrumphed in its sleep, startling the girl so much she had to bite back a shriek. She rolled up the cloak and tied it to the pommel, then slung her bow and quiver of arrows on her back and clambered up into the saddle, gripping the pommel, afraid the horse would wake before she had time to tie herself on properly. The mare slept on, however, and so she was able to lash herself on tightly, using the reins to secure her arms to the horse's neck, and a coil of rope to tie her legs and body to the saddle and stirrups. It was not a comfortable position, but the girl knew her greatest danger was being flung to the ground from high in the air. She would rather endure an aching back and arms, and the cutting off of circulation in her hands and feet, than risk such a fall.

She was tired after her exertions and rested her head on the dark flowing mane, wondering how long she had before the horse woke up or the herd found her. She even drifted off into an uneasy doze for a while, though the throbbing of her shoulder sockets and her wrists kept her from a deeper repose. At times she felt she was falling and would jerk awake, the leather biting into her flesh, only to drift asleep again. Then she heard a sound that brought her wide awake at once. It was the hullabaloo of the hunt. Although the sound was still faint, the girl knew how swift were the satyricorn. She had only a few minutes.

Frantically she began to kick the mare with her heels, and lash her neck with the end of the reins, rocking her body back and forth, urging the horse to wake, to flee. The shouts came closer. She lashed the mare harder. A convulsive shudder ran through the horse's body. She felt the satin-smooth skin ripple and twitch. Then the horse hurrumphed and suddenly jerked up onto its knees. The gril was rocked wildly, banging her chin on the pommel of the saddle and inadvertently biting her tongue as the mare bounded to her feet. She only had time to gasp and blink back tears, before the horse began to buck and rear wildly all round the clearing. One-Horn's daughter was jerked back and forth, up and down, bashing her face on its neck and with-

ers, all the breath knocked out of her. The ropes cut her flesh
cruelly. The horse galloped through the trees, trying to knock
her off against a branch. She clung on grimly, trying to control
her nausea and dizziness, feeling as battered and bruised as if
she was being beaten with a club. One of her knees whammed
so hard into a tree trunk that she thought it had been dislocated.
Her skin was scraped and torn.

Fly, she silently urged the mare. *Fly away from here else they
catch us . . .*

The mare spread her great feathery wings and leapt up into
the air. The girl's stomach flip-flopped and she could not pre-
vent a high-pitched scream from bursting out of her throat. Although it was still night-time, the moons had risen while she
had dozed and the sky was bright with stars. She could see the
dark shapelessness of the forest dropping away below her, incredibly fast, and feel the cold bite of the wind on her face. She
shut her eyes and gripped tight every muscle in her aching arms
and legs, determined not to fall.

As soon as the mare was in the air, the dreadful jolting and
jarring was over. The mare flew smoothly and steadily, higher
and higher. She could feel the smooth working of its muscles
beneath her legs, and hear the rhythmic beat of its long wings.
The sound was somehow soothing and after a while she dared
to open her eyes. They seemed suspended in black fathomless
space, stars all around and nothing below them. She shut her
eyes again with a gasp, and rested her cheek against the horse's
withers. *Don't let me fall,* she thought.

The mare's wings straightened and held steady. They hung
there in the starry sky for an inestimably long moment, hovering. The girl took a deep painful breath and tightened her grip.
Without warning the mare folded back her wings. They began
to fall, hurtling towards the ground. Suddenly her wings
snapped open again and the girl was flung backwards, crying
aloud as the bonds jerked at her wrists and ankles. The mare
neighed in distress as the jerk on the reins bruised her tender
mouth. The girl fell back into the saddle with a painful thump,
catching her breath with tears, and the mare neighed again and
tried to buck. Again and again the mare sought to dislodge her,
but the girl's knots held and she did not fall. So the mare flew

on again, shaking her mane and neighing in distress, occasionally trying to buck off the heavy weight or shake away the hard, foul-tasting metal bit in her mouth.

They flew for an eternity. Then the sun was rising ahead of them, striking the girl's tired eyes like a silver-tipped whip. She shrank back, hiding her face in the flowing black mane. There was no sound but the steady beat of wings and the whistling of the wind. She guessed they were too high to hear birdsong. Without lifting her head she opened her eyes again and looked down past the sleek black shoulder. Below were wisps of rose-tinted clouds. They drifted apart and she could see a thin, shining curve of water winding through green forest. She could not believe how high they were. It hurt her lungs to breathe.

As the day wore on, the black mare grew weary and her attempts to throw the girl off grew feebler. The girl herself was near-fainting with exhaustion and pain. When at last the horse flew down to drink at the river and rest a while, she found she could not free herself. Her skin was so chafed and swollen that the leather reins had sunk deep into her flesh and she could not reach the knife strapped inside her boot, or unbuckle the dagger at her waist. They rested together, the mare lipping at the water, occasionally shuddering as she tried to shake the weight off, and the girl lying with her head resting on her bound arms, her arms and shoulders and knees and ankles throbbing unbearably. The sight of the water tortured her, for she was very thirsty. She tried again to reach the little black knife, but her movement spooked the horse and it shied and bucked. Helplessly she jerked and flopped around, and the horse neighed in terror and took off again, galloping through the forest, using its wings to leap through the underbrush or turn a sharp corner, bashing the girl against trees and rock-faces. One-Horn's daughter cracked her head hard against a stone cliff and felt pain lance down her neck and spine, then away she spun into a deep red, roaring unconsciousness. Time unravelled.

A THING OF BEAUTY

"Such are the horses on which gods
and heroes ride, as represented by
the artist. The majesty of men
themselves is best discovered in the
graceful handling of such animals.
A horse so prancing is indeed a
thing of beauty, a wonder and a
marvel; riveting the gaze of all who
see him."

XENOPHON
On Horsemanship, 431–354 B.C.

Kingarth

L ewen straightened his aching back, pushing the hair out of his eyes with a filthy, sweaty hand, and looked with some satisfaction on the large plot of rich dark earth before him. Although digging over the vegetable patch in preparation for the spring sowing was always hard work, he enjoyed working muscles stiff after the enforced inactivity of the winter, and he loved the smell of the sun-warmed earth.

He looked with keen pleasure across the lawns, through the grey filigree of branches just beginning to swell with flower buds, past pale stars of narcissus to the glimmering water of the loch. The forest lay beyond, green and deep and secret, with the grey, cloud-capped mountains brooding darkly beyond.

The knowledge that he would soon be leaving his parents' farm to travel back to the city only sharpened his acute sense of kinship with the wild, lovely landscape around him. Although he was looking forward to returning to his studies at the Tower of Two Moons, he knew he would miss his family and his home, this little glade of serenity surrounded on all sides by a dark snarl of wilderness.

I'll go out tramping this afternoon, he thought. *Take my dinner and walk up to the waterfall. Mam will understand.*

His mother looked up and smiled. She was a slender woman with eyes as green as the new leaves unfurling on the beech tree and a great mass of twiggy brown hair that was also just beginning to bud with leaves. Her bare feet were broad, brown and gnarled like tree roots.

"Sure, o' course ye can," Lilanthe said. "I'll keep Merry from following ye and teasing ye. I ken it's some peace ye be wanting." She took a deep breath. "Soil smells good." Gracefully she lifted her brown homespun skirt and stepped into the dirt, her toes spreading and digging in. "Mmm, tastes good too."

Lewen grinned. "Merry can sow her seeds now, if she wants."

"Meriel!" Lilanthe called. "Merry! Where are you?"

The branches of an apple tree at the far end of the garden shook violently and a girl dropped down, landing on hands and knees. She was only eleven years old, nine years younger than Lewen, for their mother had trouble carrying children to term. Three had died in her womb between Lewen and Meriel, and one had lived only a scant few hours before failing to take another breath. Their deaths had grieved Lilanthe deeply, and so she treasured this last child of hers all the more, keeping her close to home and teaching Meriel's lessons herself. The little girl was a bright, winsome child, as much at home in the forest as a squirrel, and with a deep connection to all growing things. Like her mother, she was small and slight, with long, twiggy brown hair and green eyes. Around her head darted a tiny nisse, her iridescent wings whirring so fast they were merely a blur of light.

"Here I am, Mam," Meriel sang out.

"Lewen has finish digging over the vegetable patch if you want to start planting," Lilanthe said. "Come and taste the soil, it's delicious!"

Meriel came bounding across the lawn, the nisse swooping ahead of her. When she came to the edge of the dug-over garden bed, she leapt in joyfully, squelching the damp earth between her bare toes. "Yum, it is good," she said. "I'll go get my bags of seeds. Will ye help me, Lewen?"

"No' a chance," he said. "I've done my work for the day. I'm going to have a swim to get all this muck off me. Then I'm going up the waterfall one last time."

"I want to go too!" Meriel cried.

"Nay, it'll be late afore ye finish planting out those seeds, Merry," Lilanthe said firmly. "Ye can go into the forest anytime, but ye ken Nina will be here tomorrow and so this may be Lewen's last chance to go wandering in the forest afore he leaves for Lucescere."

"No, I want to go," Meriel wheedled. "Oh, Lewen, must ye be going without me? Canna ye wait for me? I won't be long, I promise."

"Aye, ye will, young lady. That's our vegetables for the summer ye've got rattling in that box o' yours, and I willna have ye spoil our harvest by being hasty in the planting. Leave Lewen be. He's worked hard this morning while ye were playing about and climbing trees and he deserves a few hours off."

"Oh but Mam . . ."

"No buts about it, missy. Remember, I'm trusting ye to sow the seeds by yourself. Plant too deep or too shallow or too close together, and ye've lost your seed."

"Aye, I ken that, Mam. It's just that it's our last afternoon alone with Lewen. Nina will have a whole caravan o' people with her and then he'll be going away with them and we willna see him again for ages . . ."

"No need to be reminding me, dear heart, I ken." Lilanthe smiled at her and ruffled her wild brown locks. "He'll be home for supper, though, and when ye've finished planting out the seeds ye can come and help me bake something special for him, if ye like."

Meriel agreed begrudgingly. Lewen smiled at her, feeling rather guilty. It was not that he did not enjoy his little sister's company, it was just that she was so full of vitality. He felt a strong desire for quietness and reflection on his last afternoon in the forest.

After he had cleaned his tools and put them away in the barn, he went back through the garden towards the house. It was a very pretty little house, with rose briars climbing over the back porch and a stone shield over the arched front door with a design of a weeping greenberry tree carved upon it. It had been built of the local rough grey stone, but so carefully that all the stones fitted together harmoniously, making sure no draughts could sneak in through gaps and cracks. Its lichen-green roof was very steep, so that the heavy snows of winter would slide off easily, and the windows were all large and paned with glass, so that the rooms were filled with sunshine in the warm, growing months. Long shutters with little heart shapes cut out in rows were now fastened securely back against the walls, but in winter they would be drawn across the windows, protecting the precious glass from hail and sleet, and keeping the warmth of the fire within. The doors and shutters and gables were all painted a soft green and the house was surrounded on all sides by a lovingly tended garden so it looked as if it had grown up from the earth rather than being assembled upon it.

Lewen came through the kitchen garden with its hedges of evergreen rosemary, grinning at Meriel as she knelt in the freshly dug garden beds, carefully planting out her seeds. His mother came out onto the porch, with a satchel of food in her hands and a bundle of clean clothes.

"Here ye are then, laddie. Do no' be late home now, do ye hear? Merry and I will be making ye a special supper for your last night at home. Will ye be home afore dark?"

"I'm just going up to the waterfall, Mam. I'm no' intending to climb auld Hoarfrost."

"Aye, I ken. And I do no' fear ye doing something foolish. It's just . . . och, it's probably naught. Happen it's because I ken ye are leaving soon and I wish to keep ye close. I'm sorry. Ye enjoy your tramp and I'll see ye at supper."

"Aye, sure, Mam. I'll be good, I promise." He smiled at her cheekily, waved a quick goodbye and set off through the garden, rummaging in the satchel to see what she had packed for him. There was fresh baked bread and hard cheese and pickles, a fat wedge of fruitcake and, much to his satisfaction, a corked jar of cold ale.

On the grassy slope by the lake, he stripped off his damp, grimy clothes and plunged into the water, which was icy cold but invigorating. He swam vigorously across the lake to the island, parting the willow fronds to slide into the cool green cavern beneath, as he had done since he was just a boy. He floated there for a moment, but it was far too cold out of the sunshine and so he swum fast back towards the shore. Greatly refreshed, he toweled himself dry and dressed again, buckling his witch's dagger in its accustomed place at his belt and polishing his moonstone ring till it shone. He then followed a narrow green path into the woods, the nisse Kalea soaring swiftly ahead of him, her wings flashing.

It was an ancient forest, and very dark and tangled. Many of the trees had been growing since long before humans came to Eileanan. They ascended into the sky like massive columns, their trunks green and velvety with moss, their branches trail-

ing shawls of fine grey lace. The path climbed past one old
giant whose girth was so vast that a dozen men standing on its
roots would not have been able to touch fingers, no matter how
they stretched out their arms.

It was quiet in the cool gloom, the only sound the occasional
call of a bird or the subtle rustle of some creature in the undergrowth. Lewen walked swiftly, for the sun was already beginning to slant sideways through the tree trunks and it was a hike
of an hour or more to the waterfall.

Kalea came down to perch on his shoulder, taking hold of his
ear and raising herself on tiptoe so she could speak into it.
"Lewen tramp-stamp the green way, the forest way, Lewen sad-
sorrowful?"

Lewen smiled ruefully. The nisse knew him well. He put up
his hand and lifted her off his shoulder, holding her before his
face so he could speak directly to her. Her eyes were the colour
of the green heart of a flame, shining in the gloom like a cat's,
and her face was triangular, with sharp-pointed ears poking
through a mass of wild dark hair.

"I do feel rather sad," he admitted. "I'm going back to
school, ye ken, and although I love the Theurgia and love being
the Rìgh's squire, I still miss ye, and my kin, and the forest."

"Why go? Stay-stop."

"I canna," he answered.

Her eyes blazed with fury. "Canna? Why canna? Canna-
willna."

"I suppose that's true," he said. "I could stay, o' course. But
I want to go to school, and learn; and I'm proud to serve my
Rìgh and hope I'll be knighted after I graduate and happen even
be appointed a Blue Guard like my da was, if I do well
enough . . ."

Kalea reached out her tiny hand and seized his nose, tweak-
ing it so hard tears sprang to his eyes. "Fool-school," she said
scornfully. "More learning-lore here, tree-wise, sky-wise,
stone-wise, water-wise. No learning-lore at fool-school."

Lewen had dropped her the moment she tweaked his nose,
crying out in surprise. Now, as he rubbed it furiously, she hovered before him, her diamond-bright wings whirring.

"That hurt!" he said crossly.

She trilled derisively, showing her fangs, and darted away as he tried to catch her again.

"Canna catch me!" she called and buzzed about his head as exasperatingly as any mosquito. Every now and again she ducked closer to slap or pinch him. "Canna catch me!"

"Stop it, Kalea!" Lewen cried. "What's the matter with ye?"

"No go," she suddenly cried, swooping down to clasp his finger with both arms. "Lewen no go?"

He cupped her gently. "I'll miss ye too, Kalea, indeed I will. But I truly do have to go. I've missed enough school these last few months, and I do no' want to fall behind. I'll come back when I can, though . . ."

Without warning she sunk her sharp fangs into his hand. He yelped and shook her off, lifting his hand to suck at the blood leaking from the little puncture wounds.

"Kalea weep-wail, Kalea sob-snivel," she cried, scrubbing at her eyes with tiny fists. "Lewen go!" And she turned and flew away into the forest, swift and noisy as a hornet. Lewen stared after her, feeling angry and exasperated and a little bit guilty all at the same time. Kalea was the great-great-granddaughter of the nisse Elala whom Lilanthe had once rescued from children in a village square. Lewen's father Niall said that was when he first began to love Lilanthe, seeing her standing alone against a gang of bullies with the poor battered nisse cradled in her hands. Although the garden and forest around the house were infested with the great-great-grandchildren of Elala, Kalea was the youngest and the boldest. She was rarely far from Lewen, having developed an abiding affection for him ever since the time he had scooped her out of a particularly deep puddle one stormy day when she had been little more than a baby. Although nisses were by nature impish and quarrelsome, delighting in spiteful tricks and teasing games, Kalea had never tweaked his nose before, let alone bitten him. It upset him that she had done so now.

As he clambered over great, writhing roots, ducked under tangled vines, and slid down a slippery slope with the satchel bouncing on his back, Lewen's thoughts returned to the journey ahead of him. He had spent the last four years studying at the Theurgia and he loved it, but he did find the noise and crowds burdensome, and his duties as one of the Rìgh's squires took up a great deal of his spare time. He was so eager to be chosen as one of the Rìgh's personal bodyguards that he took his court duties very seriously, and by the end of the last term had been exhausted in both body and mind. The Keybearer of the Coven had noticed, even if the Rìgh had not. So she had sent him home for the winter holidays. He had not been home to Kingarth since his sixteenth birthday, when he had sat the Second Test of Powers and had been accepted into the Theurgia as an apprentice-witch. Four long years spent in the midst of two hundred other apprentices, all jostling for attention, all noisy and opinionated, all hungry to prove their powers. No wonder he had been exhausted.

In the morning, the journeywitch Nina the Nightingale would be coming by the farm, so that Lewen could join her caravan of new apprentices on its way to the Theurgia. Journeywitches were a specially chosen band of witches who spent their days travelling around Eileanan looking for children with magical powers, and persuading their parents to send them to the Theurgia to be properly trained. They also performed rites for any village they passed that did not have a witch of its own.

Lewen could have easily ridden down to Ravenscraig, the castle of the ruling MacBrann clan, to meet Nina and her cavalcade, but the journeywitch was an old and dear friend of Lilanthe's and did not want to miss the chance to see her and Niall. So she and her band of apprentice-witches were all riding from Ravenscraig to Kingarth, even though the round trip would add a week to their journey.

Kingarth was the last croft before the wild mountains known as the Broken Ring of Dubhslain, which curved in a perfect crescent around the highlands of Ravenshaw. There were only two known paths through the great grim peaks. One path led west, over the exposed, wind-scoured flank of Bald Ben, to the rolling plains of Tìreich where the horse-lairds lived. The other climbed high past Dubhglais, "the black lake," and up the steep, bare ridge of Ben Eyrie, the third highest mountain in Eileanan. Dragons were said to fly over Ben Eyrie, and ogres dwelled in the caves hidden within its cliffs. Although this road was by far the swiftest route to the east, it was considered so perilous that it was only used in times of great danger and need. It was called the Razor's Edge.

Under the shadow of Ben Eyrie was the loch known as Dubhglais, where the Findhorn River had its source. The river wound its way down to a tall waterfall called Hoarfrost's Beard that fell into the valley where Kingarth was built. It then tumbled and fell in swift rapids down the length of the highlands till it came to another steep cliff where it once again fell in a roaring mass of white water called the Findhorn Falls. Ravenscraig was built above these falls, and so for centuries it had been the stronghold of the MacBrann clan, secure against attack. Originally it had been the prionnsa's winter castle, but the family had taken up permanent residence there when their summer castle Rhyssmadill had proven too close to the dangerous and unpredictable sea.

Lewen had been to Ravenscraig many times, and in fact had only recently returned from a trip there with his family. The only thing it had in common with the great city of Lucescere in Rionnagan was that it was built above a waterfall too high for the Fairgean to leap. It was rather a small castle, damp and draughty and filled with dogs. Lucescere, on the other hand, was a vast warren of a place, filled with sorcerers, nobles, merchants, thieves and faeries. The Rìgh had his palace there, protected on either side by two deep, fast rivers. In the grounds of the palace was the Tower of Two Moons, where the Keybearer of the Coven of Witches had her headquarters, and where the most famous school in the land was based.

Although Lewen wanted desperately to be a Yeoman of the Guard, like his father had been, he had ambivalent feelings about Lucescere. He knew his mother had been unhappy there, shunned and mocked because of her faery blood. It was in the gardens of Lucescere that she had been attacked with an axe while sleeping in her tree-shape. Twenty years later she still walked with a limp, and the deep ugly scar still marred her smooth bark.

Although Lewen had not inherited the ability to shapechange into a tree, as his sister had done, he was certainly unhappy if he spent too much time away from the forest. If it had not been for the palace's famous gardens, Lewen would have left the

Theurgia as soon as he got there. Although the gardens were very old and very beautiful, they were tamed and controlled, quite unlike the wild woods of northern Ravenshaw.

When Lewen had first gone to the Theurgia, at the age of sixteen, he had braced himself for the same sort of mockery and disdain his mother had faced, but to his relief his tree-changer ancestry had never been a problem. Either things had changed since Lachlan the Winged had won the throne, or else, as his father had laughingly said, he was simply too big for any of the other students to dare challenge him. Certainly Lewen had inherited his father's build, being a head above six foot tall, and broad across the shoulders. He had been taught to fight too, with fists and feet, dagger and claymore, and to shoot the longbow with uncanny accuracy. The longbowmen of Ravenshaw were famous, and Niall the Bear the most famous of them all. It was said only the Rìgh could bend a longer bow, or shoot as far or as truly, and Lachlan the Winged carried Owein's Bow, an ancient and magical weapon.

The cool, delicate touch of spray across his face roused him from his abstraction. Lewen glanced up, surprised, to see a wide curtain of white water tumbling down a high cliff. It fell sheer and foaming as a curtain of white muslin, the stone behind it dark and glistening. Here and there sunlight struck through the encircling trees and lit the spray as bright as diamonds, but most of the cliff-face and the pool below were in shadow and so the effect was curiously smooth and silent.

Lewen grinned and stretched and swung his satchel off his back. He felt a pleasant euphoric tiredness after his long walk, his exasperation at Kalea's antics having faded away. He pulled out the jar of ale first, uncorked it with his teeth, and took a long swig. After an hour in his rucksack it was not as cool as he would have liked and so he went down to the pool to set it in the icy water while he ate his bread and cheese. He knelt on the damp mossy stones and was just setting the jar securely between two rocks when he heard something that brought him swiftly to his feet.

In the dark underhang of rock by the cliff a horse was lying, its head drooping. Its breath was harsh and laboured, rasping in its throat. Its coat was so black it was hard to make out its shape in the gloom of the deep little dell, but Lewen was able to see at once that someone was draped over its withers. He scrambled over the rocks, his concern growing as he noticed first the yellowish scum that streaked the horse's damp hide, the trembling of its limbs and the twitching of its hide, signs that it had been driven to exhaustion. Then Lewen was close enough to see and recognize the blue jacket and cockaded hat of a Yeoman of the Guard, and he broke into a run. The movement spooked the horse. It shook its head, eyes rolling white in terror, and tried to rise but was too weary, collapsing back to the ground. The attempt to rise had shown Lewen two more, very strange things. The horse had wings, magnificent black feathered wings, each as long as he himself was tall. And the body slumped so heavily over the horse's back had been tied on with rope.

Lewen went forward slowly, holding out one hand, whickering softly under his breath. The horse's ears twitched and it rolled an eye towards him.

"Gently now," he said. "Gently."

Slowly, step by step, Lewen came closer. Again the horse tried to rise and shy away but Lewen reached forward and caught it by the bridle, steadying it. He smoothed one hot, damp shoulder, distressed to see the slobber round the horse's mouth was stained with blood. Gently he eased the bit out of the horse's torn mouth, keeping a firm hand on the bridle as the horse tried to drag its head away, whinnying in distress.

Once he had calmed the horse again, Lewen turned his attention to the unconscious soldier. There was a nasty gash on one temple, with blood drying thick on one pale cheek, and the leather reins had cut deeply into the flesh at the wrists. Although Lewen had his witch's knife sheathed at his belt, he was reluctant to cut the bonds here in the gloom of the spray-misted basin, so far from home. He did not think he could carry the wounded soldier all the way home as well as lead the weary horse, and he knew his parents were the best people to tend both man and horse.

Gently Lewen urged the black mare to rise. He knew it was dangerous to let the horse lie still after such exertion. So he dragged on the cheek-band and pushed at the horse's flank until at last she summoned the energy to stand. He encouraged her to walk the few steps down the slope to the pool. Then, without letting go of the bridle, he reached down to the pool and cupped water in his hand, letting the horse drink from his palm. The poor beast drank thirstily, and would have drunk more if Lewen had not restrained her, knowing too much water could be dangerous in her overheated and weakened state.

Keeping all his movements slow and steady, he rubbed the mare down with a handful of grass, then covered the horse and its unconscious rider as well as he could with the warm woollen cloak tied before the pommel. Then, regretting his jar of ale growing nicely cold in the pool, he began the long, wearisome walk home.

It was fully dark by the time he and the exhausted horse plodded out of the forest and into the orchard by the lake. Both the moons were half-full, and their mingled radiance cast a cool, colourless light across the garden. The trees were all very black, the loch was a strange glimmery silver, and warm orange light streamed from Kingarth across the dark lawn. Lewen lifted his gaze to the light, finding new energy in the closeness of home. He was bone-weary himself. Many times it had only been the strength of his hand on the bridle and his shoulder against the horse's flank that had prevented the mare from foundering. The forest at night was a frightening place, besides, for it rustled and whimpered with mysterious sounds, and occasionally was rent by the howl of the hunter and the death-wail of the hunted. He was glad to have left the nerve-wracking darkness of the forest behind.

Suddenly a huge shape loomed up out of the darkness beside him and he smelt the strong stench of bear. The horse did too, and reared and whinnied in terror, almost wrenching his arm out of its socket.

"Ursa! Back!" he cried.

"Ursa, down," his father said gently. "Go back."

The bear gave a sad-sounding snuffle and lumbered away towards the house.

"What is it, laddie?" Niall said in his deep, soft voice. "Ye're home so late, your mam was worried." He came up out of the shadows, moving quietly for so tall a man. He saw at once the stumbling horse with its heavy burden and his son, trudging wearily at its bridle. "What is this ye've found? A horse?"

"A winged horse," Lewen said.

"Winged? With a thigearn astride?"

"He wears the coat o' a Yeoman."

"Indeed?" Niall's voice rose in interest.

"He's been tied on cruelly tight. I dared not cut him loose; the bonds were too tight and the light too bad. I am afraid though . . ."

"Ye did well, my lad. Bring them to the stables. I'll call Lilanthe. She'll ken what to do."

Lewen knew his mother had learnt her healing arts from Isabeau the Red, who was now Keybearer of the Coven. Lilanthe's knowledge was so deep, she was often called away to help at a difficult birthing, or to splint a shattered bone. His family's trip to Ravenscraig a few weeks earlier had been to help ease the last painful days of the old MacBrann, who had died slowly and with ever-increasing madness.

The final few yards to the stables seemed to take forever, with the horse barely able to put one hoof after another, and Lewen's boots seeming very hot and heavy. At last they were within the dim, hay-smelling vastness, and Niall was kindling lanterns and exclaiming aloud at the sight of the winged mare in the golden fullness of their light.

She was a magnificent beast, even as worn and tired as she was, with great black wings shading through blue to violet at the tips, and long scrolled horns with the iridescence of dark mother-of-pearl. Every curve was beautiful and proud. She was delicately made for such a long-limbed animal, with a luxuriant mane and tail, and feathered hocks. She was so very weary she hardly flinched as Niall drew his dagger and carefully sawed away at the ropes that bound the rider to the beast. At last the ropes frayed and fell away, and they were able to lift the rider down and lay him in the straw and lift the lantern to examine him.

There was a long silence.

"She's a girl," Lewen breathed at last.

"And no' so very auld," Niall said. "What is she doing in the uniform o' a Yeoman?"

"And tied on to the back o' a winged horse?"

"Eà kens! Come, let us leave her for your mam and look to the horse. She's a noble beast and cruelly used. Look at her bleeding mouth."

Niall had been a cavalier for many years and knew just what to do for the exhausted beast. He kept Lewen busy mixing warm mash, applying poultices and anointing the horse's many cuts and abrasions but, despite his fascination with the winged horse, Lewen could not help casting many a glance at the girl lying in the straw. She was so dirty and bloody it was hard to see much of her face, especially with all that black, matted hair straggling all over it, but her figure was tall and lithe with a deep curve from breast to hip, and her mouth had as sweet a shape as any he had seen on a girl. She was beginning to stir as Lilanthe gently bathed her swollen, lacerated wrists, and Lewen stopped to look again as her eyes slowly opened.

They were not black, as he might have expected with all that raven hair, but a clear blue-grey colour, and fringed with very long, dark lashes. For a moment she stared up at Lilanthe blankly, and then she glanced round the dimly lit stable, seeing the winged horse tethered in its stall, and the man and boy cleaning the tack nearby.

With a vicious snarl, the girl was on her feet, knocking Lilanthe over with the violence of her movement. She looked about desperately, seized a pitchfork from its place on the wall and raced at Niall, her lips drawn back from her teeth.

Niall dropped the saddle, holding up both his hands in a pacifying gesture, but the girl only growled and drove the pitchfork towards his heart. Niall lunged forward, caught the handle just below the tines, and wrested it from her. As he flung it away into the straw, she leapt at him with her nails raking at his eyes. He managed to block her with one arm, but he was knocked off balance by the speed of her attack and fell back on to the straw-scattered cobbles, the girl on top of him.

Lewen dropped his polishing rag and leapt to his father's aid.

The Wild Girl

Though he was able to drag the girl off his father, she turned on him, biting the tender skin where his neck met his shoulder. Lewen yelped and shoved her away. She kicked him hard behind the knee and he almost went over. Niall had scrambled to his feet again and caught her from behind but she kicked back with her heel, catching him smartly in the groin. He reeled back for a moment, as much shocked as pained, and the girl then turned on Lewen, grasping a lock of his curly brown hair and pulling so hard she almost ripped it out by the roots. Lewen had to wrap his arm about her throat, trapping one arm to her side, while he held her still against him with the other. She squirmed and wriggled like an eel, and he almost had to throttle her to keep her still.

Niall rubbed his abused private parts ruefully, then took the pitchfork and threw it out the stable door. Lilanthe was trembling and he put one arm around her shoulders to comfort her. "What a wildcat!" he said. "I never thought I'd be tempted to hit a woman before, let alone a wee slip o' a girl."

"She's no' so wee," Lewen panted, having to tighten his hold on the girl as she struggled again to break free. Indeed, she was near as tall as he was, though slim and softly curved. She kicked back savagely with one booted heel and he leapt back, inadvertently loosening his hold. She spun and tried to escape, but Lewen caught her again, holding both her hands in one hand and seizing her waist with the other. "There's no need to fight and squirm so," he said gently. "We mean ye no harm. We're trying to help."

She made a disbelieving noise but, when he tightened his grasp, stopped her desperate struggling, straining away from him, panting and trying to hold back tears. He loosened his bruising grip a little, moving away so she was not held so tightly against him. "There's no need to fear," he said in the same deep, gentle voice he had used to soothe the horse. "Come, ye're sorely hurt. We do no' wish to harm ye any more than ye've already been harmed. Will ye no' sit and rest and let my mother tend ye?"

She looked up at him suspiciously, and he eased his grip and gestured to her to sit back down in the straw. "Your wrists must be sore indeed," he said kindly, "and happen ye're thirsty? Can I get ye some water?"

She moistened her parched lips with the tip of her tongue but did not answer. Carefully he let her go and moved across to the barrel of water, scooping out a cup of water for her. She snatched it from him and scrambled away, then drank thirstily, staring at him through the tangle of filthy black hair.

Lilanthe regarded her with troubled eyes. "She's like a snow-lion cub, all teeth and claws. I wonder where she came from."

"What is your name, lassie?" Niall asked. "And why do ye fight so? What do ye fear?"

She cast him a sideways look, very wary and distrustful, then returned her gaze to Lewen's face.

"What is your name?" Lewen said very gently.

She licked her lips again, her eyes darting from one face to another, then said haltingly, "Lassie."

"Aye, we ken you're a lass, we've eyes in our head," Niall said. "But what is your name? What are ye called?"

"Lassie?" she said again.

Niall and Lewen and Lilanthe exchanged rueful glances.

"Happen she's a wee touched in the head," Niall said.

The girl frowned and, with a puzzled air, lifted a hand to touch her head.

"Nay," Lilanthe said. "I dinna think so. There's intelligence in those fierce blue eyes. I wonder . . . there's something strange about her. I'd say she's a faery child. Or at least, she's has faery blood in her. And we are far from anywhere here. She must have come down out o' the mountains."

"Then what is she doing wearing the uniform o' a Yeoman?" Niall said gruffly.

The girl stared at him uncomprehendingly. He bent and took a fold of her jacket between his fingers, saying, "Where did ye get it? Who does it belong to?"

Immediately she flinched away, scrambling out of reach.

"Nay! Mine!" she cried.

"Yours?" Niall asked, his eyes on the silver stag badge of the Yeomen. "Ye say the clothes are yours?"

She crossed her arms about her protectively. "Mine! No touch."

"Well, she seems to understand what we say well enough," Niall said. He bent towards her. "Lassie? Are ye hungry?"

She nodded her head voraciously, though she sidled back nervously, keeping a fair distance between them.

"Lewen, lad, why do ye no' go and find our guest something to eat? And happen make up a bed for her? She must be sick and weary. We can question her again in the morning. For now let her sleep and recover."

"I'll fill up the bath too," Lilanthe said with a quick smile. "She's filthy."

"Nay!" the girl said emphatically.

"Ye need a bath, my lass. Ye're no' sleeping in my good sheets until I have all that blood and muck off ye."

"Nay!" the girl said again, gripping her hands into fists. She pointed one finger at the winged horse, now drowsily lipping at the bucket of warm mush with a blanket over its back. "Me stay. She mine. Mine!"

"You want to stay here with the horse?" Lewen asked.

She glanced at him and nodded, her expression clearing for a moment. "Mine."

"We do no' seek to take your horse away from ye," Niall said sternly. "Though they say one canna own a winged horse. They canna be tamed with spur and whip, or broken to bridle and saddle, like ye have tried to do." He gestured with one hand to the bridle in the straw where Lewen had dropped it, its bit be-fouled with blood and foam. "A thigearn wins the trust and re-spect of his horse, he does no' bloody its mouth and whip it till it founders."

It was clear she understood his meaning, for a crimson blush swept up her throat and face, and she dropped those disconcertingly luminous eyes. "Dinna mean to hurt," she said haltingly, searching for the right words. "No . . . no other way."

"No other way for what?" Lewen asked. "Ye have ridden a long way. Where have ye come from? Are ye fleeing from someone?"

She shook her head, not looking at him, and made another emphatic gesture. "Go away," she said. "Leave me. Me go. Soon me go."

"But ye are hurt still," Lewen said. "Will ye no' let us tend you, and give ye some food? And your mare? Ye canna mean to ride her anytime soon. She is sick and exhausted, and sorely hurt too."

She looked at him in alarm. "Hurt?"

"She's exhausted," Niall said in cool tones of condemnation. "And her flanks have been flayed cruelly."

The girl flashed him an angry look. "No' me. Thorns."

Niall grinned, his teeth flashing white in his dark bushy beard. "Ye're rather thorny yourself, my prickly lass. Nay, do no' look daggers at me. Ye may stay here in the stable if ye'd prefer. Indeed, somehow I think I'd sleep sounder tonight if ye did. It'd be like trying to cage a snow-lion cub to bring ye into the house. Lewen, lad, will ye go and get her some blankets and something to eat."

Lewen nodded and tried to smother a yawn. He had to admit he was tired and hungry after the long walk through the forest.

As he turned to go, Lilanthe knelt down in the straw beside the girl, reaching for one lacerated wrist. At once the girl snarled at her, baring her teeth like a wolf. Lilanthe started back in alarm. Lewen turned back in sudden concern for his mother.

"Do no' be afraid," Niall said, surprised. "My wife is a healer. She shall no' hurt ye."

The girl glared at them through the matted knots of her hair, her whole body tensed and ready to spring. Lilanthe made a tentative move towards her and the girl lashed out, raking Lilanthe's cheek with her filthy nails. Lilanthe gasped and shrank back, blood beading on her cheek. With a roar of outrage Niall strode forward, drawing his wife into the shelter of his arm with one hand and menacing the wild girl with his other fist. "How dare ye?" he cried. "Leave her be! She was only trying to help."

The girl pressed herself back into the wall, her eyes blackly dilated, her hands held up before her face as if seeking to protect herself from a blow.

"Do no' fear," Lewen said softly, stepping between his furious father and the wild-eyed girl. "No-one here will hurt ye. Ye are safe, I promise ye. Will ye no' let us help ye? We mean ye no harm, there is no need to be afraid."

She lifted her eyes to his face, her hands dropping. He took a few slow steps towards her, repeating his words in a low, gentle voice, and although she leant away from him she did not strike as he dropped to one knee before her. "There, there, ye see? I mean ye no harm. We only want to help. Your poor wrists look so sore. See, the cool water feels good, doesn't it? It'll wash away the dirt and make sure your wounds heal cleanly."

As he spoke, Lewen very gently took one hand and trickled the water over her abused wrist. She crouched very still, not taking her eyes off him. He turned her wrist in his big hand, and blotted it dry with the soft cloth, staining it with streaks of mud and blood. "See, is that no' better? Let me wash the other one too. It must be so sore. Look how much it is swollen. Now let me put some lotion on it. Does that no' feel better?"

She breathed out in a long sigh, and nodded her head.

Then Niall moved, easing Lilanthe away from him so he could examine her scratched cheek. At once the girl shrank back, hands flying up in a protective gesture again.

"Sssh, sssh," Lewen said. "No need to fear. All is well."

Niall sighed in exasperation. "It's your mam who needs the lotion now," he said. "Do ye see how filthy that wildcat's claws are? It's your mam's cheek that'll fester, for sure."

Lilanthe pressed her hand against her cheek. "Nay, I'll be fine," she said faintly. "Lewen, let me do that. Ye're worn out."

"Nay, no' ye," the girl said. "Me no like ye. Ye go away."

Lilanthe was taken aback, and Niall was furious. "Ungrateful brat," he said. "Fine, we'll go away. I hope ye're cold and hungry and your cuts and bruises throb all night."

"Niall, no!" Lilanthe cried.

Lewen protested at the same time. "*Dai-dein*! She's sore hurt and she's afraid. Do no' be angry with her."

Niall sighed. "Fine. Ye stay and tend to her then. She seems to like ye, at least. I'll take your mother back to the house and tend to her. I'll send Merry out with some food for her—"

"Nay, no' Merry," Lilanthe protested at once, looking askance at the filthy, wild-eyed, wild-haired creature crouched in the straw.

"Very well, no' Merry, me," Niall agreed in a long-suffering tone. "I willna be long, lad. Try to keep out o' reach o' those claws. I do no' want anyone else injured tonight."

"All right, Da," Lewen said.

"Make sure ye make up her bed well away from the winged horse," Niall warned. "That mare is as wild as the lass, remember, and though she is quiet enough now, she may no' be so docile once she recovers some o' her energy. A great beast like that can recuperate surprisingly quickly."

"Aye, that I ken," Lewen said, smiling.

"I'll be back in just a wee," his father said. Still cradling the pale and shaken Lilanthe in one arm, he rather reluctantly went out into the darkness.

Lewen turned and looked at the wild-haired girl.

"Come, sit down," he said gently. "I shallna hurt ye, I promise. Ye must be sick and dizzy with that head wound, and aching all over after the ride ye've had. Will ye no' trust me?"

She hesitated, then very gingerly lowered herself back to the floor. "Me do hurt. All over."

"Ye must indeed. Here, let me finish salving your wrists. They're raw and bloody. Those ropes must've been tied very tight."

"Had to be tight. Fall off if no' tight."

"So ye tied them yourself? You tied yourself on the horse?"

After a long frowning moment, she nodded.

He said no more, kneeling in the straw before her and lifting up first one hand, then the other, turning them to examine the lacerated flesh. Her fingernails were torn and jagged and black with dirt, but the hands themselves were slender and long-fingered, with callouses he recognized as being caused by drawing back the string of a bow. He remembered the bow and quiver of roughly hewn arrows that had been tied on to her back, and felt his curiosity grow.

Very gently he applied the soothing cream and bandaged her wrists. Then he gathered up all her hair and swept it over her shoulder, smoothing it away from her brow so he could look at the wound on her temple. She sat quietly, almost as if spellbound, as he washed away the encrusted blood, and anointed the wound with his mother's salve.

"It is no' too bad," he said softly. "Head wounds often bleed a lot. Ye may have a headache for a day or two, but naught more serious. I'll no' bandage it, it's only a scrape and the air will do it good."

She said nothing, just gazed at him with her dark brows drawn together over her eyes, though more in puzzlement than anger. With the mud and blood washed from her face, he was able to see her clearly for the first time. She had a long, thin face with bony temples and a patrician nose. Her cheekbones were so high there were little hollows beneath. Her mouth was soft and full-lipped with a deep indentation in the upper lip. It gave her a vulnerable air, at odds with the strength of the rest of her features. As he stared at her, her mouth quirked and set itself firmly. Lewen looked away quickly.

He moved back a little, taking up one of her feet and lifting an eyebrow in query. She tilted her head, then gave a little shrug and nodded. Gently he drew off the long, leather boots, and took her bare ankle in one hand, examining the bruised and swollen flesh carefully. "The boots were some protection, at least," he said. "Let me wash your feet clean and put some arnica cream on, and then ye'll be more comfortable."

She acquiesced silently. He washed her feet carefully, noting the hard soles and splayed toes of someone who customarily went barefoot, and the new red patches where the boots had rubbed skin not used to confinement. He had just finished massaging in the cream when he sensed someone watching and looked up. His mother stood just beyond the stable door, a pile of blankets in one arm, a basket in the other hand. She was watching them with a grave expression on her face. Lewen flushed but Lilanthe made no comment, limping in and putting her burdens down near her son, who lifted the girl's feet off his lap so that he could turn and reach to pick them up.

"I brought her a nightgown and some blankets," Lilanthe

said with the faintest trace of coolness in her voice. "And there's some vegetable broth, and some new bread, and a slice of the whortleberry pie that Merry and I made this afternoon."

Lewen was hot and uncomfortable in his skin. He found it hard to meet his mother's clear gaze. He busied himself winding up the unused bandages and tidying up the salves while the girl fell upon the soup and bread like a wild animal.

"Your supper is waiting for ye, when ye're ready," Lilanthe said. "Do no' be long, laddie. It's almost time for Merry to go to bed and she's eager to see ye, on your last night home with just us."

Lewen bit his lip in chagrin. "I'll no' be long, Mam. I'll just see her settled."

Lilanthe nodded and shook out some warm blankets, then piled her basket high with her healing salves and bandages. "Sleep well, lassie," she said gently to the girl, who looked up briefly from her soup before lowering her face to the bowl again. "Do no' fear. Ye are safe here. This house and garden are well protected. None will harm ye here."

The girl looked up again, considering Lilanthe for a long moment. Then she nodded in acknowledgement and went back to her meal.

"Ye're welcome," Lilanthe said with gentle irony and went back into the darkness.

"It's usual to say 'thanks' when someone does something for ye," Lewen chided gently.

"Why?" she asked.

He was nonplussed. "It just is. It's good manners. People get upset if ye do no' say thanks."

"Why?"

"They just do. It's rude."

"What rude?"

"Rude is . . . being rude is having bad manners." Lewen was conscious of talking in circles. He made a big effort. "Good manners are like the oil in the clogs of a clock, they keep things running smoothly," he said.

The girl stared at him blankly. Lewen realised she would never have seen a clock before and cast around for some other way to explain.

"Being rude makes ye seem . . . ungrateful. No-one will like doing things for ye. If ye say things like 'please' and 'thank ye' and 'bless ye' and 'may I,' then people will like ye more and like doing things for ye."

"If me say . . . this thing, 'thanks,' then people like me?" she asked incredulously.

"Aye."

"Ye too? Ye like me if me say 'thanks'?"

"Aye, o' course. I mean . . ." Fearing his tongue getting into a tangle again, Lewen came to a halt.

"Then me say thanks," she said.

"Ye're welcome," he said. "That's what you say when people have said thanks."

"Why?" she asked.

"Ye just do," he answered.

The girl absorbed this in silence.

Rather shyly Lewen directed the girl towards the clean clothes. "Would you like to change? And there's a comb for your hair." She stared at it in puzzlement as he held it up for her. He mimed combing his hair, then said, "Though happen your hair is too knotted to comb by yourself. And it needs to be washed."

He imagined himself washing it for her, and colour surged in his cheeks. He went on doggedly, "Tomorrow, happen my mam will help you wash and comb it. Now ye should sleep. Ye are tired."

She had put one hand up to her hair self-consciously. Now she dropped it, nodding and saying, "Aye, me tired. No' much sleep last night." She shook her head wonderingly and crammed another piece of whortleberry pie into her mouth.

"Why no'? Were ye riding the mare all night?"

She jerked her head in affirmation.

"How long? How long were ye on her back?"

She thrugged, then held up two fingers.

"Two days?"

"One day, one night," she answered. "Long time."

"Aye, indeed. I'll leave ye to sleep then, for ye must be tired," Lewen said, handing her the pile of soft blankets. "I hope ye will be warm enough."

She had been fingering the blankets rather dazedly. At his words she looked up at him, wiping her mouth with the back of her hand. Dimples suddenly flashed in her cheeks. She made a gesture that went from the blankets round the shadowy, lantern-lit stable with its straw-filled byres and sleepy, contented animals. "Me never so warm," she answered.

Lewen went back through the cool, moonlit garden to the house, feeling that hot, happy daze one gets from drinking too much ale at Hogmanay. His mind was so full of the girl that he had to stand outside the door in the darkness for a while to clear his head.

When he came into the kitchen, his parents and his sister were already seated at the table, eating their meal. Fires burnt at either end of the room, and candles were lit on the table and mantelpiece, filling the room with a golden glow. Ursa lay on her rug before one of the fires, her enormous bulk blocking most of its heat. She lifted her grey snout and looked at him with worried eyes, moaning a question. Both his parents scrutinised him closely too but he managed not to flush, pulling up his chair to the table and saying in his usual practical way, "She's no' badly hurt, just tired and rather bruised, I think. She'll be grand in the morning. What about the mare, though, *Dai-dein?*"

"'Twas lucky ye found them when ye did," Niall said gravely. "The mare has been ridden hard, and then allowed to founder. She'll be lucky if she does no' take a chill."

"I do no' think she meant to harm the mare in any way," Lewen said eagerly. "Ye ken the stories about winged horses, how difficult they are to tame. The mare would have fought the bit and saddle, and flown high to try and throw her off. She was bruised all over. I'd say the mare tried to knock her off against tree trunks and branches, ye ken the way they do."

"How do ye ken she's bruised all over?" Lilanthe said sharply.

Lewen went red. "I . . . she told me . . ."

"Here, lad, have some soup," Niall said calmly. "Dearling, will ye cut him some bread? He must be starving."

"Aye, that I am," Lewen responded, glad of the diversion. "I managed to eat some of my cheese and bread on the way home, but it dinna even begin to fill the hole."

He began to eat his soup hungrily, and when Lilanthe had cut him some bread he slathered it with butter.

Meriel bounced up and down in her chair with excitement. "But who is she, this girl? Where did she come from? Did she catch the winged horse?"

"I dinna ken," Lilanthe answered, taking her seat again and looking across at her son, raising her eyebrows. "Lewen? Did she tell ye anything while ye were tending her?"

Lewen shrugged. "She said she'd tied herself onto the horse, so I guess that means she caught it. She said she had to tie herself on tight so she would no' fall while the mare was in the air."

Merry gave a sigh of happiness. "Oh, I wish it had been me! Imagine, your own flying horse."

"Thigearns do no' say they *own* their winged horses," Niall said repressively. "It is a friendship, a partnership. They say to win the respect o' a winged horse, a thigearn must ride it for a year and a day without once putting foot to ground. This girl is no thigearn."

"She managed to stay on its back for a night and a day," Lewen said. "That's pretty amazing."

His father regarded him for a moment, then nodded and smiled rather ruefully. "I've done it myself on occasion, and I must admit I thought well o' myself afterwards, and I was no' riding a horse that can fly. She'll be stiff and sore for a day or two, particularly if she's no' used to riding astride."

"I wonder where she came from," Merry said, holding out her bowl for another serve of soup. "I dinna see a winged horse flying over and I was out in the garden all day. Ye'd think I would've seen it."

"Unless it came down out o' the mountains," Lilanthe said.

"But there's naught in the mountains but goblins and ogres," Merry said, wide-eyed. "Did the lass look like a goblin?"

Lewen shut his mouth on his indignation and said nothing.

"Nay, o' course no'," his father said for him. "She was a bonny lass, if rather wild."

"There are other faeries in the mountains," Lilanthe said quietly. "Corrigans, satyricorns, nixies, cluricauns, even seelies. She is certainly wild enough and bonny enough to have seelie blood in her." Lewen looked up and inadvertently met her eyes. Her face was solemn, and he clamped his jaw together and looked away. "I do no' think that is it, though."

"But ye are sure she's o' faery blood?" Niall said. "She looked human enough."

Lilanthe nodded her brown twiggy head and got up, stacking the empty bowls and taking them away from the table. "Aye, she's a half-breed, that I ken. Happen ye need to be one to ken one." There was a faint shade of bitterness in her voice. "She is hard to read, though. I canna hear her thoughts. I would say she has been harshly treated in the past, for her mind and heart are locked up tight indeed. She is well used to shielding her thoughts."

She brought the next course to the table, an egg and onion tart served with steamed green leaves and roasted roots. Lewen and Merry passed up their plates to her and she served deftly, then sat down again with a sigh. Niall looked at her closely.

"Are ye troubled, *leannan*?"

She straightened her back and smiled at him rather wearily. "Nay, nay, o' course no'."

"I am," Niall said. "What is a strange, wild lass from the blue yonder doing wearing the coat and plaid o' a Yeoman?"

Lewen thought of his father's shabby old coat and stained white buckskin breeches, stored carefully in a large chest in the attic with the rest of his uniform, muslin bags of dried lavender and lemon verbena tucked between their folds. His father was proud indeed of his past standing as one of the Rìgh's personal guards. One of the few times Lewen had ever seen his father angry was when he and Merry had opened the chest and played dress-ups with his uniform to amuse themselves one snowy winter's day. Lewen had worn the silver mail shirt, cunningly made of metal links closely woven together, and the thick blue cloak and battered helmet, while Merry had dressed up in his court regalia, the blue tartan kilt and sporran, the cockaded blue tam-o'-shanter, the long-tailed blue coat. Finding them playing at soldiers, pretending to fight with old curtain rods and dragging the hems of his clothes through the dust, Niall had roared at them as angrily as any woolly bear. Merry had been so frightened she had begun to cry, but Niall was too angry to care. He had stripped the children of their costumes with hard and hasty hands, given them both resounding spanks on their bottoms and sent them sobbing down the stairs.

Later, with Lilanthe behind them to give them moral support, they had gone with some trepidation to apologise. The heat of Niall's anger had cooled but he was still displeased, and had told them, very sternly, that they must never touch his uniform again.

"To be chosen as a Yeoman o' the Guard is the greatest honour a soldier can be given," he had said. "I fought many a weary, bloody battle in those clothes, and watched many a comrade slain. I have slept in them many a time when we dared not remove even our boots in case the alarm was called, and I wore them as I stood behind my Rìgh with my eyes hot with tears o' pride as he was finally crowned. It took a very long time for us to bring peace to Eileanan and during all that time, those clothes were my second skin. Those stains on them are stains o' blood and mud and tears and sweat, and they are marks o' honour and courage. Do you understand me, bairns? For if I ever find ye playing with them again, I swear I'll give ye a whipping ye shall never forget."

Lewen and Meriel had been contrite and overawed. Their father rarely spoke much about the long campaign to win the crown for Lachlan the Winged, and then to unite Eileanan under his banner. It was Lilanthe who had taught them their lessons, and she talked about it as if it had all happened long ago, in another lifetime. Niall's words made the Bright Wars seem vivid and immediate. Ever since then, Lewen had harboured a not-so-secret dream of becoming a Blue Guard himself.

"No Blue Guard would ever willingly relinquish his coat and cap," Niall continued. "I fear one o' my laird's men must have come to harm somewhere in the mountains, for this lass to have his gear. I must question her closely in the morning and find out how she came to be dressed so. His Highness will wish to ken if he has lost one o' his men. I wonder who it could be? I do no' ken all the Blue Guards like I used to. It has been some time since I was last in Lucescere."

"So ye think he has fallen victim to foul play, whoever the Yeoman was?" Lilanthe asked.

Niall shrugged, frowning. "I do no' ken. Happen there was an accident o' some kind. How can I tell? This lass, though, whoever she is, she has all his gear, his saddlebags and everything. Even the official saddlecloth, with the ensign o' the charging stag upon it. And she was wearing the badge o' the Yeomen." His voice was thick with outrage.

Lilanthe chose her words with care. "Do ye fear this lass may have killed the Yeoman?"

Niall's frown deepened. "Did ye notice the coat has been torn at the breast and back, as if by an arrow? And the tear cobbled together again? And she carried bow and arrows."

"They may no' be hers," Lilanthe said.

Lewen remembered the callouses on her right palm but said nothing, staring at his plate in dumb misery.

"No, they may no'. And she is only a lass." Niall sighed heavily.

"No' really," Lilanthe said. "She must be seventeen or eighteen. And certainly she kens how to fight."

"No' to mention fight dirty," Niall said.

"Aye. I'll never forget the look on her face as she went for ye with that pitchfork. I almost fainted!"

"Ye almost fainted! Think how I felt when she kicked me. I thought I was going to pass out. I'm afraid I willna be much use to ye for a day or two, *leannan,* I'm swollen up like a pair o' pumpkins."

"Why? Where did she kick ye?" Meriel asked, wide-eyed.

Lilanthe gave her husband a reproving glance and got up to clear the plates.

"She bit me on the shoulder," Lewen said, as much as to distract his little sister as because the wound was throbbing nastily.

Lilanthe put the plates down and came in a hurry to look. She pulled back the collar of his shirt and exclaimed at the round, purple-red bruise.

"What a wildcat," Niall said admiringly.

"I'll put some arnica cream on it," Lilanthe said. "It's a nasty bite. What could make her behave so? It was no' as if we were threatening her or trying to hurt her. We were trying to help! She just went mad like a rabid dog."

"Happen she was frightened," Niall said.

"Or angry because ye held her saddlebags. Happen she thought ye were trying to steal her things. 'Mine' seems to be her favourite word."

"She had only just woken up," Lewen said defensively. "She dinna ken where she was or who we were."

"Aye, that's true enough," Niall said placatingly. "Well, we'll question her in the morning. Let's leave the conjectures till then, shall we? Let's no' forget this is our last night together as a family for what may be a very long time. Merry, sweetling, why do ye no' serve us some of that special pie ye made for Lewen? And I'll get down some goldensloe wine, to toast our lad on his last night at home."

She'll probably be gone in the morning anyway, Lewen said to himself. The thought was cold and heavy as a stone, but he squared his shoulders and took the glass his father gave him with a grin of thanks. *No sense dreaming o' a lass I'll never see again.*

Her Naming

Lewen woke early the next morning, and was at once sitting up and reaching for his clothes. The house was quiet and dim. He went down the stairs in his stockings, carrying his boots. His feet were numb by the time he reached the kitchen, for the stone floors were cold, and so he built a fire on the grey ashes in the hearth and willed it into life with a snap of his fingers. Flames roared up, and Lewen warmed the soles of his feet before pulling on his boots.

Ursa yawned and stretched, and raised her enormous head, gazing at him with questioning eyes. He reached up to rub her greying snout. "Go back to sleep," he said affectionately. "All is well. I'm just going out to the stables."

She moaned softly but put her head back down on her heavy paws, for she was a very old bear now and content to sleep before the fire and amble about after Niall as he went around his chores. Lewen swung the kettle over the fire then, pulling on his coat and gloves, and went quietly out into the early morning mist. The whole garden was wrapped in cloud. The silence was uncanny. Lewen moved with great gentleness, afraid to disturb the stillness. He eased open the door of the stable and stepped quietly inside.

The stall door had been smashed to pieces, and a length of frayed rope dangled from the ring where the mare's halter had been secured. The bucket of water had been kicked over, and the dirt floor was a churned mass of hoof prints. The stall was empty.

Yet in the mound of straw where he had made up a bed for the girl, she slept, curled within the curve of the winged horse's body, the blanket slipping from one shoulder, her hand tucked under her cheek. The horse slept too, its head resting on its forelegs. One wing sheltered the girl, like a black feathered quilt. In the other stalls, the horses all stood drowsily, Lewen's stallion Argent raising his head to look at him, the others sleeping on.

Lewen stood very still. Surely it was not safe for her to sleep there, so close to those sharp hooves? The mare was wild. Everyone knew it was near impossible to tame a winged horse, and this one must surely hate the rider that had ridden it so hard and so far. Yet there she slept, tucked up against the mare's side like a foal.

As if sensing his regard, the girl stirred and sighed and opened her eyes, lifting her hand to rub away the grit of sleep. Her movement roused the horse and it moved its head, blowing gustily through its nostrils. The girl looked up and saw Lewen standing there, gazing at her. Immediately she tensed, pushing herself away from him, pressing deeper into the horse's side. Lewen put up a warning hand, but it was too late. The mare at once scrambled to her feet, rearing back on her hind hooves. She trumpeted a defiant neigh, came down, and kicked out behind.

The girl had rolled herself nimbly away, and now stood and stepped forward, her hand held out flat. "Hush," she said. "No need to fear. Me here."

The horse rolled a white-rimmed eye towards her and shied away, but the girl stepped closer still, one hand going to cup its velvet nose, the other moving up to seize the mare's ear. "Ssssshhhh," she crooned. "Ssssshhhh. No need to fear."

Amazingly, the winged horse quietened at once. It breathed in the girl's scent with flared nostrils, shivered a little and danced uneasily, but did not rear again or neigh. The girl moved closer still, smoothing the mare's satiny neck with her hand, whispering to her. The mare flicked her luxurious long tail and dropped her nose into the girl's hand, and the girl laid her cheek against the mare's neck, caressing one of the long scrolled horns, as blue as a dusk sky. "Aye, ye're bonny, aye, ye are," she whispered.

Lewen could only stand and stare. He had never seen anyone calm a horse so easily. Lewen was a horse-whisperer himself, and had tamed his own bad-tempered stallion in record time, but even that had taken him days, not hours. As he wondered and marveled, she turned towards him and said coldly, "Ye be more careful. She kick hard, she would. She afeared here."

"It was ye I was worried about," Lewen said defensively. "What were ye thinking, sleeping up against her like that? She could've killed ye."

"She mine," she said flatly. "I guard."

"Guard? Guard her against what? There's naught to fear here."

She gave him a contemptuous stare and turned back to the mare, stroking her nose and neck. At some point during the night she had removed the halter and blanket, for the mare was unfettered now. Lewen came forward a few small steps, fascinated by the mare's exotic beauty. The mare shook her mane and pranced a little. The girl laid her hand over the mare's nose again and she quietened so the girl could run her hands gently down her slender legs to check for hotness or swelling.

"Ye ken horses," Lewen said. "Ye've ridden them afore."

"Sometimes," she said. "I call them, they come to me."

"They just come? Any horse?"

She shrugged. "All I've called."

"The mare too? Then why . . .?"

She shook her head. "Me no' ken if she carry me like the wild ponies do. And if she let me, me no' ken if me stay on long enough. Me fallen off afore. Me no' want to fall off while she flying." She made a high, flowing gesture with her hand.

"Nay, o' course no'," Lewen said with a grin. He came forward another few steps and at once the girl backed away, fists clenching, baring her teeth at him warningly. The horse whinnied and sidestepped uneasily. Lewen put up both hands placatingly, stepping back. "I mean ye no harm. I just wanted to check . . . I was worried. Are ye hungry? Would ye like some porridge?"

She was suspicious. "What . . . porridge?" The word stumbled on her tongue.

"Ye do no' ken porridge?" Lewen said unbelievingly. "It's oats . . . hot, and with milk and honey. It's good. If ye'll come . . ."

He gestured out into the brightening morning. "I can make ye some, and happen some griddle-cakes too, and tea."

She narrowed her eyes. "Why? What ye want?"

Lewen was distressed. "Naught! I mean, I just . . . I thought ye might be hungry."

"Me hungry, sure enough, but what ye care?"

"Ye're our guest here . . . ye're sore hurt . . . I wanted . . ."

"What?"

"Naught! Just to be kind."

To his surprise and secret hurt, he saw contempt in her eyes. "True me hungry. Bring food here," she commanded.

He drew back, his eyes hardening. "I am no' your servant," he said. "I thought ye might be hungry so I offered ye some breakfast, but if ye want it, ye can come and get it yourself." He turned on his heel and began to walk out, his back very straight. She said nothing, but he could feel her gaze burning into his back.

He was out of the stable and halfway through the barnyard when he heard her say imperiously, "Stop!"

He turned, still smouldering with anger. She stood in the doorway of the stable, dressed only in a long white nightgown and bare feet, her black hair a matted rat's nest. She looked so young and vulnerable his anger melted away, but he held himself stiffly still, meeting her gaze. "Me very hungry," she said forlornly, "but canna leave what mine." She gestured behind her.

"Ye mean, the horse?"

"All what mine."

"Ye're afraid someone will steal your things?" Lewen did not know whether to feel anger or pity that she should be so filled with suspicion and distrust. He said more gently, "No-one will steal your things, or even touch them, I promise. Ye and your things are safe here. Ye must learn to trust us if we are to help ye."

"Why?"

"Why what?"

"Why ye want help me?"

Again Lewen could not find the words to explain. He said stiffly, "Ye are our guest. Ye've broken our bread and tasted our salt. We may no' harm one who has partaken o' our hospitality."

She seemed to accept this, for she nodded, turned back into the stable and said, with one imperiously pointed finger, "Horse, stay. Me come back."

Then she came out into the dew-frosted grass, her bare feet leaving dark streaks.

"Wait! Ye must be cold. Where are your clothes, your shoes? Happen ye'd best get dressed first." He tugged at his own clothes and indicated his own stout boots.

She looked surprised, but shrugged and went back inside, coming back a few minutes later with the long black boots pulled on under her nightgown and the plaid wrapped negligently about her shoulders. Lewen felt a now familiar bemusement. No other girl of his acquaintance would be so nonchalant about being seen in her nightgown, or so careless of her appearance. His curiosity about her continued to grow.

"So why did ye tie yourself to the mare? Did ye just wish to ride her, to tame her? Or are ye fleeing from someone?"

The girl's lips pressed together firmly and she did not answer.

"Did ye come down out o' the mountains? Where is your family?"

Still she would not answer. Lewen looked at her sideways, marveling at the stubbornness of her patrician profile, the line of brow and nose so straight, the mouth below so softly and deeply curved. It was a face of contradictions, and he did not know which part to believe, the cold severity of the upper, or the warm sensuality of the lower.

They came into the warmth of the kitchen and at once Ursa lifted her snout and moaned a greeting, lumbering to her feet. The girl froze. Suddenly a sharp silver dagger was in her hand and she had dropped into a killer's crouch, her teeth bared. Ursa hardly noticed, so accustomed was she to gentleness and affection. She lumbered forward, lowering her head for a scratch behind the ears. Quick as a snake, the girl struck. Lewen was so taken aback his brain refused to respond. His muscles were well trained, however, and he lunged forward and caught her wrist, the sharp point of the dagger a scant inch away from Ursa's shaggy breast. For a moment they struggled silently, barely moving, but exerting their strength against each other.

Then she submitted, allowing him to draw her away from the puzzled old bear, surrendering the knife into his hand as she rubbed at her bruised wrist.

"Ye strong," she said with approval. "Ye hurt me."

Lewen swallowed his instinctive apology. "Why did ye stab at poor auld Ursa like that?" he said.

She was regarding the enormous woolly bear with narrowed eyes. "Bear," she said, gesturing with one hand.

"Aye, o' course she's a bear, anyone can see that!"

He took a breath to berate her further, but the look on her face made him pause and reflect. "Did ye think her a wild bear, strayed into our kitchen searching for food? I suppose she could have been, but . . . canna ye see how tame she is, how gentle?" He gave a low growl of frustration, unable to express how troubled he was by her fierceness, yet knowing he was being unfair. Anyone raised in the mountains knew to fear woolly bears, known as much for their savagery as their stupidity.

If he had not been raised by his parents, if he was someone else, someone normal, and he had walked into a strange house and seen such an immense, long-toothed, sharp-clawed, strong-shouldered creature in the kitchen, would he not have reacted instinctively to defend himself? And this strange feral girl from the mountains had clearly not been raised with gentleness as he had been. She flinched instinctively when anyone came too near, she carried a knife under her nightgown, she was the nastiest fighter he had ever seen, more unprincipled than even the beggar-boys down near the ports. It was wrong of him to wish her something different, it was wrong to long for her to have the gentleness of his father, the sensitivity of his mother, the merry heart and sweet trustfulness of his sister. She was what she was, and he should not want her to be different just because she had a mouth that fascinated him.

She was watching him now with a calculating expression, as if reading and interpreting the play of expressions on his face, and he took a deep breath and brought his thoughts back under control.

"Ursa is my father's familiar," he said. When she clearly did not understand what he meant, he said rather vaguely, "His friend, his helpmate, his . . ." He did not want to say "pet," but could not think how to explain. "Like your horse," he said at last.

She moved her clear, intent gaze from his face to the bear's. Ursa was patiently waiting to be petted and Lewen choked back a laugh and put his hand up to scratch behind her ears. She slitted her eyes and growled deeply in her throat with pleasure. He stroked her snout and she ambled back to her place by the fire. "She's very auld now," he said, almost as if wanting to excuse her docility.

After that he did not know what to say to her. His hands suddenly felt large and clumsy, and his face hot, and his tongue thick. He busied himself making breakfast, but even that felt wrong and difficult. He dropped the porridge pot, and slurped in too much milk and had to add more oats, which turned to glue, and then he forgot to add the salt and, when he hurried to remedy the omission, fumbled the opening of the canister and spilt in too much, and all the while his ears got hotter and hotter. She sat at the table in silence, watching him with interest, her arms wrapped round her knees, the nightgown slipping off one bare white shoulder as she did not know how to tie up the laces properly. By the time Lilanthe came in, the buds of her twiggy hair bursting into green overnight as if to signal the surge of spring that Lewen was feeling in his blood, her son was as red-cheeked and miserable as she had ever seen him. She tasted the porridge, cast him one whiplash glance but said nothing, swinging the pot off the fire and beginning to swiftly mix up some batter for griddle-cakes, all the while asking the girl gently how she had slept, and was she not cold in her nightgown still, and did she prefer honey or greengage jam? Lewen could only retire in grateful confusion.

Hand-in-hand with her father, Meriel came scampering in, bright-eyed with curiosity. Her chatter filled the silence so that Lewen was able to retreat to the table and busy himself eating and drinking. Meriel peppered the blue-eyed stranger with questions, not at all disconcerted by her reluctance to answer.

"Did ye sleep well? Were ye warm enough?"

"Aye." The girl crammed a whole griddle-cake into her mouth.

"And ye really have a winged horse all o' your own? How did ye catch her?"

No answer.

"Can I have a ride o' her?"

"Nay," she mumbled through her mouthful of crumbs.

"Oh, please? I've always wanted to have a winged horse o' my own. Please?"

"Nay."

"Will she only let ye ride her? Are ye from Tìreich? How did ye get here? Did ye fly over the mountains?"

No answer. Another two griddle-cakes disappeared.

"Mam says ye were sore hurt by tying yourself on so tight. Do your wrists still hurt?"

"Aye."

"Why did ye do it?"

"So no' fall off." Her voice expressed weary contempt. She wiped jam away from her mouth and reached for another griddle-cake.

Meriel was not abashed. "But if she's your horse, surely she wouldna let ye fall? Thigearns do no' tie themselves on."

"She no' my horse *then*. Is now." She flashed the little girl a sharp warning glance.

"So have ye only just caught her? She's no' really your horse then, is she?"

"Mine."

"But, I mean, flying horses canna be tamed so easily. Thigearns must ride their flying horses for a year and a day. Ye only stayed on one day and one night. That canna count."

"She mine!"

"How come ye talk so funny?"

The stranger gritted her jaw and stared at the little girl furiously.

"Meriel," Lilanthe said warningly.

"But she does talk funny."

"No' everyone grows up learning to speak our language," Lilanthe said quietly. She served another platter of hot griddle-cakes, then turned to the girl. "I must admit to curiosity also. We do no' even ken your name. What may we call ye?"

The girl shrugged, frowning. "Lassie?" she said hesitatingly.

"But lassie is no' a name, it's . . . it's what ye are, like Lewen here is a lad. Or was, I should say," Lilanthe said, amending her sentence at a furious glance from her son. "We canna just call ye 'lassie'. Do ye no' have a name? What did your family call ye?"

The girl's face closed up and she looked away, saying nothing.

"Ye have no family?"

She shrugged. "Family like this?" An expansive gesture took in the warmly lit room, with its bright copper pans, bunches of dried herbs hanging from a rack, its collection of childish drawings tacked to the mantelpiece, the immense woolly bear snoozing by the fire. She uttered a bitter laugh. "Nay, no family like this."

"But your parents? Your mother? Your father?"

"Father dead."

"Your mother?"

The girl laughed harshly again. "Mother no' want me. No good." She paused for a moment and then said, in a rush, as if she could no longer dam up the words. "They kill me if I go back."

They were all appalled.

"Kill ye?" Lewen cried. "Why?"

"But, my lass, surely no'?" Niall said. "A bonny lass like ye?"

"Me no good. No' strong enough, no' fast enough. Have no horns."

"No horns?" Niall and Lilanthe exchanged swift glances.

The girl closed her mouth firmly and would not speak.

"A satyricorn?" Niall said. "But . . ."

"It would explain the dirty fighting," Lilanthe said dryly.

Lewen felt his heart sinking. The satyricorns were wild and fierce faeries indeed. Although the First-Horn of the largest known herd had signed the Pact of Peace, so that the satyricorns were theoretically vassals and allies of Lachlan MacCuinn, many of the smaller, more remote herds continued to raid farms and villages just as they always had, killing indiscriminately and stealing food, weapons and young men.

"But I have seen satyricorns," Niall said. "The Rìgh has an infantry troop o' Horned Ones that serve him. They have hooves and a tail as well as horns, and yellow eyes. She is naught like them at all."

"No horns, no hooves, and only one set o' dugs," she said sadly.

There was a shocked silence. Despite himself, Lewen's eyes were drawn to the womanly swell of her thin cotton nightgown. He forced himself to look away. His father was regarding his plate, trying hard not to smile, Meriel's mouth was hanging open in amazement, and Lilanthe looked disconcerted, embarrassed and amused all at the same time.

"Happen she was a foundling child," Lewen stumbled to fill the silence. "Lost on the mountain or something."

She gave a satiric snort. "Horned Ones no' save lost lassie. Eat it if hungry enough. A lost laddie, they'd save. Some use for a lost laddie, at least when grown." And she looked him up and down with such a knowing expression in her eyes that Lewen felt the blood surge up his body and into his face. He did not know where to look or what to say. Neither did his parents.

Luckily Meriel took the comment at face value, crying out, "They'd *eat* a lost bairn? Do ye mean, they'd actually *eat* it?"

"If hungry enough," she said indifferently.

"Urrgghh!"

The girl looked at her speculatively. "Me ate goblin once. Rather eat nice, plump babe than foul, stinking goblin, wouldna ye?"

"Urrgghh, no! I wouldna want to eat either."

"Ye would if hungry enough."

"Nay, I would no'!"

"Bet ye would. If it meant ye'd get to live another day. Anyone would."

"I'd rather die!"

"Proof ye've never really been hungry," the girl said, and helped herself to another griddle-cake. They all hurried to pass her more butter and jam, and Lilanthe poured her another cup of fresh goat's milk, so full it almost brimmed over. The girl ate and drank greedily, wiping her mouth on her sleeve.

There was a long silence as they watched her eat, each busy with their own thoughts.

Then Niall leant forward, frowning, one hand scratching his

bushy brown beard. "So ye have run away from your family . . . your herd. That is why ye caught the winged horse. To help ye escape."

"Herd run fast, hunt good," she said rather indistinctly, through a mouthful of food. "Me slow. They catch me, they kill me."

"So what about the saddle, the bridle? The clothes? Where did ye get them?"

She frowned, glaring at him suspiciously.

"Ye canna tell me they are what ye wore with a herd o' satyricorns," Niall said. "They are the uniform o' à Yeoman o' the Guard, the Rìgh's own regiment. Where did ye get them?"

Her frown deepened and for a moment it looked as if she would say nothing. Then she said reluctantly, "Herd hunted down man, close on a moon ago. He dead. Me took his clothes. Liked better. Soft."

Niall was watching her closely. "Who was he? Do ye ken his name? How did he die?"

She did not answer.

"I thought satyricorns usually keep male prisoners alive," he said slowly. "Having a use for them, as ye said yourself."

She did not drop her eyes, or blush, or fiddle with her knife, keeping her eyes steadily on his. "Aye, true," she answered.

"So how did the Yeoman die?"

"Try escape," she said after a moment. "Herd hunt him down."

Niall nodded. "I see." He glanced at Lilanthe. "I wonder who it could be? There'll be identification o' some kind in the saddlebags, I imagine, a family seal or signed reports. I'll look and see. We must send notice to His Highness . . ."

"Nay!"

They looked at the girl in surprise. She had leapt to her feet, sending the cup of milk cascading over the table. One fist was thrust under Niall's bearded chin. "Mine! Ye no look, ye no touch. Mine now. No' yours."

"But, lassie . . ."

"No touch."

"But they are no' your things, lassie. They belong to that poor dead soldier. His family will be wanting to have his uniform and

badge back, they are marks o' honour. They'll be wanting to ken
how he died. We have plenty of clothes here that ye can have, ye
do no' need his things anymore. I must see what news he was carrying, and send it on to my Rìgh. That Yeoman must have had
dreadful need to reach the capital quickly, to ride through Dubhslain, canna ye see that? I must make sure the Rìgh kens what has
happened."

All the while Niall spoke, she was negating every sentence
abruptly and forcefully. As he continued to argue with her, she
reached down and drew the knife she wore hidden under her
nightgown. She would have stabbed him if he had not had such
quick reflexes, catching her wrist in both hands, leaning far
back in his chair to avoid the snake-swift thrust. They wrestled
silently for a few moments, her lips drawn back into a feral
snarl, then at last Niall managed to knock the knife out of her
hand, dragging her down to her knees.

He breathed heavily, trying to regain his temper as much as
his breath. Lewen was frozen in shock and dismay, unable to
believe he had forgotten her knife, realizing how close his father had come to death because of his absent-mindedness.
Lilanthe and Meriel were frozen likewise. Violence had erupted
so quickly.

The girl took a deep shuddering breath perilously close to a
sob. Niall released her wrists and she cradled them to her chest,
her head bent. Still no-one spoke, not even Meriel, whose face
had turned the colour of unbaked dough. Then Lilanthe gave a
great sigh and went swiftly to her husband, bending over him,
pressing his head to her breast. She said softly, brokenly, "I
canna believe . . . och, *leannan* . . . if she had killed ye . . ."

"I'm a hard man to kill," Niall said with an attempt at a
smile.

The girl raised her head. Though her face was smeared with
tears and the bandages about her wrists were seeping with fresh
blood, her expression was set hard with anger and determination.

"If ye touch me or mine again, me kill ye," she said softly.

Niall sighed and put his arm about his wife's waist. After a
moment he said, very sternly, "Then let this be understood between us. If ye try to harm me or mine again while ye are here,
I will have ye taken to the reeve and tried and punished. Ye do

no' attack a man at his own table, after ye have broken bread and tasted salt with him. Ye do no' seek to settle a disagreement by drawing your blade. This is dishonourable and unlawful. Ye may have been raised as a satyricorn, but ye are among men now, and ye must and will learn our ways."

"How?" Lilanthe asked. "What are we to do with her? We have no' had time to think what is best to do."

The girl stood up, her blue-grey eyes blazing. "Ye do naught with me! Me go. Me take horse and me go."

"Where?" Lilanthe said gently. "Where shall ye go? Back into the mountains? They are no' called Dubhslain for naught. Apart from the satyricorns, who ye say shall kill ye if they find ye, there are ogres and cursehags and dragons too. It is no place for anyone to live alone, no matter how doughty. And believe me, lassie, I ken. I ran away from my home too, when I was just a lass myself, and I lived in the wild mountains as best I could for quite a few years. Being able to change shape into a tree helped, o' course, but it was a cruel hard life, ye must understand that. And lonely. Bitterly lonely. It was that which drove me out o' the mountains in the end, a longing for those o' my own kind, for love and friendship." She bent and pressed her cheek against Niall's beard and he put up one hand and caressed her leafy hair.

The girl was silent, though her chin was still raised defiantly and her hands clenched.

"Happen she should come to the Tower o' Two Moons with me?" Lewen said diffidently. His parents looked at him in surprise.

"It'll take us some time to travel to Lucescere," he went on. "Nina and Iven and I can try and teach her what we can on the way, and there'll be other apprentices too, for sure, and they'll help too. And then she can tell the Rìgh what she kens herself, I'm sure he'll have questions he'd want to ask her. And Aunty Beau will want to talk to her too, I ken."

"Why, though, laddie?" Lilanthe sounded a little puzzled. "Ye think the lassie has Talent?"

"She's tamed the winged horse," Lewen said. When his father went to say something he held up his hand in entreaty. "Nay, I mean, *really* tamed her, Dada. When I went in this morning, well, the mare had kicked out the door o' her stall and broken her headstall and torn up the whole place, but . . . well, they were sleeping together, like mare and foal, as sweetly as ye could imagine. And she talks to her. Tells the mare to stay and she does."

Niall's brown eyes and Lilanthe's slanted green ones both swiveled to the girl's face. She stared back at them haughtily. "She mine," she said.

"She says she's tamed horses afore, in the mountains. She calls to them and they come."

"Happen it's the Tower o' Horse-lairds we should be sending her to," Niall said softly.

"Happen so," Lewen agreed. "But there's plenty o' time for that, if that's the right place for her to go, isn't there? There's no-one to take her there now, and she would ken no-one there nor how to go on. And the Rìgh would want to see her first, dinna ye think so?"

"Aye, he would." Niall stroked his beard thoughtfully. "I can see some merit in this plan o' yours, my lad. Though we must make sure news o' the Yeoman's death travels faster than ye will. It'll take ye a month or so to reach the palace, and my laird will be anxious for news o' his Yeoman. I wish we could scry to him, but the mountains stand in the way. What a shame the Tower o' Ravens is so infested with ghosts and we canna use the Scrying Pool there. It would be so much easier to keep in touch with the court and Coven." Niall sighed and dug his fingers into his beard more vigorously.

"Come, we can work out the finer details later," Lilanthe said. "For now, I think it is a good plan. I would no' like to just send the lassie off somewhere all by herself, for all that she is so fierce and strong. The Tower o' Two Moons is interested in all Skills and Talents, and there are satyricorns at the royal court that may be able to help her find a place for herself."

"Lewen's right, the Rìgh will want to question her about the Yeoman's death himself," Niall said, almost as if he had not been listening to his wife. "And happen on the way Lewen can make her realise that wearing the clothes o' a Blue Guard is treason!"

The girl had been listening to all this with narrow, suspicious

eyes. At this last comment she flashed him a quick glance, but
still said nothing, her jaw thrust out stubbornly.

Lilanthe turned to her and smiled, saying in her gentle voice,
"It is for ye to decide, o' course. We have no rights over ye. I
do no' ken if ye will like Lucescere, it is one o' the great cities
o' Eileanan and very busy and noisy. They call it the Shining
City because it is so beautiful. It is built on an island at the top
o' the highest waterfall in Eileanan, a place where two great
rivers meet. On sunny days the whole city is strung with rain-
bows from the spray. Ye would like to see it, I am sure. And the
Tower o' Two Moons is very quiet and peaceful, for it is built
away from the city, set in the heart o' acres o' the bonniest gardens. It too is one o' the grand sights o' this world. Ye will meet
people o' all kinds there, both human and faery, and if ye wish,
ye can try for a scholarship to study there and learn many new
things, as Lewen does. Or ye can get back on to your winged
horse and fly away from here, we shallna try and stop ye. It's
up to ye, lassie."

It was the right approach to take. The girl's face and stance
relaxed as Lilanthe spoke, and a look of interest came into her
eyes. She glanced once at Lewen and then back at Lilanthe,
catching her lip between her teeth as she considered. Then she
raised her head proudly.

"Me like to see this city," she said. "Me go." As everyone
sighed and relaxed a little, relieved to have a plan to work towards, she looked sternly at Niall. "Ye, though—ye shallna
touch what is mine."

"But . . ." Niall began.

"No touch! Else me kill ye."

"Very well, then, lassie," Lilanthe said quickly. "We shall
touch naught o' yours if ye do no' wish it. But can I give ye
some other clothes to be wearing on your journey? For indeed,
ye canna wear the uniform o' a Yeoman if ye have no' been chosen to serve the Rìgh. It is no' right and indeed, it is treasona-
ble, as Niall said. If ye give me the clothes I will wash them for
ye and pack them up, and ye can take them with ye."

The girl nodded begrudgingly.

"Very well then. Now, we do no' have long. Nina and Iven
will be here soon, if they left Barbreck-by-the-Bridge at day-

break like they said they would. How about a bath, lassie? Believe me, ye will feel much better when ye are clean. I'll wash your hair for ye and salve your wrists again and find ye some clothes, and then we can pack a bag for ye to take with ye. Lewen, dearling, I do no' ken how long they'll be able to stay so ye had best make ready."

"He's already packed and repacked his bags about a hundred times," Meriel teased.

"Well, I wanted to be ready," Lewen said.

"Come on, my lad, let's go and get our chores done while the lassie has her bath," Niall said. "The poor auld horses must be wondering where their mash is, while I'm surprised we canna hear the pigs squealing from here."

"I feed my horse, no' ye," the satyricorn girl said, tensing up at once. "I come now. Ye touch naught!"

Niall raised both his hands. "I shallna touch a thing, lassie, I promise ye. Which reminds me. We canna keep on just calling ye 'lassie'. Ye sure ye do no' have a name? What did your mother call ye, and the other satyricorns?"

She flushed hotly. "No-Horn," she answered shortly. "No' a nice name." She struggled for words. "Mean name."

"We canna call ye that then," he said, taken aback.

"Then we must give her one," Lilanthe said. "She needs a name."

They all eyed her speculatively and she glared back at them, her jaw set firmly.

"Aye, but to choose a name that suits her, that's the trick," Niall said, scratching his beard, a humorous glint in his eyes. "Prickles? Bramble? Blackthorn?"

She tilted her chin even higher.

"Rosaleen? That means little dark rose," Lilanthe said hastily.

"She's no' so little," Niall said, grinning. "What's a name that means enormous dark rose? No' that I think a rose is the right sort o' plant, thorny as it is. How about thistle?"

"Do no' even joke about that," Lilanthe said with a little shudder. "No' even Iain of Arran calls himself the Thistle, it brings back such dreadful memories. That's a name Margrit o' Arran took to the grave with her, thank Eà."

"True enough," Niall said soberly. "I'd forgotten Margrit

NicFóghnan was called the Thistle. Indeed, that would be a sorry name to give such a bonny lass. I suppose we should be serious about this. A name is a serious thing, one carries it all one's life. Are there no names ye like, lass?"

"Ken no names," she answered.

"That makes things harder," Niall said. "Do ye ken any names to do with horses, *leannan*? A woman that rides a winged horse should have a name that suits. Is there a girlie form o' Ahearn? That means laird o' the horses and was a true naming indeed."

"I do no' think so," Lilanthe said, frowning. "And we canna call her Ahearn, or any derivative, for it is a name that belongs to the MacAhern clan."

"How about Rhiannon?" Lewen said quietly. They turned to him, surprised, having almost forgotten he was there, he had been so silent. "From the auld story, ye ken the one," he said. "She rides past the king and he is so smitten with her beauty that he sends his cavaliers galloping after her, to bring her back to him. But she rides so swiftly none can catch her. The king cannot forget her, and so day after day he returns to the same place in the forest, hoping to see her again. At last she gallops past and he pursues her. But not even his great war-charger can catch up with her, and so he calls out to her, telling her he has fallen in love with her. So she turns and reins in her horse, and lets him come near, and he makes her his wife."

"Aye," Niall said slowly. "I remember that tale. Rhiannon." He turned to the girl. She was gazing now at Lewen. Her face had softened, her mouth curving just enough for the elusive dimple to crease her cheek. "Do ye like that name, lassie?" Niall asked gruffly.

"Rhee-ann-an." She spoke the name slowly, haltingly, tasting the syllables on her tongue. "She rides so swiftly none can catch her. Aye, I like. Rhee-ann-an."

"Rhiannon it is, then," Lilanthe said. Lewen caught the slight restraint in her voice and looked up at her. She smiled at him ruefully and tousled his curly brown hair, then stroked it back away from his brow. "It's a lovely name, my lad, and well thought of. Why do ye no' all go and tend the horses now so Rhiannon can get her clothes for me to wash? Then ye can go round the farm with your father one more time and be saying your farewells."

Lewen nodded, overcome by an unexpected wave of home-sickness. Eà alone knew when he would be able to come back to Kingarth again. His eyes were suddenly hot and he had to swallow a lump in his throat.

"Go on, laddie," Lilanthe said lovingly. "Take your time. It's going to take a while to get Rhiannon clean, that's for sure!"

The Jongleurs

It was early afternoon when Meriel came skipping out to find her brother and father, who were busy grooming Lewen's big grey, Argent. The stallion was standing with one leg relaxed, his eyes half-closed in bliss, but as soon as he heard Meriel's quick footsteps, his ears went back and he lifted his top lip to smell the air suspiciously.

"Give over!" Lewen said affectionately, pushing the stallion with his shoulder. "Ye should ken Merry's step by now."

"We're ready!" Meriel cried. "Gracious me, what a job! It was like trying to wash a litter o' piglets, the squealing and squirming we've had. My arms ache from hauling so much water, and then I had to mop up the floor, which looked like the floor o' the byre, it was so wet and muddy. And it took a whole bottle o' Mam's liquid soapwort to wash her hair, and then it was so matted Mam had to use up all the rosemary herb oil to get the knots out. It took forever."

"Well, ye seem to have survived the experience," Niall said, looking her over in mock concern. "No black eyes, no bleeding nose, no bite marks that I can see. Is your mother all in one piece too?"

"Aye." Laughing, Meriel snuggled up against her father's side. "She fought a bit to begin with but Mam told her if she dared try again, she'd turn her into a tree and then she'd never be able to ride her winged horse again. Rhiannon didna believe her, so Mam pretended to turn me into a tree just to show her."

Lewen grinned. His mother could no more turn Rhiannon into a tree than he could, but Meriel had inherited her mother's tree-shifter abilities and needed only to dig her bare feet into the ground to change her shape. It was very disconcerting to watch if you were not used to it, though, and he could imagine Rhiannon's alarm.

"Well, thank Eà your mother couldna carry out her threat. Can ye imagine what kind o' tree our sweet Rhiannon would make? A very prickly goldengorse bush, perhaps. Or a blackthorn."

"Ye are silly," Meriel said. "Anyway, she's very fidgety about her horse but Mam wouldna let her come out to check it 'cause she's all clean and dressed now, so I promised I'd make sure the mare's still all right."

"She's grand," Lewen said. "I left her some warm mash and a bucket o' fresh water, and her ears pricked forwards with great interest, which is always a good sign. I think she'll be fine to set out tomorrow as long as Rhiannon does no' ride her too hard."

"That's good. Mam said to tell ye that Nina and the caravans will be here soon—her little sunbird just flew in the window and trilled us such a bonny tune."

"Almost here?" Lewen said in dismay.

"Aye, so ye'd better get hopping! Mam wants us all bonny and bright, she says. I'm to wear my new red dress and she wants ye to put on your good coat."

"But I've packed it already! And right down the bottom o' my bag 'cause I didna think I'd be needing it till we got to Lucescere."

"Better go and unpack it, my lad," Niall said. "Your mam wants to show ye off to Nina, to be sure."

"And there's so much o' him to show," Meriel said cheekily. Lewen pretended to lunge for her and she danced away, laughing. "And dinna think I'm hauling any water for your bath, laddie-boy. I never want to see that well-bucket again."

Niall tousled his son's head affectionately. "Go on, lad, go and get cleaned up. Tell your mam I'll be there in just a moment."

Lewen nodded and gave Argent one more loving polish before putting away his curry-brush. With Meriel skipping beside him, chattering all the way, he went back through the gardens to the house, trying to imprint every aspect of the landscape upon his memory—the apple tree his mother had planted for him the day of his birth, the row of beehives under the cherry trees, the loch gleaming between the willow trees. It had seemed such a luxury, having three whole months of holiday, but it had rushed past him like a runaway horse and carriage.

Meriel left him in the kitchen garden, going to hang over the vegetable patch and make sure no bird had ravished her seeds away. Lewen had to clamber over Ursa, who was sleeping on the step in the sun, snoring loudly. He came into the kitchen, stopping abruptly inside the door. Rhiannon was sitting demurely by the fire, dressed in a leaf-green dress laced down the bodice with white satin ribbons. A frill of white embroidered cotton softened the square-cut neckline and the edge of the sleeves, which were folded back just below the elbow. Her hair was combed back from her face and tied in a simple knot at the back of her head, allowing the remainder to fall free in a shining black curtain that reached past the seat of her chair.

Lewen had seen the dress many times before, since it was a favourite of his mother's, but it was a very different dress on Rhiannon. Lilanthe was a slender woman, slight as a young willow tree. Rhiannon was far taller, and her waist was as deeply curved as a double bass. The silk clung closely to every curve, so that Lewen could see clearly the exact shape and dimension of her figure. The sight of her made the bones of Lewen's chest constrict so he had trouble taking a breath, and he was all too aware of a hot rush of blood to his groin.

She was frowning down at her bare feet, set neatly side by side, below the deep white frill edging her skirt. She looked up at Lewen, her eyes reflecting the green of the silk so that they looked the colour of water over pale sand. She scowled more deeply, saying abruptly, "Me dare no' move in case it busts."

He could find no words to answer her.

Lilanthe was busy laying the table but turned then to smile at her son. She was dressed in her best gown, a forest-green silk with gold embroidery and an underskirt of cream and gold brocade.

"Rhiannon is far too tall for my clothes! I did my best but we shall have to get her some other clothes. She certainly canna be wearing my auld green silk on the road."

Lewen still could find nothing to say. He tried hard not to stare at Rhiannon but it was impossible to look anywhere else.

His heart was swelling painfully in his chest, and his hands felt hot and heavy. He shoved them into his pockets.

Lilanthe regarded him shrewdly. "Go on, laddie, ye havena time to waste. Nina will be here any moment and she has a full caravan, she says. Go and get cleaned up, and then come and help me. It's been a long while since I've had a dozen guests for lunch."

He nodded brusquely, trying hard not to show how powerfully the sight of a clean and silk-clad Rhiannon had affected him.

"And can ye dig out some o' your auld clothes for Rhiannon? She's near as tall as ye. She'll need some shirts and a jerkin, and some breeches to wear on the journey, for she'll be riding that winged horse o' hers, no doubt. Do ye ken what ye did with your auld riding cloak? For it'll rain, as sure as apples, and she'll need one."

"Ye gave it away to the village jumble sale," Lewen managed. His voice rasped in his throat.

"Och, aye, that I did. What a shame. I wonder if I can cut down one o' Niall's? But we've so little time . . ."

"Me have one," the girl said sullenly, twisting her hands together in her lap. She looked angry and miserable.

"Aye, but . . . och, well, I suppose as long as ye do no' wear the plaid or the brooch, it canna matter. A cloak is a cloak, whether it be blue or no'. Ye can wear the tam-o'-shanter too, I suppose, as long as we take off the cockade. Och, so much to think o' and so little time! Go on, Lewen, my love, please! I want ye looking all bonny for Nina when she comes, for she hasna seen ye since she delivered ye to the Theurgia four years ago. She'll be so surprised to find ye so tall and doughty now. I ken I was." Lilanthe sighed and smiled mistily at her son.

Lewen put his arms about his mother's slim waist and gave her a hearty squeeze, grateful that she had managed to cover his awkward silence and wondering if she understood all the things he found so hard to say. Then he made his escape, not meeting Rhiannon's sullen and questioning gaze.

He was clean and dressed and engaged in rummaging through his wardrobe for old clothes when he heard a commotion outside, and went eagerly to his bedroom window to look out.

Two caravans were rolling up the elm-lined avenue towards

the house. One was red and green, and the other was blue and yellow, the contrasting colour painted on decorative scrollwork around the windows and doors and roof. A big brown mare pulled the red caravan and a big grey gelding pulled the blue. A flaxen-haired man with a long, forked beard was lounging on the driver's seat of the blue caravan, playing a guitar, the reins knotted loosely over the dashboard. A little boy with curly chestnut hair was sitting up next to him, enthusiastically banging on a drum, with a small hairy creature sitting beside him, dressed in a short red dress and bonnet. The gelding plodded on placidly, occasionally twitching his ears back at the din. A woman drove the second caravan, dressed in green and vivid orange. As the caravans pulled up under Lewen's window, he saw a small iridescent green bird perched on her shoulder. Following the caravans were half a dozen horses and riders.

Lewen bundled together the clothes he had found on his bed, then went leaping down the stairs, all his incipient homesickness drowned beneath a wave of excitement. It had been four years since he had last seen his mother's jongleur friends, but he remembered them clearly. They had come to give Lewen his Second Test of Powers and to accept him into the Coven as an apprentice-witch. At first all had been solemn and rather scary, but once Lewen had proven himself, the house had been full of music and laughter and dancing. Nina was nicknamed the nightingale for her gorgeous voice, and she had sung them many songs, merry, plaintive and droll in turn. Her husband Iven was an acrobat and trickster, and knew more jokes and witty stories than anyone Lewen had ever met. Their son Roden had only been a toddler then and the arak Lulu no more than a round-eyed, wrinkled-faced baby. Nina had found her fallen out of a tree, and had nursed her back to health, saying she would teach her tricks when she was old enough. Although Nina now worked for the Coven, she had been a jongleur all her life and made no attempt to leave her past behind her.

As Lewen came out the front door, he saw Nina leap lightly down from the driving seat and seize Lilanthe in her arms, hugging her enthusiastically. Nina was a tall, slim woman with a mass of unruly chestnut hair and dark eyes. On her left hand she wore a vivid green emerald ring, the sign of a sorceress in the

element of earth. Three other rings—green, white, and blue—
decorated her right hand.

"Och, Nina, it's so lovely to see ye!" Lilanthe cried. "Heavens, is that Roden? Look how big he's grown!"

"I could say the same about your laddie," Nina said, smiling
at Lewen. "He's a man now! Is he a longbowman like Niall? He
has the shoulders for it. Heavens, it makes me feel auld, to find
Lewen so tall and doughty."

Lewen grinned at his mother. "That's exactly what Mam said
ye'd say."

Niall greeted Nina and Iven warmly, then turned to the riders
behind, saying with ritual ceremony, "Welcome! Will ye no'
stand down?"

The riders inclined their heads in acknowledgement, the
three boys touching their caps. Two of the boys were tall and
sturdy and brown-faced, and dismounted with customary ease.
The other was pale and wan. He dismounted with difficulty, and
winced as he moved.

The other three riders were girls. One was very richly and
fashionably dressed in a mud-spattered crimson velvet riding
habit, brown leather boots and gloves, and a wide-brimmed
brown velvet hat with a curled red feather. Long dark curls in
wind-ruffled ringlets hung down her back and she had a mischievous smile.

Riding close beside her was a haughty-faced blonde girl
dressed in dark brown the exact colour of her high-stepping
nervous mare. Like her companion, she rode side-saddle and so
carried a long whip in her left hand, but unlike her companion,
her right boot was spurred. Lewen could tell at a glance that she
rode her horse hard. The reins were held too tightly, so the mare
fought the bit, dancing and sidestepping, her ears laid back flat.
She was damp under her saddlecloth and Lewen could see the
marks of whip and spur against her sweat-streaked hide.

The third girl was different again. She was plump and rosy-
cheeked, with mousy hair tied in two wispy plaits. Wearing the
plain homespun dress and wooden clogs of a country girl, she
sat in the saddle like a sack of potatoes, and her short-legged,
fat pony was on a leading-rein to the tallest of the boys. He paid
her no attention, however, dropping the rein as he dismounted

so he could rush forward to help down the girl in crimson. She had made no movement to dismount herself but waited with absolute assurance that help would be forthcoming. The other brown-faced boy had also hurried forward, however, and they collided at her stirrup. Lewen saw the girl's mouth curve in a little smile as they apologised to each other, both stiff and angry and very much on their dignity.

"Cameron helped me dismount yesterday so happen ye can hand me down today, Rafferty," the girl said, holding out one small, gloved hand. The younger of the two boys took it proudly and assisted her down to the ground.

The sweat-lathered mare of the fair-haired girl shied and bucked as if the hand clamped on the rein had tightened even further. Lewen moved quickly to take the rein and help the other girl down, before the horse kicked out at one of the others, or backed into the fat pony waiting so placidly behind.

"I thank ye," she said coldly, shaking out her brown velvet skirts and casting a resentful look at the other boys. They did not notice.

Lewen nodded, smoothing the neck of her mare and murmuring in his deep, low voice until she had calmed. Then, he went to help down the dumpy girl in clogs, who everyone seemed to have forgotten.

"Come on in, all o' ye, and welcome," Lilanthe said. "It's glad I am to see ye all."

She led the group up the stairs and into the house, Meriel stricken into silence for a change and clinging close to her mother's side. The little boy, Roden, scampered happily beside Nina, holding the arak's hairy hand. She was an odd little creature, as small as a baby but with the sad, wizened face of a very old woman, and an extremely long, mobile tail. Soft greybrown hair covered every part of her except her face, her hands and feet and the very tip of her tail.

Nina stopped halfway up the stairs to exclaim at the beautifully carved wooden doors. "These are new since I was last here!" she cried. "Oh, Lilanthe, they're exquisite. Dinna tell me Lewen made them? I had no idea he was so talented."

Lilanthe smiled. "He worked on them all winter. We're snowbound here, ye ken, and it was a bad winter, very cold and snowy. There's naught much else to do here. They're lovely, aren't they?"

"Indeed they are," Nina replied, stopping to examine them closely before passing through into the house.

The door was split into two panels. A tree-changer had been carved on either side, their faces looking out from the leafy fronds of their hair. Birds and animals sheltered in their branches or looked out from behind their trunks—an owl, a lark, a squirrel, a donbeag, a wolf, an elven cat, a hare, the snout and sad eyes of a huge woolly bear. Flowers clustered around the tree-changers' roots, and when the doors were shut the fingers of the two forest faeries, man and woman, were entwined.

Lewen felt a warm glow of pleasure at Nina's words. He had worked on the doors for many days as a Hogmanay gift for his parents, and Nina was the first person outside his family to have seen them.

The apprentice-witches had all followed Nina up the steps.

Lewen noticed how the fair-haired girl's lip lifted in a condescending sneer as she glanced about, how the plump girl with plaits looked at the carved doors with admiration, and how the dark girl in crimson laughed and chatted with the two boys, who flanked her like a guard of honour. The other boy followed with a dreamy look of contentment as he gazed on the fresh green lawns, the narcissus and snowbells dancing under the bare branches of the trees, and the encircling ring of cloud-capped mountains.

"O mountains wild and high, where the eagle flies . . ." he murmured. "No, no, that willna do. O mountains wild and high, where the eagles fly, frowning down upon us here, sear, dear, mere, yes, mere . . . frowning down upon us here, the garden green, the shining mere . . ."

Lewen led the nervous brown mare and the pony along the driveway towards the stables, wondering if the boy was mad.

Iven grinned at him.

"Young Landon fancies himself a poet," he said. "He's quite harmless and Nina thinks him very Talented. Och, no' at writing poetry. He stinks at that! But he is clear-seeing and clear-hearing, and very sensitive to atmosphere. Nina thinks he'll make a grand witch in time. Come, Sure, come, Steady." He clicked his tongue and the carthorses followed him placidly like two big dogs, the caravans trundling along behind them.

"What about the others? Are they all apprentices too?" Niall asked, leading the other horses.

"Aye. Cameron is one o' the MacHamish clan and wants to be a Yeoman. He kens ye need to do your witch's training first, so he's submitting rather gracelessly to having to go to school for a few years. He's auld for it, being nineteen already, but he's been squire at Ravenscraig for four years or so, and trained as a soldier, and he has his heart set on serving the Rìgh, so the MacBrann is sponsoring him for the next few years to give him a chance."

"Rafferty is the son o' a clock-maker who shows some witch-talent, much to his family's surprise, nothing like that ever cropping up in their family afore. His father is hoping a few years at the Theurgia will help him climb a few rungs o' the social ladder. He's a good lad, though rather quick to throw a punch. They were rubbing along grandly till we picked up Lady Fèlice, but since then we've had a few punch-ups."

"Is that the lass in the crimson?" Niall asked.

"Aye. She's the daughter o' the Earl of Stratheden, one o' the MacBrann's courtiers, and has apparently caused some havoc with the hearts o' the young men in Ravenscraig. We picked her up there, and it's put the cat among the pigeons, I can tell ye. Until Lady Fèlice came, Lady Edithe o' Avebury queened over all o' us, but now her nose is quite out o' joint, I can tell ye. She comes from the MacAven family, one o' the first families in Ravenscraig and famous for their witches. Edithe thinks herself quite the sorceress and far too good for us mere jongleurs."

"Does she no' ken who Nina is?" Niall asked in surprise.

Iven shook his head, quirking his lip. "She doesna think to look beyond the surface o' things, that one, and ye ken Nina would never tell her. I think Nina's taken a dislike to her ladyship and quite enjoys watching her make a fool o' herself. I must admit I find it rather amusing too. One minute, Lady Edithe's trying to ingratiate herself with Lady Fèlice because o' all her contacts at court, the next minute she's furious at all the attention she gets."

"What about the lassie in the clogs?" Lewen asked.

"Och, aye," Iven said, as if in sudden remembrance. "Maisie.

She's the granddaughter o' a village cunning man and a sweet wee thing. She's never been away from home afore and is quite overwhelmed. Nina says her Talent is quite strong, though."

Iven's easy flow of conversation suddenly dried up, as he came to an abrupt halt just inside the stable door. The sturdy brown mare nudged his back with her nose. He did not seem to notice. He was staring at the winged mare, standing untethered in the wreck of her stall, contentedly lipping at a bucket of warm mash. At the sound and smell of the strange man, she flung up her horned head and shied away, showing the yellowish rim of her eye in sudden alarm.

"Easy, lassie," Niall said in his low, warm voice. "No need to fear. Easy now."

The horse shook her head, hurrumphing, ears twitching back and forth. The black wings lifted and unfurled with a flash of iridescent blue at the tips.

"Eà's green blood!" Iven whispered.

"Aye, she's a bonny one, isn't she?" Niall said. "Nervy, though. As ye can see, she's already kicked out the walls o' her stall. Happen we'd best untether the horses in the yard. They can graze in the garden and ye can leave the caravans there under the tree. It'll be cold tonight but they'll be fine once we blanket them."

"What are ye doing with a winged horse?" the jongleur exclaimed. "Ye canna be trying to tame it, surely?"

"Och, no' us," Niall said. "I do no' think I'd dare. Nay, we have a guest staying with us, a lassie named Rhiannon. She's the one that has dared cross her leg over the mare's back."

"I do no' think I've ever heard o' a woman thigearn afore," Iven said in interest. "Is she one o' the MacAhern clan?"

"She's no' a NicAhern, nor a thigearn, nor even a woman," Niall said. "I said a lass and I meant it. She canna be much more than seventeen or eighteen."

"Eà's green blood!" Iven said again. He shook his head in wonderment, unable to take his eyes off the mare, who was still dancing about on dark-feathered hooves, ears laid back. "We sing songs o' the black winged horses o' Ravenshaw. I thought it was only a story. I never thought I'd ever actually see one. Ye say this lassie has tamed it?"

"So it seems," Niall said.

"Och, there's a tale in that, to be sure. Where is this lass?"

"Putting Lady Edithe and Lady Fèlice's noses out o' joint in the sitting room would be my bet," Niall said rather dryly.

Iven raised an eyebrow. "Bonny, is she then?"

"Aye, though no' in the manner o' your fine misses. She's bonny like a falcon is, or even yon winged horse. Wild and fierce and dangerous to cross. Ye'll see what I mean when ye meet her."

"I can hardly wait," Iven replied.

Lewen thought of Rhiannon, sitting stiff and uncomfortable in her too-tight dress with her hands clenched in her lap and her feet set exactly side by side. His throat was suddenly dry. He wondered if he had done the right thing suggesting she come to the Tower of Two Moons with him. What would they make of her, those pretty fashionable girls, those rough and ready young men? He could not imagine any of them being as kind or as accepting as his parents.

"Happen we'd best get the horses settled and then we can take Iven back to meet her?" he suggested.

"Aye, good idea, laddie. I'm sure Iven would care for a nice mug o' foaming ale."

"To be sure," Iven grinned.

They worked swiftly and competently to unharness the horses. The two sturdy carthorses were left free to graze where they willed, but the six other hacks were put into halters with a long rein that fastened to a spike in the ground. Although Lewen was eager to get back to the house, he gave them all a good currying, especially the tired brown mare with the painful welts on her side. As he brushed away the sweat and mud, he thought he too had conceived a strong dislike of the fair-haired girl with her whip and spurs. He wished he did not have to travel with her.

At last the horses were settled and the men walked back through the gardens towards the house, Iven bringing them up to date with news of the country. The biggest tidbit of gossip he had was that a date had been set for the wedding of the young heir to the throne, Donncan, to his cousin Bronwen, daughter of Maya the Ensorcellor. The cousins had been betrothed as young children as a condition of the peace treaty between the Rìgh, Lachlan MacCuinn, and King Nila of the Fairgean, which ended decades of bloodshed. King Nila was Maya the Ensorcellor's half-brother, and had maintained a close interest in his niece, who had inherited the Fairgean ability to shapeshift in water, along with the smooth scaly skin, silvery eyes and finned limbs of the sea-dwelling faeries.

"They've set the wedding date for Midsummer's Eve, a most proper date," Iven said. "O' course His Highness wants Nina to sing at the wedding, so we have to make sure we're back in time."

"Aye, I suppose it is time. Prionnsa Donncan will have turned twenty-four at Hogmanay, wouldn't he?" Niall looked at Lewen.

Lewen nodded. "Aye. He would've sat his Third Test then. He canna join the Coven, o' course, being heir to the throne, but they will have wanted him to finish his studies afore he and Bronwen were married."

Iven shrugged. "The Banprionnsa Bronwen finished at the Theurgia last autumn, and by all accounts has been turning the court upside down with her tricks. Did ye ken it is all the fashion now for the young ladies to smear their skin with some kind o' silvery shimmering gel, to mimic the look o' Bronwen's scales? And they cut their dresses very low now, like Bronwen does, even though they have no gills to flaunt like she does. Some even go so far as to make false fins from muslin that they attach with ribbons to wrist and elbow. She has a clique o' her own now, that do naught but play and sing and dance, and stir up trouble. I heard one tale that she and her ladies have parties where they all swim naked in her pool, and do tricks like performing seals for the crowd."

"Surely no'!" Niall was shocked.

Iven shrugged. "Ye ken those ladies o' the court, all they do is clishmaclaver. Some say she's already with babe and she and Donncan need to be married afore the babe is born, which could be true. Others say the young prionnsa is hot for her, but she turns a cold shoulder on him, and His Highness wants to tie the knot afore she unravels all his treaties by running off with someone else. Who kens?"

Lewen listened with great interest. He knew the young heir

to the throne very well, being only four years younger and seeing a great deal of him in the course of his duties as one of the
Rìgh's squires. He knew Bronwen NicCuinn too, as well as
anyone could know that cool, haughty young beauty.

"It's all the talk o' the countryside, though, which must relieve
the pressure on the MacBrann," Iven continued. "Now he's inherited the crown o' Ravenshaw there's a good deal o' pressure on
him to be marrying too and producing an heir. Ravenscraig was
awash with eligible young ladies when we left. I fancy that is why
Lady Fèlice is with us. I hear she tried her feminine wiles on him
and was mortified when the MacBrann paid her no mind. Which
is no' surprising, all things considered."

At this last comment Lewen frowned and looked to his father,
not liking to hear gossip about the MacBrann being repeated. Although Dughall MacBrann's lack of interest in women had been
sniggered about for years, it was disconcerting hearing a friend of
his father's discuss it so openly.

Niall smiled at him. "Och, my lad, I ken ye think Iven as full
o' clishmaclaver as the court ladies but indeed, his tongue does
no' always run on wheels. It is his job to gather information for
the Rìgh and he kens I'm still interested in court doings, although I live so far away. He can be the very soul o' discretion
if needs be."

"Indeed I can," Iven said solemnly. "All I'm telling ye is
what ye could hear in any village inn. I ken far more than I've
said, I promise ye."

Lewen smiled but thought he would be sure never to confide
any secrets to the fair-haired jongleur. His father must have
read his expression for he put his hand on Lewen's shoulder
and said quite seriously, "Och, I mean it, laddie. Iven has
worked in secret for the Rìgh since long afore Lachlan won
back his throne. He was one o' Dide's men, and faced much
danger in the days o' the Ensorcellor, when rebels and witches
faced death by fire if they were caught. A single careless word
would've been enough to condemn them all."

Iven's face had darkened. "Och, they were bad days. Let us
hope we never see days like them again."

"Eà turn her bright face upon us," Niall said, just as sombrely.

They came silently through the kitchen garden, all busy with their own thoughts. Wood-smoke scented the cool, fresh air. The clouds on the mountains were slowly blowing down over the valley. Ursa ambled along behind Niall, raising her snout to sniff the air. Niall could hear voices from the sitting room, and then the sound of laughter.

Suddenly the nisse Kalea shot out of the sky like a maddened hornet. She tweaked one of Ursa's soft ears, so the old bear moaned in distress, tugged Niall's hair, and then grabbed hold of the two ends of Iven's long, plaited beard. She spun so fast in the air she was nothing but a blur of light. Iven cried out in pain and put up his hand to try and catch her. As suddenly as she had come, she was gone again. Iven's forked beard was now twisted into a spiral. He picked it up in his hand and looked at it ruefully. "That hurt," he said.

"That's nisses for ye," Niall said. "We get plagued by them a lot. They think o' the bairns as some kind o' pet, especially Lewen. Notice she did no' pull his hair?"

"Aye, so she didna," Iven said in mock resentment. "That hardly seems fair. Doesna she ken I'm a guest and to be treated with deference?"

"What about me? I'm the master o' this wee domain and she pulls my hair and tugs on my nose all day long."

"Aye, but she almost pulled my beard out by the roots. A man's beard should be sacred!"

"Would a nice cool ale make it feel better?" Niall asked, opening the door into the kitchen. "Or happen a wee dram?"

"The sun is over the midline, make it a dram," Iven said. "Then take me to see this bonny lass that dares ride a winged horse. What a shame we canna bide a wee so I could have a chance to put her story into song. It's been a long while since we've had a new tale to tell."

"We plan to send her with ye to Lucescere," Niall said with a grin. "Ye'll have plenty o' time for song-writing."

"Will she be bringing her horse?"

"Just try and stop her."

Iven tossed back his dram of whisky with a deep sigh of satisfaction. "My beard and the Centaur's, I can hardly wait," he said contentedly. "I can tell it's going to be an interesting journey!"

The Apprentice-Witches

Kingarth was only a small house and the sitting room was already uncomfortably crowded when the three men joined the others. Usually this room was reserved for Lilanthe, who did her sewing and the household accounts there, and wrote her letters. Beautifully worked tapestries of forests and gardens hung over the stone walls, and soft padded chairs covered in green velvet were drawn close about a low table. A sofa made comfortable with soft cushions and rugs was pushed against one wall, while a tall bookcase was crowded with books, a rare luxury so far from the city. On the mantelpiece was a collection of wooden animals Lewen had carved for his mother over the years. In moments of idleness he liked to sit and whittle, watching the shape that emerged from the wood as if it had been imprisoned inside.

The sofa and chairs were all occupied by the females, so Iven, Niall and Lewin went to crowd by the fire with the other males. As soon as Cameron and Rafferty saw Niall, they eagerly asked him if it was true he had once been one of Lachlan the Winged's own guard in the years before he had won the throne. Niall was happy to oblige them with tales of some of the Blue Guards' more romantic escapades from the days when the Ensorcellor ruled the land and Lachlan had been a young rebel, his wings concealed beneath a cloak of illusions so that all had thought him a poor hunchbacked cripple.

Lewen leant his shoulder against the wall and observed the members of the group with great interest. The young ladies were all drinking tea and listening politely to Nina as she brought Lilanthe up to date with the happenings of the royal court. Maisie was drinking in every word with rapt eyes, while

Edithe was quick to express her opinion on everything from accounts of witch-taunting in Tirsoilleir to the new tax on glass.

Meanwhile, the young poet Landon was absorbed in watching Rhiannon as she fiddled with a wooden box on the side table. Lewen grinned to himself. He had made the box at school and brought it home as a gift to his mother that Hogmanay. It was a cunningly designed puzzle box which looked as if it was merely a prettily carved cube of wood with no lid or hinge or clasp or lock that could be opened. However, it rattled when shaken, revealing something was hidden inside. Most people gave up in frustration after only a few moments, but it was possible to solve the puzzle if one looked long and hard enough. He wondered if Rhiannon would be one of the few to work it out, and by the determined expression on her face, he wagered that she would.

Meriel, Roden and the arak were busy playing spillikins on the floor, the little hairy creature showing amazing dexterity with fingers and toes and tail. Eventually she did knock over one of the sticks, however, and then the arak shrieked with rage and bounded all round the room, upsetting cups of tea and sending a plate of cakes flying. Hurriedly the children tidied up after her, apologising and trying to contain their giggles. When Edithe said haughtily that she would have thought the stable was the place for such a wild beast, and Lulu tipped her head upside down and made a rude face at her from between her hairy legs, Meriel and Roden lost control and fled the room, bubbling over with laughter. Lulu bounded after them, her long tail seizing one of the broken cakes and tossing it deftly into her mouth.

Edithe rolled her eyes and lifted her cup to her mouth, sipping delicately. "Really, that animal! As if we were all no' in enough discomfort already. I must say, I do no' understand why we all must travel in this way. My father would have preferred me to travel in my own carriage, with outriders and my maid to attend me."

"Students are no' permitted servants at the Theurgia," Nina said in a tone of long suffering. "Apprentices must learn to manage for themselves. Ye ken the rules, Edithe."

Edithe sniffed and turned her gaze to Rhiannon, who had

lifted the puzzle box to her ear and was shaking it vigorously. Something rattled inside, and she turned it in her hands, searching for a way to open it.

"So ye are to ride to the Tower o' Two Moons with us, Rhiannon? What is your Talent?"

Rhiannon shrugged, not looking up from the box in her hands.

"Ye have no Talent as yet? But ye are quite auld. Ye must have sat your first two Tests o' Powers. What element were ye strongest in?"

"Dinna ken."

"Ye do no' ken? You mean ye have no' sat your Tests?"

"Nay."

"But then, surely . . . what makes ye think ye can attend the Theurgia if ye have no' even undertaken the First Test o' Powers? I ken, o' course, that the Coven are no' as strict as they once were about whom they allow to attend the Theurgia." Edithe flicked a contemptuous glance towards Maisie, who coloured unhappily, and Landon, who did not notice. "However, applicants must still have some form o' cunning, at the very least. I, o' course, was demonstrating unusually strong powers at a very young age and passed my First Test o' Powers with flying colours."

She said this with a confidential smile to Fèlice, who smiled and murmured, "O' course," with a laughing glance aside to Maisie.

Rhiannon was not listening. Her nimble fingers had found a loose edging of wood along the bottom of the box which, when pulled out, revealed a secret compartment. Hidden within was a tiny key. Rhiannon emptied it into her hand with a gleeful smile and at once began to look for a keyhole. She found it only a few moments later by swinging aside a carved scroll which had been made mobile by the removal of the piece of edging. She glanced up at Lewen in triumph and inserted the key into the lock. Once it was turned, the lid of the box swung open to reveal another, smaller, puzzle box inside. Lewen had to bite back a grin as her face changed from triumph to chagrin. At once she began to turn the smaller box in her hands, looking for the secret to opening it, but this box had been made differently to the first, and so presented a whole new conundrum.

Edithe did not like being ignored. She pressed her lips together, then said sharply, "But ye? Ye have no' even sat your First Test o' Powers, that most sit at the age o' eight. How auld are ye now? What makes ye think ye can just turn up at the Theurgia and have them welcome ye with open arms? Have ye any Skills at all?"

Rhiannon did not answer, being still absorbed in the box.

Edithe leant forward and tapped her sharply on the knee. Rhiannon jumped violently and almost dropped the box.

"I said, do ye have any Skills at all?"

Every muscle in Rhiannon's body stiffened. She stared at Edithe warily, then slowly shook her head.

"Ye do no' go for training in witchcraft and witchcunning then? Ye are naught but a common student? Are ye no' far too auld?"

"Dinna ken," Rhiannon said, through clenched teeth.

"I see," Edithe said. "No Skills at all, and no learning either that I can see."

"Edithe," Nina said warningly.

Edithe smiled sweetly at her. "I'm sorry. I'm just curious. Is the Theurgia really so desperate for students that they will accept just anyone?" She turned back to Rhiannon, running her gaze up and down the dress which had so obviously been made over to fit her. "Your family must be eager indeed for ye to learn what ye can, and make many new friends and associates, if they are prepared to carry the costs of sending ye all the way to Lucescere to go to school."

Lilanthe drew her brows together.

"Have no family," Rhiannon said tersely.

"No family? But then who . . . ?" Edithe glanced round at the small, simply furnished room, clearly wondering how Niall and Lilanthe could hope to pay for both their son and their strange guest to attend the Theurgia. "Have ye a private independence?"

"Uh?"

"A private independence? Money o' your own? How do ye expect to pay for your board and tuition at the Tower?"

"Dinna ken."

Edithe glanced at Fèlice, who shrugged, looking uncomfortable. "I see," Edithe said again with such a nasty innuendo in her voice that Lewen took a quick step forward, though he had no idea what he could say in Rhiannon's defence.

Before he could speak, his mother said in a chilly voice, "Rhiannon shall be sitting for a scholarship. She shows unusual potential that we are certain shall flower into a true Talent. I have already written to the Keybearer about her and I am sure she shall be most pleased to welcome Rhiannon to the Theurgia. Isabeau is always excited at the discovery o' a possible new Talent."

Edithe stared at her, both brows raised. "Indeed?" she asked coolly. "Ye ken the Keybearer well, do ye?"

"Ye must realise that Lilanthe is the Keybearer's dearest friend, Edithe," Nina said. "They have kent each other since they were lassies. Lilanthe once taught at the Theurgia. The Keybearer would love her to return and teach again but Lilanthe does no' care for cities."

"Oh, I see," Edithe cooed, pulling her chair a little closer to Lilanthe. "I dinna realise. Och, please tell us more, madam. I would love to hear tales o' the Keybearer as a lass. I believe her powers were extraordinary even then?"

"Indeed they were," Lilanthe said, "but more extraordinary still were her kindness and compassion. Even today, when we are at peace with all, such consideration for the feelings o' others is rare."

It was so clearly a snub that colour flamed into Edithe's cheeks and she sat back, at a loss for words. Lilanthe turned back to Nina, saying eagerly, "Tell me, how is Dide? Is it true he has finally given up the travelling life?"

As Nina answered her with a laugh, Edithe excused herself stiffly and came over to the fire. To Lewen's surprise, Edithe did not join the laughing group round his father but came straight up to him, smiling sweetly. Up until this moment she had paid him no attention at all, but he soon realised that she had revised her earlier opinion of him as an unimportant country clodpole.

"I had no' realized your parents were so well acquainted with the court at Lucescere. Tell me, have ye visited there often?"

"Aye," Lewen answered curtly, not wanting to tell her he

waited on the Rìgh at table every night, and ran his messages, and carried his cloak and hat.

"Indeed? Tell me more," she purred. "Have ye met the Rìgh?"

"Aye," he answered again, feeling torn between amusement and embarrassment. After a moment, realising she would find out in the end, he said reluctantly, "I am one o' the Rìgh's squires, when time permits. I attend court every evening, after I have finished my studies, and I often ride out with him."

Edithe leant closer. "Ye must ken the young prionnsachan too, then? Donncan and his brother Owein?"

"Aye, and the Banprionnsa Olwynne too," Lewen said, irritated by the way she mentioned only the two sons of the family. Lewen was very close friends with the royal twins, being less than a year older than them, and in the same class at the Theurgia.

"Och, o' course," she said now, smiling. "I imagine we shall see a lot o' them once we are at the Theurgia."

"I doubt it," he answered. "They are very busy with their own concerns. And the Theurgia is very large."

She tried another tack. "And the Keybearer, do ye see her often too?"

"No, no' very often," he answered, looking for some way to escape

"Oh? I had thought your mother was good friends with the Keybearer Isabeau NicFaghan? Did I misunderstand? Or perhaps their friendship was no' kept up?"

"Aunty Beau comes here often," Lewen said unwillingly. "She travels about a lot, ye ken. She'll always come by if she's in Ravenshaw."

Edithe looked skeptical. "But ye live so far away from anywhere here! It took us three days' hard riding to get here from Ravenscraig and the MacBrann told us there is nothing beyond your farm but the wild mountains."

"Aye, that is true," Lewen said. "But Aunty Beau can take any shape she chooses, remember. It is no' far to come if ye are flying in the shape o' a golden eagle."

Edithe was impressed despite herself. She leant even closer, laying one white hand on Lewen's sleeve. "I am so glad to ken someone who will be able to teach me how to go on at the Theurgia." She glanced down coyly, twisting the small moonstone ring on the middle finger of her right hand, symbol of her acceptance into the Coven as an apprentice. Lewen wore a ring very like it, as did all of the young apprentices. "It will be so very large and overwhelming at first. It will be nice to have a friend, to help ease my first days there."

Lewen was aware of Rhiannon's gaze fixed upon them, and blushed. He was saved from answering by Lilanthe, who stood up and said, "Shall we go and eat? I can smell all is ready. Ye must be hungry."

At once everyone stirred and looked up, beginning to make appreciative noises, for indeed the smell coming from the kitchen was delicious. They all followed Lilanthe eagerly, though Lewen noticed both Fèlice and Edithe looked rather affronted at having to eat in the kitchen.

Their look of outrage deepened as all three of the young men showed a marked inclination to sit next to Rhiannon at the dinner table. Openly eyeing the voluptuous curves threatening to split the seams of her dress, Cameron scrambled to pull out her chair for her and then, when she sat, took the opportunity to gaze over her shoulder and down her cleavage. While he feasted his eyes, Rafferty slid deftly into the chair beside her and tried to engage her in conversation, much to Cameron's chagrin. Cameron hurriedly took the seat on her other side, pushing the young poet Landon out of the way. Dejectedly Landon made his way round the other side of the table to sit next to Maisie, who smiled at him shyly in commiseration.

Edithe slipped her hand inside Lewen's arm and smiled at him, saying sweetly, "Do ye always eat in the kitchen? How very quaint. Please, tell me where I should sit? I can see ye have no order o' precedence here."

He pulled out a chair for her and then tried to make his escape but she was ruthless, pulling him down to sit next to her. Fèlice at once took the seat on his other side and both young ladies spent the whole meal laughing at every remark he made, leaning close to him so he could smell their perfumed hair, and generally making him very uncomfortable.

His only hope was that their attentions would make Rhiannon jealous, but she did not seem to notice, focusing all her attention on her food as if she had not eaten twenty-three griddle-cakes earlier in the day. Edithe and Fèlice exchanged a horrified roll of the eye when they saw her cramming her food into her mouth with both hands. Lewen managed to catch Rhiannon's eye and gently shook his head, showing her as unobtrusively as he could how to wield a knife and spoon. She scowled at him but tried to copy his actions, her elbows stuck out so far side-ways the two boys had to lean the other way to avoid being poked in the face.

They were not put off, however, continuing to be assiduous in offering her more bread or another serve of pie. She did not soften with all their attention, answering only curtly, and often staring at them with scorn as if she thought their questions or comments more than usually stupid. The older boy, Cameron, was particularly attentive, leaning so close to her at times that Lewen had to grind his teeth together to stop himself from leap-ing up and protesting.

"I have no' seen ye at court afore. I ken I would remember ye if I had," Cameron said with a winning smile.

She flashed him a glance but made no reply, being too busy eating.

"Am I right?" he said, leaning closer. "If ye had been to the court at Ravenscraig, I am sure I must have noticed ye."

She cast him a quizzical look, gave a perfunctory shake of her head, and reached for another bread roll.

"Never? Are ye a country lass then? Did ye grow up round here too?"

"Near enough," she answered after a moment, cramming an-other wedge of cheese and leek pie into her mouth.

"So is this your first journey away from home?"

She nodded and elbowed him away so she could reach the jug of iced bellfruit juice. He sat back for a moment, discon-certed, then fortified himself with several large gulps of the juice and tried again. "Ye must be rather daunted at the idea o' travelling all the way to the royal court at Lucescere then."

"I think that's the understatement o' the day," Edithe said to Fèlice, who giggled, then looked a little shamefaced.

"Ye must no' be nervous. I'll be happy to show ye round and tell ye how to get on," Cameron continued.

"Like ye'd ken," Edithe said with a snort of contempt.

Cameron glared at her. "I may no' have been to the royal court afore but I've been a squire at Ravenscraig for years now."

Edithe looked down her nose. "Ye think anyone at Lucescere will care?"

Cameron turned his shoulder against her. "Do no' listen to her," he said warmly to Rhiannon. "She hasna been to Lucescere either, she just likes to put on airs."

Rhiannon stared at him blankly, shrugged and kept on eating. Cameron edged his chair closer to hers. "So ye must no' be afraid," he said in a low, confidential voice that Lewen had to strain to hear. "I promise I'll keep an eye on ye. Ye shallna be lonely while I'm there to watch out for ye."

Rhiannon laid down her knife and spoon. "Me no afeared," she said angrily, "and me no lonely. Me have my horse."

Cameron laughed, startled, then leant even closer, speaking in such a low voice that Lewen could not hear a word, despite all his efforts.

Rhiannon curled her lip. "Rather have my horse," she said.

Cameron sat back, colour rising in his cheeks. He looked dumbfounded.

Rhiannon grabbed and another handful of roast potatoes, ate them hungrily, then wiped her greasy hands clean on her bodice. As she gulped down the rest of her juice, Rafferty took advantage of Cameron's sudden silence to try his hand at engaging her in conversation.

"I havena travelled much afore either," he said. "I'm so looking forward to it. I've always wanted to travel the world. What are ye looking forward to seeing the most?"

Rhiannon shrugged. "Dinna ken."

"I canna wait to see an ogre," Rafferty said confidingly.

Her lip curled. "Why? Ogres ugly, mean and stupid."

"Ye've seen one afore?"

"Aye, o' course." She spoke as if ogres were as common as dandelions.

"Well, I've never seen one. I come from down by the sea, though. I've seen the Fairgean come into harbour, riding on the back o' their sea-serpents." He spoke rather defensively.

"Really?" Maisie squeaked.

"Aye, really." Rafferty looked across the table at her.

"I'd love to see the Fairgean." Maisie clasped her hands together. "They're said to be bonny indeed."

"If ye like that sort o' thing," Edithe said cuttingly. "Personally I find the idea o' scales and gills quite loathsome."

"The Banprionnsa Bronwen is said to have scales and gills and they say she is the most beautiful girl at court," Fèlice said. "I canna wait to see her! I've heard her clothes are just divine."

Cameron snorted in derision. "Is that no' just like a lass? Who wants to look at clothes? It's the changing o' the guard that I'm dying to see. I hope the Rìgh's captain is there and no' off fighting somewhere. I've heard so many stories about him and his cursed sword."

"Och, me too," Rafferty said excitedly. He turned to Rhiannon. "Have ye heard the tales? They say once he has drawn his sword, he canna sheathe it till all the enemy are dead. It doesna matter how many o' them there are, he'll just keep on fighting till nary a one is left."

This sparked her interest and, encouraged, he went on. "They call him Dillon o' the Joyous Sword, for the sword takes such joy in battle. He was one o' the League o' the Healing Hand, ye ken." At Rhiannon's blank look, he said, "Ye must've heard o' the League? There are so many stories about them. Ye ken, the band o' beggar children that helped the Rìgh win his throne?"

"Do ye think Jay the Fiddler will be at court?" Fèlice said with a sigh. "I'd love to hear him play his *viola d'amore*. They say no-one can play the songs o' love like he can."

"Very true," Nina said with a mischievous smile. "But I doubt whether Jay will be at court. He and Finn the Cat will be off somewhere on the Rìgh's business. Ye would think they had jongleurs' blood in them, those two, the way they travel around."

"What about ye, Landon?" Lilanthe asked then in her soft, gentle voice, for the young poet had not said a word all meal. Indeed, he had hardly eaten a mouthful either, sitting with his chin resting in his hand and his eyes fixed on Rhiannon's face. Once or twice the wild girl had cast him an irritated glance, but he did not seem to care. He seemed to find her endlessly fascinating.

Landon did not respond, until Maisie tugged his darned and

grubby shirt-sleeve. Then he looked round with an abstracted air, saying, "I'm sorry?"

"What are ye most looking forward to seeing on your journey to Lucescere?" Lilanthe repeated.

He looked back at Rhiannon and smiled wistfully. "My eyes have feasted upon the utmost pinnacle o' beauty, I have no desire to see aught else," he answered without a trace of embarrassment.

Fèlice giggled, Maisie blushed, Edithe frowned and snorted, and the other boys looked down, discomfited and embarrassed on his behalf. Rhiannon herself stared across the table at her admirer in obvious puzzlement, then set about picking her teeth with a ragged but thankfully clean fingernail. The adults exchanged wry looks.

"What about ye, Maisie? Is there anything ye particularly want to see at court?" Lilanthe asked.

The country girl blushed and fiddled with her moon-stone ring.

"I just want to see the Keybearer," she whispered. "And all the healers at work."

"Ye are interested in herb-lore and the healing arts?" Lilanthe said. "I must show ye my simple room afore ye go. I canna claim to be a healer like Isabeau or Johanna, her head healer, but I did learn what I ken from them and I do my best for the people o' the valley."

"Och, I'd like that," Maisie whispered, her face glowing.

"I guess ye're used to that sort o' thing," Cameron said to Rhiannon, with a glowering look at Landon, who was once again regarding her with intense fascination.

"Uh?" Rhiannon said.

"All that flim-flammery and flattery," he said. "I bet all the lads ye ken follow ye round all the time, begging ye for a smile or a kiss."

Rhiannon was surprised into laughter. "Who, me? Nay!" she cried, shaking her head so her glossy hair swung.

If she was striking when sullen-faced and cross, she was quite breathtaking when smiling. Lewen could not take his eyes off her, even though he was aware of how cross this made both Edithe and Fèlice. He was not at all surprised when Cameron hitched his chair closer, sliding one arm around Rhiannon's waist as he whispered something in her ear. If Lewen had not been constrained by the rules of hospitality he would have leapt up and punched the good-looking boy right in his smiling mouth. As it was, his hands clenched into fists and he had to swallow the sour taste of rage.

All the warmth and spontaneity died out of Rhiannon's face. Sitting straight-backed and stiff as a poker, she hissed, "Get your hand off me else me cut it off for ye!"

Her words rang out in one of those little lulls that sometimes come in a noisy room, and everyone turned and stared down the table. Cameron went scarlet and hurriedly moved his chair away. Rhiannon stared at him for a moment longer, then went on eating as if nothing had happened, but Fèlice and Edithe gave little embarrassed titters and Lilanthe drew her brows together in a look of trouble.

After the meal had been cleared away, the group broke up. Lewen and his father showed the other men around the farm while Lilanthe took the girls out to her herb garden and then to her simple room, lined with bottles of home-made medicines and potions.

They met again for high tea in the kitchen, then all crammed together in the sitting room as dusk rolled over the garden.

Nina sang for them, her long-billed sunbird amusing everyone by accompanying her with melodious little trills and call notes. There was much animated talking and laughing, with Iven easily dominating the conversation, telling tales and teasing the others good-naturedly. He tried to draw Rhiannon out but she stared at him suspiciously and answered only in monosyllables, so at last he gave up and concentrated on entertaining his crowd. Rhiannon sat as still and wary as a bird hiding in bracken, frowning, her mouth set firmly, her luminous blue-grey eyes moving from face to face. It was clear to Lewen that she could understand little of what was said. They were all speaking too quickly, and at cross-currents, drowning out each other's voices as they insisted on having their say. The conversation was mostly concerned with politics and court gossip, none of which meant a thing to the wild girl from the mountains.

As the night wore on Edithe and Cameron, who had both obviously taken a strong dislike to Rhainnon, began to mock her more openly, asking her opinion on the appointment of the new Fealde in Tìrsoilleir or rumours that the treaty with the Fairgean was under strain. To each question she said only, "Dinna ken," which the girls seemed to find exquisitely funny. Edithe appeared most concerned about Rhiannon's lack of a private independence, and asked her a great many questions about how she hoped to manage in Lucescere without an allowance.

"But, my dear, ye simply must have some income," she said. "Although we all have to wear an apprentice robe while at school, there will be lots o' parties and balls and picnics and one must have clothes. It is the royal court, after all." She looked Rhiannon up and down, and then said delicately, "But happen ye do no' care for clothes?"

Cameron laughed.

Rhiannon said nothing.

Fèlice and Edithe then fell into an animated discussion about the latest fashions at court.

"I heard the Rìgh's niece wears her bodice cut very low, with barely a sleeve at all, to show off her fins and gills," Edithe said. "Who would have imagined fins and gills would become fashionable! And it is most unfair, for she does no' feel the cold, ye ken, so that she wears her dresses so even in the very midst o' winter."

Rhiannon sat silently, listening, ignoring the fixed unfriendly gaze of Cameron and the fixed longing gaze of Landon as best she could. It was clear she was going to have to get used to Landon's eyes upon her face. He had spent all afternoon staring at her. Occasionally he dug out a scruffy little notebook from his pocket where he would scribble a few words, before staring in agony at the ceiling as he mouthed half-rhymes and mangled phrases. At one point Lewen heard him muttering, "Breast, west, best, nest?" and he blushed for both Landon and himself.

He heard a burst of mocking laughter a little later, and looked across the room, to find Fèlice and Edithe hiding their smiling mouths behind their hands, while Cameron grinned, looking very pleased with himself.

"What, naught to say?" Cameron was saying. "What's the matter? Cat got your tongue?"

Rhiannon stared at him in obvious bewilderment. "Uh? Cat? What cat? There no cat. And me have my tongue. See?" She poked it out at him.

They all broke into peals of laughter, even shy, sweet Maisie. Only Landon did not laugh, looking at Rhiannon in obvious pity and sympathy.

Glancing at Rhiannon, Lewen was surprised to see her eyes were swimming with tears. He got up at once and said gently, "Rhiannon, ye must be weary still, would ye like to go to bed?"

She nodded at once and got up, so tall and awkward in her too-tight green dress that Edithe twisted her lip in scorn, hardening Lewen's dislike of her into something hotter and fiercer. He showed Rhiannon out of the room as quietly and unobtrusively as he could. Her fists were clenched and her cheeks were flushed, and she did not look at Lewen but caught up her mass of entangling skirts so she could stride out with ease. Lewen did not speak at all as he gathered up the clean nightgown Lilanthe had laid out for her, and the pile of warm blankets, and carried them all out to the stable. She went straight to the black mare, which turned its head and whinnied eagerly at the sight of her. Rhiannon flung her arm about its neck and buried her face in its silky flowing mane. The mare nudged her with her nose and blew gustily through its nostrils but she did not look up.

By the time Lewen had made up her bed for her, she was calm again, though her eyelashes were spiky with tears. She wiped her nose on her green silk sleeve.

"Thank ye," she said with some difficulty.

"My pleasure. Sleep well," Lewen answered. He hesitated, then said in a rush, "And do no' fear. None o' those louts shall trouble ye tonight, for I'll set Ursa herself to guard your door."

She laughed. "That bear? Ye want horses mad with fear all night?"

Lewen said valiantly, "Then I'll guard your door myself."

"Me no afeared," she said derisively. "Those boys ken no more about mating than a babe."

Lewen's blood surged. He had to turn away, pretending to busy himself checking the food and water of the other horses, until the heat in his face and his groin had subsided enough that he should not betray himself. In the meantime he could hear

Rhiannon ripping off the despised green dress and splashing about in the water. He dared not turn round until all was quiet again. When at last he faced her she was sitting cross-legged in the straw, eyeing him speculatively, dressed only in the thin white nightgown, the laces at the bodice undone.

"I'd best get back." He could not meet her eyes. "Are ye sure ye're grand?"

She dragged up her nightgown to show her knife strapped to one long, pale thigh. "Sure," she said. "What about ye? Need me to guard ye from those cursehags?"

Lewin grinned despite himself. "I hope no'," he said.

"Call me if ye need me and me come," she said.

"Ye too. Call me, I mean. If ye need me."

"Me no need ye," she said.

"I guess no'," he said, feeling miserable. "Good night then."

She wrinkled her brow. "What this 'good night'?"

"It's what ye say last thing at night, afore ye sleep," Lewen said. "It means have a good sleep, keep safe, have sweet dreams."

She smiled, radiantly and unexpectedly. "Me see. Good night to ye then."

He nodded and went out into the darkness. He did not go back the house at once, though, finding a tree to lean against in the chilly darkness of the garden, pressing his forehead against its smooth bark, crushing its new fresh leaves in his hands so he could smell their sharp smell. His body ached, his skin was hot, his mind was all confusion. He had heard of men addicted to moonbane, who kept on tasting it for its sweet, giddy delirium when all the time they knew it was poisoning their blood and destroying their reason. Rhiannon was like moonbane, he thought, and already it was too late for him. He was addicted.

Blackthorn

R hiannon woke slowly, feeling deliciously warm and comfortable. She cuddled her cheek against the soft black feathers that lay over her like a counterpane, aware of a strange new feeling inside her. She did not know how to name this feeling, but when she thought of her horse it warmed and deepened within her, and when she thought of the boy, with his quiet, deep voice and steady, watching brown eyes, it caused her to curl her toes, her mouth lifting at the corners.

She stretched and reluctantly slipped out from underneath the sheltering wing. The mare lifted her head and regarded her with a great, black velvety eye. When Rhiannon stared into that eye, she saw within a greater blackness, a slit, an abyss without an end. It fascinated her, this black slit that did not reflect the light like the rest of the eye, but seemed to suck it inside. Everything about her mare fascinated and allured her. Every line and curve of her body, every movement she made, every twitch of ear or flare of nostril was filled with grace and strength and power, and it was hers, all hers. She did not care what the big bearded man said, the winged mare was hers.

The mare gave a soft whinny of agreement and nudged her with her nose.

Rhiannon had not had much time alone since arriving at Kingarth. When she was not sleeping, there was always someone watching her, talking at her, demanding her attention.

Even though Rhiannon was accustomed to having no personal privacy, having grown up in the midst of a large herd, nonetheless she was used to long periods of quiet and solitude. Satyricorns did not talk much. Their language was simple and used only when a grunt or gesture would not suffice. Rhiannon had always been isolated within the herd because she looked so different from the other satyricorn children. Their eyes were yellow with an oblong iris, not a soft grey-blue like the dawn sky. They had hard cloven hooves and a ridge of hair that ran down their spine, ending in a tufted tail. Her torso had been smooth and hairless, and her feet were soft and flexible. She had never been able to run as fast, or leap as far, or fight as roughly as any of the other satyricorn children, and so she had learnt to keep herself apart, spending her days roaming the high meadows alone.

Here there was no quiet and no solitude. Rhiannon had been spinning in a whirlwind of words from the moment she arrived, grabbing here and there at sounds she thought she understood, only to find they had many more meanings than she could ever have imagined. Eyes could be daggers, cats stole tongues, air could be put on like a garment. The only clue she had to meaning was the voice with which the words were uttered, and even that was deceitful. Many of these humans said one thing with their words, and quite another with their faces and bodies and voices. It was exhausting and bewildering trying to decipher it all, and to make it worse, Rhiannon did not believe them when they kept telling her she had nothing to fear. There were so many threatening undercurrents to the things that they said, so many traps in their words.

Lewen was the only one that she did not fear. His voice was deep and slow and thoughtful, and he never made any sudden jerky move to startle or frighten her. He smiled at her, and was kind, and he never said one thing with his words and another with his eyes. When Rhiannon was alone with him, she found herself relaxing the tension of her muscles and the fierceness of her concentration.

But for now she had only the drowsy horses for company. She could think over the happenings of the last few days and begin to prepare herself for the journey ahead. Rhiannon was conscious of trepidation, for she did not know what lay ahead of her, and she was suspicious of these shrill, noisy humans with their complicated ways. She meant to keep her dagger close to hand, and her wits about her, for she could see there were many pitfalls ahead if she was unwary. At least she could always escape any trouble on the back of her beautiful winged horse. As long as the flying horse was with her, Rhiannon would be safe.

She stroked the black velvety nose, then got down her saddlebags from their hooks. She had not had a chance to go through her things and make sure they had not been interfered with. She did not believe these humans when they said they would not touch her treasures. It did not matter that they had many strange and beautiful and useful things of their own. In Rhiannon's experience, the more you had, the more you wanted.

She spent a happy half-hour turning over her treasures and arranging them to her liking in the saddlebags. She caressed the gleaming brooch of the running horse, and hid it right down the bottom of the bag along with the music-box, the silver goblet, the medal with its device of a hand haloed in light and her other treasures. If anyone saw those they would take them, she knew. Anyone would.

Then she sharpened her two beautiful daggers and put them ready with her bow and quiver of arrows. She wanted them close to hand at all times. The blowpipe and pouches of poisoned barbs she tucked just inside the pocket of the saddlebag that hung on the right, so she could reach them easily. Everything else she stowed away neatly, all except her clothes and the grooming kit in its leather wallet. She was turning over the currying combs and brushes and sponges in puzzlement when she heard a noise and looked up, muscles tensing instinctively.

Lilanthe was in the doorway, carrying a basin and jug of warm water, a big portmanteau dangling awkwardly from the crook of her elbow. Outside, birds were beginning to test their voices for their coming hosanna to the sun, and mist was eddying in a rising breeze.

Rhiannon frowned and closed the flap of the saddlebag.

Lilanthe came in and laid down her burdens. "What is it ye wish to hide, lassie?"

Rhiannon did not answer.

Lilanthe sat next to her, arms wrapped around her knees. "I am troubled about ye, Rhiannon," she said. "I canna read your mind. Are ye so secretive and suspicious because ye have reason to fear honesty? Or is it just your nature? I wish I kent what it is ye are frightened o'."

Her voice was so gentle and her eyes so filled with compassion, Rhiannon felt an urge to make her understand somehow.

"In herd, must fight for what yours," she said.

"Aye, I understand that. But we are no' o' the herd, we have no desire to take what's yours away from ye."

"Aye, ye do," Rhiannon said fiercely. "Ye say clothes no' mine, ye say horse no' mine."

Lilanthe was quiet for a moment. "I think ye can say the horse is yours," she said at last. "Certainly Lewen calls Argent 'his' horse, and I call the garden 'mine', and Niall certainly calls Ursa 'his' bear. I think it is natural in us to want to own things, to forge strong bonds with them. Niall's problem with ye calling the mare yours is a philosophical one, because a winged horse is no' like other horses. But he is no' acknowledging the fact that ye and the horse have clearly forged some kind o' bond, happen even the bond that is felt between thigearn and flying horse. Certainly none o' us would dream o' trying to separate ye."

Rhiannon grasped at the words she understood. "Ye say horse mine?"

"Aye, lassie. That is if ye think ye belong to her as much as she belongs to ye."

Rhiannon shrugged. "O' course. She mine, me hers."

Lilanthe smoothed her rough brown gown down over her knees. "The clothes are a different matter, though, Rhiannon." As the girl immediately stiffened, Lilanthe glanced up, smiling a little ruefully. "Nay, hear me out, lassie. I understand that the clothes are important to ye, but ye canna keep them. They are no' yours, they belonged to the Yeoman, and after his death they belong to his family."

"Me won them," Rhiannon said, scarlet with suppressed fury. "Blood-right!"

Lilanthe leant forward. "What was that? Blood-right? What does that mean?"

"They mine," she said flatly.

"Nay, Rhiannon, tell me, what does that mean? Did ye kill the soldier? Is that why ye claim the clothes as yours? Ye must

tell me. Canna ye see how important it is that we ken? We saw
the hole the arrow made in the cloth. He was shot through the
back. Did ye shoot him? For that's a hanging offence, Rhiannon. That would be treason. Ye must tell me, ye must explain to
me how it happened. For I do no' want . . . I would no' like to
send ye to Lucescere without at least . . . canna ye tell me how
it happened, Rhiannon?"

"Clothes mine," she said sullenly.

Lilanthe sat back, her face setting hard. "Nay, they are no',
Rhiannon. Now, I have a compromise to offer ye, for I do no'
wish to be taking anything away from ye against your will.
Look what I have done here." She turned and picked up the
portmanteau she had brought from the house. "See, these are
auld clothes o' Lewen's. There are breeches and shirts, and
quite a good coat, and an auld shawl o' mine, and some underclothes, and a few other things I think ye'll find useful."

Lilanthe then turned and, before Rhiannon could stop her,
picked up the blue cloak from where Rhiannon had laid it ready
in the straw. She turned it in her hands. "Now, look. Here is the
cloak o' the Yeoman. It is no ordinary cloak. See how it is grey
on one side and blue on the other? The cloaks o' the Blue
Guards are woven with spells o' concealment and camouflage
by the witches. In need, ye can turn it inside out and it will help
ye blend into mist and darkness, or against grey stone and
bracken.

With an inarticulate growl, Rhiannon snatched back the
cloak and huddled it against her. "Mine!"

"No need to fret," Lilanthe said with a smile. "I have no other
cloak for ye to wear and so my idea is ye should wear it till ye
reach Lucescere and then give it to the Yeoman's family with
everything else."

Rhiannon looked stubborn, and Lilanthe went on quickly,
persuasively, "And the tam-o'-shanter too. If ye will give it to
me for just a wee while, I'll unpick the cockade from it, and so
then it will be a cap just like anybody else's. When ye get to
Lucescere ye shall no' need them, for if ye are admitted to the
Theurgia to study along with Lewen and the other apprentices,
ye shall wear an apprentices' gown like everyone else. And if
ye are no' . . . well, I have asked my friend Isabeau to give ye

all ye will need. I will no' insist ye give these things up to me, Rhiannon, if ye will promise to submit them to Dillon, the captain o' the Yeomen, when ye arrive in Lucescere. Believe me, it is the best thing to do."

The set look on Rhiannon's face did not relax.

"Please? Ye do no' need the soldier's uniform. I've given ye everything ye might need."

"Very well then," Rhiannon said ungraciously. "Me no' wear them then, though no' fair, they mine . . ."

Lilanthe sighed. "Happen ye will come to understand in time, lassie. It would be wise o' ye to try to understand our customs, if ye are to live among us. I ken what we do and what we believe must seem as strange to ye as ye seem to us. Ye have a long journey ahead o' ye, I would use it to learn what ye can if I were ye. Nina will teach ye, and Lewen too. He'll have a care for ye, no need to fear."

"Me no' afeared," Rhiannon said haughtily.

"Nay, I see ye are no'," Lilanthe said slowly. She paused, looking down at her hands, biting her lip. After a long moment she looked up at Rhiannon, saying hesitantly, "I said that ye need no' fear, that Lewen will look out for ye and care for ye. I want ye to promise me, Rhiannon, that ye will have a care for him too."

Rhiannon tilted an eyebrow in surprise. "Lewen quick and strong," she said approvingly. "Stronger than me. He stop me killing bear."

"I think ye understand me, Rhiannon." Lilanthe's voice was a little uneven. "Just promise me ye will no' hurt him . . ."

"He big and strong," Rhiannon said dismissively. "He no' let me hurt him."

"I hope no'," Lilanthe said under her breath. "But there are more ways than one to hurt a man."

Rhiannon eyed her speculatively, then nodded slowly in agreement.

After Lilanthe left, Rhiannon dragged the voluminous nightgown over her head and gave herself a cursory wash with the warm soapy water Lilanthe had poured into the basin for her.

She had to admit it left her feeling refreshed, though she did find the older woman's insistence on constantly washing herself rather peculiar. Lilanthe had left her a comb as well, and Rhiannon made some attempt to drag it through her hair. It hurt, though, and so she gave up after only a moment, tossing the comb onto the floor.

This left Rhiannon with the puzzle of the clothes. She had never seen underclothes before and, after a long struggle trying to figure out which limb went through which hole, she managed to drag on the drawers. The chemise completely baffled her, however, and so she threw that at one of the horses who was laughing at her, and laughed herself when it landed over the horse's head, caught on one of its ears. The horse snorted and tossed its head, then rubbed its cheek against its leg, trying to dislodge the fragile scrap of cotton, without success.

Rhiannon managed to draw the breeches over her legs, having done that before, but found that these fastened with three small buttons, unlike the metal clasp of the dead soldier's pair. She had never seen buttons before and had no idea how to do them up. She stared at them and fiddled with them for quite a while, but then gave up, leaving the flap unfastened. The shirt she pulled over her head without too much trouble, managing to work out front from back eventually, but she could not tie the laces at the front and so left them loose, untroubled by the way the neckline hung loose, exposing the curve of her breasts.

All in all, Rhiannon was pleased with her new clothes. The white shirt was soft and warm against her skin, and the loose woollen breeches were more comfortable than the white leather pants the soldier had worn. The brown coat was a little too large, but had all sorts of useful pockets in which to store things, and she could move easily in it, unlike the tight green dress she had been forced to wear the day before. Most of all, she liked the cream-coloured shawl Lilanthe had given her, which was embroidered with a beautiful tracery of green tendrils and pink and red roses, now rather faded. She was so pleased with the shawl that she felt little regret over the loss of the dead soldier's clothes.

Lilanthe had left her the soldier's long black boots, not having any other shoes that would fit Rhiannon better, and so Rhiannon drew them on with pleasure, tucking the little black knife into its hidden sheath, and strapping the long silver dagger to her belt as before. She felt strong and brave again with her knives in place, and ready to face the mocking looks of those other boys and girls.

Now it was the mare's turn. Rhiannon had observed Niall and Lewen grooming the horses the previous day, and had seen how much the beasts had enjoyed the attention and how their coats had gleamed afterwards. Rhiannon wanted her mare to look her very best before she showed her to the others. She picked up the grooming kit again, took out a brush and began to beat the dust out of the mare's coat.

She was engaged in trying to tug all the knots out of the luxuriant black mane when a sudden restiveness in the mare made her aware Lewen was leaning on the gate, watching her.

"Do ye and your mam always sneak around, spying on people?" she said without rancour.

"I'm sorry," he said. "Dinna mean to scare ye."

"Och, me no afeared," she said severely. "Me just wonder how ye walk so quiet, being so big and all."

He coloured.

She smiled. She liked making him blush.

"Being around animals so much, I suppose," he said. "They do no' like sudden noise or movement."

"Nay," she agreed, casting him a look from under her lashes. She had noticed that this sideways look often made him blush and stammer.

Lewen's colour was high and she saw his eyes were on the front of her shirt.

"Ye should tie up your shirt," he said in a constricted voice. "Ye do no' want to go out and about like that."

"Like what?" she asked, looking down.

"Showing yourself like that. I ken ye mean naught by it, but . . . human lassies hide their . . . hide their . . ."

"My dugs, ye mean?"

"Their bosom," Lewen said, blushing as hotly as anyone with such tanned skin could.

"Bosom," she said, trying out the word.

"No-one will understand if ye do no' cover yourself up. Men

will think ye are offering yourself to them . . ." He stumbled to a halt.

"To mate?"

"Aye, to mate."

"And that bad?"

He nodded. "Only whores do that. Ye do no' want them to think that o' ye, Rhiannon."

"What whore?"

He searched for words. "Whores are women . . . and men, too, o' course, who will . . . mate . . . with anyone, if they are paid enough for it. We . . . us humans . . . we do no' mate with just anyone . . . only with those we love . . . most o' us anyway. Usually, when we find someone we love enough, we promise to lie only with them, no' with anyone else, forever."

Rhiannon was nonplussed. The satyricorn women always shared the men between them, and the idea of exclusivity was entirely foreign. Rhiannon had seen many ugly fights over the men, however, and thought she could see some sense in what Lewen said, as long as there were men enough for all the women. Certainly there seemed to be. The ratio of males and females among those staying at Kingarth was startlingly exact.

"So ye must try to remember to keep your laces tied, and no' show too much o' your body," Lewen went on, keeping his gaze averted.

"No' ken how," Rhiannon said flatly.

"Och, o' course. I should've thought. I'll have to teach ye."

"Aye," she said. "What me do?"

He looked back at her, and swallowed. "I'll show ye," he said. Gently he reached out and took the laces in his hands, drawing her closer to him. She went obediently. She felt his fingers on her skin as he fumbled with the laces, and took a step closer to him. He smelt very clean and fresh, and she could see the pulse in his throat beating swiftly, and the burn of his blood under his skin. Slowly he knotted the laces together, explaining what he was doing while he did it. As she ducked her head to watch, her hair swung forward and brushed his hand, and she heard the sudden intake of his breath. For some reason her own blood heated, and she kept her gaze lowered, feeling shy with him for the first time.

He untied the laces then, and tried to make her do it herself, but her fingers were clumsy and she could not manage it. He smiled and said, with a warm huskiness to his voice that she had never heard before, "Never mind. I'll tie it for ye now, and get some string for ye to practise on later. It's no' hard once ye get the hang o' it."

"Hang o' it?" she repeated, puzzled.

"Once ye ken how."

"Hang o' it," she repeated again. "Once ye get the hang o' it."

"Aye. It must be hard for ye, all the bits o' slang we use. I'd never noticed it afore, but we do seem to use a lot."

"Slang," she repeated.

"Aye. Slang. Figures o' speech."

She laughed. "How speech have figure? This figure." She gestured down her body with one hand.

"It is indeed," he murmured. He took a deep breath and stepped away. His foot crunched on the comb she had tossed away and he bent and picked it up.

"I suppose ye canna manage combing your own hair either?" he said, glancing back at her with a rueful grin.

She shook her head.

"Would ye like me to do it for ye?"

She nodded.

His mouth quirked. He drew her to sit down on an upturned barrel and stood behind her, drawing the comb through the waterfall of silky black hair. For a while he worked in silence, gently unsnarling the tangles, and she sat still, enjoying the feel of his fingers in her hair and lingering on the nape of her neck.

"Tomorrow ye'll have to ask one o' the other girls to help ye with all this stuff," he said after a long while.

"Why?"

"It'd be better."

"Why? Me rather have ye."

"Aye, I'm sure ye would, but it's no' seemly, Rhiannon, and besides, I do no' ken how long I could stand it. I'm only made o' flesh, ye ken."

She twisted round to look up at him. "Uh? O' course ye made o' flesh. We all made o' flesh."

He nodded. "Aye, I ken. I just mean . . . Never mind. Just ask one o' the lassies to help ye tomorrow, all right?"

Rhiannon sniffed. "Me no like those lassies. Me like ye."

Lewen took a deep breath, his hand twisting in her hair. For a moment he stood very still, holding her captive against him. She tensed all over and drew herself away, looking up at him warily. Her hair drew cruelly tight, like a rope between them. After a long moment that must have hurt her, he released his breath and his hand, stepping away. He stood with his back to her, his shoulders held stiffly, breathing with difficulty.

"I'm sorry," he said at last. With great care, he laid the comb down on her saddlebags. "I dinna mean to hurt ye."

She shrugged. "Ye no hurt me."

"That's good. I'd better go."

"Why?" she asked. "Where go?"

"Anywhere," he said with an unsteady laugh. "The lake might be a good place."

"Why?"

"Nice cold water," he said with the same odd laugh.

She shrugged. "Why ye all want wash so much? Ye smell clean enough."

"Thank ye," he said and began to move towards the door.

She remembered the buttons of her breeches and lifted her shirt. "Afore ye go, ye help? Me no' ken how."

He looked back at her and his breath caught. When he spoke his voice was unsteady. "Rhiannon, do ye ken what ye do to me?"

"No, what me do?"

"Ye'd be a test to any man's resolve, do ye ken that?"

She did not understand. "Too hard? Ye canna do?"

Lewen laughed a little. "Och, I can do your buttons up all right, no problem there. Though I'd rather be undoing."

"What ye mean?"

"Naught. Here, I'll show ye how to do it. Ye'd better learn to do it yourself, though, Rhiannon, for it's too much to ask me to be doing up your breeches for ye every day."

He took a deep breath, grinned ruefully, and slipped his fingers inside the waistband of her breeches to button them up for her, slowly and with intense concentration. When he was finished he stood still for a while, his fingers hooked through her waistband, holding her against him. Then reluctantly he slipped his fingers free and stepped away, turning his back on her. "Eà's green blood," he said.

"Too hard?" she asked again.

He laughed unsteadily. "Much too hard," he agreed. "Painfully so."

She was puzzled, but shrugged. "Me want clean horse," she said, waving one hand at the winged mare. "Me no ken how. Ye show?"

Lewen nodded, rubbing the back of his neck with one hand. "Aye, that at least will be no hardship," he answered. He went first to the water-trough and splashed his face and neck thoroughly with water, then took the dipper and poured more water over his head, gulping big mouthfuls of the icy cold fluid. She watched him in bemusement and he grinned at her.

"Ye're naught but trouble, Rhiannon, do ye ken that?"

She was indignant. "Me no trouble!"

"Trouble through and through. Come on, where's that kit o' yours? It'll do me some good to burn some o' this excess energy away."

He explained to her what each comb and brush was for, and demonstrated how to use the hoof pick on Argent, who picked up his huge hoof willingly enough.

Rhiannon then tried to do the same with the winged mare, who whinnied unhappily and danced away. Rhiannon tried again, then threw down the hoof pick in disgust. "Me no good!"

"Do ye think she will let me help?" Lewen asked. "For indeed ye are making a bad job o' it!"

"Thanks."

Lewen's eyes gleamed appreciatively. Not only was Rhiannon learning human idioms fast, but also how a change in intonation could change a whole word's meaning. "My pleasure," he said just as ironically.

"Well, show me how then," she said irritably. "Me no' want to show her to those goblin-eyes till she looks bonny as can be. Then their eyes'll really stick out!"

"Will she let me come near? For she wouldna let me near her yesterday and I dinna want her to kick down any more walls."

"Be nice, horse," she said to the mare, which neighed and put back its ears, but allowed Lewen to come closer.

"Ye need to think o' a name for her," Lewen said, gingerly laying one hand on the mare's shoulder. The skin shivered under his touch but the horse did not shy away. "Ye canna keep on calling her 'horse'."

"Dinna ken any names," Rhiannon said. "In the herd, named for your . . . Me no' ken how to say. Bigness."

"Bigness? You mean, height?"

She shook her head impatiently. "Nay, nay. Though, bigness o' body helps. Like, who gets first cut o' meat, that's First-Male, then other males, then my mother, One-Horn, she One-Horn and also First-Horn, for she kills best. Five-Horns is Second-Horn, but she has to fight hard against Three-Horns, who wants to kill her and my mother. Ye see?"

Lewen had taken up the curry-brush and was very gently brushing down the curve of the mare's back. "Aye, I think so," he said quietly. After a moment, he said, "Do no' think o' the herd anymore. Ye have escaped them. Ye are free now. Think only o' what lies ahead. Ye have a lot to learn and no' only how to groom your own horse, but how to manage in society, and all sorts o' things about Eileanan."

Rhiannon nodded and relaxed her grip on the comb, surprised to find it had pressed white ridges into her flesh.

"Your horse is the place to start, I think, since ye'll be riding her every day and so ye'll need to ken how to look after her. Come, I'll show ye her feet and how to clean them and stop her from bruising them. I wonder if she should be shod?" He slid his hand down the mare's leg and she at once lifted her hoof.

For the next half-hour they groomed the black mare until her coat gleamed like silk and she was relaxed and happy. As they brushed and combed her, and polished her hooves and horns, and worked the knots out of her mane and tail, they talked companionably. Lewen told Rhiannon about his first horse, a fat pony called Star for the white patch on its nose. He had soon outgrown Star and for many years rode a sweet-tempered strawberry roan called Aurora. Although he had loved it dearly, by his thirteenth birthday he was far too heavy for it, and so his father had given him Argent, who had been a large-boned, restive colt and now stood close on eighteen hands high, with powerful shoulders and rump. For three years Lewen had hand-fed and trained the young colt, and had begun to lunge him every day, so by the time he began to break the horse in to the saddle, they were well acquainted. Argent was bred from one of his father's own destriers, a warhorse taught to fight on the battlefield with his master. The line was famous, descended from Vervain, one of Cuinn Lionheart's six great stallions. With a pale, silvery-grey coat and tail, Argent was swift and strong with a savage temper, and he allowed no-one but Lewen to ride him.

"So ye named all your horses for . . . colour?" Rhiannon said, struggling to find the words for what she wanted to say.

"Aye, I suppose so, but ye do no' have to do that if ye do no' want."

"Me want," she said. "Horse is black. What is good name for black horse?"

Lewen shrugged. "I dinna ken. Sable, perhaps, or Jet."

She screwed up her nose and shook her head emphatically. "What did your father call me? Something sharp and cruel, he meant."

"I do no' think he meant—"

"Aye, aye, he did, ye think me no understand? What was that?"

"Thistle?" Lewen replied tentatively.

"Nay, ye fool. Black something."

"Och, aye. Blackthorn, another name for sloe. It grows wild round here. It has black thorny branches and pretty white flowers this time of year, that turn into a purply-blue fruit later. The villagers make sloe-gin out of it. Just now, this cold weather we've been having, they would call that a blackthorn winter, meaning winter in springtime."

"Perfect," Rhiannon said. "That her name then. Blackthorn."

Lewen looked at the tall, delicately built mare with her two long scrolled horns that were just the colour of the sloe, and nodded, pleased.

"Two good namings then." Rhiannon smiled at him so that he blushed red and dropped his gaze, scuffing his boot against the straw-scattered floor. When he glanced up she was smiling radiantly still, but at her horse, which had tossed her head and was prancing, as if glad to be named.

The kitchen was bright and busy with activity, though outside it was all grey and hushed still. Rhiannon ate as greedily as ever, cramming in two bowlfuls of hot porridge with honey and goat's milk, and sixteen griddle-cakes with melted butter and cherry jam. After a life of lean provisions, she could not help herself. Although these last few days had been so very different from what she had known before, she could not believe she would not know hunger again. You ate when you could, even if you felt rather sick afterwards.

She was aware of scornful glances cast at her by the two other girls, who were dressed again in their ridiculous tight dresses with their hair in unnaturally perfect ringlets, like nothing she had seen before; and the yearning dreamy gaze of the youngest of the boys, who seemed to her quite mad; and the resentful, lustful glance of the oldest of the boys, which perturbed her as none of the others did. There was something very like hatred in his glance. She had seen it before and she knew it meant harm to come. All she could do was disdain his hot glance with coldness, and hope to keep away from him.

The third girl was eager to be kind, which Rhiannon was prepared to accept, though she thought the worse of her for offering it, and the second eldest of the boys was torn between his natural good nature and his desire to emulate the older, tougher boy. Rhiannon was used to reading intent in the body language of the herd. It had kept her safe and relatively unscathed for sixteen years. There was a fine balance to be kept between appearing too weak, so that you were scorned and bullied, or too strong, so that First-Horn thought it was time to take you down.

Lilanthe was hovering over her son, caressing his rough brown hair with one hand as she poured him more tea, or straightening his collar as she passed with a plate of fresh griddle-cakes. He smiled at her and did not shrug her hand away, knowing how hard this latest parting would be for her. At last she came and sat down and ate a little herself, gazing at her boy as if he had grown so tall and broad-shouldered overnight.

"Och, I wish ye did no' have to go so far away," she said. "I've missed ye these last four years! Lucescere is such a long way, all the way round the mountains and up into the highlands o' Rionnagan! I wish the Tower o' Ravens was no' such a ruin and ye could go there to study. It's only a few days from here and then I could be seeing ye often . . ."

Nina gave a little expressive shrug. "Happen one day it will be restored. The Keybearer says she hopes the time will come when all thirteen towers o' learning are rebuilt again. Already there are seven, and a small enclave o' witches are camping in the ruins o' the Tower o' Dreamers and seeking to raise it high again, so soon there may be eight. No-one dares go near the Tower o' Ravens, though, ye ken. It is weird with ghosts and banshees and all sorts o' cruel and unhappy spirits, and they say it is only growing worse with time. The auld MacBrann sent some witches there a few months afore he died to see if it could be exorcised, saying he couldna sleep with all the ghosts flocking about his bed, but they came back in despair, saying the place reeked o' blood and death, and it was beyond their strength to cleanse it."

"They didna call him Malcolm the Mad for naught," Iven said. "Apparently he kept the whole castle in an uproar with his shrieks and curses and night terrors, and they got worse in the last few months afore he died."

Lilanthe drew her brows together. "Aye, he was troubled indeed, the poor auld man. We rode down to Ravenscraig to see if there was aught we could do to ease his last days, but he was rambling indeed by then and did no' ken us, or even his poor son. What o' Dughall? Does he no' plan to rebuild the tower? I ken Isabeau would come herself if he called, and bring a circle o' sorcerers to aid him."

"Dughall says the best thing to do is pull the whole place down and cleanse it with fire. He says he had to spend a night there once during the Bright Wars and it was enough to turn his hair as white as his father's. It was always a dark place, ye ken, right from the time o' Brann the Raven himself. The MacBranns have always been a strange lot, with their experiments and machines . . ."

Niall leapt at once to the defense of his ruling clan. "What about the auld MacBrann's seafire, then? That was one experiment the Rìgh found useful in the war against the Fairgean. And it was a MacBrann that built the locks at the mouth o' the Rhyssmadill, remember."

Iven laughed, holding up both hands. "Och, I ken. Ye must admit the MacBranns have always dabbled in the arcane, though. They have always loved the darker mysteries and that is why the Ensorcellor had so many followers here in Ravenshaw and why the attack on the Tower o' Ravens on the Day o' Betrayal was so very brutal."

"Aye," Niall agreed, sighing. "That was a black day. Forty years or more ago it was, and I was naught but a bairn, but I remember it clearly. We could see the smoke from my parents' farm. It billowed up like a great dark pillar, higher than the mountains, and then hung over us all for days, choking us with ashes. No' one single witch escaped the massacre, they say, no' even the MacBrann's own wife, Dughall's mother. And she was a Nic-Cuinn herself and aunt to the Rìgh. A Day o' Betrayal indeed."

"Still, it was a long time ago and twenty-five years since the Ensorcellor was overthrown," Nina said. She turned to the apprentices and said, "Ye will see Maya the Mute at the Tower o' Two Moons, ye ken. She labours in the libraries there, helping to restore the knowledge that was lost when she ordered the great towers o' learning to be burnt. Ye must treat her with respect, for though she may be bound to silence and servitude, she is still the mother o' Bronwen NicCuinn, who will one day share the throne with Donncan the Winged."

Not understanding a word that was said, Rhiannon had been growing impatient. Lilanthe must have noticed her restlessness for she turned to her and said, "Ye must ask Nina and Iven to tell ye all the auld tales as ye travel, and sing ye some o' the songs, for ye have a lifetime o' learning to make up in just a short while."

"Where does this lass come from, that she does no' ken the story o' Maya the Ensorcellor?" Edithe said scornfully. "Does she no' have a mother, or an auld granny, to tell her bedtime stories? And even the meanest village sees a jongleur every once in a while, to tell the auld tales and sing the song cycles."

"No' all," Lilanthe said briefly.

"It must have been a hovel indeed," Edithe said under her breath to Fèlice, who looked uncomfortable.

"Me learnt other things from my mother," Rhiannon said clearly, glancing at the blonde girl with contempt. "Like how to gut a goblin with a single slash o' my knife. Ye want me show you how?" And with a flick of her wrist her dagger was in her hand, its point hovering negligently near the pulse at the base of Edithe's throat. Edithe shrieked and shrank back. Rhiannon tossed the knife in her hand. "I guess no'," she said and put the dagger away.

There was a shocked silence. Everyone stared at Rhiannon.

"Did ye see what she just did?" Edithe said in a squeaky voice. "She threatened me!"

Nina put down her fork. "I'm no' sure any o' us blame her," she said testily. "Ye have been unpardonably rude, Edithe. I would have thought better o' a NicAven o' Avebury."

Edithe went crimson, and opened and shut her mouth a few times as she tried to think of a retort.

"Though Rhiannon does ken better than to draw her dagger at the dinner table," Lilanthe said with a meaningful glance at her.

Rhiannon was unrepentant. "Me no like that girl," she said. "She mean."

"Well, I hope ye will learn to get on with one another," Nina said impatiently. "We have a long journey together ahead o' us, and it'll be unbearable if ye're at each other's throats. Can ye all no' try and be civil?"

"O' course," Edithe said grandly. "I am sorry if anything I have said was misunderstood."

Lilanthe looked at the satyricorn girl. After a while she prompted her, saying, "Rhiannon?"

"What?" she said.

"Edithe has just apologised. Should ye no' say sorry too?"

"Why? Me no' sorry."

Edithe looked shocked.

"Rhiannon," Lilanthe said wearily. "Please."

"It's considered good manners, lassie, to return the apology, even if ye do no' do so with sincerity," Niall said with his usual humorous inflection.

"Me hate good manners," Rhiannon said sullenly.

"We've noticed," Niall responded and she flashed him an angry glance and then, surprisingly, laughed.

"Tell that girl to no' be so mean and me no kill her," she said.

"I think that's Rhiannon's idea o' an apology," Niall said to Edithe.

She looked down her nose, saying in an icy voice, "I am sure my father would be horrified if he kent the sort o' company I was being forced to travel with. I shall write to him at the very first opportunity."

"Ye do that," Nina said. "But just remember that this journey we are all about to embark upon is considered the first stage o' your learning as an apprentice-witch. The Coven believes humility, compassion and self-control are necessary attributes o' any witch. Ye may have all the craft and all the cunning in the world, but ye will never be allowed to join the Coven without showing forbearance and understanding towards others. Have I made myself clear, Edithe?"

"Aye, ma'am," she said, looking crushed.

"And as for ye, Rhiannon, if ye wish to travel in my care ye shall no' threaten any o' my students with harm again. Do ye understand me?"

"Aye, ma'am," Rhiannon responded, not looking crushed at all.

"Good," Nina said.

"Happen we'd best be on our way," Iven said. "It is light enough now to see the road. Is everyone packed up and ready?"

There was a chorus of answers, and everyone got up and started wrapping themselves in their riding cloaks and saying their farewells. Lilanthe was unable to hide her tears but she did not cling to Lewen, giving him a brief, hard hug before stepping back and saying huskily, "Make sure ye send news o' yourself, ye hear, my lad?"

Niall embraced him too and then surprised Rhiannon by kissing her on the cheek and saying, "Have a care for yourself, lassie, and keep that knife in your boot!"

"Unless I need it, o' course," she replied cheekily, surprising him into laughter.

Lilanthe did not kiss Rhiannon goodbye, but detained her

with a hand on her arm. "I have written a letter o' introduction to my friend Isabeau, who is Keybearer o' the Coven," she said gravely, giving Rhiannon a thick white envelope sealed with red wax. "I have written her a full account o' ye, and I hope she will have a care for ye in Lucescere."

"Thank ye," Rhiannon said, taking the letter and stowing it away in one of the many pockets of her coat.

Lilanthe's expression softened. "I hope all will be well with ye, Rhiannon. I am sorry I could no' help ye more." She was silent for a moment, then said in a tumble, as Rhiannon turned to go, "If ye have done no wrong, then no harm shall come to ye, that I am sure o'. Isabeau will find the truth o' it."

Rhiannon's brows drew together, and she stared at Lilanthe, who looked white and tired. Then she said, very gruffly. "Me done naught wrong!"

Lilanthe's gaze fell and colour rose in her cheeks. "That's good, I'm glad. All will be well then."

Rhiannon stared at her suspiciously, but Lilanthe just put her arm about her and gave her a brief hug, before turning to say her farewells to Nina and Iven.

Rhiannon followed the others out into the frosty morning, everyone shivering and complaining as they stowed their bags in the caravan and got out their tack to saddle up the horses. Meriel clung to her brother's hand, her cheeks wet with tears, and he looked down at her kindly and spoke quietly to her. After a while she nodded and let go of his hand, going to stand with her parents.

Only Lewen and Rhiannon had to go into the stable, since all the other horses had been pastured out for the night. He saddled up Argent quickly and then turned to help Rhiannon, who seemed to be having some trouble.

He found Rhiannon sitting on her backside in the straw, the saddle clutched to her chest, her face red. Blackthorn sidled about skittishly, her ears laid flat against her skull and an evil look in her dark eye.

"She doesna want to wear it," Rhiannon said rather blankly. It was clear she had not expected the winged horse to resist her will.

"She's no' really been broken to the saddle and bridle yet,

though, has she?" Lewen said. "It took me months to get Argent to accept the weight o' the saddle on his back."

Rhiannon scowled. She got up and dusted off her bottom.

"Blackthorn, ye are my horse now, remember," she said. "Ye do what me say."

The winged mare reared and neighed, shaking her mane defiantly. Her magnificent wings unfurled, the muscles in her shoulders bunching.

"Ye do no' want to be mine anymore?" Rhiannon said miserably. "But me thought . . ."

The mare stepped forwards delicately, pushing her black velvet nose into Rhiannon's shoulder and blowing slobber all over her. Then she turned her head and tried to bite the saddle.

"Ye do no' want saddle? But . . ."

"Well, they say a thigearn rides with neither saddle nor bridle. Happen ye're meant to be a true thigearn, after all."

Rhiannon smiled.

"Me never rode with such things afore," she said. "Me no' now."

"Ye'll have less control," Lewen warned. "And ye're bound to get rather bruised."

She dismissed this with a gesture.

"The saddle and bridle belonged to the Yeoman, anyway," he said. "Ye can stow them in the caravan with the rest of his things." He picked up the saddle and bridle, then slung the saddlebags over the top.

Immediately Rhiannon frowned. "Nay! Mine . . . my things in there." She turned back to the mare. "Blackthorn? Just the bags? Me and my bags."

Blackthorn hurrumphed and put her ears back.

"Happen ye should say 'please'," Lewen murmured, trying not to laugh.

"Please? Why?"

"It's considered polite."

"Hmmph. Very well. Please, Blackthorn?"

The mare inclined her head graciously.

"Ye will have to figure out some way to tie the saddlebags on if she willna wear the saddle. I wonder if she would accept wearing a pad? We use them for breaking in young horses. It's a soft saddle without a saddletree or stirrups. It has a girth and some hooks we could strap the saddlebags to. Let's see if she'll accept it."

A short while later Lewen rode round the side of the house on the back of his tall, silver-dappled stallion. Argent was fighting the bit, eager for a gallop.

"What took ye so long, lad?" Iven called from the driving seat of his caravan, drawn up before the front steps. "I thought the young ladies were slow!"

The laughter died out of his face as he saw the winged mare come stepping delicately through the mist-wreathed trees. The two long, scrolled horns springing from the mare's brow shone an unearthly blue, like the sky at dusk, and her wings were slightly unfurled, showing the subtle gradation of colour from black to iridescent blue. Rhiannon sat straight-backed and grave-faced on her back, wrapped in her long blue cloak, her black hair falling down her back, her quiver of arrows slung over one shoulder. Her longbow was strapped to the crown-embroidered saddlebags that hung over the mare's withers, while she wore her dagger strapped to her belt. She looked like the queen she had been named for.

There was a long astonished silence.

"O my heart moves in my breast, forever after I am denied all rest," Landon whispered.

Rhiannon scowled.

A little mutter ran round the apprentices and their horses stirred restively beneath them.

"A thigearn," Fèlice whispered. "Och, I've always wanted—"

"A thigearn!" Edithe cried. "But—"

"Och, she's so bonny," Maisie said. "I've never seen a winged horse afore. Oh, I wish she'd fly. I'd love to see her fly!"

It was the longest speech any of them had heard the shy village girl say.

The boys were filled with exclamations of surprise too. "How did she catch it?" Rafferty wanted to know. "How does she control it without even a bridle, let alone whip or spurs?" He glanced sideways at Edithe, who as always had her long whip in her hand, and a sharp silver spur on her boot. Edithe looked displeased and tightened her rein, causing her mare to sidle sideways.

"I never heard o' a girl being a thigearn afore," Cameron said gruffly. "Are they allowed?"

"Why no', if she can ride it?" Nina said pleasantly. "What a bonny creature, Rhiannon! I've heard o' the black winged horses o' Ravenshaw afore, o' course, but never thought to see one. Ye look like ye've ridden out of an auld tale, the two o' ye. Have ye ridden her long?"

"No' long," Rhiannon answered, her face glowing.

"I thought ye had to ride for a year and a day without putting foot to ground afore ye could call yourself a thigearn," Cameron said, his tone very near a jeer.

"Nay, all ye need do is tame a flying horse," Niall said. "It's just that it takes most men that long to break its will. Rhiannon did no' need to." He smiled up at her. She smiled back.

"Well, we'll surely make a sensation in every village we ride through," Edithe said in a voice of long suffering. "We really are like a travelling circus now."

"Aye, and isn't it a shame that all ken we ride on the Coven's business? Think o' the money we could make!" Iven said shamelessly, and winked at Nina. "Come on, let's get this circus rolling!"

Barbreck-by-the-Bridge

As they rode down the long elm-lined avenue, the sun struck down through the pale green blossoms flowering profusely on every bare twig and branch. The mist was drawn up like smoke, revealing lush lawns and copses of silver-barked birches. Away to the left were the orchards with their clouds of sweet-smelling blossoms in white and pink, while to the right lay the lake, lined with willow trees and flowering rushes.

Lewen was filled with a bittersweet sadness as he gazed about him, knowing it may be a year or more before he returned to Kingarth again. He turned to have one last look at the little stone house with its steep roof and gables, and saw his parents and sister waving madly. He waved back, then resolutely turned his face away, looking to the road ahead.

Suddenly a tiny shape came hurtling down out of the sky like a maddened hornet. Kalea caught Rhiannon's blue tam-o'-shanter and hurled it away, then seized hold of Rhiannon's hair in two tiny, determined hands and yanked with all her strength. Rhiannon yelped in pain and swatted at the little faery, sending her head over heels. Kalea crashed into an elm branch and hung there, whimpering. Rhiannon lifted both hands to her hair, her face white with fury. Blackthorn danced uneasily.

A babble of surprised voices rose.

"What is it?" Rafferty demanded. "Did ye see how fast it came?"

"I thought we were being shot at," Cameron exclaimed, dropping his hand from his sword.

"What on earth!" Iven cried, pulling up his grey carthorse. "Och, it's the wee nisse!"

"Kalea!" Lewen said reprovingly. "What in Eà's name do ye think ye are doing?"

"Look at the wee thing, is she no' adorable?" Fèlice cried.

Kalea showed her fangs.

"Ooh, how horrid!" Edithe cried and dragged her horse's head around so the brown mare wheeled sideways, almost trampling Maisie's fat pony.

Nina laughed and brought the blue tam-o'-shanter floating up from where it lay on the grass. "Happen she's jealous," she said, letting the tam-o'-shanter drop into Rhiannon's lap. Rhiannon seized it and put it on again, scowling ferociously.

"Kalea, ye must no' do things like that," Lewen said helplessly. He held out his hand and the bright-winged faery came zooming down to cling to his finger, gibbering in distress. "I'm sorry, did I no' say farewell to ye? Do no' cry. I'll be back soon enough."

High-pitched screeches shrilled from the tiny throat. Lewen winced, but stroked the nisse's tangled mane of hair and smoothed down her indignant wings. "I ken, I ken. Never mind. Ye kent I had to go."

More screeches, and the nisse turned and shook a minuscule fist at Rhiannon. Lewen looked a little embarrassed, but did his best to soothe the enraged faery, while Rhiannon merely stared at her coldly, her mouth set hard.

Suddenly the faery swung away from Lewen's finger and hurtled towards Rhiannon again. As quickly as a striking snake, Rhiannon reached out and snatched her from the air. The speed and precision of her reflexes was extraordinary, making them all gasp. Imprisoned in Rhiannon's fist, Kalea shrieked in terror. No matter how she squirmed or wriggled, or how ferociously she sank her fangs into Rhiannon's hand, the satyricorn girl did not let go. Slowly, deliberately, holding Kalea close before her face, she began to squeeze her fingers closed. Kalea whimpered in pain.

"Rhiannon, let her go!" Lewen shouted.

She ignored him.

"Rhiannon, I mean it!" He kicked Argent forward and the stallion wheeled in close beside the nervous winged mare so Lewen could reach out and grasp Rhiannon's wrist. Holding her immobile, he used his other hand to prise open her fingers.

For a moment their strength and wills battled. Then Rhiannon gasped and relaxed her hold. Kalea shot out of her hand and went flying to Lewen, nestling behind his ear, peering out to gibber at Rhiannon mockingly.

Lewen let go of her wrist.

Rhiannon looked down at the angry red marks on her still-bruised wrist. "Ye strong," she said in approval. "Ye near broke my hand."

"Ye should no' have hurt Kalea," Lewen said, still furious.

"She hurt me."

"She should no' have done that either."

Rhiannon shrugged, cradling her abused wrist in her other hand. "No' my fault."

"No, happen so," Lewen said, his anger cooling. "But she's only a wee nisse, ye should no' have sought to kill her."

"Tell her no' to hurt me again or me hurt her," Rhiannon said indifferently and bent to stroke Blackthorn's damp neck, soothing the unsettled mare.

"Very well," Lewen said coolly, and plucked the nisse from behind his ear. "Go home, Kalea," he said sternly. "And let this be a lesson to ye!"

She made a derisive gibbering sound, then leant forward and kissed his nose. While Lewen was still recovering from his surprise and embarrassment, Kalea flew up into the air, made an extremely rude gesture towards Rhiannon, then shot off at high speed, her dragonfly wings whirring.

For a moment Rhiannon and Lewen were frozen in mutual surprise and consternation. Then both broke into laughter.

"Nisses!" Lewen said, then said awkwardly, "I'm sorry. She has absolutely no manners."

"Me no manners either," Rhiannon said cheerfully.

She looked round at the circle of faces. Edithe and Maisie both looked shocked, Fèlice, Iven and Nina were struggling to suppress amusement, and Roden and Rafferty were both laughing out loud. Landon had pulled out a grubby little notebook and was scribbling notes with a distastefully chewed quill, his ink bottle balanced most precariously on his saddle pommel, and Cameron was regarding Rhiannon with something very nearly approaching respect.

"What we wait for?" Rhiannon demanded. "Ride on!"

Fèlice laughed. "This journey is going to be fun," she cried exuberantly. "What will ye do next, Rhiannon?"

Without waiting for an answer, she dug her heel into her mare's side and moved off again down the road, Rafferty breaking into a trot to follow her.

"I can hardly wait to find out," Iven said dryly and flicked his reins at the gelding's broad back. The caravans both moved off again, the apprentice-witches falling into formation behind them.

Lewen and Rhiannon followed suit, riding side by side at the very end of the cavalcade.

"I'm sorry if I hurt ye," Lewen said remorsefully. "I forgot how sore your wrists still are."

Rhiannon gave her usual shrug, glancing at him under her lashes. "Hurt worse afore," she said dismissively and smiled at him, knowing full well she had just made him feel a whole lot worse.

The long avenue ended at a pair of massive iron gates, bounded on each side by tall thick hedges bristling with thorns. Beyond Kingarth was nothing but forest and mountains, filled with wild creatures and faeries of all kinds, many of them dangerous. The brambly hedge ran the whole perimeter of the farm, and was patrolled regularly by Ursa the Bear to make sure there were no gaps or holes through which even a polecat or hoarweasel could squeeze its lithe shape. The gates themselves were guarded by the son of Niall's old gillie, who lived in a cottage just inside the gates with his wife and two young children.

Jock MacGhillie came out to unlock the gates for the cavalcade, saluting Iven smartly and wishing them good speed. They rode out smartly, so Jock could make sure all was secure behind them, and found themselves on a narrow dirt road that wound down through dense forest along the eastern bank of the Findhorn River. The river ran fast and white along its rocky course, tumbling down in foaming cataracts wherever the hill dropped away. Looking back up the river, Rhiannon remembered how she had used to sit on the ridge by the black lake, wondering where the river went and wishing she could follow it. The thought pleased her. She smiled and pressed her heels into

Blackthorn's side so the mare lengthened her stride, cantering ahead of the others. Lewen's big grey stallion followed her at once, his heavy hooves sending up plumes of dust.

Rhiannon looked back over her shoulder at Lewen. "Ye want race?"

"No flying allowed," Lewen warned.

"What ye bet?"

His dark brown eyes sparkled. "Ye're confident!"

"Me am."

"Ye think your dainty wee mare can outrun Argent?" he scoffed.

"Try us."

"All right then."

"So what will ye give me when me win?"

"I'll clean your tack for ye tonight," he offered.

"Me clean own tack."

"What then?"

"Me want money."

Lewen raised his eyebrow. "A gambling lass? What if ye lose? Ye havena any money to give me."

"Me no lose."

"Oh-ho, we are confident. All right, ye can owe me."

"Me no need to."

"Deal or no deal?"

"What ye mean?"

"That's what ye say when ye make a bet. Ye should say 'deal', and then we each spit on our hands and shake on it."

"Shake on it?" Rhiannon frowned in puzzlement. "Shake? Like this?" And she began to shake all over, as if she was quivering with cold. Blackthorn put her ears back and sidestepped.

Lewen could not help himself. He burst out laughing. After a moment Rhiannon laughed too.

"Nay! No' like that! We shake hands. Like this," He drew Argent close by Blackthorn's side and put out his hand to Rhiannon. After a moment's hesitation Rhiannon put her hand in his, and he pumped it up and down vigorously. "That's shaking on it."

"Me shake on it," she said, and pretended to shake all over again.

He laughed out loud.

"All right, first to the big oak down there . . ." His voice died away as Blackthorn broke into a gallop. Startled, Lewen laughed and swore, and leant forward, slapping Argent's neck with his reins. The big stallion surged forward.

Shoulder to shoulder, the two horses galloped down the road, sending pebbles flying.

"Ye cheated!" Lewen panted. "Ye're meant to start together."

"Ye just slow," Rhiannon teased. She crouched lower on Blackthorn's neck and the winged horse leapt forward, passing the big bare oak scant seconds before Argent.

"Me win, me win!" Rhiannon chanted.

"All right, all right," he said, fumbling in his pocket for a coin, which he flipped to her. "Though next time I'll make ye call the start."

"Me still win," Rhiannon crowed, cheeks pink, eyes bright with excitement. She rubbed the coin with her thumb, and then very carefully stowed it away inside her coat.

"No' a chance," Lewen said. "Ye only won because I'm too much o' a gentleman to call ye a cheat."

"Och, sure," she mocked.

They dismounted and rested in the shade, letting the horses graze at will, for neither wore a bit. In a few minutes, the big grey carthorse came shambling along, pulling the blue caravan. Iven lounged on the driving seat, his feet up, the reins looped and knotted over the rail. He was playing cards with Roden and Lulu. The arak was jumping up and down, gibbering with distress at her poor hand of cards, while Roden was looking rather smug, a heap of pebbles before him.

"I wouldna race too much if I were ye," Iven said to Lewen and Rhiannon with a smile. "We have a long way to ride and ye do no' want to be tiring out your horses."

"Ye just jealous," Rhiannon said. "Ye wish ye racing too. That horse very slow." She gestured towards the enormous carthorse with his patient dark eyes and shaggy hooves the size of dinner plates.

"Happen that's true," Iven said with a sigh. "Still, dinna ye look down upon auld Steady here. He may be slow, but he gets there. Anyway, no more racing, bairns. We really do have a

long way to go today. Nina is keen to leave the Broken Ring o'
Dubhslain behind us."

"All right, Iven," Lewen said readily. "For today anyway. I
have to have a chance to win back my honour tomorrow. We
have a bet riding on it."

"Och, well, in that case!" Iven laughed. "I tell ye what, I'll
make ye a bet o' my own. One week on the road and I bet neither o' ye will have the heart for racing!"

"What ye bet me?" Rhiannon said at once.

"A gambler in our midst. Well, Roden and I bet for pebbles,
but that's only because I couldna afford to play with him otherwise, he's just too good."

Roden grinned.

"Me no play for pebbles," Rhiannon said.

"Ye are a gambling girl! All right then. If I win, ye have to
cook dinner every night for a week. If I lose, I'll . . . hmmm . . .
I'll . . ."

"Me want money," Rhiannon said.

"Ye want hard coin? But I'm naught but a poor jongleur! All
right then. A half-crown, if ye and Lewen are still racing every
day after seven days on the road."

"Deal," Rhiannon said. She spat on her hand and held it out.
Solemnly Iven spat on his hand and then shook hers. The caravans trundled on, and they mounted their horses again and fell
into place behind the others. Lewen raised a quizzical eyebrow
at her.

"Me need money," Rhiannon explained. "Me have none."

Lewen smiled and shrugged. "I guess ye could do with some
money. We are going to Lucescere, the most expensive city in
the world, after all."

Rhiannon nodded. "So me told."

Lewen hesitated. "Ye need no' worry about money," he said.
"Isabeau, the Keybearer, will make sure ye have everything ye
need. My mother has written to her, as ye ken. As a scholarship
student, the Coven pays for all your day-to-day needs, your
robes and books and food and lodging."

"That girl say me need money. For balls . . . What ball?"

"A ball is a place where people go to dance and talk. It's also a round leather toy that bairns kick around. Lady Edithe would've meant the first, though."

Rhiannon screwed up her face. "Too many words. How ye ken them all?"

"I've had plenty o' time to learn," Lewen answered. "Do no' worry, ye'll pick them up soon enough."

"Pick words up?" Rhiannon was more puzzled than ever.

Lewen sighed. "Learn them, I mean."

"So why me need money for balls?"

"Everyone gets dressed up in fancy clothes and jewels which cost a lot to buy."

"Why?"

"I've often wondered. I wouldna worry too much, Rhiannon. I doubt whether ye'll go to many. Most students do no' have much to do with the court."

Rhiannon frowned. "Happen so," she said. "Still, if those cursehags are no' to laugh at me, me need money."

"The Coven doesna like its students gambling," Lewen warned.

"How will they ken?" Rhiannon lifted one expressive eyebrow. "Unless ye mean to tell them?"

"I willna tell," Lewen said uncomfortably. "No-one likes a tittle-tattle."

"Well then." She flashed a smile at him.

"Witches are hard to trick," Lewen warned. "I'd be careful."

"How else me get money?" Rhiannon asked. "How ye get?"

"We royal squires are paid handsomely," Lewen said, with a mock attempt to emulate Edithe's high-bred tone.

"Then me be squire too."

Lewen shifted uncomfortably in his saddle. "Lassies canna be squires."

"Why no'?"

"They just canna."

Rhiannon scowled.

"I make things too," Lewen said hurriedly, eager to change the subject. "We spend an awful lot o' time sitting around and waiting for His Highness. I hate to sit idle, so I got in the habit o' whittling to help pass the time. I've always liked to make my own arrows, they seem to fly more true than those made for me by others. The other squires used to want to buy them from me, and then the palace guards did too, and now I can sell as many as I make. Even the Rìgh likes my arrows best." He spoke with quiet pride.

Rhiannon eyed the quiver bristling with arrows that hung from Argent's saddle. They did indeed seem beautifully made, being unusually long and formed from some white wood, fletched with green. They made hers seem clumsy and badly made.

"I make other things too. Chess sets, sometimes, or toys for the palace bairns. Boxes, or little figurines o' animals. I like making those."

"Ye made the boxes back there? The tricky one?"

Lewen grinned. "Aye, I made those. They were fun."

"Very tricky."

"There are lots o' things students can do to help support themselves while at the Theurgia. If ye show a Skill at something, like growing things or animals, ye can get a job working in the garden or in the stables or kennels. Ye're good with horses. When we get to Lucescere, I'll introduce ye to the stable-master. I'm sure he'd be happy to give ye some work. Horse-whisperers are always welcome there."

Rhiannon smiled. "Me like horses, me like that."

"Ye should no' say 'me like', ye should say 'I'. 'I would like that' is the proper way to say it."

"I would like that," she repeated after a moment, even though it was clear she did not like being corrected.

He smiled at her. "Very good. Ye learn fast."

She nodded. "Me try."

"Ye mean, I try," Lewen corrected her again.

She compressed her lips together, then said obediently, "I mean, I try."

Until now, the road had just been wide enough for two horses to ride comfortably side by side, but as they came down out of the forest the road widened and an eager Rafferty was able to ride up beside them and engage them in conversation. Lewen quite liked the young apprentice-witch but nonetheless he had to suppress a flash of irritation when he saw the glow of admiration in the boy's eyes when he gazed at Rhiannon.

"I say, ye can ride!" Rafferty cried. "And that mare o' yours can really go! Will ye race with me?"

"What ye bet?" Rhiannon said at once.

Rafferty's eyes sparkled. "Half a copper?"

"Ye promised Iven ye would no' race again today," Lewen reminded Rhiannon, feeling like a stern big brother.

She hunched a shoulder at him and said to Rafferty, "Me race . . . I race ye tomorrow then."

"Grand," he said. "Ye ken, none o' the lasses I ken would ever ride like that. They'd be too afraid o' falling off."

"I no' afraid o' aught," Rhiannon boasted.

"More fool ye," Lewen said, and leant forward a little in his saddle so Argent's stride lengthened, bringing him up beside Iven's caravan. He felt he had had enough of Rafferty's company.

The road wound down into softly rolling hills and pastures. Men and women were working together in every field, ploughing the rich dark earth, sowing seeds, cutting back the hedgerows and tending herds of goats and pigs. In nearly every dell was a small croft with its orchard just beginning to bud with spring flowers, and smoke wisping up from its chimney. The crofters waved at the caravans as they passed by, and the apprentices waved back, enjoying the fresh spring weather.

They reached the little village of Barbreck-by-the-Bridge late that afternoon. It was no more than a single street with an inn at one end and a mill with a water-wheel at the other, and two rows of small, grey houses with high-pitched roofs along either side, facing onto a village green where chickens wandered and children played. The Findhorn River came foaming down the hill to boil about the stone ramparts of a great bridge composed of six arches, with crenellated gatehouses at either end.

A crowd of grim-faced people milled about at one end of the bridge, all looking down at something that lay on the ground in their midst. A man wearing an enormous sword strapped to his back was ordering them about, his black eyebrows drawn close over his eagle nose.

"That's the reeve," Lewen said in alarm. "I wonder what the matter is?"

"Barbreck-by-the-Bridge has a reeve?" Iven asked in surprise.

"Och, nay, it's far too wee. Odran the reeve will have come over from Cullen, the town on the far side o' the bridge. I wonder what can have happened?"

"I guess we'll soon find out," Iven answered, slapping the reins on Steady's back. The carthorse quickened his pace.

It was only a day since the caravans had driven through Barbreck-by-the-Bridge to Kingarth, but still the sight of the gaudily painted vans was enough to draw the eye of everyone in the village. As they turned to stare, Rhiannon was able to see the naked body of a man lying on the ground, water spreading a dark stain across the pavement. Her heart jerked. She averted her eyes, trying to control the sudden rapid beating of her pulse, her ragged breathing. Around her were cries of alarm and horror.

Nina drew Roden against her, hiding his face in her skirt, though the little boy strained away, saying, "But Mam, I wanna see! What happened to him? Is he dead?"

"Aye, honey," she answered. "Do no' look!"

Iven jumped down from the drivers' seat and went to greet the reeve.

"Trouble?" he asked. "What's the problem?"

"Murder," the reeve said tersely. "Man shot in the back, and thrown in the river. We havena had a murder in these parts for nigh on ten years, and this one looks a right nasty one."

"I am Iven Yellowbeard, a courier in the Rìgh's service and a former Blue Guard," Iven said. "Can I be o' any assistance?"

The reeve cast a suspicious eye at the jongleur, noting his frivolous beard and brightly coloured clothes. Iven bowed ironically. "No' all Blue Guards become farmers when they retire," he said. "I was born a jongleur and a jongleur I shall die, and all the life betwixt spent in service to Lachlan the Winged."

Still the reeve looked unconvinced.

Lewen dismounted and went to join Iven, leaving Argent untethered. "How are ye yourself, Odran?"

The reeve straightened his back, saluting smartly. "Sore troubled, sir, and ye?"

"Well enough, until I saw what ye have here. May we take a

look? Iven was once a Blue Guard, and he kens more than any man should ken about violent death. Also, I fear . . . I suspect Iven may ken who it is. For we've had intimations o' a Blue Guard gone missing, shot through the back, we suspect. We would like to ken if this is he."

"Indeed?" Odran raised one thick, black eyebrow. "In that case, please, be my guest."

Iven went down on one knee beside the naked corpse, and examined him carefully. There was evidently a strong stench for his nose wrinkled involuntarily, and he tried not to lean too close. "Arrow wound here through the back," he said in a voice stiff with distaste. "And look, chafing here at wrists and ankles. He was bound up tightly. He's been badly beaten too. Looks like he may have a broken rib or two. I'd say the injuries occurred afore death. It's hard to tell, though, for he's been in the water a while. By the degree o' putrefaction, I'd say it's been a few weeks, happen even a month."

There was an unhappy murmur from the crowd. A plump woman hid her face against a man's broad shoulder.

"Look at his hand," Odran said gruffly. "He looks like he's been tortured."

Iven very gently picked up the dead man's right hand, which was missing its smallest finger. He frowned. "I think the finger might have been cut off after death. I canna be sure though." He laid the hand down again, and wiped his fingers on his handkerchief, looking very pale.

"But why?" Odran asked.

Iven shrugged. "A souvenir?"

He carefully turned the dead man over, to examine the ragged exit wound in the chest. The corpse had once had corn-yellow curls, though now they were dark with water and bedraggled with water-weed. His face was a sickly grey and grossly swollen, and his glazed eyes were wide open and stared out from their sockets. His skin was marked with putrefaction like mould-flowers on canvas. His mouth hung open and they could see the blackened ruin of his toothless gums.

"Eà's green blood!" Lewen cried, and gagged.

"Nay! Och, nay!" Nina cried from the caravan. "Nay, it canna be!"

"Do ye ken who it is?" Odran the reeve asked.

Iven and Lewen both nodded. Lewen was sallow with shock. "It is Connor the Just, one o' the Rìgh's general staff," he answered. "He was once squire to the Rìgh, as I am now. He is brother to Johanna the Healer."

"Och, it will break her heart to lose him," Nina cried. "He is all she had." Tears streamed down her face. She wiped them away and got down slowly from the caravan, making her way through the crowd, which drew back respectfully. She knelt beside the dead body, taking the slack hand in hers.

"His teeth have all been drawn," she said in a constricted voice. "Why? Why?"

"Torture?" Odran asked. "Or souvenirs, taken after death? I dinna ken. I've never seen aught like it."

Nina sobbed and Iven put his arm about her, drawing her head down onto his shoulder. Fèlice and Edithe both looked sick and upset, and Maisie had her hand pressed against her mouth. Landon had climbed down from his horse and hidden his face against its hot hide. Even Cameron and Rafferty, normally so cocky, were white under their tans.

Rhiannon, meanwhile, sat very still, wanting to look away, but so fascinated by the sight of the limp, grey body that she could not force her eyes to move. Her stomach felt like it had been turned upside down. Lewen had turned to stare at her in miserable doubt and suspicion, and hot tears stung her eyes. She had never expected to be faced with the corpse of what she had done, or for it to affect her so powerfully. She thought of the necklace of teeth and bones coiled at the bottom of her bag, and suddenly her stomach heaved. She bent over, trying to control her revulsion, but it won out and she vomited her breakfast in a vile splatter on the road.

"Yurk!" Edithe cried and spurred her horse away.

"Nina, the girls should no' be seeing this, or Roden either. Will ye take them away? Lewen and I will come and join ye when we can."

Nina nodded and got up, wiping her eyes. "Poor, poor Johanna," she said. "I remember what she was like after Tòmas died, and he was no' even her true brother. To lose Connor too, and in such a horrible way. Och, it's just too awful."

She came up to the caravans, looking white and woeful, and lifted Roden down, saying, "Come, my wee dearling, let's get ye away from here. Ye're too young to see yet the evil men can do to other men. Let us go to the inn and warm ourselves by the fire, and have a hot toddy."

Roden nodded soberly, staring back at the dead man with huge dark eyes, and Lulu slipped her paw into his hand, making little whimpering sounds. With Sure and Steady following along behind, Nina walked slowly towards the little grey inn with its steep roof and bright red shutters. She looked as bowed and spiritless as an old woman. Rhiannon followed close behind, her hand on Blackthorn's warm silky hide. She had never seen sorrow before, and it gave her a strange feeling inside, as if she had been punched in the stomach and was now all sore and tender.

They tethered the horses outside the inn, loosening their girths and pumping the trough with water, then traipsed inside. Rhiannon took her saddlebags with her, feeling as if the dead man's plundered bones glowed with guilty heat, threatening to accuse her. When she sat with the other apprentices at the table, she shoved the bags underneath and put her feet on them.

"A murdered Yeoman!" Edithe murmured. "Who would do such a thing?"

"They'll hang the murderer if they catch him," Cameron said grimly. "It's treason to even waylay a Yeoman, let alone kill one."

Rhiannon did not know what it meant to be hanged, but to drive his point home, Cameron mimed it for her. He hung an imaginary rope around his neck, then demonstrated the sudden jerk, the choking and gargling, and then the cruel death, eyes bulging, tongue protruding, head awry on the limp neck. Feeling faint and nauseous, Rhiannon looked away.

"Why would they kill him? And beat and torture him?" Maisie said pitifully. Her face was blotched white and red, and her eyes swam with tears. "He was only young too, did ye see? He canna have been more than thirty."

"I kent him when he was just a lad, no' much more than Roden here," Nina said, sitting down beside them and resting her head in her hands. "He was a bonny, bright lad, and so brave. He was one o' the very first pupils o' the new Theurgia. Och, His Highness will be furious! Heads will roll, I guarantee it. Connor was his page and then his squire, and then one o' his bodyguards, and now one' o' his most trusted lieutenants. They called him the Just because he had such a way o' enforcing law and order wherever he went. Everyone liked him and trusted him. Who can have killed him, and why?"

"He was at Ravenscraig a month or so ago," Fèlice said in a tear-choked voice. "I danced with him. He was such a bonny dancer."

"Happen he discovered a plot against the Rìgh," Edithe said. "So the plotters killed him."

"But why torture him?" Nina cried. She looked ravaged with grief. "Why!"

"Happen to discover how much he knew," Rafferty said. He was quickly recovering his spirits, and was beginning to look rather excited. "Will the Rìgh send soldiers, do ye think? To discover who the murderer is?"

Nina nodded. "I would say so. Or perhaps he will ask the MacBrann to look into it, since it happened here in Ravenshaw. It will take a long time to get news o' Connor's death to the Rìgh. Witches canna scry over high mountains, ye ken, no' without a Scrying Pool o' great power. The MacBrann will have to send messengers, and that could take weeks. For even carrier-pigeons have trouble getting over the mountains here, they are so high and wild. Och, they will all be distraught when they hear the news. Connor was well loved." She wiped her eyes and blew her nose, and smiled wanly at the innkeeper as he brought a tray of steaming mugs. "Drink up, bairns, it'll do ye good. We've all had a nasty shock."

Cameron reached for his mug eagerly. "That hit the spot," he said with a sigh after taking a long draught. "Naught like a wee dram to calm the nerves, or settle the stomach." He cast Rhiannon a mocking glance.

"I'm not much o' a whisky drinker," Nina said, "but ye're right, Cameron, hot like this, with honey and spices in it, it's the best thing for us all now." She passed a mug to Rhiannon, saying gently, "here ye are, this'll help. Never mind, Rhiannon, a sight like that is enough to give anyone the shivers."

Rhiannon nodded and tried to smile, taking the cup in her trembling hands. She wondered if Nina would be so kind if she knew it was terror that caused her hands to shake. All their talk of treason and hanging frightened her terribly. She resolved to get rid of the damning necklace at the very first opportunity. No-one must guess that she was the one who had shot the Yeoman dead.

She lifted the cup and tasted the hot whisky toddy cautiously. It was like drinking liquid fire. At first she coughed and choked, but by the third sip, it went down her throat easily enough and warmed her body all through.

"Connor the Just was with the auld MacBrann when he died," Fèlice said. "He rode out that very night, he did no' even stop to say goodbye. We were all rather chagrined, all us lassies o' the court, when we heard, for he was rather a favourite among us. I canna believe he is dead."

"What was he doing up here, in the highlands?" Edithe asked. "There's naught up here but goats and peasants."

Nina sighed. "Happen he was trying to cross the Razor's Edge."

"The what?"

"It's a pass through the mountains to Rionnagan," she answered. "Though pass is no' quite the right word. It's more like a high bridge o' stone, very dangerous to cross. It is by far the quickest way to Rionnagan. Few go that way, however, unless their need is desperate. A dragon roosts at Ben Eyrie, ye ken, and the mountains are filled with ogres and goblins and wild satyricorn."

Rhiannon thought Nina's eyes turned towards her as she spoke, and hurriedly she lifted the cup to her mouth and drank again, afraid her face would give her away.

Fèlice shuddered. "How horrid! Surely he wouldna have gone that way!"

"If his need was great enough, he might have," Nina said. She gave a little shiver. "I must say, the ripping out o' his teeth could be the work o' satyricorns. I do no' ken much about them, but I'm sure I've seen them wear necklaces made o' teeth and bones. I wish Lilanthe were here, she would ken."

"Surely Lewen's mother is no' a satyricorn?" Edithe asked,

scandalized. "I mean, I ken she's some kind o' faery, ye only have to look at her to ken that, but surely no' one o' those dreadful wild horned women?"

Nina was exasperated. "Lilanthe is a tree-shifter, do ye ken naught?" she snapped. "Eà's green blood! Nay, I say Lilanthe would ken because she's an expert in the faeries o' the forest. She raised them to fight for Lachlan in the Bright Wars, did ye no' ken? Then, after peace was won, she lectured in their ways at the Theurgia. She was the one that persuaded them all to sign the Pact o' Peace, tree-changers, seelies, satyricorns too. She kens their customs better than anyone." Again she glanced at Rhiannon, with frowning black eyes.

"How strange," Edithe murmured. "Though, o' course, she is a faery too."

Rhiannon gritted her teeth and looked down into her cup. She was torn between a hysterical need to laugh, and a desire to grind Edithe's face into the table. She wondered what the fair-haired girl would say if she realised she was sitting at the same table as one of those dreadful wild horned women. She could just imagine how Edithe's nostrils would flare and her lip would curl with distaste.

Iven and Lewen came slowly into the inn. Roden ran to his father and Iven lifted him up to his shoulder, hugging him closely.

"Well, what a dark end to our day," he said, coming to sit near his wife. "Nina, my love, how are ye yourself?"

"Terrible," she answered. "I canna believe it is true. Was that really Connor lying there all battered and bruised, or was it all just a bad dream?"

"No dream," he answered shortly, signaling to the innkeeper to bring them more mulled whisky.

"To think we have lost one more o' the gallant League o' the Healing Hand! There is only Finn and Jay left, and Johanna, and Dillon." Tears welled up in her eyes and she pressed the heels of her hands to her face.

"Come, it is getting late," Ivan said. "I do no' think we should ride any further today. Have they enough room here at the inn for the girls at least to sleep in comfort? I see they have a field where we can let the horses graze, and where we can make camp."

"What have they done with Connor?" Nina asked. Her voice was so piteous Lulu stopped spinning the apple she had been given, and came to her side anxiously, looking up into her face and making little whining noises. Nina petted her absent-mindedly, her black eyes fixed pleadingly on Iven's face.

"One o' the boatmen has taken him to Ravenscraig, to show the MacBrann," Iven said unwillingly. "He needs to be buried fast, he's in bad shape after all that time in the water, but we thought the prionnsa should see him first."

"I've had a thought," Nina said. "Iven, could Connor have been trying to cross the Razor's Edge? And if so, what news drove him to take such a risk? Do ye ken if there were any papers among his things?"

Iven glanced at Rhiannon, and shook his head.

Rhiannon pressed her feet into the bags under the table, feeling a slow burn creep up her face. Nina and Iven both knew, then, how she had come riding down out of the mountains, dressed in the stolen clothes of a dead soldier. She should have guessed they would be told. She wondered if they knew she was the daughter of a satyricorn too. Unable to help herself, she gazed at Lewen pleadingly, and he refused to meet her gaze. Apprehension slithered through the pit of her stomach. Was she to stand accused of murder? Would they hang her? She slid her hand down to the knife she wore strapped to her belt.

Nina sighed. "I guess it was too much to hope for. We're lucky any o' his things were found at all." Once again her eyes returned to Rhiannon's face, filled with questions. Rhiannon looked back warily, her jaw thrust forward. "Och, well, it is almost dusk already and I feel weary unto my very soul. Let us have an early night, and we'll ride out with the dawn."

"My love, I've been thinking. Happen we should ride down the eastern side o' the Findhorn River. I ken the roads are said to be bad that way, but we need to get back to Lucescere just as soon as we can. The Rìgh will want to hear all we ken about Connor's death."

"But, Iven, should we no' go back past Ravenscraig, as we planned? The MacBrann may wish to question us."

Iven shrugged. "This is a matter for the Rìgh, Nina, no' for the MacBrann, even though it happened here in his land. Even if we go to Ravenscraig we will need to hurry on to Lucescere just as fast as we can. The murder o' a Yeoman is a matter for the royal courts."

Rhiannon gripped her knife hilt. She was amazed how Iven and Nina were able to speak of one thing and seem to speak of another. To her, and to Lewen, she imagined, it was clear they were debating whether it was best to take her, Rhiannon, to Ravenscraig to face the reckoning, or head straight to the capital, for her to explain herself to the mysterious and powerful Rìgh they all seemed to admire so much. To the other apprentices, though, there can have been no trace of the dark undercurrent of suspicion that Rhiannon heard so clearly.

"We will head down the eastern bank then," Nina said tiredly. "We'll save a week or more if we do no' have to cross the Findhorn."

Iven nodded. "More, probably, for once we get to Ravenscraig we'd have to stay for days, no doubt. Ye ken how slowly things move there, with all the confusion after Malcolm's death. The Rìgh will want the news as fast as possible. Which reminds me, my love, do ye think ye can send a bird across the mountains with a message?"

Nina sighed. "I do no' want to be the one to tell the news. It'll break Johanna's heart."

"They must be anxious about Connor already. Surely it's kinder to let them ken than keep Johanna in a fret o' worry for the weeks it'll take any message to get there from Ravenscraig."

"I suppose so," Nina said unhappily.

She got up and shook out her skirts. "I'll need a hawk at the very least. I had better go and start calling."

Fascinated, the apprentices all followed her outside. As Rhiannon went past Lewen, she cast him a look from under her lashes. His set expression suddenly broke. His hand shot out and caught her arm, in the crook of her elbow, and he pulled her aside, letting the others pass by.

"Rhiannon," he whispered, his voice breaking. "Ye had naught to do with Connor's death, did ye? Did ye?"

She dropped her eyes, saying, "Nay, it was no' me."

He lifted her hand in both of his, smoothing his thumb over the callouses on her palm. "Ye have the hands o' an archer."

Her colour deepened. "I can shoot a bow and arrow, aye. I bet I can out-shoot ye! That does no' mean I killed him."

He dropped her hand, and very gently touched the saddle-bags she had clasped under her arm. "Are there papers in there?"

She shook her head. "Nay." A memory returned to her. "He had papers. They used them to feed the fire."

He sighed and dropped his hand. "Rhiannon?"

"Aye?"

He shook his head. "Naught. I'm just glad it was no' ye who killed him. I kent him well, ye see. When ye spoke o' a Blue Guard that the herd took prisoner, I never imagined it would be Connor. I saw him only a month or so ago, at Ravenscraig. I canna believe he rode right past Kingarth and did no' stop to see us. He must've had urgent news indeed!"

Rhiannon said nothing. She remembered how Reamon had begged her to help the captured soldier. "He has news he must take to the court—the Rìgh is in dreadful danger," he had said. But now the soldier was dead and his news lost. There was nothing she could do about it now.

"Rhiannon, the Rìgh will want to ken all ye can tell him about Connor's death," Lewen said. "He will be angry and upset, he loved Connor well. Ye . . . ye will tell all ye can, won't ye? And be polite and respectful? I would no' wish . . ." His voice trailed off, and he sighed. "Happen we had best try to teach ye some court manners afore we arrive in Lucescere."

Rhiannon nodded her head. "Aye, happen so," she answered, surprising him. His head came up and he scrutinised her face closely.

"I no' want offend him," Rhiannon explained.

"Nay," Lewen said and laughed. "Very wise, wild girl."

Together they went out of the warm inn and into the chilly afternoon. The sun was setting behind the mountains and long blue shadows were cast by every tree and hill. Nina was standing out in the centre of the field behind the inn, her eyes closed, her hands loose by her side. Her long chestnut curls were blown about wildly by the wind. The others all sat on the fence, a respectful distance away, watching in silence. The sunbird perched beside them, occasionally giving a little questioning trill. Whenever it did so, Iven tapped its beak with his finger and it would quieten, though it never took its bright eyes off Nina.

"What's she doing?" Rhiannon whispered after a while.

"Calling a bird," Edithe answered curtly.

"But she's no' making any sound."

"She's calling it with her mind," Fèlice explained with a quick smile.

A few minutes later, Rhiannon heard a high, yelping call. She looked up into the sky but could see nothing. The sun was balanced in a cleft in the mountains, sending wide golden rays high up into the colourless sky. The yelping cry came again, and then Rhiannon saw, far up above, the shape of an eagle. It swung in the air as if suspended from a string. Without opening her eyes, Nina suddenly raised one hand. The eagle folded its wings and came plummeting down. Involuntarily everyone flinched back as it landed heavily on Nina's hand. It was enormous, with strong talons, a cruel beak and golden-bronze feathers. Only Nina did not recoil. She opened her eyes and stared into the fierce golden eye so close to hers. For a long moment they communed in silence, then Nina brought it to stand on the fence so she could attach a message-tube to its great clenched claws. Then it spread its beautiful, barred wings and launched itself into the air, climbing swiftly up into the grey vault of the evening sky.

"If anyone can cross the mountains and come safely to Lucescere, it will be her," Nina said, sounding tired. "I wish she carried happier news."

Iven nodded and put his arm about her waist, and slowly they made their way back to the inn.

Ardarchy

They were up and away early the next morning, leaving the river behind them as the road swung east through the hills. Occasionally they saw a small huddle of houses round a village green, or a solitary croft set among old plum trees, and midmorning they saw a goose-girl driving a flock of great white indignant birds along the road, hissing and honking, and terrifying the horses with their aggressively held heads on long, snaky necks.

Blackthorn was startled into the air, the first time she had flown since Rhiannon had captured her. Rhiannon was almost jerked off her saddle-pad, clinging to the mare's mane so desperately the coarse hair cut her flesh. She had refused to admit she was rather frightened of flying on the mare's back again, and so she hoped no-one noticed how pale and cold her skin was when at last Blackthorn dropped down to the ground again. To her relief, no-one seemed to have noticed, being too full of the mare's beauty and grace to pay her rider any heed at all.

The sun had slipped behind the mountains by the time Iven finally called the halt, drawing up his gaudy caravan in the shelter of a copse of trees by the road. The riders were all stiff and tired and cold, but the horses had to be attended to and firewood gathered before they could at last sit down and rest. Iven and Nina made camp with swift efficiency, and so it was not long before the campfire was burning merrily and the enticing smell of hot stew was filling the air.

While Nina stirred the big iron cooking pot, Fèlice showed Rhiannon where she was to sleep. The blue caravan which Iven drove was the one set aside for the journey-apprentices. Inside were four hard, narrow bunks, one set above the other on either side. Fèlice had lit a lantern hanging by the door. By its smoky, uneven light, Rhiannon peered into the dimness, noting the girls' clothes hanging from the rails, the shoes and bags shoved under the bunks, the piles of securely bound trunks and barrels and sacks of supplies. It was all very cramped and dark and smelly, and Rhiannon did not like it at all.

"Where others sleep?" she demanded.

"Nina and Iven and Roden sleep in the red caravan," Fèlice said, "and the boys sleep round the fire generally. I dinna ken what they'll do if it rains. Sleep under the caravan, I guess. It's no' very salubrious, is it?"

Rhiannon did not know what salubrious meant, but she agreed with Fèlice's tone.

"Me no sleep here," she said flatly.

"But where else would ye sleep?" Fèlice asked in surprise.

"Me sleep outside."

"With the boys? Surely no'? It wouldna be seemly, Rhiannon."

"What this seemly?"

Fèlice was lost for words. "No' . . . no' proper. No' appropriate. Boys and girls do no' sleep together. I mean, no' unless they . . . no' unless they're married." She blushed rosily.

"Why?"

"It's just no' appropriate."

"Me no care . . ."

"Ye should say 'I do no' care,' " Fèlice said.

Rhiannon cast her a look of irritation. "I dinna care! I no' sleeping here."

"But why no'? I mean, I ken it's small and rather crowded with all our luggage . . . and I must admit I'm used to having a room to myself and found it hard to grow accustomed to sharing." She giggled. "I hardly slept a wink the first few nights for Maisie's snoring. And Edithe kept banging on the bottom o' her bed to try to make her stop. But I've got used to it now, I hardly notice it anymore. Or maybe I'm just so tired from riding so far. And it's only for sleeping in. We spend all our time till we go to bed sitting round the campfire, talking and listening to Iven's stories and songs. It's rather fun, actually."

"I canna sleep in here," Rhiannon said. "It's too small, too close." She gave a little shiver and backed out of the caravan, into the fresh air. Above her was a vast arch of starry sky, and a sharp cold wind blew through the leaves, making the flames dance. Rhiannon took a deep breath and a tension she had not known was there seeped away.

"Nina, Rhiannon says she canna sleep in the caravan," Fèlice said, sounding troubled. "She wants to sleep out here with the boys."

"I always sleep out here," Rhiannon said, indicating the wind and the stars and the trees with a sweeping gesture of her arm. "I do no' like being all . . ."

"Cooped up?" Nina said, when Rhiannon's vocabulary failed her.

"Makes I feel . . . trapped," Rhiannon said.

"Makes *me* feel trapped," Fèlice corrected automatically.

"Makes *me* feel trapped? Why me? And no' I? I all other times."

Nina smiled. "Do ye ken, Rhiannon, I have no idea why. But Fèlice is right. Happen I should set her to teaching ye the rules o' grammar, for to tell ye the truth I've never really understood them. I grew up naught but a jongleur lass, ye ken. I probably make Fèlice and Edithe shudder with the way I speak too."

"Oh, no," Fèlice said, horrified. "I mean, I would no' presume . . ."

"Och, no need to blush. I'm no lady, no' me. Or should that be 'no' I'?"

"No' I," Fèlice said apologetically.

"There ye go. Ye're hereby appointed as Rhiannon's language teacher."

Fèlice looked at Rhiannon a little dubiously but could not help laughing at Rhiannon's scowling expression. "I'll be gentle, I promise," she said.

"And about sleeping outside, I see no reason why Rhiannon canna sleep under the stars if she so wishes. I often do in summer, I must admit. The ground's a little too cold for me at this time o' year but if Rhiannon does no' mind, I do no' see why we should."

"But . . ." Fèlice said doubtfully.

"Are ye worried about the proprieties? I wouldna be concerned, Fèlice. Witches rarely worry about such things. I for one ken Rhiannon can look after herself."

Rhiannon smiled at her radiantly. "So I can," she asserted. "Or should that be 'So me can'?"

Fèlice sighed.

The other apprentice-witches were huddled by the fire in their cloaks, surreptitiously rubbing at their bruises and complaining about their aches and pains. Nina passed around a jar of salve and promised to warm up bags of dried herbs for the girls to take to bed with them, apologizing for the hard pace they were being set.

"Weather's chancy in the highlands," she said, "and we want to make good time while we can. Last time Iven and I were in the Broken Ring o' Dubhslain, we ended up being stuck in a goatherd's cottage for two weeks while a snowstorm raged."

"But it's springtime," Fèlice cried. "Surely we shallna get snowed in now?"

Nina shrugged. "Like I said, the weather's unpredictable here. It's something to do with being circled by mountains on all sides."

"Cold the wind blows and bleak the raven cries, down the stony glens o' black Dubhslain," Landon murmured. "What rhymes with 'slain'? Wane? Fain? Pain?"

"I think ye could do something with 'pain'," Fèlice murmured, rubbing her backside ruefully. Everyone laughed.

"Do ye ken why it's called the Broken Ring of Dubhslain?" Iven asked. "I dinna ken if it be true, but they say there was a great act o' sorcery in these hills, many years ago, in the time o' Brann the Raven himself."

He paused for effect, taking a sip of ale. "Now Brann was one o' the First Coven, as ye ken. But many o' his people hated and feared him, for he was a cold-hearted ruthless man and much given to dabbling in mysteries that would have best been left undisturbed. One summer, it was said, Brann and his retinue were here in the highlands for he had decided to hunt down and capture the fabled black winged stallion for himself."

He nodded and smiled at Rhiannon, who was listening, rapt.

"Some o' his men decided to lay a trap for him and murder him, making it seem like an accident. Brann's son Dugald was only thirteen then and they thought they could rule through him. Brann saw into their hearts, though, and laid a trap of his own. In those days this valley was surrounded on all sides by mountains in a perfect ring. They had a hard journey climbing up here, but Brann urged them on, taunting them with their cowardice and weakness until at last they climbed the last cliff and came inside the ring. On they travelled, towards the high peak o' Ben Eyrie where it was said the black winged horses flew. Three days they travelled, and always the rebels waited for their chance to slay the Raven. He never seemed to sleep, however, and they dared not face him awake.

"On the third night, Brann at last seemed to rest and they drew their knives and crept upon him. Just as the ringleader raised his blade, Brann leapt up and sent him flying back with the force o' his magic. The rebels turned to flee but Brann struck the ground with his staff, enacting a great spell o' incredible strength by using the perfect ring o' mountains as his circle o' power. The earth itself groaned and shook, and a great crack opened up in its flank.

"A fountain o' water burst up from the deepest depths o' the earth and swept away all that lay afore it, including all o' Brann's men, traitorous or no'. And the ring o' mountains was broken and the land cleared all the way to the sea, farms and villages and towns all drowned in the flood. And where Brann's staff had struck was a great black fathomless lake, which he called Dubhglais.

"Then Brann came down alone from the mountains, following the new river, which he named the Findhorn. And where the river fell through the broken ring in a great roaring waterfall he built a castle and named it Ravenscraig. And on the far shore, in the shadow o' the broken mountain, he built his witches' tower. And no-one ever dared rebel against him again."

"I'm no' surprised," Landon said, looking up from the fire with dreamy eyes. "He was a cold, strange man, by all accounts. Did ye ken he swore he would outwit Gearradh in the end, and live again?"

Everyone sighed and shivered and looked up at the tall icy

peaks surrounding them on all sides but one, and hunched closer to the fire.

"Who that?" Rhiannon whispered to Lewen.

"Brann? He was one o' the sorcerers from the Other World, who brought humankind here to Eileanan. We call them the First Coven. Ravenshaw—this country we're in now—that was Brann's land and is still ruled by one o' his descendants, Dughall MacBrann."

"I meant t'other. The one that made everyone shiver."

"Gearradh? Oh. She is the one who cuts the thread, the third of the weird sisters, that we call the Three Spinners." Seeing Rhiannon's puzzled face, Lewen tried to explain again. "She . . . I suppose she is like the goddess o' death. She decides when it is time for us all to die."

"No wonder everyone shivered."

"It was as much at the idea of Brann the Raven living again," Lewen said. "He was a scary man."

Nina laughed at their sombre faces and bade Iven play something to cheer them up while she served the stew. "Ye willna fancy ye hear ghosts crying on the wind with a bowl o' hot stew in ye," she said.

Iven strummed his guitar and sang lustily:

> *"O Eà let me die,*
> *wi' a wee dram at my lip,*
> *and a bonny lass on my lap,*
> *and a merry song and a jest,*
> *biting my thumb at the sober an' just,*
> *as I live I wish to die!*
> *So drink up, laddies, drink,*
> *and see ye do no' spill,*
> *for if ye do we'll all drink two,*
> *for that be the drunkard's rule!"*

Despite the merry tune and the hot stew, the shadow of the tale lay on them all still. That night, as she lay rolled in her blankets by the fire, Rhiannon could still hear the wind sobbing in the trees and feel the dark gaze of the mountains upon them. It took her a long time to find sleep, and she heard the sighs of the other apprentices as they too sought sleep that would not come.

The next day they were all tired and heavy-eyed, and quick to snap at each other, but no-one demurred when Iven began harnessing the carthorses to the caravans before any of them had even finished scraping their porridge bowls clean. All were eager to leave the Broken Ring of Dubhslain behind them.

They rode hard that day, for clouds were pouring in over the great peaks like a grey flood, dimming the thin spring sunshine and swallowing the steep banks of pines and hemlock. When the road rolled out before them Rhiannon challenged them all to race and, to her great delight, beat every one of them. Her pocket began to jingle with coins and she often slipped her hand inside to caress them, liking the cool round perfection of them.

Most of the day they all rode quietly, though, pacing the horses and nursing along their saddle sores. Rhiannon kept close and quiet, listening to the conversation and later asking Lewen to explain anything she did not understand. Hardened by her upbringing, she did not suffer as much as the other girls from the long hours in the saddle and so she was glad to look about her with hungry eyes, and listen to everything that was said, sucking out its pith of knowledge. Rhiannon was determined to never again be mocked for her ignorance. If learning was the currency of power in this land, then Rhiannon would learn all she could.

They came to a town late on the third day, as the gloom of the cloud-hung day darkened to dusk.

"Thank Eà!" Fèlice cried. "A proper bed tonight! Proper food!"

"Ye do no' like my cooking?" Iven said, pretending to be hurt.

"Well, ye ken ye canna do much with a pot hung over a fire," Fèlice said disarmingly. "Stew, stew, or stew."

"Och, but such delicious stew!"

"Aye, the very best. It will be nice to have something different, though, don't ye agree?"

"Mmm, a wee dram o' whisky would be nice," Iven agreed. "Ye girls take up so much room with all your fimble-fambles I

havena any room for anything but a keg o' ale and that just
doesna quench a man's thirst the way a dram does. Let's hope
there's an inn."

The town seemed quite large and prosperous, sprawling
round a square of green grass with a big old tree at one end and
a small white rotunda at the other. Behind the houses were little walled fields devoted to vegetables and orchards and a few
grain crops, running up to steep hills that disappeared into forest. The mountains behind were hidden in mist.

Many of the houses had large gardens, some hidden behind
walls overgrown with ivy, others with nothing but a low
wooden pole fence to separate them from their neighbours.
Coming down a low hill, they were able to see how the town
sprawled along a small river, following its curve. At the far end
of the main street they saw a water-mill, and a hunchbacked
stone bridge across the river, and then, away from the houses,
in a big garden all bright with spring blossom, a small round
turret built of stone.

"Aaah, they have a tower witch," Nina said, pleased. "She'll
give us a bed for the night if there's no' room for us all at the
inn."

Rhiannon stared about her with interest. Six boys, two girls
and a mob of goats surrounded their cavalcade now, all the
children chattering happily in high, piping voices, the goats
bleating and leaping about madly. A woman came to the door
of one of the little grey cottages, wiping red, damp hands on her
apron, a cluster of children peeping out round her skirts. She
exclaimed aloud and called to her neighbour. Soon there were
faces at every doorway or window, pointing at the long-billed,
iridescent bird perched on Nina's shoulder and the arak leaping
about on the roof of the red caravan, and exclaiming with awe
at the magnificent winged horse. Blackthorn curved her neck in
pleasure, lifting her feathered feet daintily. Rhiannon smiled
and waved at the crowd, but did not answer any of the shouted
questions, not knowing what to say.

They came down the main road by the village green, past a
row of shopfronts with big glass windows filled with all sorts
of amazing things. One, with the sign of a bee hanging above
it, had windows filled with candles of all shapes and sizes and

colours, many lit so the window glowed golden, and jars of honey with fabric tied over the top, some pale as sunlit water, some yellow as pollen, others dark as a forest pool. There was a honeycomb dripping with fresh honey, and large jars filled with round dark things Lewen said were toffees.

Another shop was filled with tools of all descriptions, hoes and scythes and enormous two-handled saws, and sacks of flour and meal, and bright saucepans and kettles and ladles, and mops and brooms and feather dusters, and brown bags of seeds tied with string. Another had stiff brown dried fish hanging from hooks alongside smoked hams, and huge round cheeses, and jars of preserved fruit and pickled vegetables and jam.

There was a tired-looking baker, giving away handfuls of sugar-dusted pastry twists to the children before locking up his shop for the night, and an apothecary's shop, the window filled with jars of pills, and bottles of potions, and bowls of dried herbs and flowers and muslin spell-bags, and hooks hanging with bunches of bright feathers to sweep away bad dreams, and myriad charms and talismans dangling from leather thongs.

Next to it was a shop filled with bolts of lovely coloured material, spread out to show their silky weave. In one corner of the window was a headless wooden mannequin wearing a gorgeous dress made of blue shimmering fabric tied up with silver ribbons. Rhiannon gazed at it longingly. Though she pretended not to care, it bothered her that she had to wear hand-me-down boy's clothes when Edithe and Fèlice were always so beautifully dressed in fabrics as soft as thistledown. It was a constant irritation to her, like a burr under a saddlecloth, and her only consolation was the embroidered shawl that Lilanthe had given her, which she wrapped around her shoulders every night as they sat round the campfire talking and singing.

"It'd look bonny on ye," Lewen whispered shyly with a nod of his head towards the dress. Rhiannon scowled at him. She hated the way he always seemed to know what she was thinking, no matter how carefully she kept her feelings hidden. She gritted her teeth, waiting for one of the others to mock her, but they had not heard above the noise of the crowd and so she was able to pretend Lewen had not spoken and ride on, head held high.

They came to the inn in the very centre of town, facing the village green with its big old oak tree and its pretty white rotunda where, Lewen explained, the musicians would sit to play for weddings and festivals.

The inn was small and quaint, with an enormous blue-painted door, big windows with blue wooden boxes filled with herbs and flowers, and a very steep roof with two gabled windows in it like beetling eyebrows. Outside the inn were long benches where old men were sitting, hunched up in their heavy coats against the evening chill, smoking long pipes. Over their heads hung a brightly painted sign depicting a cat playing a fiddle.

The innkeeper stood in the doorway, beaming. He was a solid, red-faced man with a big apron tied over his breeches. Behind his square shoulder stood a thin woman, her hands clapped together in glee. It was clear they saw a good profit ahead of them that night.

Everyone was very chilled and stiff, and glad to dismount.

"Jongleurs!" the woman cried. "We havena had jongleurs in Ardarchy for years. And such a large company! Will ye be putting on a show for the town? Ye may have the use o' our taproom, for sure. Everyone will come. And a flying horse! Gracious me! Does it perform too? Och, I dinna ken if we have room for it in here!"

"My wife and I are minstrels and will be glad to give ye a show, but I'm afraid our companions are only travelling with us and willna be performing," Iven replied. "They are apprentices journeying to the Theurgia at the Tower o' Two Moons."

"Witchlings? What are they doing in Ardarchy? There's naught here but goats and geese," the innkeeper asked. His voice rose incredulously. "Ye do no' mean to cross the Stormness River, surely?"

"Aye, we do," Iven answered. "Why shouldna we?"

"The bridge is barricaded shut," the innkeeper answered. "No-one goes that way anymore. The land across the river is haunted, did ye no' ken?"

Nina and Iven exchanged a glance. "Surely the barricade can be taken down for us?" Nina said gently.

"Och, ye willna want to be doing that," the innkeeper said.

"Ye'd be best off riding back to Barbreck-by-the Bridge and crossing there."

"But no' tonight," his wife said firmly. "Ye're cold and weary, and will be wanting a sup o' something hot, and happen a dram or two to warm your blood. And no point wasting a good audience. The whole o' Ardarchy will turn out to see ye perform—it's rare we see a minstrel or jongleur here. A shame ye're no' all performers, but no doubt the witchlings will still want a meal and some ale too, and will watch the show with the rest o' us. We'll want a cut o' the takings, mind. And ye'll want stabling for the horses, no doubt, and that's a few extra pennies too. I'll call my laddie to come take the horses for ye."

"We'll see to the horses ourselves, thanks, but if ye could rustle up some hay and happen some bran mash for them, we'd be grateful indeed," Iven said. Fèlice moaned audibly. He grinned at her. "Come, lassie, surely ye were no' expecting to eat and drink until ye've cared for your horse yourself? She's had a long hard ride today and she's chilled through. What if this lad kens naught about horses? Ye wouldna like to think o' her shivering in a cold draughty stall without her blanket and nothing but a bit o' auld musty straw to chew on, would ye? No, o' course, that I'm wishing to cast aspersions on our good host here," he added with a charming smile to the innkeeper. "I'm sure your stable is warm and snug enough for a prince. It's just the principle I'm wishing to teach."

"Och, and fair enough," the innkeeper replied jovially.

He turned to the crowd of followers then and motioned away with his hands. "Go on, get along home, there'll be no show now. Come back after supper."

Iven had vaulted down from the caravan to speak to the innkeeper but now he turned and faced the crowd, his voice ringing out clearly. "Good people o' Ardarchy, I am Iven the Magnificent, and I have great pleasure in introducing the incomparable Nina, called the Nightingale by the Rìgh himself for the indescribable sweetness of her voice. You may wonder what we do here, so far from the royal court, but only a few days ago we heard we were called back to Lucescere by royal decree, for Nina to sing at the wedding o' the royal heir Donncan MacCuinn to his bonny cousin Bronwen."

There was a murmur of delight and astonishment.

"Aye, I am glad to be the one to tell ye the happy news . . ."

As Iven continued on, captivating the crowd with his patter, the innkeeper helped Nina down from the caravan, saying: "I'll go and stoke up the fire for ye, and pull ye all some ale, and add a few extra potatoes to the roasting pan, and we'll have all ready for ye when your horses are seen to."

"We do no' eat meat," Nina said. "Would ye have some vegetable broth or stew that we may eat instead?"

"I have bean stew," the innkeeper's wife said, her voice falling in disappointment, as bean stew was worth quite a few pennies less than roast mutton and potatoes. At the word 'stew' an audible sigh was heard from the apprentices. Nina flashed them an admonitory glance and allowed the innkeeper to show her into the warmth of the taproom.

Lewen helped Maisie down from her fat pony and, leading his horse and hers, followed the innkeeper's plump son round the back to the stableyard, the others trailing tiredly behind.

"I wish my groom was here to look after Regina for me," Fèlice grumbled. "I am so cold and so tired. Cameron, will ye no' do it for me?"

Before Cameron could reply, Maisie said in her gentle way, "Och, we're all cold and tired, aren't we, Cameron? And poor Regina must be even tireder, for she was the one that did all the walking."

Lewen looked at her with approval and she blushed and did her best to take off her pony's tack by herself. Lewen helped her, and then unsaddled Argent, who was looking very bad-tempered, not liking being ridden for such a long time on such stony roads. Fèlice sighed and started to undo the buckles and Cameron left his own horse standing with steaming hide and hanging head to help her.

By the time the horses were unsaddled and groomed and tucked into their blankets, with fresh straw forked into their stalls and buckets of warm bran mash and fresh water to lip at, and all the tack cleaned and hanging on hooks, and the caravans secured, it was fully dark and everyone was weary indeed. The work had kindled some sort of camaraderie between them, however, and they all talked and joked comfortably as they made their way back to the welcoming warmth of the inn.

"A proper bed tonight," Fèlice sighed in ecstasy.

"I just hope they've aired the sheets," Edithe said.

"I doubt there's room for all o' us here," Lewen said, looking up and counting the number of windows streaming light. "Some o' us will have to go and stay at the witch's, I think."

"I will," Edithe said. "Less chance o' bedbugs, I bet."

"She'll probably rather have Nina and Iven, so she can hear all the news from court," Fèlice sighed regretfully.

"I doubt the innkeeper and his wife will let them go," Edithe said ironically. "I'd say Iven the Magnificent is the most exciting thing to happen round here in a decade, and they'll want to be the ones to hear all the gossip firsthand."

"Forget Iven, it's Rhiannon and her fabulous winged horse that's attracted most o' the attention," Rafferty shot back, with a quick sideways grin at Rhiannon. "I bet Iven is wondering how he can incorporate ye into his show. He'll have ye doing levades and caprioles by the next village we pass through."

Rhiannon had no idea what he meant but she smiled back anyway, deciding she rather liked Rafferty. At least he did not leer at her, or sneer at her, or compare her breasts to mountain peaks.

"Well, I'm happy to stay at the inn," Cameron said. "Ale, ale and more ale for me, please!"

"I'd like to see the witch's tower," Maisie said rather wistfully. "I've never seen one afore, ye ken."

They came into the taproom and hurried to warm themselves by the fire, the boys gratefully accepting the mugs of foaming ale the innkeeper tapped for them, the girls sipping hot spiced wine. Rhiannon had never tasted mulled wine before and drank deeply, feeling a pleasant euphoria fill her veins. By the time they had been served a substantial meal of bean stew and roast vegetables, followed by a surprisingly delicious treacle pie, she was feeling quite light-headed and was surprised to find herself giggling at one of Edithe's sarcastic asides. Edithe was equally surprised but rather gratified, while Lewen surreptitiously moved the jug of wine away from Rhiannon's elbow.

The boys began a game of chance with some dice which Cameron pulled from his pocket, and Rhiannon went eagerly to join them. Soon their corner was noisy with laughter and the calling of bets, Rhiannon's face alight with eagerness as she challenged Cameron to another toss. Lewen was content to sit back and watch her, sipping his ale and enjoying the warmth of the fire on the soles of his boots.

"I just canna understand why it is we have to travel round Eileanan in this ridiculous fashion," Edithe said as she watched Roden and Lulu practicing their juggling and Iven walking round the room on his hands. "It really is naught better than a circus. My father would've happily paid for me to travel to the capital in comfort and it would no' have taken me months to get there! Do ye no' agree, Lady Fèlice?"

"Well, it's true my *dai-dein* was no' very happy about it," Fèlice said. "He wondered how safe it was, particularly, ye ken, with the boys . . ." She nodded towards Cameron and Rafferty, who were eagerly gesturing for the landlord to refill their ale tankards. "But the Coven insists on it, ye ken. Diantha, the court sorceress at Ravenscraig, says it knocks any nonsense out o' us afore we get to the Tower and gets us used to doing things for ourselves and rubbing elbows with all kinds o' people."

"Well, that at least is true," Edithe replied and for once her voice was free of scorn, sounding only resigned.

"Diantha told me that the council o' sorcerers believe it was because the Coven had grown arrogant and isolated from the common people that the Day o' Betrayal was able to happen at all. So now all apprentices must travel slowly through the countryside afore they ever reach the Tower, learning what it means to be cold and hungry and afraid. We are lucky we are allowed to ride. Diantha said the council debated whether it would be wiser to make us walk the whole way on our own two feet."

"Eà forbid," Edithe said faintly.

"Probably if each country had its own Tower, we would have had to, but as the only Tower in all o' western Eileanan is the Tower o' Horse-Lairds and their wisdom is no' what most wish to learn, we all have to travel a long way and so they allow us horses. Indeed, she said we were lucky indeed to get to travel with Nina and Iven, for they at least are great fun to be with, and will teach us much along the way. Besides, she said we should be honoured to be travelling in their company, and somehow I do no' think she was joking."

"Honoured?" Maisie and Edithe echoed.

Fèlice shrugged. "So she said. Iven is some sort o' war hero, ye ken. He fought with Lachlan the Winged in the rebellion against the Ensorcellor, and was there when they rescued Daillas the Lame and many other adventures they now sing about. And Nina . . . well, Diantha would no' say too much about Nina but there was this note in her voice that made me wonder . . ."

"What kind o' note?" Edithe said skeptically.

Fèlice shrugged. "I dinna ken. Awe. Respect." She turned to Lewen, favouring him with her most dazzling smile. "Lewen, your family kens the royal clan. What can ye tell us?"

"About what?" Lewen said warily.

"About Nina. She's no' just an ordinary jongleur, is she?"

Lewen choked back a laugh. "Well, ye only need to hear her sing to ken that," he said.

"I mean more than that," Fèlice coaxed. "Ye should've seen the way the MacBrann himself bowed to her. The young MacBrann, I mean, no' the auld mad one who's dead now. There's some mystery about her, I just ken it."

Everyone was staring at Lewen now. He wondered how to respond. If Nina wanted her family history told, would she not tell it? But perhaps it was hard for her to tell, just as it was hard for Lewen's own father to talk about his part in the war. And if they knew, these arrogant aristocratic brats, would they not treat her with more respect? He glanced at Nina, warming her voice at the far end of the room with the most exquisite rills of music, her sunbird trilling away with her in sublime accompaniment. She glanced at him with her bright dark eyes, and Lewen realised she knew exactly what they spoke about, huddled here in their own fire-lit end of the inn. She smiled at him ruefully, shrugged her slim shoulders, and turned away.

"So?" Edithe demanded. "What's the big mystery?"

"Ask her to sing the song o' the three blackbirds tonight," Lewen said at last, his chest muscles constricting tight.

"Why?"

"Because no-one sings it more beautifully, my mother says. And because her brother wrote it."

"But . . ." Edithe sounded puzzled.

Fèlice, court-bred, knew at once. "Ye mean the Earl o' Caerlaverock?" Her voice came out in a squeak. "The Rìgh's own minstrel?"

"Wasna he the one who found the Rìgh, when he was still a blackbird, and saved him, and helped transform him back into a man?" Landon asked, eyes shining.

"It was Enit Silverthroat who did that," Lewen said. "Dide and Nina's grandmother. Dide was still only a lad and Nina little more than a babe. Lachlan travelled with them for years in their caravan, learning to be a man again. Dide was the first to swear allegiance to Lachlan and promise to help him win the throne."

"Wasna Enit Silverthroat the auld Yedda who masterminded the rebellion against the Ensorcellor?" Edithe said. "And then taught Jay Fiddler the song o' love, which he played at the Battle o' Bonnyblair, enchanting the Fairgean into peace?"

Lewen nodded. "Though she was no' a Yedda," he said. "She was a jongleur."

They all turned and looked up the room at Nina, her head bent over her shabby old guitar, her messy chestnut curls tumbling down onto a gaudy orange and gold brocade dress, stained around the hem and darned here and there with mismatching thread.

"Ye're telling me *Nina* is the sister o' the Earl o' Caerlaverock?" Edithe's voice was dazed with amazement.

Lewen nodded. "And Roden is his heir, for he has no children o' his own, ye ken."

"*Roden* is a Viscount?"

Lewen could not help smiling as everyone stared at the grubby little boy juggling balls back and forth with the arak, his chestnut curls uncombed and his grimy jerkin missing a couple of buttons.

"Well!" said Edithe at last. "I would never have guessed it."

Edithe's expression of dazed wonderment stayed on her face all through the jongleurs' performance, which was concluded with a storm of clapping from the townsfolk crowded into the long smoky room. Nina was begged for encore after encore, but at last she had to desist, hoarse-throated and heavy-eyed. Reluctantly the crowd filed out into the frosty night, talking and marvelling, and Nina sat down limply, drinking one last cup of honeyed tea, Roden nestled sleepily against her side.

A tall woman in a flowing white gown came to sit next to her, talking quietly. Her brown hair was tied back in a long plait that hung to her knees, and as she lifted her hand to gesture, light flashed off the rings on her right hand. Rhiannon came shyly closer and, at Nina's welcoming smile, sat next to the woman on the bench.

"Come, ye must be weary indeed," the witch was saying. "Will ye no' bring yon lassies and come spend the night with me? Arley Innkeeper has only two rooms here, no' nearly enough for all o' ye, and I have room to spare."

"I thank ye," Nina answered. "Indeed we are all worn out. We've been riding since dawn and had a day like it yesterday and another one ahead o' us tomorrow."

"I do no' understand why ye have come this way," the witch said. "Do ye no' ken the road past here is rough indeed, for none o' us travel that way? It is a dark and evil land across the bridge. Ghosts walk there, and evil spirits. Ye would be better off travelling back up the river to the bridge at Barbreck and crossing there, to travel down the western bank of the river. There is another bridge at Tullimuir where ye can cross again, and then ye need no' travel under the shadow o' the Tower o' Ravens."

"But we would lose weeks in the travelling," Nina said wearily. "We would have gone that way from Ravenscraig if we had not had to go up into the highlands to pick up young Lewen and Rhiannon here. But since we had to go that way, it made more sense to cut through the hills and save crossing the Findhorn again twice. This way we can travel close round the base of the hills to Rhyssmadill, and then up along the flank o' the Whitelock Mountains to Lucescere. It will be much faster than having to follow the Findhorn south again, and then cross the river at Tullimuir Bridge, right at the mouth o' the firth."

"But have ye no' heard? Do ye no' ken? No-one goes that way anymore. It's a cursed land. They say the dead walk again there and what few people are left keep their shutters closed and their bolts shot, even in the heat o' summer, for fear o' what may come knocking on their door."

Nina frowned and unconsciously nestled her sleeping son closer to her. "We've heard the tower is haunted, o' course, but we do not intend to go there, just pass through the gap in the hills at its foot."

The witch shuddered and made an odd gesture with her hands, circling the thumb and forefinger of her right hand and crossing it with the forefinger of her left hand. "Truly, it is no' safe, my lady, no' even to pass under its shadow. The people o' Ardarchy do no' go that way at all—we go north to Barbreck-by-the-Bridge and south again on the far side of the river with our goods, aye, even to go to the ports we go that way, rather than cross the Stormness."

Nina looked troubled. "I thank ye for your warning, Ashelma, but we do no' have time to retrace all our steps. As I'm sure ye've heard, we've been summoned to the palace for Prionnsa Donncan's wedding on Midsummer Eve, and I would no' miss it for anything. And I do no' fear ghosts. Ye o' all people should ken that ghosts do no' have the power to hurt us, they are naught but memories."

The witch Ashelma looked very grave. "Memories have as much power to hurt as any sword, if they are cruel enough," she said. "And it is no' just ghosts that haunt the land beyond the Stormness River. We have heard tales of corpses that will no' rest in their grave but seek to return to warmer beds, and children stolen and found murdered."

Nina looked down at her sleeping son and smoothed his tangled curls away from his flushed cheek. "Does the MacBrann no' ken o' these tales?"

"Aye, o' course, but his hands are full enough already, having only just inherited the throne from his father. Auld Malcolm was no' a good laird, ye ken, being more interested in his dogs and his experiments than in the problems o' the people. He grew more vague and eccentric with every year that passed, and by the end was raving mad, by all accounts."

Nina sighed. "It's hard to ken what to do. Your news troubles me greatly, but I ken the people o' Ravenshaw and how melancholy and superstitious they are. There have been wild stories about the Tower of Ravens since the time o' Brann himself, and that's a thousand years o' unfounded supposition. And two days o' hard riding and we are past the tower and into the lowlands. And I am no' without magic, as ye ken. I think we must risk it, though I thank ye for the warning."

Ashelma sighed and rose to her feet. "Well, let me see what I can do to make ye comfortable tonight, at least."

Nina rose too, lifting Roden in her arms and laying him across her shoulder. "My thanks," she said. "Rhiannon, will ye call the other lasses? We shall spend the night with Ashelma and meet up again with Iven and the lads in the morn. Is there aught ye need for the night?"

"I canna leave Blackthorn," Rhiannon said. "She fret without me. I sleep in the stable."

Ashelma looked at Rhiannon for the first time. Her eyes were dark and very serious, and seemed to see everything there was to see in a single searching glance. "Are ye the rider o' the winged horse I've been hearing so much about?" she asked.

Rhiannon nodded.

"Ye may bring your horse too, if ye ken," the witch said. "All beasts are welcome in my tower, as ye will see."

Rhiannon thought for a moment, reluctant to rouse her drowsy horse and take her out of the warmth of the stable into the cold night. She felt a great desire to see the witch's tower, however, and so she nodded abruptly and went to rouse the other girls from their sleepy repose by the fire. They got up, yawning and stretching. Fèlice and Edithe wrapped themselves up in their fur-trimmed cloaks and pulled on their gloves but Maisie had nothing but an old shawl to wrap about her against the cold. She pulled it close about her round face, her eyes shining with excitement at the thought of staying with a real witch.

"Sweet dreams, my ladies," Cameron said rather unsteadily, looking up from the depths of his empty mug. "Dinna miss me too much."

"Miss ye?" Edithe said haughtily. "I doubt we'll notice ye're no' around."

She saw Rhiannon's mouth curve and flashed a quick smile at her, so that Rhiannon was unable to help smiling back.

Lewen stood up and looked at Rhiannon a little anxiously.

She frowned at his look, and he quirked his mouth, saying severely, "Ye willna stab anyone, will ye?"

She laughed at that, and said, "Nay, o' course no'. No' unless I have to, that is."

"Nina will have a care for ye," he said.

"Me need no-one to care for me," she snapped back and then, when he grinned, realised he was teasing. She would not relent, however, scowling at him as she pulled on her blue tam-o'-shanter and huddled the thick, warm cloak about her.

"Good night," he said. "Sweet dreams."

She looked back at him from the doorway and her expression softened.

"Good night to ye too."

The Witch's Tower

It was bitterly cold outside, with a nasty snippety wind that found every gap in their clothing and sent the fog swirling up around their ankles. Rhiannon led Blackthorn, the big blanket still flung over her withers and concealing her wings. Ashelma had a small two-wheeled trap pulled by a sturdy, shaggy-maned pony. She tucked Nina and Maisie and the sleeping boy up under some soft goat-hair blankets, saying to the other girls, "Ye're well-wrapped enough to walk a few blocks, I think?" as she took the pony's bridle and began to lead the way.

As they went down the ill-lit street, past dark shop windows and sleeping houses, a lantern hanging from the pony-trap's seat flickered into life by itself, making every hair on Rhiannon's body stand erect in sudden superstitious terror. No-one else seemed to notice, though, except Blackthorn who shied sideways, almost knocking Rhiannon over.

"It's hard to believe it is spring," Fèlice said with a shiver. "It feels like winter. Look, I'm breathing smoke like a dragon."

"It's always cold in the Ring o' Dubhslain," Ashelma said. "We have a saying here: 'Do no' put your plaids away, until the last day o' May'."

"It's more than a month to May Day!" Fèlice said. "I would've been crowned May Queen if I had stayed in Ravenscraig, ye ken. I was hoping, if we got to Lucescere in time . . ."

"Indeed?" Ashelma turned and gave Fèlice that grave, penetrating glance so that the girl flushed a little and lost her smile.

"Well, I was," she said a little defiantly. "Though I hear the Banprionnsa Bronwen is all the rage there now. Apparently she's quite a beauty, though no' in the usual style. Anyway, never mind. There would no' be much o' a May Day celebration in Ravenscraig this year, anyway. The auld laird had just died and the court's in mourning."

"There'll be other May Days," the witch said, quite kindly.

They came to the Stormness River, moving sinuously under the mist like a great black-scaled snake, and turned to walk down a smooth narrow road along its bank. Trees and well-clipped hedges loomed over them. The last few lights fell behind and all was dark and quiet and cold. Their lone lantern bobbed along, its light little more than an orange blur through the fog. Rhiannon shivered inside her cloak. The words the witch had spoken in the inn echoed in her mind. *Tales o' corpses that will no' rest in their grave but seek to return to warmer beds . . . children stolen and found murdered . . .*

She looked across the silent river but she could see nothing but wisps of mist floating up from the darkly glinting water like the ghosts the witch had spoken of. She wished they did not have to cross the bridge in the morning but she would have cut off her tongue before she ever admitted it.

They came to a high stone wall with an iron gate standing open. The witch led them inside and the gate shut itself behind them. On either side stood tall trees covered in frail white blossoms like new snow. The air seemed suddenly warmer and sweetly scented. Through the mist Rhiannon could see lights shining towards them, golden as sunlight. They came into a wide cleared area before the house, a long, low building built of grey stone with a peaked roof covered in silver-green lichen, beside a tall round tower that rose higher than the trees. The light came from the windows and door of the house. A young woman stood in the doorway, the light of the lantern she held throwing bright colour up onto her face and hair.

"Come in!" she said. "Ye must be chilled to the bone. What a dreadful night. Morogh says bad weather is coming and indeed I think he's right. It's cold as winter."

Her voice was soft and kind with a warm undercurrent as if she had just this moment stopped laughing. She came running down the stairs, wrapped in a woolly red shawl, and took the pony's bridle. "I'll look after Drud," she said. "You go on in and get warm. I've got the kettle whistling on the hob if ye'd like some tea."

"Lovely," Ashelma said. She helped a drowsy Maisie down from the pony-trap and up the stairs. Edithe and Fèlice followed her eagerly, Nina bringing up the rear more slowly, carrying the heavy weight of her sleeping child.

"I will stable my horse myself," Rhiannon said.

"Of course," the girl answered. "What a bonny beast she is! So tall and finely made, and with such magnificent long horns. I have never seen a horse like her."

"No' many like her," Rhiannon said.

"No," the girl agreed. "A rare beast indeed. Ye and her are akin, I can see that."

They had walked round the side of the house and in through a stable door as they spoke, and so when Rhiannon looked up in sudden keen interest, she was able to see the other girl clearly in the light of the lanterns hanging on either wall.

Rhiannon's first thought was one of surprise. She had thought the other girl young and beautiful but now she realized she was at least six years older than Rhiannon, and quite short and plump, a big-boned young woman with mousy-brown hair, a round face and fresh, rosy skin. She looked with great frankness and openness at Rhiannon, however, and as soon as she spoke again, the illusion of beauty returned, for her voice was so warm and merry, and her smile so wide and friendly. "My name is Annis. I am Ashelma's apprentice."

"My name is Rhiannon," she answered, hearing the ring of pride in her own voice.

"And ye have tamed a winged horse," Annis said admiringly. "Och, the town was full o' it. I am so glad ye came to stay the night here for I would have been sad indeed to miss my chance to see your bonny horse and meet with ye. I could no' come to hear Nina the Nightingale sing, for I couldna leave the children, so I was hoping ye would all come home with Ashelma."

"Children?" Rhiannon asked.

Annis had been swiftly unharnessing the pony from the trap, rubbing it down with a cloth and filling its bucket with grain. All her movements were quick and neat, and she was surprisingly light on her feet for such a big-boned girl. Rhiannon noticed she wore the white luminous stone on the middle finger of her right hand that they all seemed to wear, as well as one made of some dark green stone.

She nodded. "Aye, we run an orphanage here, ye see. We have two bairns from Ardarchy, but the others are all from across the river. No' all are orphans. Some were brought here by their parents for safekeeping. Mainly boys. For some reason it is boys that are in the most danger over there, we do no' ken why."

Annis pumped some fresh water into a bucket for Blackthorn, who had settled comfortably into a straw-filled stall, her head drooping drowsily, and then quickly checked the water buckets of the other animals. Apart from the shaggy pony Drud, there were a tall chestnut mare, three goats, a tabby cat, and a large number of fat hens with glossy feathers.

"It snows heavily here in winter," Annis explained, "and so it is easier to keep them all under the one roof and close to the house. The hens have had to learn not to lay their eggs under the horses' hooves but otherwise they are all friends and get on well."

She led the way through an internal doorway into a long fire-lit room. Overhead were carved wooden beams holding up an arched ceiling, and tall gothic windows looked out on to the garden all along one side. An immense scarred table ran down the centre of the room, decorated with fat, sweet-scented candles and vases of spring flowers. Around the fire at the far end were drawn some deep, shabby, cushioned chairs where Nina and the witch Ashelma were sitting, drinking tea and talking like old friends. Another cat lay sleeping on Ashelma's lap and by her feet was a large hairy mass which, on closer inspection, proved to be three dogs, one of them a huge deerhound and another a tiny white terrier, smaller than the cat. The other was some kind of mongrel, spotted and brindled and patched with black, and missing one leg. An owl sat hunched on one of the rafters, while a bandaged hare lay sleeping in a box by the wall.

Maisie, Edithe and Fèlice were all sitting curled together on a couch, covered by a soft blanket. Only Edithe was still awake, and she had her head pillowed on her hand and her cup resting in her lap, looking as if she would slip off into sleep at any moment.

Annis led Rhiannon to the only remaining chair, made her sit and poured her a cup of some kind of pale, flower-scented hot tea. She sipped at it suspiciously.

"Chamomile," Annis said, smiling. "It will help you sleep. Go on, drink it up. Ye all look worn out." She sat down on the ground at Rhiannon's feet, fondling the spotted ear of the three-legged mongrel, and nodded at her encouragingly. Rhiannon drank obediently.

Ashelma turned to her and smiled. "I was just telling the others about all the animals. They think I keep some kind o' menagerie but indeed it is no' my fault. Annis collects wounded animals but somehow, once they are healed, they do no' wish to leave. The only creature that is mine is Strixa the owl, and believe me, it is only because o' the deep love she bears me that she tolerates all the other animals. Particularly Serena the hare, our newest guest. We have to keep a close eye on Strixa in case she forgets herself and swoops on her for her supper."

The owl hooted contemptuously and spat a hard pellet towards the sleeping hare, who at once sat up, her long ears twitching nervously.

"The orphanage is Annis's idea also," Ashelma went on. "I do no' ken quite how it happened, but we now have nine boys and one girl staying here with us. Most are from across the river. Nina, I do no' wish to alarm ye but ye must ken that it is dangerous for little boys over there. All o' the murdered bairns were boys, most around five or six years auld. Quite a few o' our lads were brought here by their parents for safekeeping. I wish ye would reconsider crossing the Stormness. I ken ye wish to reach the capital in time for the royal wedding, but surely your wee laddie's safety is more important?"

Nina was white. "That's no' fair, Ashelma," she said angrily. "Ye must ken Roden is the most important thing in the world to me. O' course I feel anxious with all these tales o' lads going missing and being found murdered. But we are only passing through. In two days we'll be gone. I think Iven and I can keep Roden safe till then. We shallna let him out o' our sight."

"I'm sorry, I dinna mean to offend ye," Ashelma said.

Nina took a deep breath. "That's all right," she said after a moment. "The fact is, Ashelma, we did no' choose to come this way lightly. If our only concern was getting back to Lucescere in time for the wedding, we would've gone the usual way. We have plenty o' time, the wedding is no' until midsummer."

Ashelma nodded, looking an enquiry.

"Nay, the truth is we were forced to change our plans. As we came through Barbreck-by-the-Bridge, we found the body o' a murdered Yeoman, one o' His Highness's most trusted and beloved men. He had been beaten and tortured cruelly afore he died. Both Iven and I kent him well. There will have to be an enquiry into his death. His Highness will be most anxious for us to make our report, and Connor's sister . . . she will want to ken all we can tell her."

"How terrible!" Ashelma exclaimed. "I'm sorry, I dinna realise."

"How could ye?" Nina asked. "Ye must see now that we shall save more than a week in the travelling coming this way. And I must admit it was in my mind to try to find the Scrying Pool at the Tower o' Ravens and use it to speak to His Highness."

"Och, nay, ye must no' do that," Ashelma said. "The tower is haunted, do ye no' ken? Few who go into the ruin come out again, and those that do are stark raving mad, they say. The ghosts there are malevolent and cruel, and hate the living."

Nina frowned. "I have heard that," she admitted. "I was hoping it was all an exaggeration, however."

"Och, nay," Ashelma said. "It is all true. And only getting worse, it seems. The land that lies beneath the Tower o' Ravens has been an unhappy place since the Day o' Betrayal but recently it seems the whole valley is cursed. No-one is safe, no' man, woman or child. Particularly not young boys. Nina, in the twenty-five years since Lachlan the Winged won the throne thirty or more lads have gone missing."

"Thirty or more boys? Vanished?"

"Murdered. Their bodies were found, but there's no sign o' what killed them and no witch or skeelie nearby to examine the bodies more closely. Do ye wonder that the mothers o' boys dare no' stay in Fetterness anymore? Those that canna leave bring their babes across the river to me, but I have no room for any more and besides, they shouldna be with me, they should be safe with their families. Indeed, I do no' ken what can be done."

Nina shook her head, looking appalled.

"And that's not the worst o' it. Nina, the dead canna rest there. Graves both auld and new are found open and the corpses walk around in broad daylight, dragging their rotting flesh behind them, seeking to come home again." She shuddered and wrapped her arms about her body in a vain attempt to warm herself. Rhiannon shuddered too.

"And we fear the evil shall find a way to cross the river and shadow all o' us here. Already we've found two graves robbed, or broken out o', though we have no' seen the dead they once contained walking about, thank Eà! And our town watchman has disappeared. We have his children here, Casey and Letty. He went out one night to investigate a noise and did no' come back. We never found his body. Since then the town reeve has put a gate across the bridge and locked it, and only those that come across in daylight and can satisfy him they have true business here are allowed through. Most are wanting work this side o' the river but we canna take any more, and so now they head south towards the ports. No-one has come knocking on the gate for close on two weeks now, and we've had no news since then."

Nina looked shaken. "I had no idea it was so bad!" she exclaimed. "We heard rumours, o' course, but . . . surely the MacBrann should ken o' this?"

"We sent a message to Ravenscraig last market-day, but have heard naught from the laird. Who kens if he even heard it? When the carrier returned from Ravenscraig it was with the news o' Malcolm MacBrann's death and all the court was in mourning. Our messenger had no chance o' seeing the new laird. He passed the news on to a guard at the gate and came away. What more could he do? And I canna scry to the court sorceress, even though we are so close, for we are bounded by two rivers here and both are deep and fast. Just as it is too dangerous to try to cross in a boat, so it is too noisy for my thoughts to cross." She sighed. "So we do what we can to help the people o' Fetterness, those who have no' fled, and shelter their children and guard our own doors and hope the MacBrann will send his guards to investigate when he can. Happen ye will tell the Coven yourself, if . . . I mean, when . . ." Her voice trailed away unhappily.

"I will," Nina said firmly. "Now we must to bed, for my lasses are asleep in their chairs and I myself am sick with weariness. I am sorry for your trouble. I will certainly tell the Key-bearer and when she can, she will no doubt come herself to listen in the ruins and see what the ghosts have to say. For now, do no' fear for us. I ken the songs o' sorcery. We shall be safe."

Ashelma nodded, looking tired and troubled. She stood up, gently tipping the cat in her lap to the floor, and helped Annis rouse Edithe, Maisie and Fèlice. Nina lifted Roden to her shoulder, his curly head nestling into her neck, and followed the witch and her apprentice up a broad flight of steps to a bedroom on the upper floor.

Rhiannon followed quietly behind, her head ringing with the witch's words. Satyricorns were afraid of nothing living, but had a profound horror of anything supernatural. They spilt a little blood every day in supplication of the dark fiends they believed dwelt in every shadow and cleft, and if they had failed in the hunt that day, they would open their own vein to make sure the sacrifice was made. Rhiannon had not spilt blood once since leaving her herd, having been determined to leave all of that part of her behind like a snake's cast-off skin. Her whole body was shuddering now, though, down to the very marrow of her bones. She swore she would slice open her vein this very night and make an offering to the dark walkers of the night.

There was only one bed in the room but it was enormous, standing on its own platform with a velvet canopy hanging overhead. Annis helped the other girls sleepily strip down to their shifts and climb up into the bed, which had been warmed by long-handled brass-lidded trays filled with hot coals. They were to sleep two at either end, with a trundle bed made up before the fire for Nina and Roden. Rhiannon allowed herself to be tucked up under the white counterpane, pretending to be almost asleep so Nina or Annis would not try to speak with her. The sheets were stiff and smelt of herbs, and the pillow was very soft. She was so very tired it took a strong effort of will not to succumb to the insistent weight of sleep on her limbs.

She lay quietly, watching from under her eyelashes as Nina tucked up her son, washed her face and hands, and shed her own clothes.

The jongleur did not climb into bed at once, though. She picked up the small bag she always wore tied to her belt and rummaged inside it, taking out a small stick and a few little cloth bags tied up with string. She opened one and threw what looked like dead leaves on the fire. Little green-hearted flames sprung up and curled away, scenting the smoke sweetly as they died.

She then drew her dagger from its sheath, a gesture that made Rhiannon's eyes open wider and her muscles tense. Nina hesitated and turned to look towards the bed, as if she had heard the subtle change in the rhythm of Rhiannon's breath. Rhiannon breathed slowly, pretending to sleep.

After a moment Nina knelt before the fire and gathered together a little handful of ashes from the hearth, spreading these around her in a circle. She shook salt from one of the bags and sprinkled it on top of the ashes, then sprinkled water about her as well. Then, with her back straight, she swept the stick in her hand all round her, tracing the shape of the circle, then repeated the gesture with the dagger, muttering words under her breath. She knelt naked in the centre of the circle in silence for quite some time, unmindful of the cold, her unruly red-brown curls her only covering. At last she opened her eyes and rose up onto her knees, her wand in one hand, the knife in the other. Facing the fire, she chanted in a low, sweet voice:

> "Goddess o' life, Goddess o' death,
> Goddess o' all power that is the universe,
> Shine your light o' white upon me and mine,
> Shield all within this house from that which is evil,
> Give to me peace and protection from harm,
> By the power o' the fire, by the life in this blade,
> By the power o' the earth, by the life in this wand,
> By the powers o' air and water, cup and bowl,
> By the powers o' stars and moons and cold distances,
> Shield us, Eà o' the green blood, and keep us safe."

She then reversed the movement of wand and dagger, and swept up the salted ashes with her hands, pouring them into a little muslin bag with some of the dead leaves. She tied the top of the bag with blue ribbon and then slipped the cord about the neck of her son, kissing him gently on the forehead. He murmured in his sleep and turned, tucking his hand under one round cheek. Shivering, Nina dragged her shift back on over her head and then crept into bed beside him, pulling the boy close against her body.

Rhiannon felt an odd prickling in her eyes, a hot ache in her throat. *It's the smoke,* she told herself irritably, and set herself to waiting till Nina was asleep. The jongleur seemed comforted by her little charade by the fire and soon slipped into sleep. Rhiannon waited patiently a while longer, listening to the sound of the wind in the branches outside, the sudden wash of rain. When she was sure all was quiet and still, she slipped out of the warm bed and went to kneel where Nina had knelt, in the half-obscured circle of ashes and salt. She gazed into the black and orange puzzle of glowing coals, unsheathed her dagger and slashed it quickly across her outstretched wrist. Blood welled up, thick and dark, and dripped from her wrist onto the flagstones.

Walk elsewhere, dark lords, Rhiannon said silently. *Drink this blood I freely offer you and seek not to take our souls. Walk elsewhere.*

Then she raised her wrist to her mouth and sucked at the cut, tasting the saltiness of her blood. She used her dagger to tear a strip of material from her shift, having nothing else to hand, and bound the wrist thoroughly. Almost immediately the white material was blotched with a growing stain. She shrugged, slipped the dagger back into the sheath strapped to her thigh, and crept back into the warmth of the bed, feeling faint and sick yet obscurely comforted, ready now to brave the falling shadows of sleep.

Next morning, the rain fell so heavily it was like a curtain of water drawn across the windows. Rhiannon had slept badly, her wrist throbbing and her dreams troubled. When she woke her eyes felt hot and scratchy as if filled with sand. It was so cold and grey outside, she could not find the will to throw off the counterpane and get up, and neither could the other girls. They all lay there drowsily, talking desultorily among themselves.

"Listen to that rain!" Fèlice murmured, and a while later moaned, "Och, my legs! I swear I am chafed raw."

"I wish I could lie abed all day," Edithe muttered, "but I guess there's no chance o' that. They'll make us ride all day in the rain, just to make sure we really ken what misery is."

"Surely no'?" Maisie poked her head out from under her pillow, her plaits all tousled. "I would like to bide here a wee. I was so sleepy last night I didna see a thing."

"Just a whole lot o' smelly animals and that disgusting owl that kept spitting things at me," Edithe said crossly.

They all burrowed back under the counterpane and were quiet. Rhiannon cradled her wrist against her breast and, when no-one came to rouse them, allowed herself to hope they would not have to ride out that day. She closed her eyes, feeling herself slipping back into sleep.

The door crashed open.

"Rise and shine, slug-a-beds," Nina called, holding the door open with her foot, a tray in her hands. "It's long past dawn and time to be getting on our way."

A chorus of groans met her.

"But it's *raining*," Fèlice said.

"And I ache all over," Edithe said.

"Surely we should wait for the rain to stop?" Maisie pleaded.

"Blackthorn does no' like the rain," Rhiannon said firmly. "And she is still tired. Niall said I must no' ride her too hard. He wouldna want me to ride her in the rain."

"Is that so?" Nina said. "So ye lassies think we should wait for the rain to stop?"

"Aye!" they all cried.

"What if it doesna stop for days?" Nina said. "The Stormness is already swollen with the melting snows. If it rains like this for much longer it could break its banks and then we'd be marooned here for weeks and weeks."

"Weeks?" Edithe cried in dismay.

"Aye," Nina replied severely. "Didna ye notice how high it

was last night? If ye wish to be witches, ye must learn to look about ye."

"I was too tired to notice anything except how much my legs ached," Fèlice said. "No' to mention the chafing. I'm rubbed raw!"

Nina pushed the door shut behind her and put down the tray. They all sat up a little, their eyes brightening, and one by one Nina passed them a steaming cup of tea. As they drank gratefully, Nina sat on the edge of their bed and regarded them with frowning black eyes, as dark as polished jet. Her face looked rather pale and haggard as if she too had been troubled by nightmares.

Refreshed by her tea, Fèlice said with her most winning smile, "We really are tired. We're no' used to riding so far every day. Please, could we no' rest today, and wait for the rain to stop? I'm sure Ashelma willna mind."

"Ye do look rather white, the lot o' ye. Especially ye, Rhiannon. Are ye no' feeling well? I would no' like any o' ye to take a chill."

Edithe immediately coughed, and laid her hand on her chest. "I am feeling rather unwell."

Nina cast her a stern glance but turned back to Rhiannon, first laying her hand on Rhiannon's forehead and then lifting her wrist. Rhiannon flinched and Nina looked down, her eyes at once widening in horror. "Rhiannon, what have ye done to yourself! Ye've cut yourself—ye're bleeding!"

The makeshift bandage was heavily stained and so was the sheet where Rhiannon had slept. Nina held Rhiannon's wrist in her cool fingers and stared into her eyes with a look as sharp and penetrating as a sword.

"What did ye cut yourself on?"

"My dagger."

"How?"

"I cut." She demonstrated with one swift movement.

"Ye cut yourself on purpose?"

Rhiannon nodded, not dropping her gaze. There was a long silence. Rhiannon was conscious of the other girls shrinking back.

"Why?" Nina's voice was neutral.

"To make peace with the dark walkers."

"Ye cut yourself to make peace with . . . the dark walkers? What—or who—are they?"

Rhiannon shrugged, unable to hold Nina's gaze any longer. Not knowing how to describe what she meant, she used the word she had heard so often in the last few days. "Ghosts."

Nina let go of her wrist. It was smarting cruelly, and Rhiannon cradled it in her other hand. Her cheeks felt hot and she knew she was perilously close to tears. She could not look at Nina or any of the other girls.

"Did ye bleed much?"

Rhiannon nodded.

Nina stood up. "Stay in bed, Rhiannon. I will make ye a blood-strengthening tea. We shall no' ride anywhere today. It really is no' the weather for riding out. Ye other girls can get up or stay in bed as ye please. I should tell you though that I willna allow Annis to be bringing up trays to ye, so if ye wish to eat, get up, get dressed and come on down. I'll make an exception for ye, though, Rhiannon. Stay in bed and rest."

Rhiannon refused to be singled out, however. She got up when the other girls did, though she felt a wave of dizziness wash over her, and washed and dressed herself and went downstairs with the others, holding on to the banister rather tightly. Nina made no comment at the sight of her, though her frown deepened.

The long room was raucous with the games and fights of ten small children, most of them no more than six years old. Roden was in the midst of it, shrieking with laughter, while Lulu was leaping about like a mad thing, having stolen the only girl's rag doll. The little girl was sobbing despairingly and trying to snatch it back, her younger brother enthusiastically helping. The three dogs were barking, and a white and black cat was hissing and spitting from the mantelpiece. Strixa the owl huddled on one of the rafters, occasionally spitting out a hard pellet at one of the children. Her aim was excellent.

Annis had a bowl of porridge in one hand and a dripping ladle in the other, and was trying to make herself heard above the racket, while Lulu and the little boy dodged round her. The arak gibbering in rage, the rag doll cradled close to her breast.

When the other boys joined in the chase, she suddenly jumped up onto the table, sending a jug of milk flying, and leapt up to catch hold of the iron-wrought chandelier, swinging from side to side till she was high enough to leap up into the rafters. There she crouched, rocking the doll and humming a tuneless lullaby.

"Oh, dear," Nina said. "I'm so sorry. Lulu! Naughty girl! Give back the dolly right now."

The arak shook her head, mumbling something in her own guttural language.

"Lulu, I am ashamed o' ye. We are guests in this house. Come down now and give back the doll to the wee lassie."

Lulu gave a sorrowful moan and very slowly and sadly swung down, hanging from her tail before dropping lithely onto all fours. She raised the doll and kissed its painted face and then offered it back to the little girl. The girl snatched it and cuddled it close, glaring at the hairy little creature, who was looking very shamefaced.

"Good girl," Nina said. "Never mind. I'll make ye a dolly o' your own if ye'd like one."

Lulu immediately danced in joy, shrieking in approval.

"I am sorry," Nina said. "Lulu forgets her manners sometimes."

"No' to worry," Annis said, looking rather harassed as three of the boys raced past her, almost knocking her over. "Would ye prefer to have your breakfast in the kitchen? Mealtimes are rather wild here, I'm afraid."

"I think we would indeed," Nina answered. "That is, if ye young ladies do no' think it beneath ye?"

"No' at all," Edithe said sweetly. "Please, lead the way."

"Thank ye, then, Annis, that would be grand," Nina said. "Roden! Settle down! Poor Annis should no' have to be worrying about ye as well as all the others. Sit down and eat your breakfast quietly, there's a good lad."

Roden reluctantly gave up the chase and came to sit at the table, dragging Lulu with him, and Nina and the older girls thankfully made their escape.

The kitchen was a haven of peace and warmth. A skinny old man with doleful dark eyes and a very long straggly grey beard meandered back and forth, getting them bowls, stirring various pots on the squat little stove and occasionally shovelling in another spade of coal. A grey cat was sleeping on one of the kitchen chairs, and in a box by the fire were seven adorable yellow ducklings, all squawking and trying to climb out over each other's backs.

Breakfast was a simple affair—porridge ladled out into bowls, tubs of honey and jugs of goat's milk, and a big brown pot of tea. Rhiannon felt much better after she had eaten her second bowl of honey-drenched porridge, and Nina stopped regarding her with a crease between her brows. Rhiannon was just finishing her third cup of tea when the door opened and Annis came in, plumper and rosier than ever.

"Morning, everyone," she sang out. "I hope ye've all had a more peaceful breakfast than I did!"

"I'm sure we did. I hope ye do no' mind us abandoning ye," Nina said.

"No, no, o' course no'. I kent Morogh would look after ye. It's bad enough that I have to suffer the bairns' commotion without inflicting it upon ye as well. I warn ye, though, it's only going to get worse. They're planning a re-enactment o' the Battle o' Bonnyblair, and are about to descend on the kitchen in search of pots and pans to make armour. Ashelma is in the tower, if ye would like to go through and visit her there? She is no' teaching today so she's free, for the morning at least."

"Thanks, we would like that," Nina said, standing up.

They followed Annis down a corridor to a large, arched doorway that led through into the tower. Built of stone, the tower was three stories high, with a staircase that wound up around the inner wall. On the ground floor was the witch's study and reception room, with another iron-bound door out into the garden and four tall arched windows that could be opened to let in fresh air and sunshine. There was a large desk littered with scrolls and calendars and writing implements, a few straight-backed chairs and, by the fire, two soft-cushioned, deep-seated chairs drawn close together, each with a little wooden table just large enough for a cup or goblet.

Bookshelves had been made to fit the curved walls of the room, and these were filled with spell-books and scrolls and maps, jars of dried herbs and powders and polished stones, bottles of precious oils and distillations, skulls and bones and sticks and lumps of crystals, and candles of all sizes and colours. The room smelt faintly of incense and dried herbs.

Ashelma was sitting at her desk, writing, but she rose with a smile as Nina and the four girls came in. She let them browse amongst the shelves for a while, exclaiming and asking questions. Edithe and Maisie were particularly fascinated, the first becoming absorbed in a leather-bound book of spells, the second busying herself looking through the jars of herbs and medicines.

After a while, Ashelma took them upstairs to show them the other two floors. The middle storey was a workroom and storeroom, with all the equipment necessary to grind powders, distill potions and prepare spells. The girls browsed around for a while, then followed Ashelma as she led them up the staircase to the upper level.

They all exclaimed in surprise. The walls and domed roof of the tower were made entirely of clear glass, supported by slender spans of steel, so that they could see for miles in every direction, including up into the black, roiling clouds of the storm. On the floor a mosaic of coloured tiles and thin strips of silver metal traced out the shape of a five-sided star set within a circle. The four directions were each marked upon the perimeter of the circle with arcane symbols in yellow, red, blue and green, and set at each of these symbols was a twisted wooden wand made of willow, a ceremonial dagger made of iron and moonstones, a silver chalice, and a beautifully made clay bowl inscribed with a six-sided star and filled with charred ashes.

"This is extraordinary!" Nina cried. "It really is a miniature o' one o' the great towers. How on earth could Ardarchy afford such a well-set-up witch's tower?"

Ashelma smiled. "I won a grant from the Coven," she answered. "I studied at the Tower o' Two Moons, ye ken, and heard about the grants while I was there. It's a new initiative o' the Keybearer, to encourage witches to go out into the countryside and help remote towns and villages and teach them the ways o' the Coven. Ardarchy has no' had its own witch since before the Day o' Betrayal so I've had a great deal to do since I came here. Certainly the townsfolk are proud o' their tower and they profited from the building o' it, because a condition o' the grant is that it must be used on local craftsmen and products. Only the glass had to be shipped in, o' course, which was enormously difficult and expensive, but worth it, I think."

"Oh, do ye think I could apply for a grant like that?" Maisie said with shining eyes and clasped hands. "My village is very poor and we have no-one to teach the children or do the rituals, or even help the women in their labour. My mother used to do what she could, but she got sick with the fever and my grandfather kens naught about healing, only about weather magic and blessing the crops, and so she died . . . oh, if I got a grant, I could go back and build a tower like this for us. It would mean so much to all the villages in the valley."

"O' course ye could, that's what the grants are for," Ashelma said. "Most o' the common folk canna be travelling to the High Towers for help in times o' trouble, and so the Keybearer hopes that one day every town or region will have its own tower, and everyone will be taught to read and write, and have access to healers, and celebrate the Sabbats as they should be celebrated. It has made all the difference to Ardarchy. I've started a village school, and I sit on the town council, and I bless the crops, and organise the parades and festivals, and often I mediate between the villagers so that the reeve does not have to be called in."

"And ye've started an orphanage and a hospital for injured animals," Nina said with a smile.

Ashelma smiled back ruefully. "A witch for all seasons, that's what I am!"

Crossing the Stormness

The storm raged so violently the next day that even Nina had to admit it would be dangerous to ride out. Hail rattled against the windows, and the trees swayed and bent like sword-fighters in a duel.

Iven and the boys braved the storm to come and join them, and arrived windblown, mud-splattered, and eager to get out of the pelting rain. Ashelma welcomed them warmly, helping them find dry clothes to put on, and advising them strongly against riding on.

"Once a storm like this sets in, it'll take a day or two for it to blow itself out," she said. "Stay and rest up, and set out again once it's blown over."

Nina looked at the streaming windows and thanked her with a sigh.

They were all glad to have a respite from riding, even Lewen, who was used to spending hours of every day in the saddle. They sat in front of the fire, playing cards or dice games, cleaning their boots, or in Landon's case, writing in his dog-eared, ink-splattered notebook. "Growing among trees o' blossom white, her tower shines out with blessed light . . ." he murmured to himself.

The girls all had a long soak in a hot bath, and helped wash and comb each other's hair. Their clothes were badly travel-stained, and so they took the opportunity to do their laundry, though Maisie had to show them how to use the boiler and wringer. Nina gave them all some more salve for their chafed thighs and bound up Rhiannon's wrist for her with fresh bandages.

The storm was fiercer than ever by nightfall, and so Ashelma made up pallets for the boys before the fire. They had a riotous meal with the orphans, who were bursting with energy after a day spent indoors, and went early to bed, hoping for a clear dawn.

Rhiannon had determined to undo her bandage and open her vein again that night, once all the others were asleep, but in the end this was not necessary, for Annis brought her a half-dead mouse one of the cats had caught. She gave the mouse to Rhiannon with a very grave face but said not a word, and Rhiannon was able to slit the mouse's throat and spill its blood without causing any commotion.

The next day was even wetter and wilder, and once again they delayed their riding out. Like the apprentices, Iven was quite content to lie around and read, or play with the orphans, or strum his guitar, eating and drinking to his heart's content, while the rain streamed down against the windows. Nina, however, was clearly anxious. She went out several times to check the height of the river, coming back drenched to the skin, shivering with cold and frowning.

The sorceress decided to put their enforced rest to good use, and so the apprentices had to spend the morning in the study and practice of witchcraft. Rhiannon found these lessons fascinating, though it made all the hair on her arms rise to watch the apprentices lift a wooden ball and set it spinning in midair without touching it.

Annis was set to listen to the students stumbling through the seven languages of birds and beasts, a skill Nina apparently thought they were all very weak in. Then she and Lewen spent an hour brushing up their knowledge in mathematics and alchemy, subjects they obviously detested.

Discovering Rhiannon could not read or write, Ashelma undertook to teach her, and soon Rhiannon's eyes and head and wrist were aching, the witch being a hard taskmistress. If it had not been for Edithe's raised eyebrow, and Cameron's snigger, half-hidden behind his hand, she would have rebelled but, having set her will to prove them wrong, Rhiannon learnt surprisingly fast. By the end of the day she could recognise her own name and Lewen's, as well as a few key words like bread, horse, witch and school. This gave her immense satisfaction, only equalled by her triumph over Cameron in the wrestling ring after lunch.

A morning spent in study had made all the apprentices very cross and quarrelsome, and so Iven had decided they needed some exercise. He pushed the table in the dining room to one side and asked the apprentices to demonstrate *ahdayeh* to Rhiannon. Although primarily used by the Coven as a form of meditation through movement, *ahdayeh* was also a system of hand-to-hand combat, and Iven set the students to pitting their skills against each other. After watching a few rounds, Rhiannon was eager indeed to test her own fighting skills. It took her only a few seconds to thrown Cameron flat on his back.

He was furious and sprang up at once, challenging her again. Three times she threw him down, until he was white-faced and dangerous with rage. Iven separated them then, and challenged her himself, and Rhiannon took great enjoyment in laying him flat on the carpet as well. After that the competition began in earnest. Rhiannon found the only one she could not throw down with ease was Lewen, something which gave her a degree of secret pleasure. They struggled together for close on half an hour, hot and panting, half-angry, half-laughing, before Iven at last stopped them and declared his intention to teach them all how to dance instead.

It took Rhiannon only a minute to decide dancing was not for her, primarily because she was taller than most of the boys and had absolutely no sense of rhythm, having never heard music before she met the jongleurs. She had no desire to sit and watch Fèlice flirting and laughing with Lewen as he spun her round the room, and so as soon as the music stopped and everyone changed partners, she stepped forward and laid her hand on his sleeve, asking him in a low voice if he minded if she had a look at his longbow.

Rhiannon had been fascinated by Lewen's bow from the moment she had seen him strapping it to his pommel. It was the tallest bow she had ever seen, almost a foot longer than hers. The arrows he whittled for himself were also longer than usual, and she had longed for a chance to try her hand at them. Her determination was only piqued by Lewen's surprised laugh and shake of his head.

"Ye willna be able to draw my bow," Lewen said. "Few can, ye ken. Ye need to be very strong."

"Me strong," Rhiannon said indignantly.

"No' that strong," he answered.

"Lewen's a famous longbowman, like his father," Iven said, lifting his fingers from the strings of his guitar so he could join the conversation. "It wouldna be a fair contest, Rhiannon."

"Iven!" Edithe protested, as she and Cameron came to a halt nearby. "Play on! We want to dance."

Rhiannon lifted her chin. "Me shoot ogres afore, bet Lewen hasna!"

"Well, no, I haven't," Lewen admitted, "but it still wouldna be a fair contest."

"Oh, ungallant," Rafferty jeered, taking his hand from Fèlice's waist so he could join the conversation. "I'd put my money on Rhiannon any day."

"Rafferty!" Fèlice cried. "Do ye no' want to dance with me? Iven, please, will ye no' play on?"

Iven did not hear her, turning to Rafferty and demanding whether he had ever seen Lewen shoot. "For I swear his arrows can fly round corners. Ye'd lose your money."

"I'm a fair shot too," Cameron said belligerently, eager to overcome his humiliation in the wrestling ring. "I bet I can out-shoot any lass, no matter how much o' a tomboy she is."

"Let's set up a target," Rafferty said eagerly. "I wouldna mind trying my hand at Lewen's bow too. It's mighty tall."

"Iven!" Fèlice wailed.

"I'll play for you, lassies," Nina said, looking over from the couch by the fire, where she was busy writing in a leather-bound book. "Ye'll never drag Iven away from a shooting contest."

"But we need the boys to dance with," Edithe said waspishly, glaring at Rhiannon.

"If ye can persuade them to keep on dancing with ye, I'll be happy to play for ye," Nina said. "But, indeed, Edithe, I doubt they'll pay ye any heed."

Nina proved to have the truth of it. The boys hardly heard the girls' entreaties, being busy looking for something to make a target out of, and entreating Lewen to go and get his bow so they could all try their strength and skill. Lewen agreed with good humour, and he and Rhiannon went to get their bows and arrows out of the stables, where they were stored with the rest of their luggage. Iven, Cameron and Rafferty busied themselves rigging up a board at the far end of the room, drawing rough concentric circles on it with chalk. Edithe went to sit down next to Nina with a sour expression on her face, but Fèlice joined the others, asking questions with great animation and much laughter. Even shy Maisie grew interested, and found the courage to ask Lewen, when he returned with his bow and quiver slung over his shoulder, why his arrows were so much longer than usual and why he fletched them with green.

"My arrows are longer because my bow is longer," he explained with a smile, "and I fletch them with feathers plucked from my mother's rooster's tail. They are very even and strong, see?"

To Rhiannon's chagrin, she did indeed find it impossible to bend Lewen's bow. Her only consolation was that none of the other apprentices could either, not even Cameron, who almost burst a vein trying. Lewen grinned and obligingly gave them a demonstration of his bow's range and power. He was a superlative archer. No matter where he stood in the long hall, he was able to send arrow after arrow right into the heart of the target. He even, at Iven's laughing prompt, shot an arrow from outside the room, its flight path curving round the doorframe and flying straight to the target, splitting one of Rhiannon's arrows right down the middle.

"That's impossible," Rafferty exclaimed in awe.

"It's witchcraft," Cameron said, aggrieved. "It shouldna be allowed."

"I told ye he could shoot round corners," Iven grinned.

"It's part o' my Talent," Lewen said apologetically. "Anything I make from wood with my own hands is sort o' . . . magicked. I did try to warn ye."

"Shoot with my bow and arrows then," Rhiannon cried. "We'll see how good ye are with a bow and arrows ye havena magicked."

"Magicked really is no' a word," Fèlice pointed out apologetically, but they were all too excited to listen to her.

"It willna make any difference," Iven said. "I bet ye a whole gold crown Lewen still beats ye hands down."

"I'm no' betting," Cameron said sulkily. "He's got an unfair advantage."

"I'm no' betting either but only because I havena any gold crowns," Rhiannon said, her cheeks flushed and her eyes bright. "I'll back myself against ye, though, Cameron, any day. I bet ye three coppers that I can split your arrow down the centre just like Lewen did mine."

"All right then," Cameron cried, seizing her bow. "You're on."

"Deal?"

"Deal!"

Rhiannon spat on her hand and held it out and, his ears crimson, Cameron seized it and shook it angrily.

He took her bow, fitted an arrow to it and bent the bow, making a visible effort to calm his temper before firing a very neat shot into the centre of the target. Rhiannon applauded him along with the others, but then, with extraordinary swiftness, lifted and fired her bow in a single smooth movement. The arrow Cameron had shot fell apart, split neatly in two.

"Bravo!" Rafferty shouted. "Beautiful shooting."

"Go, lassie!" Fèlice cried. "Ye show those cocky lads."

Edithe said to Nina, who was watching the competition with as much interest as anyone else, "Do ye no' find her forward behaviour very unbecoming? It is so very unladylike, don't ye agree?"

Nina cast her an irritated look. "No, no' really. She is a very accomplished archer, why should she no' take as much pride in that as the lads do? Really, Edithe, witches do no' much care for archaic social proprieties. If ye wish to be a sorceress, ye must try to put aside such silly prejudices."

Edithe flushed crimson and pursed her lips tightly.

Only Iven did not join in the general praise, standing back, his brows drawn over his eyes in a most uncharacteristic frown. He looked from the arrow, embedded deep in the centre of the target, back at Rhiannon with a sudden hard glare of suspicion.

"Where did ye learn to shoot, Rhiannon?" he asked. "Long-bows are no' usual among your people, are they?"

Rhiannon's bright colour faded. "The bow was my father's," she answered gruffly.

"And he taught ye to shoot so well?"

"My father dead. Me taught myself." As usual in times of emotional stress, her newly acquired language skills deserted her.

"Ye taught yourself very well," he said, still staring at her with those hard, angry eyes.

"Thank ye," she said, her eyes flashing up to meet his, then dropping again. "I did have help, to begin with. There was a man who showed me . . ." Her words faltered away.

"I guess the fact ye had to teach yourself shows that I was right, and bows and arrows are no' common among those o' your kind?"

"What kind is that?" Edithe asked Nina, her eyebrows raised. Nina motioned her to silence, looking distressed.

"No, no' common," Rhiannon answered after a moment.

"Any other longbows in your herd apart from yours?"

"Herd?" Cameron asked derisively.

Rhiannon shrugged, turning away to gather up her quiver of arrows. "A few, I suppose. I've never really noticed."

Iven clearly did not believe her, but the restive curiosity on the other apprentices' faces seemed to check any other questions he wished to ask her. He picked up his guitar and went out of the room, and after a moment Nina rose and went after him.

Everyone left behind felt confused and dismayed, not understanding why Iven had been so curt and angry. Rhiannon finished packing away her arrows, and said to Cameron, "Do no' forget ye owe me three coppers."

He scowled and fished in his pocket, saying sharply, "So where do ye come from, Rhiannon? What did Iven mean, calling your folk a 'herd'?"

"I'm sure he was just speaking metaphorically," Edithe said sweetly.

Rhiannon flashed her an angry look, hearing the barb beneath the honeyed tone even if she did not understand the figure of speech.

"Are ye o' faery kind, Rhiannon?" Fèlice asked with lively curiosity. "A Khan'cohban or something, like the Banrìgh?"

"My mother was a horned one," Rhiannon answered shortly, not looking at anyone.

There was a surprised murmur.

"A satyricorn, does she mean?" Cameron demanded.

Edithe said, "Well, that explains a lot!"

"Shouldn't ye have horns?" Rafferty asked.

Cameron thrust his coins back into his pocket, saying angrily, "Ye should've told us earlier, it was an unfair contest! I'm no' paying ye anything."

Lewen had been quietly packing up his own quiver of arrows, but now he looked up and said, "What difference does it make if Rhiannon is half-satyricorn? Iven just told ye a longbow is an unusual weapon among the satyricorns. It takes naught away from Rhiannon's success to ken her background, in fact, it makes it even more remarkable. Ye owe her those three coppers, Cameron."

"It wasna a fair contest," he said sulkily.

"Yes, it was," Fèlice said. "Ye always kent Rhiannon was tall and strong, Cameron, ye only have to look at her to ken that."

"That's true," Landon said. "It would be dishonourable to refuse to pay." He spoke with such clear certainty that Cameron was abashed and thrust his hand into his pocket to retrieve the coins and throw them at her. Rhiannon caught them out of the air, again startling them with the speed of her response. Lewen looked at Landon and gave him his slow, warm smile, which the young poet returned shyly.

Maisie was looking at Rhiannon with frightened eyes, and Edithe looked as if she had just found something foul on the bottom of her shoe. Rhiannon's face had settled back into its sulky lines. She did not look at any of them but went out of the room, her back very straight.

"Ye will find folk o' all kinds at the Theurgia," Lewen said in a voice made gruff with anger. "Often those born o' mingled human and faery blood have the most extraordinary powers o' all. Like the Keybearer and the Banrìgh who, as Fèlice said, are half-Khan'cohban. Or the Banprionnsa Bronwen, whose mother was half-Fairgean. There is a Celestine in my class, and a corrigan, and a girl who is a tree-shifter, like my own mother. Ye will have to get used to seeing faery folk about at the Tower o' Two Moons."

"Aye, but a *satyricorn*," Edithe said. "No wonder she is so uncouth."

"Ye would be uncouth too if ye had been raised by satyricorns," Lewen said angrily. "We canna help our birth or our upbringing, but we can help the kind o' people we are now."

Edithe raised her eyebrows, smiled coldly, and went to sit down by the fire. After a moment or two, Cameron went to join her, saying, "Well, no wonder she's such a lanky longlegs. A satyricorn!"

"I wonder she was allowed to travel with us," Edithe said. "I hope she is no' dangerous."

"She bloody well is," Cameron said moodily. "Did ye see the way she snatched those coins out o' the air?"

Maisie was asking Fèlice much the same thing, and the pretty brunette was saying doubtfully, "No, I'm sure Nina and Iven would no' open us to any real risk. I'm sure she's a *tame* satyricorn."

Lewen gritted his teeth together, and went in search of Rhiannon. As he expected, she had sought comfort with her flying mare. She looked up as he came in, and said sullenly, "What ye want?"

"Naught," he answered. "I thought I'd come and visit Argent. I wish I could take him out for a gallop. It's always such a bore, being shut up inside four walls."

Her expression softened. "Aye, I wish too."

"Happen it'll clear tomorrow and we can ride out again."

"Happen so."

He had got out his currying brushes and was grooming the grey stallion, which half-shut its great dark eyes in bliss. He said no more, and after a moment Rhiannon got out her grooming kit and began to pet and pamper her mare too, although Blackthorn's coat already shone like silk. They worked in companionable silence for some time, and Lewen was pleased to see Rhiannon's face lose its hard, angry lines. By the time they went back into the house for supper, she had regained her composure, though not the bright, open, merry face she had worn during the archery contest, an expression Lewen would very much like to see again.

As they went towards the hall, they saw Iven was waiting for them in the corridor. Rhiannon's step slowed. The jongleur stepped forward to meet them, saying, "Rhiannon, I just . . . I need to ken. Was it ye who shot Connor down?"

She looked straight into his face and said angrily, "Nay."

"Who was it, Rhiannon? Can ye tell me? It was one o' your herd, wasna it?"

"I do no' ken who," she answered. "I was no' there."

"But ye have his clothes, his daggers," Iven said.

"I won them gambling," she said.

His face relaxed. "That'd be right! I should've guessed."

She jerked her head and went to move past him. He detained her with one hand on her arm. "I'm sorry, I did no' mean to imply I suspected ye o' murder. I just . . . I really did need to ken, Rhiannon."

She nodded, removed his hand from her arm and went into the long hall, her head held high, her face set and expressionless.

Iven looked at Lewen and shrugged, his hands held wide. "I had to ask her."

Lewen nodded. "I did too."

"I'm glad it was no' her."

"So am I."

"Do ye think she's offended?"

"Wouldn't ye be?"

"I suppose so," Iven said unhappily.

"Never mind," Lewen said. "It canna be helped. Ye had to ken. Ye could no' ride with her for weeks suspecting her o' murder. Better to get it out in the open."

"I suppose so," Iven said again. "Nina thinks I'm hasty and indiscreet. Happen I am a blabbermouth after all." He hesitated. "How are the other bairns? Kenning she's a satyricorn, I mean."

"It is naught to be ashamed o'," Lewen said stiffly. "The satyricorns have shown themselves loyal and true to the Crown, just like any other faery."

"Aye, but . . ." Iven halted himself mid-sentence, tugging at his forked beard with both hands. "Auld prejudices die hard," he said then, half to himself.

Lewen nodded.

Iven flung an arm about his shoulder. "Let us go and eat," he said. "At least we're enjoying some variety to our diet staying here with Ashelma. That man o' hers is a very good cook."

Together they went in to the long hall, where the dining table was back in its usual place and the babble of high, childish voices filled any awkward silences. Roden and Lulu had spent the afternoon with the orphans and seemed to have made life-long friends with the two eldest boys. One of them had fashioned himself a slingshot and was amusing himself shooting Annis in the bottom with paper pellets, and pretending it was Strixa the owl, much to the other children's amusement.

Nina had drawn Rhiannon down to sit with her and was doing her best to banish the stiff wariness of her face. Rhiannon would not be coaxed, however, and ate her meal in unbroken silence, sat through the usual evening games and storytelling in unbroken silence, and went to bed in the same cold unfriendly silence. It was only when Nina brought her another half-dead mouse to sacrifice that her expression relaxed. She took the warm, limp body and said "Thank ye."

"I do no' like to see small creatures being killed," Nina said. "It is against everything the Coven believes in. But I ken it is the nature o' the cat and the owl to hunt and kill, and I ken ye do so, no' from some kind o' cruelty, but because ye truly believe ye are keeping yourself safe by doing so."

"Not just me," Rhiannon said. "Us all."

"Then I thank ye," Nina said. "I hope I can one day teach ye other ways to keep yourself safe from the dark forces o' this world."

Rhiannon gazed at her for a long moment, then suddenly smiled, a swift, small, shy, surprising smile.

"Happen so," she answered.

Overnight the steady thrum of the rain slowed to a mere pitter-patter, and by dawn it had stopped altogether. Nina roused them all early and bade them dress for riding, and come down for a quick hot meal, for she wanted them on the road by first light. By the time it was bright enough to see the road without the need for lanterns, the carthorses were harnessed to the caravans and they were making their goodbyes to Ashelma and Annis, who came out in the cold, sharp wind in their dressing-gowns.

"Have a care for yourselves," Ashelma said. "I hope ye have a swift, safe journey."

"So do I," Nina replied with her quick smile. "Thank ye so much for putting us all up. I'm sorry it was for so long."

"It was our pleasure, wasn't it, Annis? We rarely get to enjoy the company o' other witches. I hope ye will come and visit us again."

"We'd love to. Until then, goodbye!"

"Goodbye! Thank ye!" the others all called and then, wincing as their boots sank deep into the mud, mounted up and rode away down the drive, the gates opening and shutting behind them of their own accord.

The lane from Ashelma's house was hock-deep in muddy brown water, and one of the caravans was bogged almost immediately. By the time they had heaved it free, they were all wet and filthy and out of temper, and they were not even out of sight of the witch's tower. They rode on, hunched in their cloaks, more than a little perturbed at the sight of the river, brown and foamy as gushing ale, and carrying along great broken branches at immense speed.

They came to the crossroads and paused for a moment, looking back along the road to Ardarchy. Warm golden light glowed in the windows, and wood-smoke rose from the chimneys, torn into fragrant rags by the wind. Some children were playing with hoops in the street, and a smell of fresh bread came from the bakery. A wagon was drawn up in front of the inn, with three men rolling big barrels down a ramp and manhandling them in through the huge door. Four old men sat on the bench in front, puffing on their pipes, while further down the street two women stood gossiping, laden baskets on their arms, as a little girl dressed in a red hooded coat jumped gleefully in the puddles, unnoticed.

They glanced the other way. Only a few feet away the stone humpbacked bridge crossed the Stormness River. A high, stout gate had been fastened across it, locked tight with heavy chains and an enormous padlock. The river flung itself against the bridge angrily, throwing up gouts of brown foam. Beyond was a desolate landscape, grim and drear and empty of all life. The mountains loomed over it, purple-hued and draped with thick cloud. The road wound down away from the river, narrow and rutted and stony, running with water like a stream-bed.

"Could we no' stay a few more days in Ardarchy?" Fèlice pleaded. "Indeed, it looks like rain again."

Nina nodded. "Aye, I ken. But we've been delayed far too long already. Two more days on the road and we'll be past the Tower o' Ravens and back in the lowlands, where the weather is fairer."

"What about the ghosts?" Cameron said sullenly.

"Most ghosts are only memories," Nina said gently. "When a place has seen great sorrow or great joy, often the emotion soaks down into the very stones and leaves a shadow of itself behind—and those that have the gift o' clear-seeing or clear-hearing can pick up fragments o' those memories. Some people see ghosts everywhere, and must learn to close their mind's eye to them. The Tower o' Ravens is built on a place o' power, like all the witches' towers, and it has seen much horror and blood-shed. Because o' where it is built, the memories o' those killed are magnified and so even those with very little talent can sense or even see the ghosts that remain. It can be awful, I will admit that, particularly if ye are very sensitive to such things. Ye feel as if ye are there, watching the battle again, hearing the shrieks o' the dying. But it is only a memory."

There was a short silence, everyone staring across the river at the barren windswept moors beyond.

"Ye said *most* ghosts are only memories," Fèlice said waveringly. "What about the others?"

Nina hesitated. "It is true that sometimes a soul refuses to go on and be reborn, but clings to its life here, for whatever reason—hatred, grief, horror, even a thirst for life that canna be quenched. These ghosts are more than just memories o' a soul, they are the soul itself. They are trapped between worlds, unable to go on because they canna forget their lives here. That is tragic indeed, for then the circle o' life and death is broken and all is unbalanced. A trapped soul can be dangerous, I canna deny it. Even those that are no' malevolent but only wracked with grief or horror can cause harm, for they press upon our nerves, they swamp our souls with their own negative energy, and can drive those already prone to melancholy to deep depression or madness."

"What about the ones that *are* malevolent?" Edithe asked, her voice shrill.

Nina sighed. "Few ghosts have the strength to actually harm ye, Edithe. They have no hands to hold a sword, they have no feet to kick or teeth to bite. Sometimes, if their will is strong enough, they can cause objects to move, just as a witch can, but just clinging to this world saps their strength and their will and so it is rare, I promise ye. Their only weapons are fear and horror. If ye do no' fear them, they canna drive ye to madness or infect ye with their misery. Stay close, stay strong, and naught can happen to harm ye."

The only sound was the wind rattling the branches, the angry roar of the river and the occasional clink of metal as one of the horses shook its mane or stamped its foot. Then Edithe sighed and said facetiously, "Very reassuring, thank ye, Nina."

"My pleasure," the witch answered, not smiling, and shook the reins so her patient horse leant into the weight of the caravan and began to draw it forwards once more.

The town reeve reluctantly unlocked the barricade for them, after shaking his head and telling them sternly it was his duty to warn them that the road that passed the ruined Tower of Ravens was not safe and he hereby abjured all responsibility for them. Nina thanked him with a strained smile. Then one by one they crossed the bridge, the horses baulking at first, then shying nervously at the flying spray and the thud of storm-wrack swept against the pylons. The reeve locked the gate behind them.

It began to rain again half an hour later. It came down in long slanting lines, beating at their backs. There was nowhere to shelter and so they rode on, enduring in silence. The clouds were so dark and heavy it was like dusk, and all they could see ahead of them was the long, empty, winding road and the closing ranks of steep, bare mountains. They passed a ruined croft, its windows gaping like blinded eyes, its roof fallen in. A little further on they passed a broken fence, the fallen slats covered in brambles. The road was treacherous with mud and rocks, and the horses had to pick their way carefully, sometimes splashing into puddles so deep the water was up to their withers.

The riders had all unconsciously drawn together close behind the caravans, the hoods of their cloaks drawn over their heads. Rain spat in their eyes, and trickled down their necks.

"I do no' like this place," Landon said nervously.

"It doesna inspire ye to poetry?" Cameron jeered, though it was clear he was edgy too from the way he turned his face from side to side, scanning the misty horizon, his hands fidgeting with the reins.

"I do no' like it either," Fèlice said. "I wish we had no' come this way."

Blackthorn pranced uneasily, tossing her head and refusing to go forwards. Rhiannon leant forward to pat her neck. "What is it?" she murmured.

All the horses had to be urged onwards, and Rafferty had to tug hard on the lead rein before Maisie's fat little pony would submit to following him. Ahead was another abandoned croft, its garden and orchard choked with weeds, its gate hanging off one hinge.

Blackthorn shied sideways, banging into Edithe's mare Donnagh, who reared and plunged sideways.

"Keep your horse under control!" Edithe snapped, bringing her mare round smartly with a vicious dig of her spurred boot, the reins drawn so tight the mare's chin was forced in to her breast.

Rhiannon's nostrils flared. "Bad smell," she said.

"I beg your pardon?" Edithe demanded coldly.

"Bad smell." Rhiannon nodded towards the abandoned croft, her brows drawn in over her nose, breathing in deeply through her nose. She dug her heels into Blackthorn's side, so the mare leapt forward into a canter. "Us get away from here."

"What is it?" Lewen asked, as she cantered past him, leaping over the ditch beside the road to the rough soil of the untilled fields.

She looked back at him over her shoulder. "Bad smell. Bad feeling. Something hungry. Us better get away."

The other apprentices were alarmed and began to try to urge

their horses forward, but they all plunged and reared, fighting the rein.

Suddenly, a pack of snarling, yammering dogs came hurtling out of the gate, skeleton-thin, with hunger-crazed yellow eyes.

Maisie screamed, and kicked her wooden clogs into her pony's sides. The pony bucked violently and Maisie fell off. The dogs leapt upon her, jaws gripping and tearing, and the shrill sound of her screams rang through the air.

A PALE HORSE

"And I looked and behold a pale horse: and his name that sat on him was Death."

Revelations, chapter 6, verse 8

Forest of the Dead

Everyone shouted in horror and alarm. The caravans were all over the road, the big carthorses rearing in terror. The other horses were neighing loudly, and bucking wildly. Edithe and Cameron's horses both bolted, the apprentices clinging desperately to their pommels. Iven was almost run down as he leapt to the ground, his unsheathed sword in his hand. He had to press himself to the side of the caravan to avoid being trampled.

Landon and Rafferty's horses had shied sideways into each other, almost knocking Landon out of his saddle. The young poet grabbed his horse's mane and hauled himself upright again as his horse leapt the ditch and galloped away over the rough fields. He had almost lost his seat again, his stirrups bouncing against the gelding's sides, his reins flapping. Blackthorn flung open her magnificent wings and soared up into the air, as Rhiannon flew in pursuit.

Argent neighed a challenge and kicked out at the dogs, sending one rolling over and over, yelping. Lewen leapt from the stallion's back, catching one dog by the ruff of its neck and hurling it away, fending off another with his arm as he laid about him with his long dagger. One of the feral animals he killed at once. Others turned to attack him, bearing him down onto his back, and he struggled to keep them from ripping out his throat. Argent reared above them, lashing out with his hooves.

Then Iven was there, his sword flashing and darting. He ran through the dog at Lewen's throat and dragged the corpse away, so Lewen could roll over onto his feet, then turned to slash and stab at the dogs still tearing at Maisie's flesh. Maisie had instinctively rolled herself into a ball, her arms about her face, so the dogs had not been able to get at her throat or stomach. Her legs and buttocks and arms were badly bitten and bleeding heavily, however, and one ear had been half-torn from her head.

"Eà's sweet eyes," Nina sobbed, flinging herself on her knees beside the moaning girl. "Help me get her into the caravan!"

Fèlice had been struggling to bring her panicked mare back under control. One big dog had leapt up at her, seeking to drag her down from the saddle, but although her skirt was rent and muddied, she had not been hurt. She slid down from her horse now and, keeping a tight grip on the reins, ran to help Nina.

Rafferty's horse had slipped and fallen in the mud, but Rafferty had managed to fling himself free. Attacked by three dogs at once, he laid about him with his sword while trying to help his panicked mount to its feet. The rain made the ground so treacherous that he almost slipped and fell himself, but saved himself by hauling on the horse's reins. His gelding heaved itself to its feet, and Rafferty managed to kill one dog and wound the others enough that they ran off, tails between their legs.

"Someone help us!" Nina wept, another dog worrying at Maisie's foot while she and Fèlice did their best to drag her away.

Rafferty let go of his horse's reins and limped forward, seizing Maisie under her armpits and dragging her towards the caravan. His gelding plunged sideways, and Fèlice caught hold of its reins and held both trembling horses still. She was white as skimmed milk.

Driven off their prey by sword and dagger, the dogs prowled nearby, snarling. As one darted towards them, Iven lunged forward and drove his sword through its breast. At once another one leapt and closed his jaws upon the jongleur's arm. Iven fell to one knee as Lewen fought to drag the dog away. For a moment all was confusion, Lewen stabbing the dog wherever he could. Then at last its jaws relaxed and he was able to pull Iven's bloodied arm free.

"Iven, we need help!" Nina called frantically. She and Rafferty were trying to lift Maisie up the steps into the caravan, but the dogs were lunging and snapping at them, and the brown carthorse was rearing in her traces, sending the caravan rocking wildly. Roden had brought the other carthorse under control, and was staring round at them with a white, horrified face.

With his hand pressed over the ragged wound in his arm, Iven ran to her aid. Lewen, left to face the pack of dogs alone, crouched down and drew Iven's sword from the body of the dead dog, swapping his dagger to his left hand.

With his lips drawn back from his teeth and his powerful shoulders hunched forward, Lewen gave such a terrifying growl that the dogs paused, startled. They sniffed the air, then circled round him, snarling, the hairs on their skinny backs standing up in a ridge. Lewen growled again and suddenly lashed out at the largest and most ferocious of the dogs, drawing blood along its shoulder. It yelped and slunk back, tail between its legs. After a few more feints and a lot more vicious growling from Lewen, the pack of wild dogs suddenly turned and fled back into the ruined croft, a few limping and whining.

Nina and Iven together managed to lift Maisie into the caravan. "She's been badly mauled," Nina said, wiping tears from her cheeks. "The poor lass! Lewen? We need to find the others, quickly."

Lewen nodded, and whistled to Argent, who came up at an easy canter. Reaching up with one hand, he seized hold of the pommel and swung himself up into the saddle, no mean feat considering how very tall his big grey stallion was and how long his stride. Then they were off, galloping down the road.

Lewen caught up with Cameron fairly quickly, for his gelding Basta was generally a steady, well-mannered horse and had already slowed from his headlong pace. Lewen was easily able to catch his bridle and bring him back to a walk, acknowledging Cameron's rather curt thanks with a nod and a rapid question about Edithe. Cameron, who was sickly white and clinging rather tightly to his pommel, managed to raise one hand and point down the road.

"Go back to the others, get them moving fast. Those dogs are starving and will attack again. I'll try and catch up with Edithe afore that bloody skittish mare o' hers throws her."

Without any discernible signal, Argent began to lope forward again, moving quickly into his thunderous gallop. Mud and stones flew up from his hooves. Lewen leant forward,

anxiously scanning the mist-wreathed valley ahead. Finally he
saw the silhouette of the running mare outlined against the sky
as she bolted over the crest of a low hill. His heart jerked as he
realised the mare was riderless. With a low murmur and a pat
on Argent's shoulder he encouraged him to an even greater
speed. Then he saw Edithe lying on the road before him. As he
pulled Argent to a halt and jumped down beside her, she
moaned and moved, lifting her hand to her head. He helped her
sit up. Blood trickled from a nasty gash on her temple.

"Can ye stand? Any bones broken?"

She tried to stand, with his help, and grimaced with pain.
"Ow, my ankle!"

He helped her limp to the side of the road so she could sit on
the low wall, then knelt and took her foot in his hand. "I'll have
to take off your boot," he warned.

Edithe nodded. He tried to do it gently but she cried out and
began to weep as he managed to wrench it off. Her ankle was
discoloured and swelling rapidly. "I hope it's no' broken, only
sprained," Lewen said. "I'm no healer, I'm afraid. Nina will
ken better than me." He glanced back up the road but the rest
of his companions were still out of sight on the other side of the
hill. "Do ye have a dagger?"

Her pupils dilated blackly. "I? Nay, I have no dagger. Why?
What do ye want it for?"

He bent and drew the little black dagger from his boot and
passed it to her, hilt forward. "Just in case," he answered. "I
must ride on and catch your mare afore she damages herself.
I'll be back, never ye fear."

She nodded, her breath a little unsteady. "Ye expect trouble?"

Lewen gave her his lopsided grin. "Better safe than sorry."

He vaulted into the saddle again, gathered up the reins and
gave Argent a sharp tap in the sides with his boots. Argent
neighed and took off, galloping down the road, ears pricked forward. The mare was still running, but was worn out with her
terror and already beginning to founder. Argent was able to
catch up with her before she plunged into a thick forest of dark
trees that filled the bottom of the valley, where she might have
hurt herself among the branches. Lewen caught her trailing
reins and hauled her to a shuddering, blowing halt, her front

legs stretched out before her stiffly. Her dark brown coat was scudded with sweat, and her breath was harsh.

Lewen dismounted slowly, not wanting to spook her into running again, and left Argent to recover his own breath as he sought to calm the mare. She was trembling violently and so he unpinned his cloak and laid it over her, damp and mud-spattered as it was, then began to coax her to walk slowly in circles. She stumbled wearily and he talked to her in a low, soothing voice.

As they circled closer to the forest he caught a whiff of something foul and wrinkled his nose. The mare smelt it too, for her nostrils flared in alarm, showing the red hollows within. She tried to shy away but Lewen held her firm. Argent whinnied and cantered round them in a big circle, as if striving to head them away from the forest.

Surprised, Lewen glanced towards the trees. He had thought the smell must come from some dead animal that had crept into the wood to hide. Instead, with an instant shock of horror, he saw a half-rotting corpse shambling out from under the leafy shadows, one putrid decomposing hand held out as if in entreaty. It still wore the filthy tattered remains of a shroud. One shriveled breast showed through the rags. Its eye sockets were empty, eaten out. Its hair hung down in long, dirt-caked waves. Slowly it stumbled towards Lewen, the stench coming over him in waves that made him retch.

The bay mare neighed and reared, tearing her head free of Lewen's loosened grasp, and bolting back in the direction she had come. Knocked off balance, he fell to his knees in the mud, the dead woman lurching closer to him with each ungainly step.

Rhiannon crouched on Blackthorn's back, forcing herself to watch as the ground fell away below her. Even after almost a week on the winged horse's back, she had not managed to control the instinctive cower of terror as she felt Blackthorn's muscles clench and release beneath her, felt substantial ground fall away and the precarious power of air lift and hold her. She had nightmares of falling, dreams so real that she would rouse with a jerk and have to open her eyes and reach out her hand and

clench on to the roots of grass to reassure herself she was safe
on the earth. The only fear more profound was the terror that
the others might guess and mock her, saying she was no true
thigearn.

Blackthorn beat her long powerful wings, rising higher in the
air. The wind was cold and made tears start to Rhiannon's eyes.
She pressed with her knees, directing the mare to veer left, as
she rubbed away the tears, searching for some sign of Landon.
Clouds were rolling down from the mountains, and there was a
low insistent rumble of thunder. Rain washed over them,
drenching them to the skin. The only sign of life was a raven
flying high above the forest in the valley, occasionally calling
out in his harsh, melancholy voice. Otherwise all was still.

Rhiannon crouched lower on the winged mare's back as
Blackthorn shivered, her wingbeats faltering. "No need to fear,
my bonny," she murmured, stroking the damp black hide. "We
just need to find Landon. Can ye see Nuinn anywhere?"

Blackthorn whickered and began to circle lower. Rhiannon
leant forward and saw Landon below her, looking rumpled
and muddy, leading his grey gelding back towards the road.
Nuinn was limping badly. Landon heard the beat of wings and
waved his hand in urgent greeting. Blackthorn landed lightly
before him.

"Nuinn hurt his leg," Landon said anxiously. "It's bleeding.
I dinna ken what to do, whether to make him walk on it or not."

"Storm coming," Rhiannon said. "We walk him back
slowly."

Landon nodded. "That's what I thought too. Oh, Rhiannon, I
do no' like this valley. It makes me feel . . ." He gave a little
shudder and tightened his grip on the bridle. "I do no' ken how
to describe it. My skin is all a-prickle."

Rhiannon nodded. "Me too."

She dismounted and cast a quick eye over the gelding's foreleg. Blood oozed from a long red gash, and it was clear it hurt
the gelding to put weight on that leg. Then she looked up at
Landon. "What about ye? Were ye thrown?"

Landon blushed and nodded. "I'm no' a very good rider," he
said miserably. "No' like ye."

"Hurt?"

"Shaken up a wee," the boy said, "and bruised all over, for sure, but nay, no' hurt. I just wish Nuinn had no' been injured. If I'd been a better rider this wouldna have happened."

Rhiannon shrugged, leading the way back towards the road. "All riders thrown sometimes. Dogs' fault, no' yours. Horses no' like dogs."

There was a quick flash of lightning, and a few moments later thunder growled again. The rain was coming in waves over the hills, flattening the grass and the brambles. A grey twilight hung over the landscape, and the encircling mountains were hidden in great, roiling clouds.

"Bad storm coming," Rhiannon said sombrely. "Bad feeling here."

"I feel like someone's watching us," Landon said with a shiver and pulled his damp, muddy cloak about him. They heard the raven cry again and looked up in sudden superstitious apprehension.

"Something is watching us," Rhiannon said.

They felt very alone and exposed in the middle of that rough brown field, and unconsciously quickened their step, forgetting Nuinn's injury. The raven flew over their heads, and then the rain swept over them as if tied to the bird's black wings.

"There's the others," Rhiannon said, seeing the two caravans pulled up haphazardly on the road. "Let's hurry."

They ran forward over the tussocks of grass, Nuinn limping badly. Iven came out onto the caravan steps and greeted them thankfully.

"We've driven the dogs away for the moment. Lucky for us Lewen can speak the language o' dogs!" he said. He glanced at the pack of feral animals crouching just inside the gate, their yellow eyes intent, the hair on their spines stiff. One crept forward a few steps, snarling. Iven frowned.

"It won't be long afore they attack again. Let's get moving. Roden, ye and Lulu get in our caravan and do no' come out for anything. Fèlice, ye go on in and see if ye can help Nina," he said. "Landon, ever driven a caravan? No? Och, there's nothing to it, just hold the reins and Sure will do the rest. Rafferty, can ye help Rhiannon lead the other horses? We must get away from here, those dogs are gathering courage to attack again, sure as apples."

"Throw them some food," Rhiannon said. "That'll keep them busy while we get away."

"Good idea," Iven answered, as the growling rose in volume and ferocity. The horses all sidestepped nervously, ears laid back.

"Pity ye have no meat to feed them," Rhiannon said with feeling. Iven cast her a rueful glance, knowing how much she had missed eating meat since joining company with the witches, and scrummaged in the store-barrels for something to throw the dogs.

As soon as Iven flung some hunks of cheese and bread and onion pie at the dogs, the starving animals leapt upon the food. At once the two carthorses began to jog away down the road, Rafferty and Rhiannon close behind, leading the other horses. They met Cameron at the crest of the hill, and after a hurried consultation he climbed up onto the driving seat of the red caravan, taking the reins from Landon, who was looking white and frightened. Behind them they heard vicious snarling and barking as the dogs fought over the remnants of the food. The carthorses quickened their pace, the caravans swaying precariously.

Halfway down the hill, they found Edithe, sitting white-faced and bleeding on the ground, a dagger clenched in her hand.

"My mare!" she cried. "My horse! I just saw her, bolting away again. That way!"

"Where Lewen?" Rhiannon asked.

Edithe shrugged, pointing down the road, which dipped and then rose again over the crest of another low hill. Behind them they heard yelping, a lot more snarling, and then, ominously, the long, drawn-out howl of dogs on the hunt. For a moment they all froze, listening, then everyone leapt into movement. Iven half-carried Edithe up the stairs of the red caravan, shoving her through the door, then scrambled up into his driver's seat again. He brought the reins down on the gelding's rump with a thwack and the big, shaggy grey began to jog forward, whickering in distress.

"I get Donnagh," Rhiannon said and thrust Basta's reins at Rafferty, before wheeling Blackthorn round and urging her into the air. The great black wings rose and fell rhythmically, horse and rider soaring high into the air. Rhiannon could see the terrified mare stumbling blindly across the rough fields, and followed her, calling out to her with her mind. *Stop! Ye will fall. Ye will break your leg. Do no' fear. I come. Me and Blackthorn, we come. Stop . . .*

The mare's headlong pace faltered and she came to a halt, shuddering with exhaustion, her head down, her legs braced. Blackthorn folded her wings and went spiralling down, landing lightly next to her. Donnagh flinched but was too exhausted to shy away. Rhiannon reached out her hand, grasped the bridle and forced the mare to walk along beside her, her hide scummy with sweat, her legs trembling. As they walked, Rhiannon scolded the mare and she hung her head in shame. When the brown mare had caught her breath, Rhiannon coaxed her into a stiff-legged trot, conscious all the time of the howling of the pursuing dogs.

By the time they reached the road again the dogs were racing along just behind the caravans, which were swaying roughly over the ruts in the road, all of the horses galloping at full speed, necks stretched out. Rhiannon let go of Donnagh's bridle, warning her sternly to keep close and not bolt again, then unhitched her bow from her pommel. She drew an arrow from the quiver on her back and lifted the bow, aiming carefully. There was a twang and then a dreadful yelping. One of the dogs went down under the wheel of the red caravan. Some of the pack turned on the injured animal, tearing it to pieces, but the others kept on running, snapping at the horses' heels, trying to hamstring them. Rhiannon shot another arrow, and another. Two more dogs fell.

Then Landon's horse stumbled, his injured foreleg giving way. He fell heavily into the road, almost dragging Rafferty down with him. As the dogs leapt upon the terrified horse, tearing out its throat, Rafferty heaved himself back into the saddle and forced his own horse's head around, whipping him forward. He had let go of all the lead reins but the horses were run-

ning together now, as a herd, and did not need to be led. Blackthorn galloped behind them, keeping them all together.

"Where Lewen?" Rhiannon asked again, anxiously.

No-one could answer her.

Lewen scrambled to his feet just as the dead woman lurched
forward, decaying arms held open as if to embrace him. As
her bony fingers seized him and drew him closer, the foul
stench almost overwhelmed him. For an instant he stared into
the empty eye sockets so close to his, where he could see the
wriggle of white maggots still feeding. Violently he pushed
her away, staggering backwards. She fell, her mouth open as
if to shriek, and as she hit the ground her skin burst open like
an overripe plum, putrid flesh spilling out with a liquid splash
that caused Lewen to bend and vomit violently. Again and
again he retched, until his stomach had nothing left to give,
and then he broke into a stumbling run.

Blinded by the heavy rain, he slipped in the mud and fell into
a long shallow pit. The bottom of the pit was covered in water
and he was drenched to the skin and smeared with clay. He
hauled himself upright and dragged himself out of the ditch,
clutching at the slippery muddy sides for purchase. Wiping the
slimy muck from his face he saw he was right up under the
shadow of the trees. There were other mounds of disturbed
earth nearby, and a few long pits like freshly dug graves.

Lewen's skin was crawling, and he scraped away as much of
the mud as he could, feeling sick. Something moved under the
shadow of the low-hanging branches and every nerve in his
body jumped. Lewen peered under the branches fearfully. Seeing a dark, man-like shape lurching towards him, he spun on his
heel to run.

A corpse stood right before him. Lewen cannoned into it before he could help himself. He cried aloud in horror and recoiled, as the rotting cadaver reached out with pleading hands,
grasping his arm. Lewen wrenched his sleeve away, feeling it
tear. "Stop it!" he cried. "Leave me alone!"

For a moment he stared into the cavernous, half-rotted face,
seeing beneath the grey skin and the staring hollow eye sockets

something of the man it must have once been. The stench was so overpowering his breath snagged in his throat. He pressed his hands over his nose and mouth, trying not to vomit again, and backed slowly away. He felt something, or someone, right behind him, and froze. Very slowly, his limbs trembling violently, he turned.

Close behind him stood an old man. White hair still clung to his blackened scalp. Filthy scraps of shroud hung from his bony shoulders. Bones gleamed palely through the withered skin. He was crying, his mouth hanging wide open, his hands held up in entreaty. A horrible keening sound filled the air. Lewen thought he could hear words among the sobbing and wailing. "Help us, save us, avenge us," he heard. "Heeelp us!"

Lewen backed away, turning on his heel. On all sides stood emaciated corpses, their hands held out pleadingly, their decomposing faces twisted in grief. More came shambling out of the forest. A few were mere skeletons, their jerking bones held together by some invisible force, their jaws clacking horribly. Many were no higher than Lewen's thigh.

He heard Argent's trumpeting neigh and ran that way, dashing tears from his eyes. The stallion was in a terrified sweat, the white rim of his eyes showing, his ears laid back. Somehow Lewen managed to haul himself into the saddle before his legs gave way. The stallion swerved and began to run. Lewen made no attempt to control the stallion's headlong pace, using all his strength just to stay in the saddle.

Then he saw the caravans hurtling towards him down the rough, stony road, swaying so violently it seemed they must topple over. He leant forward, pressing one knee into Argent's hot, damp side, pulling gently on one rein. Obediently the stallion veered round and came galloping alongside the blue caravan.

"Stop! Stop!" Lewen cried. He could not frame the words to describe what he had just seen, but knew only they must not go any further.

Iven was driving the caravan. "Lewen! What's wrong?"

"Must stop," Lewen panted.

"Canna stop," Iven shouted back. "Dogs at our heels."

Lewen glanced back over his shoulder. Behind the swaying

caravans, behind the galloping wild-eyed horses, came the mob of dogs, howling with blood-lust.

"They took down Landon's horse, you'd think that would hold them off for a while," Iven said. "But they're mad with hunger, poor mutts." One wheel of the caravan hit a pothole and he was almost jerked off his seat. He hauled himself upright and concentrated on the road, such as it was.

"No' safe ahead," Lewen said. "Iven, there's . . . walking dead ahead. Dead people, corpses, walking around in broad daylight."

Iven's eyebrows shot up. He hauled back on the reins instinctively, but the grey carthorse had the weight of the caravan at his back and could not easily stop.

"Dead people?"

Lewen nodded. "One took hold o' me." He shuddered involuntarily, feeling nausea rise in his throat. "I pushed her off me and she . . . sort o' fell apart. But there were others, Iven. I saw them moving in the trees and . . . arrgh, I smelt them." His stomach won out and he leant over, retching. Argent neighed in protest and swerved sideways, almost unseating Lewen.

"Mad dogs behind, walking corpses ahead," Iven said ruminatively. "Delightful place, this."

"What are we going to do?" Lewen cried. "Look, those trees just ahead, that's where they are, the walking dead."

Iven whipped his carthorse back into a ponderous gallop. "Ride, Lewen!" he cried. "Ride for your life!"

The road ran straight through the spinney of trees. Trees crowded close on either side, forcing them to fall into single file. Branches slammed into the sides of the caravans, scraping away paint and tearing free some of the decorative fretwork. They made no attempt to retrieve it, the horses behind driving it deep into the mud with their hooves. As the horses were forced to slow by the deep ruts and sucking mud, the dogs swiftly gained ground on them. Lewen and Rhiannon turned and fired arrow after arrow into the pack. Nearly every one found its mark and those that fell were meat for the other dogs to fight over. Soon there was only a handful of dogs still pursuing them, led by a big yellow brute with crazed eyes and blood-slavered jaws.

Rhiannon had only one arrow left. With her body twisted right round, rising and falling to the rhythm of Blackthorn's powerful gallop, she raised the bow and squinted along the arrow's length. Just as she was about to let the arrow fly, a low tree branch knocked her from her horse's back. With a scream she fell.

"Rhiannon!" Lewen shouted and brought Argent wheeling round on his haunches. Just as the big yellow dog leapt upon Rhiannon's fallen body, Lewen shot an arrow straight through its chest, knocking the dog head over heels. Then Lewen flung himself down on the road on his knees, pulling Rhiannon into his arms. With frantic hands he brushed away the tangled mess of her hair, looking down into her face. "Rhiannon, Rhiannon," he whispered. "Are ye hurt?"

She opened her eyes and looked up into his face. "No' me," she said.

Lewen bent his head and kissed her.

The world went still and quiet, all the clamour of snarling dogs, stampeding horses and jolting caravans fading away. Rhiannon reached up her hand and cupped it round the back of Lewen's head, fingers threading through his curls. Lewen's breath caught and he pressed his mouth down harder upon hers, feeling her body curl into him.

Then a shrill neigh of anxiety penetrated his dazed senses. He jerked upright, in time to see another dog leaping upon them. Instinctively he felt for his *sgian dubh*, the dagger he wore in his boot, but as his fingers found the sheath empty he remembered giving his knife to Edithe. He had time only to seize the dog's throat in his hands and hold it off, even as the weight of the dog bore him down onto his back. Then suddenly the dog jerked and went limp, falling upon his chest, blood gushing all over his hands. He thrust the dog away and saw Rhiannon withdraw her dagger from its chest, and wipe its bloodstained blade on her breeches.

"Best go," she said.

He nodded, bereft of words. Together they ran and vaulted up onto the backs of their horses, leaving the dead dogs behind for the remnants of the pack to fight over. Then they were galloping down the road again, eager to catch up with the caravans.

Lewen risked a glance at Rhiannon as they rode. Her black
hair whipped out behind her like a living cloak and her hands
and face and body were smeared with blood and mud. She
turned and smiled at him, and he felt the hot clench of desire.
He looked away, finding it hard to breathe. *So beautiful,* he
thought. *So dangerous . . .*

Rhiannon laughed.

The next instant they were once again having to rein their
horses in to a violent halt. The blue caravan had hit a deep rut
and was bogged in the mud. Iven and the boys were all desperately trying to drag it free, Rafferty pulling at the big gelding's
head, Iven and Cameron trying to lift the caravan with their
shoulders while Landon knelt in the mud, thrusting branches
under the wheel.

Lewen dismounted. To his surprise his legs almost gave way
beneath him. "Here, let me help," he said, coming across to put
his shoulder to the wheel.

"Quick! Quick!" Iven cried.

"The dogs are all dead, or gorging themselves on their kin,"
Lewen said wearily.

"It's no' the dogs I'm worried about now," Iven said. Lewen
looked up in surprise. Only then did he smell the rank odour of
rotting flesh. Something moved in the grey dusk under the
trees, something out of rhythm with the blow of leaf and rain.

"Oh, no," he said blankly.

"Oh, yes," Iven shot back. "Now, heave!"

With a will Lewen heaved. The caravan came up out of the
mud with a sucking sound and rolled forward. The boys scrambled back to their feet. Then all went still and quiet as stone.

All round them stood the company of the dead. Some were
nothing but bones and staring skulls, others were freshly risen
from their grave and bore only the faintest purple bloom of putrefaction on their chalky skins. Some even had eyes still,
filmed over, their eyelashes clogged with grave-dirt. These
were the ones who reached out their cold hands as if begging,
who stretched their mouths into moans and shrieks, who groped
their way forward, lifting their limbs in a grotesque parody of

living movement. It was not the jerking skeletons that caused the most horror but those most newly dead, who had skin and hair and eyes still, and features recognisable still as old man or young woman or little boy.

Rafferty made a gagging noise and swayed where he stood. Iven strode quickly to stand by him, holding him up with one hand. "Nina!" he called softly. "Nina!"

The door of the red caravan opened and Nina stood upon the step, looking out into the twilight forest where, step by stumbling step, the host of the dead closed in upon them. She stood frozen for a moment, horror on her face. Then she reached back into the caravan and pulled out her guitar. "Close your eyes and your ears, my dears," she said gently. "And throw your cloaks about your horses' heads. I am going to sing the songs o' sorcery and I do no' want ye ensorcelled too."

For a moment no-one moved, their muscles paralysed with dread. Then everyone sprang to obey. They wrapped their heavy, rain-wet cloaks about their horses' heads and then huddled their own faces under the muffling folds of cloth, pressing their hands over their ears. There they hunched for an excrutiatingly long time, hearing nothing but the thunder of their own blood in their ears.

At last Lewen felt a gentle touch on his shoulder. He stifled a shriek and sprang away from the touch, fighting his way free of the folds of his cloak. Argent neighed and reared back, spooked by Lewen's fear. It was only Iven though, his fair hair and beard bedraggled with rain.

"All is well," he said. "Nina has sung the dead home."

Lewen looked about him in amazement. Lanterns had been lit at the front and back of both the caravans, casting a warm circle of light over the road. The dead lay in crumpled heaps where they had fallen. Nina sat on the steps of the caravan, her guitar drooping from one hand. She looked ill and haggard, with deep blue rings under her eyes. The sunbird stroked its long, curved beak against her cheek affectionately.

"How?" was all Lewen could say.

Iven shrugged. "Ye think I ken, lad? I had my ears well plugged, I assure ye. I am naught but a jongleur. It is my wife who is the sorceress. All I ken is she has drained her strength. I have to get her to warmth and shelter, and quickly. I do no' want her getting sorcery sickness! Help me rouse the others and let us get away from this accursed wood."

"Aye, away from here," Nina said in a dull, flat voice. "Away from the stench o' death. Oh, Iven! Find us a house, a barn, somewhere with walls and a roof. For there are more out there, I can sense them. I do no' want to camp in the open tonight, when we are all so weary."

Iven swallowed and rubbed his hand over his face. "Go and rest, my darling. I will find us somewhere safe, I promise."

She nodded and stood up, swaying for a moment as giddiness overcame her. Moving like an old, sick woman, she hauled herself up the stairs, the guitar dangling from her hand.

Fetterness Valley

Lewen went to Rhiannon, gently drawing away her cloak. He was surprised to find her sickly white and trembling all over, her pupils so widely dilated her eyes looked black in the flickering lantern light. To his surprise and pleasure, she flung herself into his arms, choking on sobs.

"Why, what's wrong, *leannan*?" he asked, stroking her back.

She shuddered, unable to speak.

"Dinna be afraid," he said. "All is well. Look, Nina has sung the dead to sleep, or true death, what, I really do no' ken. But they are quiet now and willna bother us again. All is well."

She pulled herself away from him, her hands clenched into fists. "No' afraid," she said.

Puzzled, he put his hand on her arm, trying to draw her round to face him. "No, o' course no'. Naught to be afraid o' now. Come, ye're shivering. Ye're wet through with rain, and the wind is cold. No wonder ye canna stop shivering!"

He put his arm about her, but she jerked away. "Call this cold?" she jeered. "It's no' even snowing!" She huddled her arms about her body, trying to control the shudders that racked her.

Nina paused on the top step of the caravan. "Let her come into the caravan with me. I canna heat us a hot drink, but I do have dry clothes and warm blankets. We're all exhausted."

"No' exhausted," Rhiannon said stubbornly. "I fine."

"Rhiannon, ye're trembling," Lewen said. "Go in with Nina and get dry and warm."

"Nay. I stay with horse, I ride. Ye go in and get warm, if ye so cold."

"But Rhiannon . . ."

"I said I ride!"

"But it's raining . . ."

"Ye think I melt in a wee drop o' rain?"

"Nay, o' course no! I just—"

"Ye no' worry about rain, why must I? I just as strong and brave as ye."

"Of course ye are, I dinna mean to—"

"Then shut up and ride. Horses get cold."

"What's all this clishmaclaver?" Frowning, Iven came up to them, the other boys close behind him. "What's wrong?"

"Naught," they both said stiffly, moving away to grasp their horses and swing themselves back up into the saddle.

"Rhiannon?" Nina called from inside her caravan. "Will ye no' come in and get warm?"

"I plenty warm," Rhiannon said through her chattering teeth. "I ride."

"Are ye sure?" Iven said.

"Aye, I sure," Rhiannon snapped, wheeling Blackthorn round abruptly. "Why ye doubt me?"

"I do no' doubt ye," Iven said, taken aback. "I just—"

"Talk, talk, all any o' ye ever do is talk," Rhiannon said and kicked her mare into a gallop. Mud sprayed up from Blackthorn's hooves and splattered against Iven's face, but by the time he had indignantly wiped his face clean and opened his mouth to retort, girl and horse had vanished down the road.

"She's got a shocking bad temper, that lass," Iven said, shaking off gobs of mud from his hand. "Well, we'd best get after her. It's a bad night to be galloping about in." He cast a shrewd look at Lewen, who was so baffled and angry that he felt unable to speak or look at anyone, then sighed.

"I guess she doesna like admitting she's afraid," Iven said to no-one in particular. "Silly lass. Everyone feels fear sometimes. May as well admit it. It's like love. No point trying to hide what ye feel. It'll break through in the end, regardless."

Lewen felt a slow burn of shame and embarrassment spread over his body. He stared through Argent's ears grimly, saying nothing.

"Come on, let's get on the road," Iven said, clambering up into the drivers' seat and clicking his tongue at the big, grey horse standing so patiently between the shafts. Landon was hoisted back onto the driving seat of the girls' caravan, and the other boys forced themselves to remount, groaning as their aching muscles complained. Only their fervent desire to get away from this place of death gave them the strength they needed. They rode on into the damp gloom of the wood, staring all around them, flinching at every creak of branch or rustle of wind. Lewen could not help peering anxiously down the shadowy road, looking for Rhiannon, but when she came cantering back up to them, jeering at them for being so slow, he neither spoke nor looked at her, instead concentrating on spying out the road ahead. She fell in behind the caravans on the other side, as far away from Lewen as she could get. Lewen's chest tightened with misery.

He did not understand what was wrong with her. One minute she had been fighting by his side, kissing him passionately, laughing as they galloped side by side through the rain-swept forest. Then, the very next instant, she was cold and angry, rejecting him fiercely.

Lewen did not know what he had done to offend her. He hoped it was not his kiss that had changed her so profoundly. He had not meant to kiss her. He knew how much she hated to be touched. He had longed to take her in his arms from the very moment he had seen her, but she was like a wild creature caught in a trap, ready to bite any who tried to free her. He knew she needed gentleness and patience before she could be tamed, not the urgency of desire that sometimes threatened to overwhelm him. And she was only a lass, and she had been placed under the protection of his mother's best friends.

It did not matter that Rhiannon was unlike any young lady he had ever met, half-wild, and innocent of society's etiquette. He knew that if Nina should find him kissing Rhiannon, she would be troubled and upset. He knew his mother would be horrified.

If he was to do what society expected of him, he would wait till Midsummer and then ask her to jump the fire with him. When they were properly handfasted, he could take her to his bed and keep her there, at least for a year, when he would ask her to jump the fire again. If she said yes, then they would be wed, and he could have her in his bed for ever after. He could not imagine anyone approving. Not his parents, nor his Rìgh, nor the Coven, who liked their apprentices to finish their training before they got distracted with affairs of the heart. Certainly not Dillon of the Joyous Sword, captain of the Blue Guards.

Yeomen of the Guards swore to serve the Rìgh as their first and only master, and those who wished to marry usually left the Rìgh's service, as Lewen's father Niall had done when he jumped the fire with Lilanthe. Often they were given a small estate to manage, or given some other role at court, but they forfeited the right to wear the blue cloak and the badge of the charging stag.

He did not need to marry her, of course. The people of Ravenshaw were not like the Tìrsoilleirean with their fear and hatred of the natural desires of the body. Indiscretions of the heart were usually smiled at, unless there was a babe, and even then neither party was reviled if they chose not to marry. Witches of the Coven were even more relaxed in their attitudes. If Lewen decided to stay with the Coven, he could do as he pleased, as long as his affairs did not cause too much disruption. The Yeomen did not have the same freedom. Dillon of the Joyous Sword kept very strict discipline and would frown on any amorous indiscretion. Particularly one with a wild half-satyricorn who was suspected of being implicated in the murder of a Yeoman of the Guard. Lewen could not imagine it helping his career prospects.

Lewen would never have kissed Rhiannon if he had not spent the last few hours at the very extremities, fighting for his life and facing death squarely in the face. She had not seemed to mind. She had kissed him as passionately, opening her mouth to his, pulling him closer with an urgent hand, curling her body into his. The memory of it was enough to make hot blood flood Lewen's groin. He stifled a groan and shifted in the saddle, glancing sideways at her cool patrician profile. She did not glance back.

On and on the horses plodded with hanging heads, following the swaying lantern at the back of the caravans. They came out of the false dusk of the wood into the true dusk of the sinking sun, the sky behind them flaming with brilliant reds and oranges that slowly faded to crimson, and then to pink and at last to violet, as they rode through untilled fields, past abandoned crofts and ruined cottages, all gaping open to the wind and rain.

On and on they rode in the darkness, till Landon was asleep on the bench, the reins flapping loose, and Rhiannon and the boys were jerking about on the backs of their horses, only kept awake by the cold rain trickling down their necks.

Then the jongleurs' caravans ground to a halt. Lewen, jolted awake by the cessation of movement, looked up, rubbing his eyes. They had come to a gate in a high wall, topped with upright shards of glass that glinted in the light of the lanterns. Inside the wall was a steep, peaked roof, and a low window from which candlelight shone, welcoming and warm, and the soft sound of voices.

Shivering in their damp cloaks, the boys watched hopefully as Iven climbed down from the caravan and went up to hammer on the gate. Lewen smelt wood-smoke on the breeze and something delicious that made saliva spring in his mouth. He had not realised he was hungry.

At the sound of Iven's fist, the faint murmur of voices faded away. Iven hammered louder. There was no response. At last he cried out angrily, "For pity's sake, open the gate! We have an injured girl here and we are all exhausted. Please, let us in!"

There was an exclamation and then a swift exchange of low voices. Then they heard a soft, cautious step, and a man said, "Who's there? What do you want?"

"Just shelter for the night," Iven said, his voice hoarse with exhaustion. "We were set upon by a pack o' ravening dogs and were hard pressed to fight them off. One o' us was badly mauled, a girl. She's no' yet sixteen. Please, let us in!"

There was no response.

"Please!" Iven called. "It is raining and we are all cold and hurt. We can pay. We have money."

"Who are ye?" The man's voice was surly with suspicion.

"I am a jongleur, called Iven Yellowbeard. I have my wife and son here, and a party o' lads and lasses, who have ridden far and fought hard today. Some o' us are hurt. Please, for Eà's sake, have mercy and let us in."

"A jongleur? Here in Fetterness?" They heard the bolt scrape back and the gate opened barely a crack. A man's face peered out at them. He was dark-eyed and dark-haired, like most people in Ravenshaw, and carried a long double-bladed sword, nearly as tall as himself. He held it out threateningly, his eyes running over the garishly painted caravans, the weary, mud-spattered horses and the hunched shapes of Rhiannon and the boys, the youth of their faces evident in the glow of the lanterns. The door of the caravans had opened, Nina looking out of one and Fèlice out of the other, her dishevelment not disguising her fresh young beauty.

"By my beard and the beard o' the Centaur!" he exclaimed. "Well, ye look live enough. I suppose ye can come in." He dragged the gate open, staring suspiciously out into the darkness, his sword held high. Gratefully they rode through and the man shut the gate quickly behind them, slamming home the bolts.

"The stable is over this way," he said. "Ye'll have to pay me for the hay. We have little enough left after the winter. Your horses look fair foundered. Come, I'll help ye unharness them and rub them down. Look, those lads are riding in their sleep! What on earth are ye doing out after sundown? Do ye no' ken the dead walk these hills?"

"Aye, we ken . . . now," Iven answered heavily.

"I guess ye meant to make Fetterness afore they shut the gates," the man said. "They willna open after the sun has gone, no' even for the laird o' Fettercairn himself. Here, lad, take this bucket. There's a well in the yard. We'll just get these horses settled and ye can come in and rest by the fire. It's late, we've eaten our supper already and were readying ourselves for bed, but I'm sure my wife can find something for ye to eat. There's always bean soup."

Bean soup sounded heavenly.

They were all so tired, the settling of the horses seemed to take forever. For once Iven did not insist on every piece of leather and steel being polished to a high sheen, but let them wipe away the worst of the dirt and hang the tack on pegs to be cleaned in the morning. He then carried Maisie out of the caravan and into the house, trying hard not to jolt her as he hurried through the pelting rain. Maisie was white with shock and pain, and the bite wounds on her arm and legs and head were still bleeding sluggishly through their bandages. The others trailed behind, too worn-out and hungry to notice more than the warmth of the fire in the candlelit kitchen and the good smell of soup.

The farmer was named Tavish MacTavish, and his wife, all bones and cavernous hollows, was named Alice. For a while all was bustle and hustle, as Maisie's ugly bite wounds were cleaned and re-bandaged, Iven's arm and Edithe's head and sprained ankle attended to, home-made healing potions and a few mouthfuls of soup swallowed, and the two injured girls tucked up to sleep in the sitting room, where the fire still glowed on the hearth. The others were allowed to wash in the scullery and then fed black bread and soup in deep bowls. Nina was so exhausted that she sat in silence, Roden asleep on her lap, wrapped warmly within the shelter of her plaid. Iven managed to coax her to eat a few mouthfuls of the soup, and then Alice, noticing her pallor, got down a bottle of goldensloe wine and poured her a tiny glassful. Nina drank it obediently and a little colour came back into her cheeks and she stirred, reaching for her spoon. The plaid fell away from Roden's head of chestnut curls, nestled sweetly into Nina's breast, and Alice stopped in mid-movement, staring at him, her sudden pallor making her face seem gaunter than ever.

"A wee laddie," she whispered. She put down the precious wine bottle with such nerveless fingers it almost toppled from the table. Tavish reached out and caught it.

"Now, now, Alice," he said anxiously.

She sat down, staring at the sleeping boy with an expression of such pitiful yearning on her face that her husband came round to stand behind her, resting both hands on her skinny shoulders.

"We lost our boy," he explained awkwardly. "Just afore Hogmanay. She grieves still."

"I'm so very sorry," Nina said, so tired and overwrought that quick tears of sympathy welled up in her eyes.

"What are ye doing riding the moors at night wi' a laddie?" Alice said accusingly. "Do ye no' ken? How can ye no' ken?"

Nina made a helpless gesture. "We heard stories but . . ."

"No lads are safe in this valley, do ye no' understand, ye fools?" Her voice rose hysterically. "We thought we could keep our boy Dooly safe, with our high walls and our long sword and the strength o' our love, but nay! He was taken from his bed, even while I slept only a few feet away, and though we searched high and low, calling and calling, we did no' find him, no' for weeks, and when we did he was dead." She began to weep, slow desperate tears that did nothing to relieve the hot knot of her grief. "I should have kent! I should have kent! The moment he began to toddle about and call me 'mam', I should've taken him and gone."

"Alice had a brother that was stolen too," Tavish said unhappily. "When she was just a lass o' six or seven."

"Twenty-six years ago, he disappeared," Alice said, raising her gaunt face from her hands. "By the Truth, ye'd think I would've kent better than to stay near that witch-cursed tower. It casts its foul shadow over us all."

Iven frowned at her words. "Why did ye stay?" he asked.

Tavish flashed his wife an unhappy glance. "My father farmed this land afore me, and his father afore him, and his father afore him. There has been a Tavish MacTavish living in this house for six generations. I could no' just abandon it."

"There'll be no Tavish to inherit when you're dead and gone," his wife said brutally. "Our wee Tavish would be alive still if ye'd only agreed to go. I should've taken him and the lasses and gone. But like a fool I stayed with ye and now we have no son, no wee Dooly!" She began to weep again.

Everyone was silent, not wanting to even move or cough, embarrassed to be witnessing this scene.

Alice turned to Nina, her face ugly with grief and spite. "Have ye no care for your wee laddie that ye risk being out after dark? Do ye no' ken the dead will no' sleep here, but walk the hills, looking for live bodies to take wi' them? We buried our Dooly, when we found him, but he would no' rest in his grave, did ye ken that? He dug his way out and came sobbing back home, wanting us to let him in, though the flesh rotted on his bones. We shut the gate on him but he knocked and cried all night, every night, for a month, until at last my man could bear it no more and cut his head from his body with his sword. Can ye imagine doing that to your son?" Her eyes turned feverishly from Nina's horrified face to Iven's. "We buried him again, head and rotting body together, but his spirit will no' rest. I hear him sobbing outside every night, crying for his mam. Do ye wonder that every croft in the Fetterness Valley lies abandoned, when our dead will no' rest, no matter how often we kill them?"

There was a long, strained silence. The wind howled in the chimney and rain rattled the shutters. Rhiannon, her nails cutting into her palms, thought she could hear a little boy's voice, crying pitifully outside the wall.

"I'm so sorry, I'm so very sorry," Nina said at last, helplessly.

"Why should ye be sorry, when your son still lives?" Alice said. She stared longingly at the profile of the sleeping boy, his soft curved cheek flushed and rosy. "Ye canna love him like I loved my Dooly, when ye bring him into our valley without a care."

"We are just passing through," Nina said pleadingly. "We heard the stories but . . . I thought I could keep him safe."

Tavish gestured towards the window. "Keep him safe against *them*? No-one is safe!"

Nina frowned. "Do ye mean the dead who walk? But they are no' the ones who took your laddie. It is no' the souls o' the living they seek, but peace. They have been ensorcelled from their natural rest, those poor dead people."

"What would ye ken?" Alice said scornfully.

"We met with some in the wood," Nina said gently. "They came to us begging us for help. They did no' seek to hurt us. I went down among them and I saw they walked against their will, compelled by some unnatural spell. So I sang the spell o' reversal, to unbind them from the enchantment, and then I sang the songs o' death and o' farewell, so their bodies could rest and their spirits go free."

Tavish and Alice stared at her, taken aback and horrified. Then a dark mottled flush spread up Alice's thin, bony face. "Ye sang spells? I thought ye were jongleurs!"

"We are," Iven said. "Though that is no' all we are. My wife is also a journeywitch, who travels the land working on behalf o' the Coven. These bairns that travel with us, they are apprentices travelling to the Theurgia to study."

"A witch!" Alice spat. She got to her feet, backing away from the table. "Get out," she cried. "Get out o' my house and take your witch-brats wi' ye."

Nobody moved, all stunned with surprise.

"Ye heard me! Get out!"

"But . . . it's late, it's raining," Iven said. "Ye canna mean to turn us out into the storm."

Alice's face was distorted with hate. "I can indeed. Witches! I should've kent. No-one else would be riding out on the moors after dark, wi' the ghosts and evil spirits and walking dead. Get out, get out, afore ye curse this house."

"But where could we go?" Nina asked, nonplussed. "Maisie is hurt sorely, and needs to rest, we all need to rest, we are exhausted. We have done ye no harm."

"No harm! Harm is all ye witches ever do."

"Ye canna believe that! Why, since the Coven threw down the Ensorcellor it has done nothing but good, surely ye must ken that? Why do ye hate witches so?"

"Nothing but good!" She snorted with scorn. "All the evil that has ever happened in this valley is because o' the meddling o' those blasted witches. Go on! Get out o' my house."

Nina rose hesitantly. "Please, may we no' sleep in your stables? It is so late, and listen to that rain! We have ridden so far already today."

"No, no! I want ye gone!"

"Ye canna throw us out into that storm," Iven said angrily. "It would no' be right."

"Ye're witches, surely ye can drive away the storm?" Tavish said sarcastically. He took a few belligerent steps forward, a big burly man with clenched fists.

Nina shook her head. "I am no weather witch to command the storm." Her voice was very tired and sad. "Even if I could, I doubt I'd have the strength now. I've already worked strong magic today. Please do no' drive us out. I am sorry if we have distressed ye . . ."

Tavish shook his head. "Alice wishes ye gone. Gather up your things and get out."

"I will go if ye wish, but my wee laddie? Ye would no' turn him out into the storm? And Maisie . . . and Edithe . . . they are sore hurt . . . will ye no' shelter them for the night at least? They are naught but lassies, and sleeping. And the other bairns? They are all so weary. There is no' room for them all in the caravans. Please, will ye no' let them stay? "

Alice shook her head, eyes red-rimmed, arms folded.

Nina's black eyes sparked with sudden anger. "Ye ken I could force ye to shelter us, I could sing ye to sleep, or compel ye against your will, or I could even tell the boys to draw their knives and force ye into some cold storeroom to spend the night thinking about the meaning o' kindness and compassion. But I shallna do any o' those things for that is no' the way o' the Coven. I will wake those poor injured girls, and I will take these poor weary bairns, and we will all go out into the rain and the storm and the darkness. But I hope ye never rest easy in your bed again, for ye are a cruel, hard woman."

Alice's face twisted and she tried to speak, but her grief and rage and hate was like a boulder in her chest and she could not draw breath around it.

Nina looked round at the pale, miserable faces of the apprentices.

"Come on, my dears. I ken it is hard, but I for one do no' wish to spend another minute under this roof!"

As everyone slowly and unhappily got up, and gathered together their wet cloaks, Nina took out her purse with fingers that trembled. "Here, for the hay, and the soup, and for your trouble."

She held out a heavy gold coin.

Alice reached out and snatched it.

It was close on midnight and a foul wind was blowing. The horses refused to go out into the storm, and they had to whip their flanks and drag at their heads, all the while the rain beating on them through the open stable door. It was not until Lewen and Rhiannon seized their bridles and whispered cajolingly in their ears that the horses at last consented to leave the warmth of the stable.

Cocooned in blankets, Maisie and Edithe had been carried through the sleet by Lewen and Cameron and deposited on their

narrow bunks in the cold, draughty caravan, frightened and
questioning. Fèlice ran behind them, cloak over her head, tears
running down her face. At Rhiannon's insistence, Landon took
the fourth bunk and he was so exhausted he did not argue, just
thanked her and lay down, huddling the blanket about him.

"Ye'll have to hold on tightly," Cameron told them grimly.
"It's as black as Brann's waistcoat out there, and the roads are
rough. I'll do my best, but I canna promise ye won't be jolted."

He then put up the hood of his cloak and climbed up into the
drivers' seat, gathering up the reins dourly. Rafferty climbed up
next to him, too weary to ride any further. Iven was driving the
other caravan as usual, having first made sure Nina and Roden
were safely tucked up in their bunks inside. Nina had protested,
feeling she should drive the caravan since it was her fault they
had all been turned out, but Iven simply told her not to be a
goosecap, and to get in and comfort Roden, who was wailing in
the thin, high tone used by very tired young children.

So that left Lewen and Rhiannon, the horse-whisperers, to
lead the horses and keep them calm in that thunder-rumbling,
lightning-stalked night. It was a difficult job. The horses shied
at every crack and flash, sometimes rearing up on their hind
legs in terror, sometimes trying to bolt and almost dragging
their arms out of their sockets. It was so dark they had trouble
seeing the road, and so the horses stumbled into every pothole
and water-filled rut. Only the swaying orange blur of the
lanterns in front of them kept them from wandering off the road
altogether.

They stumbled along for half an hour, shivering in the icy
wind. The road was covered with water now, swirling around
the horses' hocks and sometimes splashing up to their withers.
Once Edithe's nervy bay mare Donnagh reared as a great white
sheet of lightning illuminated the sky. Lewen realised with a
shock that they were making their way round the shore of an
immense, wind-tossed lake. He only had time for one quick
glance before he had to leap out of the saddle to help drag Donnagh to her feet, the mare having slipped in the mud and fallen
on her side. That one glance had been enough, though. Lewen
knew where he was. That lake filled the mouth of the valley,
spilling down through the narrow gap in the Broken Ring of

Dubhslain to fall in a great roaring waterfall called the Find-horn Falls.

Somewhere on the far side of the lake, hidden behind the spray thrown up by the roiling waters, was Ravenscraig, built on its high crag of rock. That meant they must be coming close to the Tower of Ravens, for Brann had built his witches' tower on the crag facing the castle across the waterfall. Once, the castle and the tower had been joined by a great arched bridge of silver-bound stone, like a cold grey rainbow, so that Brann could cross as he willed. So high was the bridge, and so terrible the fall, that few had ever dared cross with him, the old stories told, even though it was the only way to cross from one side of the lake to the other. The waters were simply too wild and the currents too strong for any boat to risk crossing so close to the waterfall, which was more than one thousand feet wide from crag to crag and fell almost three hundred feet to the lowlands below. The bridge across the waterfall had been a marvel of engineering, but was destroyed on the Day of Betrayal by the Ensorcellor's Red Guards, toppling down into the maelstrom below and taking with it a hundred fleeing witches.

Knowing where to look now, Lewen waited for the next flash of sheet lightning, then raised his head, peering through the driving rain. Involuntarily he cried out, for ahead he could see the walled town of Fetterness, built against a high ridge which rose and rose and rose into a great, forbidding pinnacle of stone. Perched high on this bare, stern crag was the ruin of a huge building, its stone blasted black with fire. Only for an instant could he see it, then the lightning was gone, leaving coloured midges dancing in Lewen's eyes, and he could see no more.

"What is it? What wrong?" Rhiannon cried.

"Naught," he answered, his lips stiff with cold. "Look, ahead, there's the town. Fetterness, they call it. Happen we'll be able to rouse someone to open the gate and let us in. There must be an inn where we can stay, even so late as this."

But the town of Fetterness would not be roused. Though Iven pounded and pounded on the gate, and shouted until he was hoarse, no sleepy gatekeeper or surly guard came to open it up and let them in. At last they had to admit defeat.

"We'll find a croft somewhere," Iven said, his hair dripping into his eyes, his shabby clothes wet through to the skin. "Do no' worry, Nina, there must be somewhere we can shelter, even if it's only an auld ruin. Why, if the worse comes to the worst, we'll brave the tower! It canna all be burnt and broken down."

Nina, standing in the caravan doorway with a gorgeous green-and-gold shawl wrapped round her head, shuddered and shook her head. "No, thank ye! I've had enough o' ghosts for one night. Iven, that farmer said something about the laird, do ye remember? The laird o' Fettercairn, he said. If there's a laird, there must be a castle."

"Aye, Fettercairn Castle," Iven said slowly. "I remember hearing about it, ages ago. It guards the pass down into the low-lands. It canna be far away. Do ye really wish to look for it, at this hour o' the night?"

Nina nodded. "Surely the laird willna have forgotten all the laws o' hospitality, no matter how surly his people? And I need to sleep, Iven, we all need to sleep. It's impossible to rest with the caravan jolting and swaying the way it does, and we canna all cram in, the vans are simply too small. I hate to think how poor Maisie is doing, all torn and bitten as she is. Let us find this castle and if they willna open to us, I swear I'll sing the gate open, if I have to! Never have I been in such an unhappy place!"

So on they trudged, following the road past the town and zigzagging up the side of the ridge. The wind plucked at them with icy fingers, dragging at the caravans as if seeking to throw them off the side. The road was steep and narrow and cobbled with stone, all slick and wet from the rain, and in the darkness it was hard to see their way. Iven got down and led the grey gelding, afraid they would miss a turn and drive right over the edge of the cliff. Nina got out and walked with him, to relieve the strain on the horse, and called to those who were not injured to do the same.

The higher they climbed, the more vicious the storm became. The wind sent their cloaks fluttering and snatched Iven's hat from his head, taking it whirling up into the sky. Thunder grumbled all around them, and flash after flash of lightning tore the sky from end to end. The horses were terrified, rearing and neighing and fighting to be free of the firm hands that held them steady. They came to the last turn of the road and, in a great stabbing stroke of lightning that made that them all jump and swear, saw before them a long driveway, running through tall gateposts topped by stone ravens.

"No' that way!" Iven called back to Cameron. "That must be the way to the haunted tower. Turn this way. Down the road. Down!"

The road wound down the side of the ridge, protected by tall battlemented walls all the way along. Lewen could only see over the wall by standing up in his stirrups, and he sat down abruptly again for the drop down into the valley below was many hundreds of feet.

The road was so steep they had to lean on the brake to stop the caravans from sliding down on top of the weary carthorses, who could barely lift one great hoof after another. Down another turn of the road they went, and then the road ended at a tall gatehouse with a enormous iron door. They looked around them, suddenly feeling trapped in that narrow ditch of a road, and realised that they had been passing under the outer wall of the castle, which reared grim battlements and towers far above them on the left side.

"Well, we found Fettercairn Castle," Iven said. He cleared his throat, smoothed down his wind-ruffled hair, twirled his fair beard into its usual fork, both twists dripping water down his front, and tried to brush away some of the mud.

"Big castle," he said.

"Plenty o' room for all o' us," Nina answered.

Iven squared his shoulders and strode up to the enormous door. A bell hung beside it and he rang it loudly, catching his breath as echoes sounded from the abyss below. Again and again he rang the bell, and was just turning to Nina with a dismal shrug when a little doorway cut into the gate opened. An old, stooped man dressed in a nightgown and nightcap peered out, holding high a lantern. "Aye?"

"Please, we're travellers, in desperate need o' shelter," Nina cried out. "Please, let us in!"

"O' course, o' course," the old man said. "Bad night to be lost in. What arc ye doing here, o' all places? Och, ye canna go wandering round here at night, it's a bad dangerous place, it is. Come in, come in, out o' the rain. What have ye got there? Caravans? I'd best open the big gate."

With a loud groaning noise, the gate swung open, revealing a narrow passage beyond, guarded by a portcullis. Looking up nervously at the sharp iron prongs above his head, Iven led the carthorse along the passage into a large stone room, the others following close behind.

Rhiannon slipped off Blackthorn's back to lead her through last of all, feeling a shiver run through the mare's delicate frame that she felt in her own bones. This was a grim, dark place indeed, the gatehouse of Fettercairn Castle. Its walls seemed to ooze fear and misery as much as they did dampness. Rhiannon imagined she could hear cries and groans and the clash of arms, and looking round at the white, anxious faces of her companions, she thought they heard them too. There were no windows, only small apertures in the ceiling and walls through which arrows could be shot, or boiling oil poured. Weapons were hung all over the walls, broadswords and axes and spiked clubs and flails. On the far side of the room, the cramped passageway continued along to another great iron door, which presumably opened out onto the road down into the lowlands.

To the left, the room opened out into the ground floor of the barbican. An enormous hearth on the eastern wall lay cold and empty. The old man opened another fortified door beside it to show a narrow grassed area between the inner and outer walls.

"The stables are along that way," he said. "I willna take ye, I have no desire to get soaked to the skin. Rouse up the grooms to help ye. Do no' fear, ye canna get lost. There's no way in to the inner ward from here. Ye'll have to spend the night here in the gatehouse with me, o' course, I dinna wish to be waking my laird at this hour and I canna take ye through to the castle myself, I'm just the gatekeeper. It's rather rough and ready, but there's plenty o' room. We dinna keep men-at-arms here anymore, no' being at war, ye ken, so there's just me and a messenger lad, who's still sleeping, despite all the racket ye lot made."

"Oh, I canna thank ye enough," Nina said. "We've had a long day o' it, and a few o' us are injured, and we have no' been able to find shelter anywhere."

"Aye, so I can imagine," the old man said. "Bad times in the Fetterness Valley, these past few years. Anyone who wishes to leave must come past me, and I've seen many o' them, all o' them weeping and wringing their hands. Och, well, it's keen I am to get back to my bed, for it's awful cold and my bones feel it these days, indeed they do. Come, I'll show ye where ye can sleep. There's firewood if ye wish to light a fire, and some blankets in a chest. Let the horses bide a wee, while I show ye. In the morning I'll send the lad up to the castle to tell the laird ye're here, for he'll want to ken."

Nina nodded dumbly, and they followed the old man's flickering lantern up a spiral staircase to the second floor, where he showed them into a bare dormitory with rows of narrow beds.

"Ye'll be comfortable enough here, I imagine," the old man said. "Better than camping out in the rain."

"Aye, indeed," Nina said gratefully. "Thank ye!"

"Och, it's my job," he answered with a shrug of his skinny shoulders. "No' that I've been roused at night for a long time, mind ye."

He kindled a candle on the mantelpiece, nodded goodnight, then went out, leaving them staring at the cold, bare room, while outside the wind howled like a flight of banshees. Rhiannon shuddered and wrapped her arms about her body, feeling a dark foreboding pressing on her spirits.

Nina sighed and looked at Iven.

"We've slept in worse places, my love," he said.

"Och, I ken. I just hope those mattresses aren't full o' lice."

"Doubt it, looks like they havena been slept in for years."

"They'll be damp, for sure."

"Well, so are we all. Come, *leannan,* this is no' like ye, ye're worn to a shadow. Let's get a fire going and get ourselves dry and warm, and tomorrow we can drive on, and shake the mud o' Fetterness off our feet. It's only one more night."

The wind shrieked in the chimney, as if in derision.

Fettercairn Castle

R ain lashed at the mullioned windows, an occasional sheet of lighning irradiating the sky, before the heavy gloom descended again.

"I have never kent such foul weather," Fèlice said discontentedly. "Is it always like this?"

Nina was trying to blow the sullen coals into flames with the help of wheezy old bellows. She looked up and tried to smile. "No' always. If I did no' ken better, I'd think the Broken Ring o' Dubhslain sought to keep us here. At least it is no' hailing."

"In April!" Fèlice cried.

Hail suddenly clattered against the glass.

"I spoke too soon," Nina said, and sat back on her heels, wiping one hand across her brow and leaving a dirty smudge.

It was midmorning already. Everyone had slept very late, for little light penetrated the thick walls of the gatehouse and they had all been exhausted. It was the sound of Maisie's moans that had woken them in the end. She was sick with fever, and when Nina carefully dampened and peeled away the bloody, grimy bandages, it was to find the wounds beneath festering and green. Landon was unwell also, racked by a hacking cough, and aches and pains in all his joints. When Nina felt his forehead, the little crease between her brows deepened and she bade him stay in bed. Cameron was coughing also, and complained he had not been able to get warm all night, and so he was abed also, and Edithe too, while Iven had gone to ask the gatekeeper for water and a kettle, and any herbs or medicines he might have.

"I'll go and check the horses, Nina," Lewen said, pulling on his boots. "We were so tired last night it was all we could do to get their tack off them. I want to make sure the grooms have fed and watered them properly."

"I'll come too," Rafferty said.

"Me too," Rhiannon said. She had been standing by the window with her forehead pressed against the glass, staring at the hail, but now she turned and looked at the others.

"Ye'll get wet," Lewen said to no-one in particular.

"Think I care?" she answered.

"We willna melt," Rafferty said with forced cheerfulness.

Nina nodded and gave a ghost of her usual merry smile. "Thanks. Would ye mind bringing me some stuff from my caravan? I'm worried indeed about poor Maisie. I wish I were a better healer. I wish Isabeau were here, or your mam, Lewen."

"Me too," he said. After Nina had told him what she needed, he led the way down the dimly lit stairs and out the door into the outer ward.

"Poor Maisie!" he said. "Even if Nina can clean out the infection, she'll be left with nasty scars. It's such a shame, she's a sweet lass."

Rhiannon frowned, but said nothing. Rafferty made a murmur of agreement, then said anxiously, "Do ye think Maisie will be fit to ride out soon? Because glad as I am to be safe behind high walls, I canna wait to get away from here. It's creepy. I wish we'd never come this way."

"I'm sure everyone does," Lewen answered. "But how were we to ken? I mean, they may have tried to tell us, back in Ardarchy, but who was to ken how bad it really was? I am just glad we've come through safely."

"We're no' through yet," Rhiannon said harshly.

"No," Lewen answered, looking at her thoughtfully. Rhiannon did not return his gaze. They came to the door to the outer ward and pulled up their hoods against the rain.

Rhiannon could not have explained why, but she was angry with Lewen, and with all the others too. When she thought over the tumultuous events of the previous day, she felt such a confusion in her emotions that anger and fear, her two most familiar emotions, were the only ones she recognised. Since Rhiannon hated to feel afraid, or to have others know that she felt fear, her only refuge was anger. She stayed angry all through the trip to the stables, a vast stone building constructed within the double ring of walls that encircled the castle, and protected by its own gatehouse and bailey. In times of war, the horses could be fed and exercised within the outer ward, and if the first wall was breached, either taken inside to the castle grounds, or used to escape through the back gate. The stable itself had room enough for a hundred horses, though most of the stalls were now empty.

An old, wizened groom called Shannley, with a face set in lines of sour suspicion, grunted at the sight of them. He and his stablehands had not been pleased to be roused in the early hours of the morning, and by the expression on his face, he was not pleased to see them now. Even Lewen, who could win over most people with his deep warm voice and pleasant ways, could not soften the head-groom's manner. Shannley showed them where the bins of grain were with a jerk of one spatulate thumb, then shuffled back to his rooms, grumbling under his breath. The stablehands, meanwhile, got on sullenly with their work, casting many a curious look at Lewen, Rhiannon and Rafferty.

The horses were tired and bad-tempered after their hard usage, and so Rhiannon tried to work away her own ill-temper with a stable rubber, curry-comb and tack-brush. She groomed horses and carried buckets of mash and polished tack till her arms ached and her head throbbed, but it did not help. She was in a fouler temper than before, with most of her rancour directed at Lewen. If it was not for him, she would never have made this ill-starred journey into a land haunted by evil spirits and the walking dead. All night she had thought she could hear the sound of a young boy crying, and sobs of grief, and wails of fear, and the moans of the dying. It had done no good telling herself it was only the wind, or Maisie crying out in her fevered sleep, or her own overwrought imagination. Even driving her fingers into her ears or pulling the musty-smelling pillow over her head had not helped. She had not been able to silence the echoes in her brain.

Rhiannon was shaken to the core by these supernatural terrors. Dark walkers stalked her imagination, and not even the slicing open of her wrist and the spilling of her own blood on the hearth had relieved her dread.

As they went about their business in the stables, she often felt Lewen's eyes on her face, puzzled and questioning, but in his usual fashion he did not say anything, which only infuriated her more. By the time they were making their way back to the gate-house, loaded down with supplies from the caravans, even un-observant Rafferty was shooting her anxious glances, and beginning to be wary of addressing remarks to her.

They came into the dormitory to find Fèlice doing her best to keep Roden and Lulu occupied and out of Nina's way as the witch tended to the sick and injured. The sunbird was asleep on the back of a chair, its head tucked under one iridescent green wing as it was so dark and cold in the long room the bird thought it was still night-time. The fire flickered dully on the hearth, for all the wood was wet, and sent out unpleasant puffs of smoke every time the wind shifted.

"Iven's gone up to the castle, to speak with the laird," Nina said, looking tired and pale. "I dinna ken what we are to do, for Maisie is only getting worse, and I havena all the medicines she needs, and I'm worried about Landon too, he's no' as sturdy as ye other lads, and he was chilled through last night. I do no' ken if we should go on, and seek help from the apothecary in the nearest town, or wait here until the bairns are feeling better. I must admit I'd rather no' stay. This place makes me uneasy. It's like a fortress! The laird sent down soldiers to insist Iven attend upon him, and the gatekeeper seems to dread his displeasure. If only it would stop raining! I canna feel easy about going on in such weather but I just want to get away from this place!"

Seeing how anxious they all looked, Nina laughed ruefully, saying "I'm sorry, I'm all out o' sorts from such a late night and the anxiety over poor Maisie. I'm sure there is no need for us to worry."

Poor Maisie, Rhiannon mimicked and then realised that Lewen had been watching her, as usual, and had seen her ex-pression. He frowned and she glared at him, wondering what right he had to disapprove of her behaviour. His frown deep-ened, and she turned away and went to stand by the fire, pre-tending to warm her hands before its sullen glow. Tears prickled her eyes.

"The laird sent down soldiers? That seems odd," Lewen said.

"I suppose it's no' so peculiar when ye think o' all those missing and murdered," Nina responded. "They must be suspicious o' strangers. I must admit I dinna like to see Iven go, however, flanked on all sides by guards armed to the teeth. If they decided to keep him, I'd never get him back!" She sighed, unconsciously pressing her hands together in a gesture of rare anxiety.

"I canna help but wonder how it was the Red Guards were able to take the Tower o' Ravens by surprise on the Day o' Betrayal," Lewen said. "If the only way in and out is through the castle's own gatehouse, ye would've thought the witches' tower impregnable to surprise attack."

"They could've come over the Stormness River like we did," Rafferty pointed out.

"Aye, I suppose so. Only . . . well, the tower looks over the Fetterness Valley, any force o' arms coming that way would have been seen. And they would've had to have passed the town."

"There was some kind o' trickery, or betrayal," Nina said. "I do no' remember the tale. It all happened afore I was born."

"Heavens, that long ago?" Fèlice said teasingly.

Nina cast her an amused look. "Aye, hard to believe, is it no'?"

They heard Iven's quick steps running up the stairs and turned to him expectantly as he came in, looking a far different figure than the drenched and disheveled man of the night before. He had changed into his very best coat, a long-tailed blue velvet and silver-buttoned creation, over a fresh white shirt with a fashionably soft and flowing collar. His boots were rather worn but had been freshly polished, and he wore baggy black satin trousers tied under the knee with ribbons. The ends of his moustache curled upwards and his beard had been forked and plaited into two, with his long hair tied back with a ribbon.

"So what was the laird like?"

"What did he say?"

"Was the castle very grand?"

"Iven, what did he say? Those guards were so grim-faced, I've been afraid . . ." The last question came anxiously from Nina, who had gone to him and grasped his arm tightly.

"What, did ye think he meant to throw me in his dungeon? Nina! Ye must be tired to fall prey to such imaginings."

Nina quirked her mouth. "I ken, I'm sorry. I am tired, I must admit, and this place is grim enough to make anyone imagine horrors."

"Well that's true enough," Iven looked around the circle of expectant faces, as always enjoying having an audience. "The castle is just as grim, and very grand—or may have been, half a century ago. Now it is rather damp and cobwebby, and very much out o' style. The servants are either auld and grouchy or young and nervous, and there are far too few o' them for such a large place. The laird himself is a very affable gentleman and surprisingly well informed on court matters, considering how far away from anywhere we are here. He was most distressed to hear o' our misadventures and has offered us his hospitality until we are all fit to travel again. Indeed, my love, even if Maisie was well enough to travel we couldna leave, for he says the storm has caused a big auld tree to fall across the road, which may take a few days to clear, as it's awkwardly placed. We are stuck here, willy-nilly, and so I thanked him most graciously. He is having rooms made up for us, and has promised to send over some sturdy footmen with a pallet for Maisie, and some auld nurse who he says is as good as any skeelie with her herbal remedies, that he swears will break the infection quick smart."

"Well, that at least is a relief," Nina said. "I am no healer, as ye ken and I'd begun to imagine us wandering the countryside looking for succour while gangrene ate away poor Maisie's leg. I suppose, if we must be marooned somewhere, it may as well be at a castle! Come, lads and lassies, let's pack up our things and make ready. I wish we could have a bath and scrub ourselves clean afore we need meet this laird. I feel damp and itchy and slovenly indeed, even with a quick wash and a change o' clothes."

"Ye look most bonny," Iven said. She seized his nose and tugged it. "Why, thank ye, sir! I could say the same about ye."

Iven twirled his moustache. "Aye, indeed ye could," he answered complacently, so even Rhiannon had to smile.

*   *   *

Fettercairn Castle loomed high behind its battlemented walls, a
great grey fortress with narrow slitted windows and two round
towers, one looking into the Fetterness Valley, the other down
into the lowlands of Ravenshaw, many hundreds of feet below.
It had stopped raining, though the sky still looked ominously
dark and the wind was strong enough to drag the girls' skirts
sideways and blow their hair wildly.

The gatehouse led into the inner ward, a large square courtyard surrounded on all sides by lofty walls. To the south were
the kitchens, staff quarters and workshops, all built no more
than one storey high so that the sun could strike in over the
peaked roof and fall upon the garden built in the centre of the
yard.

A long, green rectangle of lawn with an apple tree at one end
and a greengage tree at the other, the garden was surrounded by
low hedges and bushes sculpted into balls and spirals. Narrow
beds ran the length of the garden, filled with white roses un-
derplanted with blue lavender and thyme. An old lady bent over
the storm-ruined roses, tying them up with some twine. She
turned her soft, crumpled face towards them as they made their
awkward progression round the courtyard, all of them carrying
bags and bundles, and craning their necks to look up at the
crenellated towers looming over them.

"A garden planted for peace," Maisie murmured, gazing at
the sweetly scented flower beds with pleasure. She was lying
on a makeshift stretcher carried by two footmen, and had been
much more comfortable since drinking a pain-killing elixir
given to Iven by the laird's old nurse. In fact, since swallowing
the elixir, Maisie had had a strange, dreamy smile on her face
and had even hummed a few bars of an old folksong as she was
carried along. Only the feverish glitter of her eyes and her scarlet cheeks showed the insidious advance of the poison through
her bloodstream.

"There's another garden behind the kitchen," Iven told her,
walking along beside her, holding her hand. "When ye are better I'll take ye there and show ye. Ye'll like it. It's full of herbs
as well as vegetables, for the laird's nurse is as skilled a skeelie
as any I've seen. She has hyssop and sage and pennyroyal

planted there, and comfrey and feverfew, and many others I do no' ken."

"Hyssop, sage, pennyroyal, feverfew," Maisie repeated vaguely. "A garden for healing. Will I ever walk there? Will I ever walk again?"

As she hummed a few more bars of music, Iven said uncomfortably, "O' course ye will," and exchanged a glance with Nina, who walked on the other side of the stretcher, Roden skipping along beside her.

"Can I go play in the garden, Mam? Please?" he asked, pulling against her hand. The old lady was regarding them with great interest, the twine falling from her hand, and he smiled at her brilliantly, for she looked like the sort of old lady that kept a box of sweetmeats in her pocket.

"No' now," Nina said absently. "Remember we are guests here, Roden."

"Aye, Mam," he answered in a long-suffering tone.

The procession rounded the garden and came into the paved area before the main part of the castle. Surrounded by a square of chains was a pyramid of rocks, a little higher than Rhiannon's knee. A raven perched on top of the cairn, head tilted, regarding them all with one bright black eye. The deep, plaintive cry of ravens echoed all round the courtyard and, glancing up, Rhiannon could see black-winged birds circling the towers far above.

"Have ye heard the tale o' the ravens o' Fettercairn?" a deep, melodious voice said at her elbow.

Rhiannon turned. An elderly man stood beside her, dressed in a black kilt under a black velvet jacket. Under the skirt he wore long black hose and black brogues with silver buckles. Only his stiff white collar and the crisscross of fine white and grey lines in the kilt broke the severity of his dress. He was clean-shaven, an unusual trait in a country where men were proud of their beards, and his short dark hair glinted with silver.

"Nay, I have no'," she answered warily.

"It is said the first laird o' Fettercairn was a page in the service of Brann o' Ravenshaw. One day, during the building of the Tower o' Ravens, Brann and his retinue came to oversee its progress. As always, Brann had his familiar with him, a large raven he called Nigrum. He had brought the raven with him in the journey from the Other World, and so it was a very auld bird but still went everywhere with Brann, sitting on his shoulder and whispering cruel nothings in his ear. Or so they said, those who served him. They also said Brann loved this bird more than his own children and indeed, as ye ken, his eldest son did in time rebel against him, and so their saying may be true."

Rhiannon did not know, but said nothing, regarding the old man gravely.

"The raven Nigrum flew from Brann's shoulder, whether because he was hungry and wished to find food, or because he was bored, who kens? Anyway, a screech o' gravenings nested nearby and saw the auld bird and came flying out to attack. My ancestor, who was then a lad o' sixteen, picked up a large rock and flung it at the gravenings, striking and killing the one which had seized the raven in its claws. Rock after rock he threw, until the gravenings fled and Brann's raven fluttered back to Brann, injured but alive."

Everyone was listening now, and the old man moved his piercing black eyes, set deeply under strong black brows, from face to face, smiling a little as he noted their interest.

"The sorcerer was most impressed with his page's quick thinking and strong arm, and knighted him then and there, naming him Sir Ferris, which means 'rock'. He then promised the lad a nestling from the raven's next breeding which, given the bird's age, was to be his last. "Ye shall stand guard over my witches' tower as ye stood guard over my raven," Brann said then, and ordered that a great castle be built to defend the approach to the tower, and that Sir Ferris be its laird and protector. The rocks Sir Ferris had thrown were gathered together and made into a cairn to mark the spot where the castle was to be built." He indicated the little pile of mossy rocks with a graceful gesture and everyone turned to gaze at it.

"Brann always had a wry sense of humour, and so he decreed the castle be named Fettercairn, for Sir Ferris and his heirs would be bound here for always, guarding the pass. Then he made a prophecy, as Brann was wont to do. He said, "As long as ravens on Fettercairn dwell, tower and castle shall never be felled." So we let the ravens nest on our towers and feed them and protect them, so that Fettercairn Castle shall always stand. They are quite tame. Look."

The old man held out his arm and whistled, and the raven on the cairn spread its wings and flew across to land on his outstretched wrist. It was an enormous, glossy black bird, with a cruel curved beak and knowing eyes. Fèlice gave a little shriek and jumped back, and everyone else exclaimed in surprise. The old man smiled and stroked the raven's back.

"But the tower did fall," Rhiannon said abruptly. She was frowning, for while the old man spoke the air had seemed to thin about her so she could hardly breathe. She had heard faint cries and screams and the clash of arms, and the sound of a woman wailing in such terrible and profound grief that every hair on Rhiannon's body had sprung erect and she had shivered with sudden acute cold. She was shivering still.

The smile faded from the old man's face. After a moment he said, rather curtly, "Aye, that is true, but then Brann the Raven also prophesied that he would outwit she who cuts the thread and live again, and that is most manifestly untrue."

He was quiet for a moment, preoccupied with thoughts that caused his thick dark brows to draw down and his mouth to twist, and then he looked at Rhiannon again and smiled. "Besides, the tower did no' really fall. It was built too well. Despite all the efforts o' the Red Guards, and close on forty years o' neglect, most o' it still stands. Happen one day it will be rebuilt and witches will study their craft there once again. If ye listen to village gossip, which I urge that ye do no', they will tell ye the witches have never really left, that one still lives somewhere in the ruins. They say they have seen lights and smelt smoke, and even seen a mysterious hooded figure in the forest, gathering herbs and mushrooms."

"Is that true?" Nina asked, raising one brow in quick interest.

The old man sighed. "We o' the Dubhslain are said to be more superstitious than most, and those o' the Fetterness Valley more superstitious than any. Ye really canna believe aught that is said in the town or valley. The winters are long, and the auld folk tell tales to amuse and frighten the young, and seek to outdo the tale that was told afore. It is all fables and fabrications, nothing more."

"The dead that walk are no' mere fabrications," Nina said. "We all saw them, and I myself went down and walked among them and tried to speak with them. And we have all heard the tales o' the lads that disappear from their beds at night. We met one who had lost her son that way and her grief was real enough."

The old man's piercing black eyes went from her face to her son's. Roden was standing quietly for once, holding on to Nina's hand and listening with great interest.

"Aye," the old man said slowly. "That at least is true."

The old lady had come out of the garden to join them and now she reached out a gentle hand to ruffle Roden's chestnut curls and stroke his cheek. "What a bonny lad," she said.

Roden submitted to the caress, though reluctantly.

The old man drew the old lady to him, tucking his arm through hers. "But I have been most remiss," he said. "What are we doing, standing here and telling dusty auld tales? Please, come in and be welcome. I am Malvern MacFerris, laird o' Fettercairn, and this is my sister-in-law Lady Evaline NicKinney, who was married to my brother who was laird afore me, and is now chatelaine o' my castle."

"Ye are most welcome," Lady Evaline said sweetly, smiling round at them all. "We do no' get visitors very often, I am afraid. I hope ye will be comfortable, and that the ghosts do no' disturb ye too much."

Everyone had begun to murmur an answer, and move towards the door, but at Lady Evaline's last words every head swivelled to look at her.

"Ghosts?" a chorus of voices repeated.

Lord Malvern looked uncomfortable. "I am sorry. My sister-in-law is getting elderly now. She was always rather a daydreamer, but in recent years I'm afraid . . ." He paused, searching for a kind way to say what he meant.

Lady Evaline turned to him reproachfully. "But Malvern, ye hear the ghosts too, I ken ye do!"

He shrugged a little and smiled. "Come in out o' the wind, my dear, and let me call Harriet for ye. Please, everyone, come in, come in. Harriet!"

At his call a big-boned, red-faced woman came bustling along the hall and took the old lady by the arm. "Time for your nap, Lady Evaline," she said firmly.

"But our guests! I must see them to their rooms and make sure all is comfortable."

"The maids can do that," Harriet said.

"But that would hardly be very hospitable." Lady Evaline looked distressed.

"Ye will see all our guests again at dinner, my dear," Lord Malvern said. "Ye must rest, else ye will be too tired to preside over the table tonight."

Lady Evaline resisted for a moment longer, her face looking more crumpled than ever, then submitted unhappily, allowing Harriet to lead her away towards the stairs.

The entrance hall was a vast, shadowy room, with large doors leading off on either side, and another set at the far end, under the stairs. The walls were hung with ancient shields and spears, stag heads, and a tarnished genealogical table adorned with swathes of black and grey tartan. A big man with greying hair and beard stood to attention a few steps away from the lord, wearing a metal breastplate and shin-guards, and a claymore strapped to his back. As Lord Malvern led the way down the hall, he fell into place a few steps behind him, his face impassive.

Footmen stood against the walls, staring straight ahead, and another man stood before the stairs, his head bowed, waiting for his orders. He was dressed in immaculate, dark livery, and his very large, very white hands were folded before him.

"Could our guests be shown to their rooms, Irving? I am sure they would like to wash and rest awhile."

"Certainly, my laird," Irving replied in a very smooth, unctuous voice. He made a gesture with one hand, and at once a skinny young woman came scurrying forward to make an awkward curtsy.

"Wilma is the chambermaid assigned to care for your needs, sir, madam," Irving said without actually looking at Nina and Iven. "If ye should require aught, please just ring the bell and she shall come to assist ye. Wilma." He jerked his head. At once Wilma bobbed another curtsy and said rather breathlessly, "If ye could come this way. Please. Sir and madam. Ladies and gentlemen."

"I hope ye will find your rooms comfortable," Lord Malvern said and, with a nod and a smile, he walked through into the next room, the armed man following silently behind.

"A laird o' the auld school," Iven said to Lewen in a low voice, as they followed the maid up the stairs. "It is usually only the prionnsachan that still keep a gillie-coise at their heels."

"What's that?" Rhiannon asked, not recognizing the word.

"A bodyguard, I suppose. Once upon a time all the lairds had one, for times were dangerous, but we have been at peace now for years and most dinna see the need for them. I ken the Mac-Seinn has one still, and the NicBride, for their lands are troubled still, but the MacThanach never does. I bet the laird has a cup-bearer too. Even the Rìgh does no' use one nowadays."

The maid Wilma cast them a curious glance over her shoulder and Iven said no more, falling back and allowing the others to exclaim over the rich, ornate tapestries and artifacts that crowded the dimly lit gallery. They were led through a veritable maze of dark, damp halls and rooms, and up another flight of stairs till at last they reached a corridor with a number of rooms opening off either side.

The footmen carried Maisie into one of the rooms and shifted her to the bed, which had been freshly made, and Iven helped Edithe hop in and sit down gratefully in a big chair by the unlit fire, Lewen finding her a footstool on which to rest her sore and swollen ankle. The maid Wilma kindled the fire deftly, kneeling on the flagstones and blowing the sparks with a pair of bellows until the kindling caught and yellow petals of flame burst open all along the sticks. She then stood and, curtsying, offered to show the others their rooms.

Landon and Cameron, both heavy-eyed and hoarse-throated, were glad to be tucked up in their beds in the room next door, but the other apprentices followed Nina and Iven into the large chamber they were to share, with views across to the waterfall and the burnt-out hulk of the tower. The room was cold, for the windows had been flung open to allow fresh air in, and the floors had been freshly scrubbed so were damp and chill underfoot. Wilma frowned at the view and drew close the windows, so that the shapes of crag and tower were obscured behind small, thick, rippled panes of glass. The room was immediately filled with a greenish gloom, for the glass was so old it tinted the air like water. Wilma knelt by the fireplace and pulled out her tinder and flint, chasing away the watery shadows with warm golden flames.

The sight pleased her. She stood up, smiling, and rubbed away the smudges of charcoal on her stiff white apron.

"Ye need no' worry about the sheets, we aired them this morning," she said proudly. "And Lady Evaline came through herself to check all was nice for ye. She picked the flowers for ye herself."

Looking at the pretty tussie-mussies laid on the pillows, white roses tied with lavender, newly opened lily-in-the-valley and silver posie thyme, Nina exclaimed with true pleasure. "That was kind o' her," she said.

"Lady Evaline loves her garden," the maid said with a sigh.

"It's a lovely wee garden, no' at all what one expects to find inside these grim grey walls," Nina answered.

"Nay," the girl agreed with a giggle, then added, "Dedrie tends the garden for my lady."

"Who is Dedrie?" Nina asked. "Is that the laird's auld nurse?"

"The auld nurse, aye," Wilma answered, "though she was never the laird's nurse. Why, she'd have to be ancient! Nay, she was nurse to the former laird's son. Lady Evaline's son."

"Lady Evaline had a son?" Nina asked, unconsciously drawing Roden to her and wrapping her arms about his shoulders. He was young enough still to press close and return the embrace.

"Aye. He died, och, a long time ago. Afore I was born."

"And that was such a long time ago," Iven teased, and the maid giggled again.

"Well, 'twas," she insisted. "I'm seventeen now. Lady Evaline's son died twenty-five years ago. He was just a bairn."

"Och, that's sad," Nina said. "How did he die?"

The maid shrugged and grimaced. "In the wars," she said vaguely. "Poor Lady Evaline, she's never got over it really."

She seemed about to say more but a sound from the corridor startled her and she blushed, dropped her eyes, fiddled with her apron, and then said with a hasty curtsy, "But if ye'll excuse me, madam, sir, I must be getting back. I'll bring ye up some jugs o' hot water so ye can wash. I hope ye'll all be comfortable."

"I'm sure we shall," Nina said and Wilma went out, bobbing another curtsy at the door.

"Indeed, I think the Rìgh should be paying ye, no' me," Iven said. "Ye are far better than me at loosening people's tongues, my love."

Nina smiled a little ruefully. "Happen it's just habit," she said. "Though, Iven, are ye implying . . . do ye think we are upon the Rìgh's work here?"

Iven hesitated, then shrugged. "Happen we are," he said slowly. "Though I do no' ken why I feel so. My skin is all a-twitch, though. That crofter's wife last night and her talk o' cursed witches—and she called upon the Truth, remember? Maxims like that, they stay in the language, they can be hard to shake, we all ken that . . . but still, she said it fervently, as if the words meant something to her."

Nina nodded but raised her finger to her mouth, casting a quick glance at the door. Iven nodded and turned to smile at Rhiannon, Fèlice, Lewen and Rafferty, all warming themselves by the fire and listening with interest. "Go on, bairns, go find your own fires," he said cheerfully. "Have ye naught better to do than hog all the warmth?"

Fèlice dimpled at him and moved away from the fire, shaking out her skirts so the hot material would not burn her legs. "We do no' ken where our own fires are," she said.

"Go find one!" Iven said, flapping his hand at her. "There seemed to be plenty o' room in this castle, there must be some way Nina and I can be rid o' ye. We need some adult time, away from all ye young things."

Fèlice sketched a curtsy. "O' course, we understand. Shall we take Roden for ye?" she said cheekily.

"Now there's an idea," Iven said, his blue eyes kindling.

"No!" Nina said and then coloured as everyone, including her son, looked at her in surprise. "I'm sorry. I just want to keep Roden near me. Until we are out o' the valley."

"Och, Mam," Roden said in disgust.

"I'm sorry, laddie. It's just . . ." she trailed away, not wanting to put it in words, her hands unconsciously tightening their grasp about her son's shoulders.

There was a knock on the door. Iven raised one eyebrow at

his wife and sauntered over to open the door. After a low murmured conversation, he turned his head and called to Nina, "*Leannan,* it is Dedrie, the skeelie I told ye about. She has been to see Maisie."

"Och, ask her to come in, please, and tell me how Maisie does," Nina said eagerly. "I've been worried indeed."

Iven stood back and held open the door for a small woman dressed in a crisp white apron and cap, with a heavily laden basket on her arm. Her eyes were brown, her hair was brown, and her dress was brown, her cheeks as round and rosy as apples. She came in with a quick, supple step, looking round her with great interest. As her eyes fell on Roden, both her step and her smile faltered.

"Och, no, a laddie," she whispered.

"Aye, a laddie," Nina answered stiffly, her own welcoming smile fading. "What o' it?"

"Has no-one told ye?" Dedrie said, her face creasing in anxiety. "Och, my lady has no' seen him, has she?"

"Your lady? Do ye mean Lady Evaline? Aye, she saw us all arrive. She seemed quite taken with my boy." Nina's voice was still stiff and offended.

Dedrie sighed. "Aye, well, she would be, wouldna she?" She put down her basket blindly, groped in her sleeve for a handkerchief and wiped her eyes.

Nina regarded her curiously, while Roden looked red and uncomfortable. All the conversation in the room had stopped. Dedrie was oblivious of their curious glances. She blew her nose thoroughly, tucked the handkerchief away, and went to kneel by Nina's side, reaching out a rather tremulous hand to touch Roden's ruffled curls.

"Ye should no' bide here," she said. "This is no' a happy house. Ye should pack up your things and go."

"Are ye saying we are no' welcome here?" Nina replied in a cold voice.

Dedrie shook her head impatiently. "Nay, nay, I'm saying this is no' the place to bring a young boy. Particularly one with red hair and dark eyes. Our boy Rory, he had hair this colour. Happen a wee redder, though it's been so long, it's hard to remember." She sighed and took out her handkerchief again, wiping her eyes.

"Rory was Lady Evaline's son?" Nina asked, her voice and manner softer now.

Dedrie nodded.

"Her son that died?"

The nurse nodded again.

"Ye are afraid the sight o' my lad will hurt your mistress? Stir up unhappy memories?"

"Aye, my lady," Dedrie said, and hesitated for a long moment as if wanting to say more but unable to formulate the words.

"I'm sorry for that, truly I am, but what are we to do? Maisie is sorely hurt, ye've seen her, ye ken she should no' be travelling, and besides, Laird Malvern says the road is blocked. We canna go on until it is cleared."

Dedrie looked up, alarm on her face. "The road? Blocked?"

"Aye, that's what he said. Why? Do ye mean it isna blocked?"

"Nay, nay, I just . . . if my laird says the road is blocked, o' course it is. I do no' go away from the castle much these days, I wouldna ken about the road." She stopped and took a corner of her stiff, starched apron and began to pleat it between her fingers. After a moment she said awkwardly, "I do no' wish to alarm ye but I am wondering if ye have heard the tales . . . did ye come past the town on your way here?"

"Nay, the town had closed its gates for the night and would no' open for us," Iven replied, a trace of anger in his voice.

Dedrie seemed to consider. "Happen ye have no' heard then. I wish I did no' need to say this, but my conscience would no' rest easy if I did no' tell ye. It is no' safe here for young boys. Lads—many lads—have gone missing from hereabouts . . . for years now. If I were ye, I'd be on my way just as fast as ye can."

"But surely we are safe here, in the laird's own castle?" Iven said. "This place is a fortress!"

"Nowhere is safe," she answered harshly.

"Lady Evaline's son . . . is that how he died?" Nina asked gently. "Did he go missing too?"

Dedrie hesitated, then said roughly, "He was the first to die."

Nina would have asked more, but the nursemaid got up, blowing her nose defiantly. "I have done what I can for the lassie. They are nasty bites, deep and unclean, but I have washed them with water boiled with adder's tongue and St. John's Wort, and bound on a poultice o' bruised wintergreen, a herb which grows freely in these parts and which is very effective for healing open wounds. I have given her a hot tea I made myself, with feverfew and powdered willow tree bark for the pain and the fever, and chamomile and valerian to help her sleep, and devil's bit to expel the poison. I gave my borage syrup to the lads, washed down with a dose of elderflower wine, with peppermint and vervain in a basin for them to steam their faces. The lass with the sprained ankle, I made a poultice o' elder leaves, trefoil and figwort. An afternoon's rest and she'll be walking by nightfall, I promise ye."

"Thank ye," Nina said, sounding a little dazed. "So when . . ."

Dedrie snorted. "There is naught wrong with the laddies that a little rest and warmth willna help, but the lass . . . rattling round in a caravan willna do her any good, she's in pain and shall be for some time. I did no' wish to give her too much o' the poppy and nightshade syrup, for it shall give her nightmares, and too much can be dangerous, but if ye find ye must be gone quickly, I will give ye a bottle o' it and it shall help her endure."

Nina nodded. The blood had ebbed away from her face, leaving her eyes black and glittering. She looked down at Dedrie, saying in a constricted voice quite unlike her usual melodious tones, "Will ye ask about the road for us, Dedrie?"

"Aye, that I will," the nursemaid answered. "I will come back at dusk, to change the lassie's poultice. I will speak with ye again then."

"Thank ye," Nina said.

As soon as Dedrie had curtsied and taken her basket of medicines away, Nina turned to the others. "Go and rest, my dears," she said. "I think we will be setting out again in the morning, Eà willing, and so ye should enjoy a soft bed and warm fire while ye can."

They all nodded and murmured, without a smile or a joke between them, and went quietly to their own rooms, where the dancing flames of a freshly kindled fire helped, to some degree, to drive away the sudden chill that had shadowed them.

The Nursemaid

R hiannon woke slowly from a strange dream.
She had been in the castle garden, sitting under the apple tree, watching a young boy dressed in stiff, formal clothes rolling a hoop along the pavement with a stick. He had run to her, laughing, and she had held out her arms, gathering him in close for a kiss and a hug. At first she had thought he was Roden, but when she held him away, she saw it was some other boy. He had tugged at her hand and, smiling, she had got up and followed him. As they passed through the great door into the castle hall, chill air had struck at her, the bee-humming sunshine behind her swallowed. There was a confusion of noise, shouting, steel crashing, screams of pain, and she was running, the little boy's hand in hers. "All will be well," someone whispered. "I'll be back soon."

Then she had been kneeling in a dark, icy space, stone walls pressing close all around. Weeping, she had beaten her fists on the stone, screaming to someone to release her. "So cold," the little boy sobbed. "Mama, I'm so cold."

Small, cold hands touched her face. Somewhere ravens were crying. "So cold," a voice whimpered in her ear. "Please, I'm so cold."

Rhiannon woke, tears on her cheeks. It took a while for her shivering to ease. She rubbed her damp eyes, realising she was lying in a warm bed under a soft quilt, with firelight playing on tapestry-hung walls. She sat up. Rain drummed on the diamond-paned windows and the sky was dark. Ravens were calling weirdly. Fèlice was sitting in a hipbath by the fire, her hair twisted up into tight knots all over her head, washing her arms and softly humming. Rhiannon watched her for a while, unable to completely shake away the cobwebs of the dream. There had been a boy, she remembered, a crying boy. She shivered.

Fèlice looked across. "Och, ye've woken at last. Ye've slept all afternoon."

Rhiannon was surprised. "Have I?"

"Aye."

"I was exhausted."

"Ye slept like the dead. No' even the servants bringing in the bath roused ye. I was debating whether to try and wake ye for dinner or let ye sleep on."

"The dead do no' sleep in this valley," Rhiannon said.

"Ouch! Must ye remind me? I was just beginning to feel a wee bit better. Come, have a bath and borrow some o' my perfume. That'll take your mind off such gruesome things."

"I had a dream . . ." Rhiannon clutched the coverlet to her chin.

"What kind o' dream?"

Rhiannon shook her head. "Gone now. Something about cold hands touching me . . ."

"Gruesomer and gruesomer. Mind ye, this castle's creepy enough to give anyone nightmares. I'm glad we're leaving tomorrow, even if it does mean poor Maisie shall be all rattled about." Fèlice stood up, water streaming off her, rosy in the firelight. She shivered, clambered out of the bath, and hurriedly wrapped a bath-sheet about her. "Come and have a bath, and I'll wash your hair for ye," she said winningly. "Do ye want me to put it into ringlets?"

"Is that why ye have all those knots in your hair?" Rhiannon climbed reluctantly out of bed.

Fèlice put one hand up to her head. "O' course. Dinna tell me ye've never seen anyone with their hair papered afore?"

Rhiannon shook her head.

"Gracious me, where have ye sprung from, my sweet?"

Rhiannon's mouth shut firmly, but Fèlice had no real interest in an answer. She went on gaily, "I'll do it for ye now, if ye like."

"Doesna it hurt?"

"Well, yes," Fèlice admitted. "It does make my scalp ache a

wee, and I canna lie down and sleep like ye did very comfortably. But it's all the fashion, ye ken. The Banrìgh and the Keybearer both have the curliest hair ye ever did see, apparently,
and now it is all the craze to have curls too."

"I canna," Rhiannon said. "I must go and see to Blackthorn.
She shallna like being confined within these high stone walls."

"Ye canna go now, it's close on dusk already," Fèlice said in
alarm. "The laird keeps country hours here. We were told to be
ready for dinner at sunset and it's nearly that now, look at the sky."

Rhiannon looked out at the bruise-coloured sky, hesitating.

"Do no' fear, Lewen was going out to check on the horses
when the servants came with my bath. He would've come to
rouse ye if he was concerned, ye ken he would."

Rhiannon bit her lip but submitted, knowing Fèlice was
right. She stripped off her chemise and stepped into the bath,
which was cooling fast. Dressed in petticoats and pantaloons,
Fèlice brought her soap, but stopped abruptly at the sight of
Rhiannon's wrists, which were roughly and inexpertly bandaged, the cloth stained with seeping blood.

"Eà forbid! Rhiannon! Why do ye cut yourself so? It's horrible. Look at your poor wrists. Have ye done it every night?
Why? I do no' understand."

Rhiannon said nothing at first, but she liked Fèlice and found
to her amazement that she wanted Fèlice to like her too. This
was a new experience for Rhiannon, and it caused her to blurt
out unhappily, "It's the only way I ken how to . . ." She
searched for a word. "Quiet down . . . the dark walkers. They
demand blood."

"Ye said that afore, the dark walkers. What does it mean?
Ghosts? Ye think ghosts want to drink your blood?" There was
incredulity in Fèlice's voice.

Rhiannon tried again. "Dark walkers the things that lurk . . .
evil spirits . . . unhappy spirits . . . they hungry . . . they
angry . . . they hunt at night, want blood. Spill blood, they
drink, go away."

Fèlice shook her head. "Who told ye all this? It's rubbish.
Ghosts do no' want to drink your blood. It's naught but an auld
faery tale."

"Happen dark walkers no' ghosts," Rhiannon said. She searched for the best word. "Happen they gods."

Fèlice stared at her, then came and knelt by the bath, taking Rhiannon's sore, abused wrists in her hands. "None o' it is true, Rhiannon, I promise ye. Whoever told ye this was tricking ye. Wounding yourself like this does ye no good. Ye will make yourself ill and scar yourself, to no avail. Please do no' do it any longer."

Rhiannon looked stubborn. "Must. I see dark walkers at the edges, everywhere. They want blood."

"Must it be yours?" Fèlice asked helplessly.

Rhiannon looked surprised. "Nay. Any blood will do. Only I have no time to hunt. Ride, ride, ride all day, all night, and no eating meat, no hunting. So only my blood left."

"I will find ye something else tonight," Fèlice swore. "If no', ye can cut me."

Rhiannon looked at Fèlice's soft white wrists, with the blood pulsing gently through a delicate tracery of blue veins. "Och, nay," she said. "I couldna do that."

"That's good," Fèlice said rather tremulously. "Because I really do no' want ye to. We'll find something else, much as it hurts me to wantonly kill another living creature."

"Why?" Rhiannon was perplexed.

Fèlice shook her head, all her tight ringlets dancing. "Where did ye come from, Rhiannon? Do ye ken naught about the Coven?"

Rhiannon set her jaw. "No' much," she admitted angrily.

"Well, a conversation for another day. We're late and ye're still very grimy. Let me wash your hair and bandage your wrists and make ye bonny, and we'll worry about all this serious stuff tomorrow."

Rhiannon submitted to Fèlice washing her hair and then tying it up into hard little knots that made her feel as if her hair was being pulled out by the roots. Fèlice then laid her hot little hands over Rhiannon's head, explaining as she did so that this was one sorceress trick she had learnt at court, to hasten the drying of the hair. "Otherwise it can take hours to dry, when our hair is all so long."

Rhiannon was amazed at this magic trick, and so Fèlice

amused her by causing the candles on the mantelpiece to flicker out, then spring back into life again, and then warmed the cooling water by swirling her finger round and round. "Surely ye must've seen such tricks afore?" she asked. "The challenge o' the flame and the void is an elementary exercise—any novice can do it. Can ye no' do it yourself?"

"I do no' think so," Rhiannon answered.

"Have ye had no lessons in magic at all?"

Rhiannon shook her head.

"Nina must think ye have Talent though, else she'll no' be taking ye to the Theurgia," Fèlice said thoughtfully. "O' course, ye've tamed a flying horse and no lass has ever done that afore."

Rhiannon smiled at the thought of Blackthorn. She hoped her horse was safe and comfortable in that great, draughty stable. She stared at the candles on the mantelpiece and imagined putting them out with the power of her mind alone. Nothing happened. She scowled.

"It takes time," Fèlice said, dressing herself in a long dusty-pink evening gown and hanging a delicate, sparkling necklace about her slim neck. "Ye need to learn how to draw upon the One Power, and that is no easy task."

"What's the One Power?"

Fèlice hesitated. "It is the life-force o' the universe, the energy that exists inside all matter, whether it be stone or tree, star or moon, wind or water. It is the wheel that drives the motion o' time and the seasons. It is in us too, our soul or our spirit, and when we die, our life-force dissolves again in the world's life-force, bringing with it all the gifts o' wisdom we have acquired in our life, to be born again in another shape, another time."

She fell silent and Rhiannon was quiet also, thinking.

"What about ghosts?" she asked after a moment. "Why do the spirits o' ghosts no' dissolve?"

"I'm no' sure," Fèlice admitted. "Happen they are no' ready to go."

Rhiannon thought she could understand that. She too had a hunger for life that she could never imagine being satiated. If she was to die now, in her youth, before ever having had all the things she wanted, would she not cling to her empty shell of a body with fierce hands, refusing to let go?

Fèlice noticed her shiver. "Hop out now, that water's getting cold and I do no' want to use all my energy keeping it warm for ye."

Rhiannon climbed out obediently and huddled herself into the warmed bath-sheet Fèlice held ready.

"So these witch-tricks o' yours, they take energy, just like running or fighting?" she asked.

Fèlice nodded. "O' course. Working magic is very exhausting, and no' just for the witch. The greater the magic, the more energy ye draw upon—and no' just from your own reserves but everything around ye, even other people if ye are no' careful. That is why witches must be taught to be canny in their use o' the One Power, for misuse can be very dangerous. That is why we go to the Theurgia." She gave herself a little shake, setting her ringlets dancing. "But all this talk is very boring. Let's let your hair out and see what it looks like."

With Fèlice's help, Rhiannon put on her green silk dress, the other girl smoothing away the creases with her witch-warm hands. Then Fèlice took out the papers from her hair, Rhiannon biting the inside of her mouth to stop crying out in pain. By the time Fèlice had finished fussing, Rhiannon's hair hung in long, dusky ringlets to the small of her back, and her mouth and cheeks had been subtly rouged.

Looking at herself in the mirror, a device she had never before seen, Rhiannon smiled, and for the very first time saw the flash of her dimples in her cheeks. They surprised her and, after a few more tentative smiles at herself in the mirror, pleased her. The face that looked back at her looked nothing like the stern, unhappy face that she had sometimes glimpsed in the satyricorns' lake.

"Well, ye scrub up well," Fèlice said, sounding very pleased with herself. "Though the dress is a wee bit too tight for modesty. If ye were no' so tall, I'd lend ye something o' mine."

Rhiannon stood up, once again conscious of how much bigger she was than the dainty dark-haired girl beside her. Fèlice smiled up at her. "Here, let me fold down your sleeves to hide those bandages. We do no' want anyone to see ye've been wounding yourself. Now, look, are ye no' bonny? Let us go show the lads!"

Together they left their room, going next door to Nina and Iven's room, where they could hear the sound of voices and low laughter. Rhiannon felt eagerness rise in her. She felt so much better after her sleep and a bath; it had made her realise how tired she must have been, and how very cranky and bad-tempered. She felt sorry now, and resolved to smile at Lewen as soon as she saw him.

But although Lewen looked up when she came into the room, he only coloured and looked away when she smiled at him. Rhiannon scowled at his averted profile and smiled at Rafferty instead, who went scarlet and jumped to his feet, saying incoherently, "Ye look bonny indeed, Rhiannon, like a narcissus. All slim and green, I mean, not narcissistic. No' that ye're green, o' course, except in the dress. I just mean . . . ye look bonny. Like a lily-of-the-valley." He gulped and managed to stop himself, and Rhiannon laughed and let him pull out a chair for her next to Nina.

Both Cameron and Landon were there also, exclaiming over the efficacy of Dedrie's herbal remedies, and telling Nina she must get the recipe for the elderflower wine.

"It was the most delicious thing I've tasted, and cleared my head something marvellous," Cameron said. "I feel so much better now."

"Aye, happen so, but drinking too much o' that willna help any," Nina said pointedly, looking at the glass of whisky in Cameron's hand.

He flushed but drank a mouthful defiantly, saying, "Och, my granddad said a dram o' whisky is the best thing for any ailment. That's why they call it the water o' life."

"And your granddad was a healer, was he?"

"Well, nay, but he lived to be sixty-four years auld," Cameron said defensively.

"Well, my lad, let's hope ye live to be a lot aulder," Iven said, taking the cup out of Cameron's hand. "Do no' forget we are guests in this castle and I doubt the laird wishes drunk and rowdy young men at his table."

"I'm no' drunk," Cameron said angrily.

"No' yet," Iven answered, still smiling. "But I'll wager ye two gold crowns that Dedrie's elderflower wine is as potent as it is effective, and ye look like ye've been drinking it all afternoon."

"I had a few glasses," Cameron replied, on his dignity. "To clear my head."

"To muddle your head," Iven teased.

"I must give this wine a taste," Rafferty said. "Any left, Cameron?"

"O' course! I dinna drink the whole damn bottle."

"Well, when we come back up after dinner I'll come and have a swig," Rafferty said.

"Maybe I should have custody o' this famous bottle o' wine?" Nina said. "I'm sure Dedrie did no' mean for ye all to get sozzled on it."

"Ye just want it for yourself," Rafferty said teasingly.

"No' I," Nina said. "My father was both a fire-eater and a drunkard, a combination that does no' work well. I will drink Isabeau's goldensloe wine at Midsummer, but naught else, ever."

Her words cast a pall of sobriety over the room. She looked up and smiled. "Do no' fear, he did no' burn himself to death or anything awful like that. He just could no' work his trade, and he was a jongleur to the bone, it hurt him to have to leave the travelling life. Luckily my brother Dide had a house where he could stay and do his best to drink the cellars dry. He died comfortably in his bed when Roden was a babe."

"Thank Eà for that!" Fèlice said. "I was imagining the worst."

Nina smiled. "I think my da would probably have preferred to go out in a blaze o' glory. Dying in bed is no' the way a jongleur wishes to go."

"What is it about this place that makes us keep talking about death?" Fèlice wondered. "Canna we find aught else to talk about?"

"I was happy talking about the wine," Cameron said. Fèlice laughed and moved to sit down next to him by the fire.

Nina smiled at Rhiannon. "Ye look the very picture o' courtly fashion. I fear it is wasted on the laird o' Fettercairn. Did ye notice he wears his hair short and his chin clean-shaven? He wears the fashion o' thirty years ago. He willna like all the long curls and soft clothes o' today."

She cast a rueful hand down her own gown, a low-cut, cap-sleeved orange velvet dress that brought out fiery tones in her long chestnut hair. Round her neck she had clasped an amber and gold necklace. Roden stood between her legs, squirming and protesting as she tried to comb out his unruly curls. He was neatly dressed in a clean white shirt with a flowing collar and full sleeves, under an embroidered brown velvet jerkin.

"If the laird willna like it, why do I have to wear it, Mam?" the boy complained, tugging at his collar. "It's tight. It itches. I dinna like it. Ow! Mam!"

"Sorry!" Nina freed the comb from his hair and tried again.

"Please, Mam? I dinna want to."

"We're guests here, Roden, and must mind our manners. I canna have ye coming down to the drawing room all in a tangle, and wearing a shabby auld shirt."

"I dinna like this one. I want to take it off!" He pulled violently at his collar and a button pinged free.

"Roden!" Nina sighed in exasperation and pulled him onto her lap, as Lulu uncurled her long, dexterous tail, retrieved the button from under the chair, and gave it back to Nina, all without moving from the table, where she sat eating her way through a bowl of small green apples.

"Can I have my sewing kit too, please, Lulu?" Nina said, twisting Roden round so she could see where the button had come loose. Obligingly Lulu leapt across the room, rummaged through one of the bags, and brought back a little floral-topped basket. Roden had become engrossed in looking at Nina's necklace and so his long-suffering mother was able to deftly sew back the button without any more trouble.

As Rhiannon sat down next to them, he turned and showed her the pendant. Frozen inside the large amber stone was an orange-and-black butterfly.

"Mam says its thousands o' years auld," he whispered. "It must've been sipping at the sap o' the tree and got stuck, and slowly the tree-sap flowed all over it and set hard, and the butterfly was trapped inside. We do no' have butterflies like this here in Eileanan, Mam says. This necklace came over with the

First Coven. From the Other World, ye ken. So it's no' just thousands o' years auld, it's from millions and millions o' miles away! Is that no' amazing?"

As Rhiannon nodded in agreement, Nina turned to her and smiled, dropping a kiss on Roden's curly head. "He loves this necklace," she said. "It belonged to my grandmother. I do no' ken where she got it from, but I remember her telling me the story when I was just a bairn. I always loved it too."

"It's beautiful," Rhiannon said, putting her hand up to her bare neck. For the first time in days she thought of her necklace of teeth and bones, hidden away inside her saddlebags, and felt a cold shudder of revulsion. Her face must have reflected her feelings, for Nina's brows contracted and she leant forward, her eyes asking a question. Rhiannon shook her head and tried to smile, pushing away the memory forcefully. She was not a satyricorn anymore, she told herself. She would throw the necklace away the first chance she got.

The door opened and Edithe limped in. She had put her hair into ringlets too, and was wearing a very striking dress of gold lace, with a beautifully worked amulet hanging on a long gold chain round her neck.

Cameron whistled. "Going all out, Edithe! Trying to impress the laird?"

"What, with this auld thing?" she replied coolly, though the colour rose in her cheeks. "No' at all. I only brought a few clothes, we were no' allowed to bring more than a trunk each, as ye ken. The material o' this dress is so fine, it folds very small and doesna take up much space." She twirled about, holding the skirt so the material glimmered in the dim glow of the candles.

"Well, ye look mighty grand," Cameron said.

Edithe smiled and thanked him, genuine pleasure on her face.

"A daffodil, a rose and a lily," Landon said. "The spirits o' spring." A thought struck him and he groped in his coat pocket for his notebook and the disgracefully chewed quill. Finding he had left them in his everyday coat, his face fell, but Iven tossed him a scroll of paper and a quill, and it lit up again. He went to the desk, found an ink-bottle and began to scribble, his handwriting looking like an insect had fallen into the ink and managed to scrabble its way free.

There was a soft knock on the door. Lewen got up and opened it, to let in the nursemaid Dedrie. She came in briskly, looking with approval at Edithe and saying, "Och, your foot is all better, I see. That's good. And ye lads? A lot more colour in your cheeks this evening, I'm glad to see."

"I think that may be due to the elderflower wine," Nina said rather apologetically, putting Roden down so she could rise to her feet. "Cameron has taken rather a liking to it."

Dedrie smiled. "He wouldna be the first young man to sneak a few extra glasses o' it. It is delicious indeed, and will do him no harm. No' even a headache in the morn."

"I must have the recipe!" Cameron cried. "Dear, dear Dedrie, will ye no' write it down for me?"

"I canna write, sir. But if ye like, I can tell ye the recipe, which is simple enough, and ye can write it down yourself."

As Cameron thanked her exuberantly, Nina said to her softly, "Were ye never taught to write nor read, Dedrie? Do they no' have a school here?"

"No' since the fall o' the witches' tower," the nursemaid answered stiffly. "That was nigh on fifty years ago, when I was but a bairn. There has been no school since then, nor any healers, which, Truth kens, we have need o' here. That is why I set myself to gathering what skill I could in herb-lore and healing, since there was no-one else to do it."

"I will let the Coven ken," Nina promised. "Ye have no need o' a healer, for ye clearly ken your craft well, but the bairns need a school, and Eà kens ye need a good exorcist!"

She spoke lightly, but Dedrie did not smile. "What do we need a school for?" she said bitterly. "There are no bairns left to teach."

Nina's smile faded. "Happen there will be in the future," she said gently. "Eà willing."

Dedrie looked up at her. "My lady, I would no' be so quick to throw around your witch-words, if I were ye."

"Ye are the second person to say so to me," Nina said, drawing herself up to her full height, her face stern. "Why so?"

Dedrie looked away, the rosy apples of her cheeks darkening.

"Witches have brought naught but trouble to Fettercairn," she said roughly. "I mean ye no disrespect, my lady, I ken you are a sorceress and I am sure ye mean well. But . . . we have long memories here, and Fettercairn has no' been well served by witches. There are those that will mislike ye for your powers, and it would be wisest no' to remind them."

"But why are witches so disliked? What have they done?"

"Och, it was grand in the auld days, when the Tower was strong and people came from everywhere to study here," Dedrie said. "We were a rich valley then, and able to put up with the wildness o' the students and the arrogance o' the sorcerers for we had money in our pocket. But then the Red Guards came and burnt down the Tower and put all the witches to the sword, and anyone who protested was killed too, without hesitation."

"They bided here in the castle, the soldiers, and no-one in the valley could mumble a witch-word in their sleep without them hearing it. We soon learnt to mind our tongues, we did. And the Seeker walked among us and told us all the wickedness the witches had done, under our noses all the time, and promised we would be rewarded for keeping faith with the blessed Banrìgh, as she was called. So we did what we were told, and it was true, we all prospered better than ever afore, for the Banrìgh came to live in Ravenshaw, at the blue castle by the sea, and needed guards and servants and food—and we are close to the blue castle here, only two days' ride away.

"But then the witch-rebels came and attacked Fettercairn Castle, and our laird was killed and his son too. Since then it is has been a cold, unhappy place, filled with ghosts, and each year it only grows worse, so that no-one dares put their nose outside their doors after dusk. Ye've seen the walking dead, I ken, and heard the tales o' robbed graves and murdered children. All o' that has happened since the witch-loving rebels stormed the castle and killed our laird. It is said the witches have long memories, and will no' forgive or forget our support o' Maya the Blessed."

"The people o' Fetterness blame the witches? But that makes no sense! Why would the Coven rob graves and murder bairns? That is ridiculous."

Dedrie shrugged. "If it was no' for them, the auld laird would still be alive, and our dear Rory too."

Nina was silent, though her black eyes glittered with anger under her knotted brows.

Dedrie looked at her appealingly. "So ye see, they do no' like witches here, and though it is mostly foolishness and superstition, ye canna blame them. I do no' mean that ye should hide what ye are, it is too late for that, but just . . . mind your words. Words can jab as sharp as any thorn and, when the wound is already deep, cause fresh blood to flow."

"That is true," Nina said evenly. "I must admit I mislike hearing ye call upon the Truth. That was one hypocrisy I thought never to hear again."

Dedrie went scarlet.

"Enough!" Nina said, taking a quick step away. "I heed your warning and thank ye for it. I will mind my tongue. Tell me, how does Maisie? I sat with her a while and she seemed to sleep easy enough. I did no' dare remove the poultices to see the wounds, no' wanting to undo your good work."

"She does well. She is young and strong and will heal quickly. There will be scars, there's naught I can do about that, but the one on her face is only small and will no' mar her too much."

"Will she be well enough to ride out tomorrow?"

Dedrie pleated the edge of her apron. "I fear the road shall no' be cleared in time, my lady. It would be dangerous to try and leave afore the tree is taken away."

Nina regarded her with frowning eyes. "Happen Iven and I shall ride out tomorrow morn and inspect the road for ourselves," she said silkily.

"As ye please, my lady."

"Thank ye for enquiring."

"No' at all, my lady." Dedrie curtsied, then said, with colour again rising in her plump cheeks, "My lady, if I may be so bold . . . happen your laddie would rather have his dinner up here, on a tray? I've already asked the kitchen to bring up some broth for the poor wee lass. It would be no trouble for them to bring up some more for the boy. 'Tis just . . . my laird is rather auld-fashioned in his ways, he has had no bairns o' his own, he is no' much used to their ways . . ."

Nina hesitated. "Normally I'd agree like a shot," she said. "Roden is no' good at formal dinners. But . . ."

"Och, please, Mam?" Roden cried. "I wouldna have to wear this bloody shirt then!"

"Roden!" Nina cried. She cast a vexed glance at Iven, who shrugged and held up his hands.

"If ye like, I could stay here with the lad?" Dedrie said. "I'd like to stay close to the lass too, her fever still worries me."

"I want to keep my laddie near me," Nina said, almost inaudibly. "I'm afraid . . ."

Dedrie nodded. "Aye. I understand. I'll have a care for him, though, my lady, I promise." There was a fierce note of passion in her voice.

There was a long pause. Just before it grew embarrassing, Lewen bent his head and coughed into his hand. "Och, I fear I've caught Cameron's cold," he said. "Do ye think I could be excused from dinner too, Nina? I really am no' much good at formal dinners, either, and I do no' want to cough all over my laird."

Nina looked relieved. "Very well. O' course. Happen ye feel well enough to sit up with Roden for a wee while and tell him some stories afore he goes to bed?"

"Yippee!" Roden shouted. "Lewen, will ye tell me some o' the tales from when your *dai-dein* was a rebel with the Rìgh? Please?"

Lewen grinned at Roden. "Sure!"

Dedrie was frowning but when Nina turned back to her, one eyebrow raised, she nodded her head, smoothing down her crumpled apron with work-reddened hands. "Sure, and that's a happy solution for everyone," she said. "Happen the young man can help me with the lassie too. I thank ye all. My lady . . . my lady forgets sometimes, ye ken. It is no' good for her to be reminded o' the past. She is happy enough, in her own way, if she does no' remember."

Nina nodded, her dark eyes softening with sympathy. "It is a terrible thing, to lose a child."

"Aye," the nurse said and, for one moment, crushed her apron between her two large, red hands. Then she smiled ruefully, smoothed it down again, and moved towards the door,

which Iven opened for her. Just before she crossed the thresh-
old, she turned back and regarded them all with those troubled
dark eyes, at such variance with her round, rosy cheeks and
brisk step.

"Ye'll all stay close, won't ye? Fettercairn's a big place, and
very auld. Ye willna go wandering about, will ye, or play any
silly games like hide-and-seek?"

Rafferty and Cameron exchanged mischievous glances and
Fèlice had to bite back a giggle, but they all agreed solemnly
that they would stay close to their rooms.

"Och, good," Dedrie said. "I wouldna want aught to happen
to ye. Wait here, I'll send Wilma to direct ye. She willna be but
a moment."

The door shut behind her.

"What a weird auld lady," Fèlice said. "I swear my blood ran
cold when she said 'stay close', with *such* a meaningful look.
What do ye think she's afraid will happen to us?"

"Ye might get lost and spend the rest o' your life wandering
the halls o' Fettercairn, looking for a way out," Rafferty said
solemnly.

"Happen they have dungeons. Or an oubliette," Cameron
said. "Ye could fall in and no-one would ken where ye were.
Someone would find ye in a hundred years, naught but a skele-
ton wearing a rose-coloured gown."

"Happen the ghosts would get ye," Roden said in his high,
treble voice. "Oooooooooooooooooooh, ooooooooooooooooooo-
ooh." He pulled his shirt up over his head and ran round the
room, wailing and flapping his arms.

Fèlice shuddered. "Enough!"

"Aye, that's enough, laddie," Nina said. "Ye can go and get out
o' your good shirt now. I just wish I hadna asked for it to be
ironed. Look at ye! Ye're grubby already. Ten minutes on your
back, and ye look like ye've slept in it. I dinna ken how ye do it."

Roden whopped with joy, dragged the hated shirt over his
head and flung it on the ground. Lulu leapt on top of it, jumping up and down, howling with glee. Laughing, Roden joined
her, the little bag of muslin he wore about his neck bouncing up
and down on his thin chest.

"Roden!" Nina cried in exasperation. "Ye've got your boots

on! Look at it now. It'll have to be washed again. Why do ye do these things?"

"I don't have to go to dinner!" Roden sang. "Yippee!"

"We'll go and check on the horses," Lewen said, "and give them a bit o' a walk in the grass, then have dinner just the two o' us."

"And a story."

"Sure, and a story."

"Ten stories!"

"Three," Lewen compromised. "And only if ye do no' give me any cheek!"

"I wouldna do that," Roden said in all sincerity, his eyes wide. "Would I, Mam?"

"Never," she said with a smile, and drew close to Lewen so she could thank him.

"I do no' wish to upset anyone, but I canna be easy about leaving Roden with a stranger," she said softly. "I ken I'm probably over-anxious but all these tales we've been hearing . . . and those poor ensorcelled corpses . . . I just canna be easy in my mind."

"Och, that's grand," Lewen said. "I'm happy to have a quiet night by the fire. *I* have no desire to get myself all fancied up."

He caught Rhiannon's eye and looked away, and she turned her back, feeling unaccountably snubbed. She smoothed down her green silk, shook back her ringlets, and smiled at Rafferty, who shielded his eyes, saying, "All this beauty, I am blinded!"

Rhiannon did not glance at Lewen again as she allowed Rafferty to show her out of the room.

The Great Hall

The maid Wilma was waiting anxiously outside to show them down to the dining room. They went down two-by-two, and were shown into a huge, gloomy room panelled from floor to ceiling in wood so dark it was almost black. Each lofty wall was crowded with the stuffed heads of dead animals—stags, hinds, boars, sabre-leopards, snow-lions, woolly bears, hoar-weasels—their glass eyes shining awfully in the dull flicker of the iron chandelier suspended from a chain in the centre of the ceiling.

Nina's step faltered as she took in the sight of all the disembodied heads and antlers, and Fèlice made a face. Rhiannon looked round in interest. She had never seen the taxidermist's art before but she understood the desire to display such trophies of one's hunting prowess.

In the centre of the room was a long table spread with a yellowing linen tablecloth and decorated with ornate silver candlesticks and an enormous silver epergne. Lord Malvern sat at one end, looking with displeasure at his watch, and Lady Evaline sat at the other, her face unhappy. There was an old man wearing round eyeglasses sitting on her right hand, and a thin, brown, drably dressed woman sitting on her left, fiddling with her fork. Another elderly man with thin, gnarled fingers and anxious, grey eyes sat a little further along, a middle-aged man with the same grey eyes sitting beside him. All the other guests looked apprehensive, and Lord Malvern was frowning heavily, two white dents driven down from his hooked nose to the sides of his mouth.

"I'm sorry, are we late?" Nina said, crossing the room swiftly.

"Your maid's fault, no doubt," Lord Malvern said, standing up and bowing stiffly.

"Nay, I'm afraid we were all rather tired and slow to get ready. I am sorry."

"No matter," Lord Malvern said.

The seneschal Irving was there in his sombre livery, carrying a white-tipped stick in one hand. He bowed to Nina and lightly touched the back of the chair on Lord Malvern's right hand. At once a footman sprang forward and pulled out the chair for Nina, who sat obediently. Irving touched another chair, and a footman pulled it out for Iven. One by one, the seneschal indicated where each person was to sit, showing himself uncannily aware of the order of precedence owed to each and every one of them.

Rhiannon found herself sitting right down the end of the table, next to the old man with the eyeglasses. He peered at her over their rim, mumbled, "My, my!" and then introduced himself as Gerard the Sennachie. Not knowing what this meant, Rhiannon smiled and nodded her head, and discovered, in time, that this meant the old man looked after the family history and papers, and kept the clan registers and library in order. He rambled on for what seemed like a very long time, telling Rhiannon all about the long and distinguished genealogy of the MacFerris clan. They were one of the few great families of Eileanan to have an unbroken line of inheritance, father to son, for a thousand years, he told her.

"Is that important?" Rhiannon asked, bored.

He was surprised. "O' course! Though the line is broken now, unhappily. Hopefully my laird can repair the break and restore the line. I ken it is his dearest wish." Just then the first course arrived, and he thankfully subsided into silence.

Lady Evaline was scanning all their faces with anxious eyes. "Where is the lad?" she asked piteously. "Did I no' see a lad with ruddy hair and dark eyes, just like my wee Rory? Is he no' here? Was he a ghost too?"

Nina hardly knew how to answer, and everyone else sat feeling troubled and uncomfortable. Then Lord Malvern said very lightly, from the far end of the table, "There's always lads run-

ning about, my dear, ye ken that. It must have been some pot-
boy ye saw."

Lady Evaline shook her head. "I never see lads anymore,"
she said sadly. "No' anywhere. No' living boys, anyway.
Ghosts, only ghosts. Sometimes it is my Rory that haunts me,
sometimes other boys that come and go like will o' wisps, never
here for long but always crying, always cold and crying."

Lord Malvern stood up, the white dents appearing beside his
mouth. "My dear, ye are unwell. I shall call Harriet."

Lady Evaline shrank back. "Nay, nay, I am well, indeed I
am," she said. "No need to call Harriet. I am sorry, it's just . . .
I'm sure I saw a lad, a living lad, but no' to worry, never mind,
I must've been mistaken. I am sorry."

Lord Malvern sat back down again, his face unreadable. He
indicated with a jerk of his head that the footmen continue serving the soup and everyone was able to hurry into comments
about how hungry they were, and how good the soup smelt, and
how lovely was the table setting.

Lady Evaline's clouded gaze moved back to Nina's face
plaintively. Nina smiled at her, and turned her gaze to the soup
bowl being placed before her.

Rhiannon found her composure unbalanced by the mention
of the cold, crying boys, which brought her own dream back to
her vividly. She also found the table settings very intimidating,
for there were at least four spoons and knives, some quite oddly
shaped, and any number of glasses and bowls and platters and
tureens. She wished fervently that Lewen was there to show her
what to do. She watched what the other girls did and tried to
mimic them, with mixed results, since this line of defense was
complicated by the fact that Fèlice and Edithe, as apprentice-
witches, were not permitted to eat meat. There was barely a
dish on the table without the flesh of some animal in it, which
made it hard for Nina and the apprentices to eat without dis-
courtesy. The soup at least was made of some sweet orange
vegetable, but otherwise there was a large roasted fish on a bed
of spinach, a chicken and leek pie, baked pigeons with aspara-
gus and fennel, a dish of lamb and minted peas, and a buttered
freshwater lobster. Rhiannon had been hungry for meat since
leaving her herd and so she made an excellent meal despite

never being quite sure if she was using the right knife and spoon. She noticed that Cameron and Rafferty also tasted many of the dishes, even if rather surreptitiously, and that Nina noticed too and was displeased.

The drab woman on the opposite side of the table from Rhiannon watched her chomp her way willingly through everything on offer, and said faintly, "Heavens, the appetite o' the young. How one forgets."

Rhiannon regarded her thoughtfully, but said nothing. The old man with the anxious grey eyes, who was apparently the clan harper, smiled at her, and said, "I always enjoy watching young people enjoy their food. I wish I could eat with such joyous abandon, but that is one more pleasure lost to me, I'm afraid."

"Here, *Dai-dein,* try some o' the fish, that is no' too rich," his son said.

Further up the table, Lord Malvern was enjoying a lively conversation with Edithe, who had been placed at his left hand, in accordance with her noble birth. The young apprentice was smiling demurely as he said, "But what is your father thinking, to let ye go off to court all by yourself, with no-one to protect ye?"

"It is the way o' the Coven," Edithe said with a sigh. "Indeed, my father was concerned but I was determined to go to the Theurgia and so at last he gave in and let me have my way."

"Indeed, I can see it would be hard to resist ye," Lord Malvern said. "But why must ye go to the Theurgia? Surely a lovely young lady like yourself must wish to be married?"

"To whom?" Edithe asked, raising her eyebrows. "There is none with whom I would wish to jump the fire."

"But surely ye must be inundated with suitors?" Lord Malvern said.

"None my father considers suitable," Edithe said, wrinkling her nose.

"Too auld or too young?" Lord Malvern asked with a smile.

"Too poor," Edithe answered.

Lord Malvern laughed. "Och, well, that is a problem for any father. I pity him. Ye say ye have three sisters? No wonder he has permitted ye to go to the Theurgia. To spend eight years so close to court, it'll be a wonder if ye do no' meet some handsome young laird who will sweep ye off your feet."

"One can only hope," Edithe replied.

Lord Malvern laughed again, causing both Lady Evaline and her drab companion to look up at the table at him. "Och, if I was just forty years younger, I'd be wooing ye myself."

Edithe replied sweetly, "And if ye were forty years younger, I'm sure I'd be most flattered, my laird. Tell me, do ye no' have a son or nephew as charming as ye, that ye could introduce me to?"

"I have no son," he answered harshly. "And though I had a nephew once, he died afore ye were born, my lady."

"I'm sorry," Edithe said, looking down at her plate.

The smile returned to his face. "Och, no matter. Ye will have to make do with me, as ancient and creaking as I am."

"Ye're no' ancient!" Edithe responded with an arch smile.

"Compared to your young loveliness, I'm auld indeed, though I do no' feel it, basking in the warmth o' your smile. Indeed, it is a shame ye must ride on as soon as the road is cleared. If ye and your friends were to bide a wee, I swear I would shed years each day ye were here."

"That would be lovely," Edithe said with a giggle, "but I am afraid we must go. We have a wedding to attend!"

"Och, aye, the wedding o' the young prionnsa," Lord Malvern said. "To his cousin, the deposed Banrìgh. That is a canny political liaison. I canna be the only one in Eileanan that remembers she was named heir to the throne when her father died."

"She ruled for only six hours," Iven interjected angrily. "And she was only a newborn babe at the time."

"But the only offspring o' the Rìgh," Lord Malvern reminded him. "I have never heard that youth was a reason for disinheriting the rightful heir to the throne. Eleanore the Noble was only eight when her father died and she inherited the Crown and the Lodestar, if I remember correctly. Her mother ruled as Regent till she was twenty-four. And Jaspar himself was only fifteen when he inherited the throne. Why should his daughter be disinherited just because she was a babe-in-arms?"

"We needed a strong man to rule," Iven said quickly. "We were at war on every front, a land divided."

"True," Lord Malvern answered, "but why could the Banrìgh's uncle no' act as Regent and rule in her name until she reached her majority? Which I believe she has done just recently. No wonder her uncle wishes to marry her off to his son."

Iven half-rose. "She is the Ensorcellor's daughter!" he roared.

"And Jaspar's," Lord Malvern pointed out. "If the fact that she is the Dowager Banrìgh's daughter sticks in his craw so much that he will no' allow her to rule, why is Lachlan the Winged marrying his son to her?"

Iven said nothing, though his blue eyes blazed with anger. Nina laid her hand on his arm.

"Besides," Lord Malvern continued, unperturbed, "when has it ever mattered what evil acts one's parents have been accused o', as long as one's right to the throne is legal? Donncan the Black was no' disinherited simply because his father Feargus was accused o' terrible crimes."

"Ye seem to ken your history well," Iven said coldly.

"We were taught well when I was a lad," Lord Malvern answered. "It was thought that if we kent history, we could try to avoid the mistakes o' the past. That is obviously no' what is believed now." There was a trace of bitterness in his voice.

"Come now," Lady Evaline said in her sweet voice. "*I* was taught it is rude to discuss politics at the dinner table. Tell me, my lady, how are your sick bairns? Has Dedrie been o' use to ye?"

"Aye, indeed," Nina answered, her cheeks rather flushed. "As ye can see, the boys are both well enough to join us here for dinner, and Edithe is only limping slightly. Dedrie seems to ken her craft well."

Lady Evaline sighed. "Aye. I do no' ken what we would have done without her all these years."

"She's a skilled healer, ye are lucky. So many remote villages and towns are still without properly trained healers, even so long after the witch-burnings. Indeed, it was an evil thing, the killing o' so many harmless skeelies and cunning men. Most o' them had done no more wrong than do their best to help the poor and auld and sick." Nina's eyes sparkled with anger. It was clear the lord's comment had cut her on the raw too.

Another uncomfortable silence fell. All of the castle folk stared at their plates, and Lord Malvern's thick, dark brows were drawn down angrily. He laid down his knife and leant forward, as if about to speak.

Lady Evaline spoke first, hurriedly. "But ye have no' yet told me what ye do, travelling through Fetterness Valley? We are so pleased to have guests, it has been a dreadfully long time since anyone has come to visit us. Ye say ye are travelling to Lucescere, for the wedding? Why come this way? Most people seem to prefer travelling down the far side o' the Findhorn, where the roads are so much better and where there are no ghosts."

Lord Malvern's frown deepened and once again he made to speak.

Iven cut across him. "Indeed, we would normally have chosen to go the other way too, my lady, since it is difficult travelling with caravans on rough roads. However, we have news we were most anxious to take to His Highness, and so we decided to come this way, since it is so much shorter. Or, so at least we hoped. We have had nothing but bad luck and foul weather since we chose this road."

"What news may that be?" Lord Malvern demanded.

Iven turned to him politely. "One o' the Rìgh's Blue Guards was found murdered in the highlands, my laird. He was one of His Highness's most trusted lieutenants and both Nina and I kent him well. His sister is the head of the healers' guild and is a dear friend o' ours. We wished to take the news to her, and to His Highness, as quickly as we could."

"Oh, I see," Lord Malvern replied, his frown relaxing.

"How very sad," Lady Evaline said and the other castle inhabitants murmured also.

"How did he die?" the harper's son asked.

"He was shot," Iven replied.

"And ye kent him well?" the drab lady asked.

Nina nodded. "I've kent him since he was just a lad. He was one o' the League o' the Healing Hand. Have ye heard the tales about them? They were a band o' beggar children that joined the rebellion in Lucescere, och, many years ago, and did many brave deeds to help Lachlan the Winged win the throne."

"The League o' the Healing Hand?" the harper asked with great interest. "What a strange name."

"One o' the lads, Tòmas, had the power to heal with the laying on o' hands. He was only a wee laddie, six or seven, perhaps. Connor, the Yeoman whose body we found in the highlands, was just his age and his best friend. They formed the League to help and protect Tòmas."

"And where is this lad now? He must be a man grown?" Lord Malvern asked with sudden interest.

"He died at the Battle o' Bonnyblair," Iven said. "It was a great tragedy. He died saving the Rìgh's life."

Lord Malvern turned his attention back to his lobster. "Very sad," he said.

"It was his second death," Iven said, noticing the eager interest in the eyes of the harper and his son, who were naturally stirred by such a story. "There is a beautiful song about him, written by the Rìgh's minstrel, who is now the Earl o' Caerlaverock. I will sing it for ye later, if ye like."

"I would like that," the harper's son said eagerly. "We hear so few new songs here."

"What do ye mean, it was his second death?" the harper asked, his grey eyes alight with curiosity.

"Tòmas died earlier, during an ambush by the Bright Soldiers. He had used all o' his powers to save the Rìgh, who was sorely wounded. Lewen should tell this story, it was his mother Lilanthe who saved him. She had been given a flower o' the Summer Tree by one o' the Celestines. The flowers have immense power in them, it is what gives the Celestines their magical ability to heal by the laying on o' hands, an ability that Tòmas had inherited. Lilanthe roused Tòmas enough so that he could eat the flower, and it brought him back to life and made his miraculous powers even greater. He saved the lives o' thousands o' soldiers during the Bright Wars, so many I think it is fair to say we could never have prevailed without him."

Lord Malvern had looked up from his plate again. "So those *uile-bheistean*—the faeries ye call Celestines—they can bring people back to life?"

Nina and Iven both stiffened at his use of the word. Nina in particular looked outraged, her cheeks flushing red, her black eyes shooting out dangerous sparks.

"We do no' call those o' faery blood *uile-bheistean* anymore," she said coldly.

Lord Malvern waved his hand dismissively. "Whatever. Ye were saying they can bring people back to life?" His gaze was fixed with disconcerting intentness upon Nina's face.

"They can heal," Nina said stiffly. "Particularly those o' Stargazer blood. The Stargazers are those who have eaten o' the flower o' the Summer Tree. They are like the royal family o' the Celestines."

"I see," the lord said thoughtfully. "But they can heal even those so sorely wounded they are close to death?"

Nina nodded. "If they are powerful enough."

"What a fascinating story," he said, beginning to eat again. "We must certainly hear the song after dinner. Some music would be a most pleasant diversion. And perhaps the young ladies would like to dance? My piper and my harper would be glad to play a few reels."

Fèlice clapped her hands in delight. "That would be wonderful!"

"I'm sure my ankle will be able to stand a few turns," Edithe said.

"Then it's arranged. In the grand drawing room after dinner, Borden!"

"As ye wish, my laird," the old harper said, bowing slightly.

Once the meal was cleared away, Lady Evaline and her companion rose and left the room, Nina and the three girls following her. They sat in one of the drawing rooms and drank tea, and made stilted conversation. As soon as the seneschal had indicated the footmen could remove the tray and had left the room himself, shutting the door behind him, Lady Evaline leant forward.

"My dear madam, please will ye no' tell me, ye did have a boy with ye, dinna ye? A laddie with red hair?"

"My lady," the drab companion protested weakly.

Lady Evaline kept her eyes on Nina's face. The journeywitch pressed her lips together and reluctantly nodded. "My son, Roden," she answered.

Lady Evaline clapped her hands. "I thought he was no' a

ghost! Och, I am glad. I had begun to think I must really be going mad."

"Evaline, my dear," her companion said anxiously.

Lady Evaline waved a hand at her. "I just wanted to be sure, Prunella. Tell me, did he no' come down to dinner because they warned ye to keep him away from me?"

Nina nodded, looking very uncomfortable.

"I knew it!" Lady Evaline cried. "They do worry about me. But ye must no' worry, my dear. I would never hurt your son."

"I hope no'," Nina said steadily, a spark igniting in her black eyes. "For I am a sorceress, ye ken, and one should never enrage a sorceress."

Lady Evaline nodded wisely, though her companion looked scandalised. Edithe and Fèlice exchanged glances, trying not to giggle.

"Believe me, I ken how to protect my son," Nina went on, her colour high.

"More tea?" Miss Prunella asked, lifting the teapot. She had a soft downy moustache above her lip, which quivered.

"Nay, thank ye," Nina answered, putting down her cup. "I think I have had quite enough."

"I thought I could protect my son too," Lady Evaline said. "I thought the strength o' these walls and the strength o' my husband's arm, and my own love would be enough to keep him safe, but I was wrong."

"Evaline," Miss Prunella quavered. Nina and Lady Evaline both ignored her.

"I'm sorry for that," Nina said gently. "I ken how much ye must grieve for him."

"They try and make it up to me, but there's naught they can do," Lady Evaline said in her soft, plaintive voice. "A mother kens her own son, dead or alive."

Edithe rolled her eyes and made a little corkscrewing gesture beside her ear that almost made Fèlice giggle out loud. Nina shot them a fierce look. "O' course," she said.

The door opened and Lord Malvern came in, smiling.

"That was quick," Lady Evaline said. "Would ye like some tea?"

"None o' my guests were smoking men," he answered

equably, scanning them all with his fierce black eyes set under bristling grey brows. "Do we feel like some dancing? Shall I send for my harper and piper?"

Edithe and Fèlice squealed and clapped their hands. Lord Malvern rang the bell and Irving came, bowing, to smoothly arrange the removal of various chairs and tables from the large drawing room.

"We have a ballroom, but that is too large for only a few couples," Lord Malvern said. "For a friendly little dance, this is more comfortable, I think."

Then the harper and his son came, carrying various instruments, and an old man with a set of bagpipes, and for the next hour, the time passed merrily enough, with no more talk of ghosts or dead boys. Rhiannon was the only one of the girls not to enjoy herself thoroughly, for she could not dance. Also, she could not rid herself of the weird feeling that all this talk and laughter and music was a sham, and that under the smiling faces and lively chatter, other darker thoughts hid, like a snake in the grass. She felt like she was being watched all the time. Refusing every exhortation to join the dancing, she sat against the wall, listening and observing. The candlelight wavered in her tired eyes, and she thought for a moment she saw a little boy standing forlornly in the shadows. She started and blinked, and the mirage was gone, but she could not shake the nervous tension that kept her muscles all in a knot.

Landon did not much enjoy dancing, either. Dutifully he danced with Edithe, managing to tear the hem of her gauzy gold gown, and with Fèlice, who laughingly pretended to limp away afterwards, declaring her feet were black and blue with bruises, and then he thankfully sat down against the wall too. After a while, when he thought no-one was paying him any attention, he drew out his dog-eared notebook and his quill and, balancing the inkpot on the gilded, satin-covered chair beside him, began to scribble with great intentness.

Rhiannon watched him with interest. She had begun by thinking Landon a very peculiar young man, but she had grown to like him very much, something which surprised her. He was not strong, or fast, or brave, or handsome. He sat on a horse like a sack of potatoes, and showed no interest in wrestling or hunting. He did not like being wet or cold or tired or hungry. He was, in fact, the sort of person she would normally view with contempt. Yet, despite his physical frailty, despite his shyness and oddities, there was something about him that made her warm to him, and want to look out for him and keep him from hurting himself.

After a while she slid along the seats towards him, noticing with amusement that his inkpot was leaving a round dark stain on the lord's straw-coloured satin chair.

"What ye write?" she asked.

He glanced up at her, looking a little cross, but then when he saw it was Rhiannon interrupting him, he blushed and stammered and almost tipped his inkpot over. Rhiannon rescued it with a grin, and he said shyly, "It's only rough still, but I could read it to ye if ye like?"

When she nodded, he cleared his throat and read aloud,

> *"How dark this place, how grim!*
> *Where the black wings o' ravens shadow the sky*
> *Where the wind sobs round the tower high*
> *Like the desolate cries o' a murdered child.*
> *My own life, once so keen and bright, grows dim.*
> *My own song falters; my pulse is wild.*
> *In my dreams I hear the toll o' death's bell,*
> *Beneath my feet yawns a bottomless well."*

Rhiannon stared at him in true amazement. "Ye feel it too?" she whispered.

He stared at her in surprise and pleasure. "My poem means something to ye?"

She nodded. "I hate this place. I wish we could get away."

"Me too. But I dinna ken why. It's all dreams and shadows. I dinna like to say aught, I ken the others would just laugh at me, but . . ." He paused, and then said, "It's no' a happy place, this castle."

"No," Rhiannon agreed. They sat in silence for a while, watching the dancers twirl about the room, then Landon said, very shyly, "I'm so glad ye liked my poem."

*   *   *

After Lady Evaline and her companion had retired for the night, and the musicians had packed up their instruments, Lord Malvern offered to show them around the castle and they agreed eagerly. He led them through various vast picture halls, a ballroom with a music gallery, a library filled with books and maps and a great desk piled with papers, the grand dining room which was far larger than the private room they had just dined in, and then, lastly, the great hall. This was an immense cold shadowy room that made Rhiannon shiver and edge closer to Nina. The witch seemed to find the atmosphere of the room unpleasant also, for she hugged her arms with her hands and looked about her with troubled eyes. "Do ye use the hall much?" she asked politely.

"No' these days," he answered. "It has unhappy memories."

As Lord Malvern spoke, Rhiannon felt a strange, disturbing thinning of the atmosphere. Her breath puffed out white. For a moment her companions faded away, and she saw a room filled with men, weary and bloodied with battle. One wore long red robes, others wore the livery of the MacFerris clan, but a few were dressed in shabby, stained motley, little better than rags. Two men faced each other across the points of their swords. One was young and dark, with a hunched shoulder, and a surly, unshaven face, wrapped in a filthy black cloak from head to foot. The other was older and dressed formally in a velvet doublet and black kilt, with embroidered stockings and neatly combed hair and beard. Rhiannon heard a snatch of voices, shouts, curses, a hysterical-sounding ranting from the man in red. Then the swords rose and clashed, there was a sharp cry of horror, and then the older man slowly fell to his knees, both hands clutching his stomach. Then he toppled sideways and blood spread across the paving-stones.

"Blood," Rhiannon said, and clutched at Nina for support. "Blood was spilt, just there."

"Blood spilt, here?" Nina repeated, and looked at the floor as if expecting the stain to remain. Edithe gave a little shriek and leapt back.

"Aye," Rhiannon said. "A man was killed."

"She is right," Lord Malvern said unwillingly. "It was my

brother's blood that was spilt. He was murdered here on this very spot."

Everyone exclaimed in shock and moved back uneasily.

"It was a very long time ago," Lord Malvern said. "I do no' like to come here myself, but I am surprised the lass should be able to sense aught. I daresay she has the witch-sight, though, heh?" His voice was heavy and sarcastic.

"I daresay," Nina said, drawing Rhiannon close.

"Was no' murdered," Rhiannon said in a clear, calm voice that sounded to her own ears as if it came from a very great distance away. "Was fair fight."

Lord Malvern turned on her in sudden rage, two white dents on either side of his mouth. "A fair fight!" he cried. "The laird o' the castle, cut down in his own hall by a mob o' filthy rebels? How is that fair or right?"

Rhiannon was coming back to herself in wracking shudders. She leant heavily on Nina, her voice as tottery as her legs. "I do no' . . . ken the laws o' your land. In my land, if one raises hand or weapon against another and . . . is killed, is no' called murder. Is called fair fight. Fancy man . . . your brother . . . he struck first blow . . . was no mob . . . fair fight with dirty man . . . dirty man won."

"Indeed, the dirty man did win," Lord Malvern said very softly, looking away into the gloom. There was a very long silence. Rhiannon tried to still the trembling of her arms and legs. She saw nothing now, but the memory was vivid in her mind's eye. Half-fearful, half-curious, the others glanced about the ill-lit room, its hearth swept clean and bare as if it was never warmed with dancing flames.

"Did ye see aught?" Cameron whispered to Fèlice, who shook her head reluctantly.

"I *felt* something," she whispered back. Landon nodded, eyes wide.

"Sure ye did," Edithe said caustically. "The damp and the cold."

Fèlice cast her a cutting glance but dared say nothing else, for Lord Malvern had stirred and brought his stern gaze back to them.

"It is cold in here. Let us withdraw to the drawing room," he said with great politeness. "May I offer ye some mulled wine, my lady?"

"No' for me, thank ye, my laird," Nina said just as politely. "I find I am rather tired still and would like to retire to my bedchamber. I thank ye for a most delicious meal, though, and for your hospitality."

"Tell me," Iven said, "what news o' the road? For we are anxious to be on our way, as we explained. We really must get to Lucescere as fast as we can, the Rìgh will be looking for us."

Lord Malvern grimaced and shook his head. "No good news, I fear, sir. The road was badly damaged and is hard to repair because o' the steepness o' the slope. I have all my spare men working on it though, and hope ye will be on your way again as soon as can be."

Iven inclined his head. "I ken something o' such things, my laird. Happen I may be able to help?"

"Thank ye for the offer but I'm sure my men have all under control," he answered.

"Nonetheless, I would like to have a look, my laird, if only to give me something to do while we wait. I fear I am unused to much rest."

"Ye should enjoy the chance to relax while ye can," Lord Malvern smiled.

Iven sighed. "True, but I fear a lifetime o' habit is hard to overcome in only a few days. And I am curious. It must indeed be a difficult job, to repair a road in such conditions. Happen your men can teach me something."

"Very well." Lord Malvern bowed stiffly. "I shall instruct my men to show ye the road in the morning."

They had come back through to the main wing of the castle and stood now at the base of the grand stone staircase that led up to their rooms. Lord Malvern bade them a rather grim goodnight and rang for a footman to show them the way back, even though Iven protested that there was no need, they knew the way.

"It is a very large castle, and much o' it is empty these days," Lord Malvern responded. "I would hate ye to become lost, particularly so late at night when most o' the servants are sleeping."

"Then thank ye," Iven said, allowing a footman carrying a great branch of candles to lead them towards their rooms. Rhiannon felt odd, as if her feet were weighted with lead and her head was as light as a bellfruit seed. It was very dark and quiet in the corridors, and bitterly cold, so all were glad to reach Nina's warm suite, lit generously with scented candles and a roaring fire. Roden was fast asleep in Nina and Iven's great canopied bed and Lewen was sitting drowsily before the fire, his boots off, his shirt undone at the collar and rolled up to show his powerful brown forearms. He had been whittling arrows, a great pile of them lying beside him, waiting to be fletched.

"How was dinner?" he asked, standing up and yawning.

"Creepy," Fèlice answered, coming to stand close to the fire, and smiling up at him. "No' as creepy as the great hall, though. Rhiannon had a fit, and saw blood everywhere, and ghosts, and the laird was furious. He doesna like talk o' ghosts, it seems."

"Who does?" Lewen answered, looking past her to Rhiannon, who was now so exhausted she could barely stand upright on her own feet. "How are ye yourself?" he asked.

"Grand I am, indeed," she answered, and fainted.

The Dream

Rhiannon woke with a jerk. For a moment she was disorientated. Everything was dark. The fire had fallen into ashes. She lay still, temples throbbing. Her mouth was dry.

Someone stood by the bed.

Rhiannon's heart slammed hard, and she said with a sharp rise in her voice, "Roden? What's wrong?"

The boy said nothing.

"Roden?"

"So cold," he whispered. "So cold."

Rhiannon lay very still. "Who are you?"

He stepped closer. In the darkness he was nothing more than a pale shape. She could feel him trembling. "Please . . ." he whispered. Then an icy cold hand touched her face.

Rhiannon screamed.

Fèlice sat bolt upright beside her. "What is it? What's wrong?"

"A boy . . . a ghost!"

"Ye're just dreaming," Fèlice mumbled. The candles on the mantelpiece flickered into life, showing the bedchamber was empty. "There's naught here. Ye were just dreaming. Ye're sick. Go back to sleep." The candles snuffed themselves out, and Fèlice rolled over and was instantly asleep again.

Rhiannon lay, every muscle rigid. Then she slowly brought one hand up to cover her cheek. It was chill to the touch. She shuddered.

After a moment she very slowly and carefully put back the bedclothes and got up. In the darkness she pulled on her woollen stockings and boots, and wrapped her cloak about her. It was so dark she had to feel her way to the door, but the hallway was lit dimly by a lantern left on a side table, turned very low. For a moment she stood, listening. Then she picked up the lantern, turning up the wick so it cast a circle of warm light into the frigid darkness. Immediately her heart began to slam against her ribs again.

At the far end of the corridor the boy waited. He was dressed in formal clothes, and his feet were shod in buckled brogues that seemed to rest solidly enough on the carpet. He had dark, sombre eyes and ruddy hair. He was shivering, and had his arms wrapped tightly about his skinny body. He looked back at her, then made his way slowly round the corner. Rhiannon followed him.

He led her away from the guest quarters towards the northern tower, which Rhiannon knew was set aside for Lady Evaline's use. He went swiftly and steadily, but not so fast that Rhiannon had trouble keeping up with him. She was just beginning to think that he was perhaps a real boy, a pot-boy who liked to play silly tricks on guests, when he passed straight through the great oak door that led into the tower. This discomposed her so much she stopped, fighting to regain her breath, her heart galloping like a runaway horse. Her nerve almost failed her, but her hunger to understand was greater and so she went on again, opening the door as silently as she could. There was no sign of the ghost, and she was angry with herself. She moved on through the narrow stone corridor anyway, its walls hung with faded tapestries. She came to a spiral staircase and began to climb it, her shadow preceding her up the round walls like some black, formless giant. Then she rounded the central pillar and saw the ghost standing there, only a few steps ahead, staring at a door half-concealed behind a tapestry. As she shrank back, instinctively shielding the light of her lantern, he looked back at her, beckoned urgently, then stepped forward and vanished through the solid wood.

It took Rhiannon a long time to find the courage to open the door. Her hand was trembling so much the lantern's flame flickered and shook, sending shadows swinging everywhere. She steadied it at last, and saw a sight which chilled her to the very marrow of her bones.

Inside was a boy's bedroom. There was a little bed with a

patchwork counterpane, a rocking horse, a wooden castle with tiny soldiers lined up along the battlements, a puppet theatre, and a basket filled with balls and wooden animals and toy swords. There was a big barred window with a cushioned window seat and faded curtains covered with prancing red horses. Against one wall was a cupboard painted with stars and moons, and against the other was a toy chest, its lid propped open.

The room was filled with the ghosts of boys. One rode the rocking horse back and forth, back and forth, its rockers creaking. Another examined the puppet theatre, a few more were crouched over the castle. One was curled up in the big chair, trying to look at a book. One crouched on the window seat, sobbing into his arms. Another lay weeping on the bed. One boy was dripping wet, sitting in a puddle, shivering and crying. Another rocked back and forth in silent terror beside the door. Some were dressed in nightgowns, others in rough homespuns, a few in neat suits with collared shirts, a few others in heavy winter coats and red woolly hats. The more she looked, the more ghosts she saw, some as insubstantial as heat rising from a sun-baked stone, others looking like living boys, except that as they moved about the room, their bodies merged into each other and materialised again on the other side, like flickering shadows.

The ghost Rhiannon had seen first was standing in the centre of the room, his arms huddled about him. He turned his face towards her and said pitifully, "All lost. Canna find their way home. Lost." He shuddered violently and said in a thin whisper, "So cold. Mama, it's so cold."

It was cold. Rhiannon's inner ears ached painfully. Her breath came out in frosty plumes, and she was shivering so violently the oil in the lantern slopped about and the flame sunk away into darkness. All she could hear was the muffled whimper of crying and the creak, creak of the rocking horse.

Slowly Rhiannon backed out of the room, the lantern dropping from her nerveless fingers. The sound of it breaking went through her like a shock of lightning. She slammed the door closed, then ran down the stairs. She felt faint and sick, so faint she was afraid she might lose her wits again. Back through the dark hallways and galleries she ran, and ran, and ran, down unlit stairs and through cavernous chambers, banging into furniture, becoming entangled in hanging curtains, bruising her hips on unexpected hall tables, and, horribly, coming face to face with the gloomy eyes of ancient paintings, until the stitch in her side forced her at last to slow, fighting for breath. Only then did her panicked mind admit that she had no idea where she was, or how she was to get back to her room. She was lost.

For a while she huddled on a couch in an immense, high-ceilinged room, her cloak wrapped tight around her, overcome by such terror that unconsciousness passed over her in black, roaring waves. The muscles of her urinary tract had relaxed involuntarily, so that she felt a sopping patch on her nightgown grow, the initial warmth passing to bitter cold. All she could do was fight to get breath into her paralysed lungs and try not to lose control of her other bodily functions, which threatened to shame her further. No-one could endure such extremities of emotion for long, though, and eventually she was able to control the shudders that wracked her, wipe the tears from her face and get up. She felt her way to the paler oblongs of the tall windows, looking for some clue as to where she was in the vast, silent castle. There was no moon to help her but the sky swarmed with stars. She wrenched the window open and leant out, breathing in great gulps of fresh, cold air, fixing her eyes on the familiar constellations above. When her eyes adjusted to the darkness, she was able to see the shape of battlemented walls and the pointed roofs of towers silhouetted against them. She gave a smile of pure relief, realising she was back in the main part of the castle, looking across the inner ward to the gatehouse.

She made her fumbling way through the room and out to the gallery above the main stairs. Here another lantern glowed softly in the darkness, lighting the landing. More light spread out in an arc from a door down on the next floor. Rhiannon hesitated for a moment with her hand upon the lantern. With its help she thought she could find her way back to the warmth and safety of her own bed. But she could not help wondering who in the castle was awake at this late hour, and what they were doing. Since seeing the ghosts of so many little boys, Rhiannon could feel nothing but the deepest horror and suspicion of everyone in the castle, but it only sharpened her desire to know, to understand. So she made her slow, tentative way down the stairs and put her eye to the crack of the door.

She saw high shelves of books, flickering in the dancing shadows of flames, and the high back of an old leather chair, and the gleam of a wooden desk. The air breathing out of the room was warm and smelt pleasantly of smoke. Everything was quiet.

After a while she gently pushed the door open. Still there was no sign or sound of life. She looked about her warily. Long wooden cabinets lined the walls. She pulled open a drawer. Inside were hundreds of old bones, all laid out neatly and tagged. Another drawer held a collection of desiccated claws and paws. She recognised the black massive hand of an ogre and the yellow claw of a goblin, a snow-lion's heavy white paw, and a scaly webbed hand that she guessed must belong to one of the sea-folk. In the drawer beneath it were rows and rows of human hands, all severed at the wrist. Some were badly preserved, some bare bones, but most looked as if they had just been cut away from a living body. Her stomach quivered uncomfortably. Rhiannon touched one. It was cold and hard and left an oily residue on her fingers. She swallowed and wiped her fingers on her nightgown. She felt, suddenly, very cold and frightened.

The warmth of the fire drew her irresistibly. It had only just been built up with fresh wood and roared away merrily on the hearth. She tiptoed towards it. A dead baby floated in a jar on a shelf. An ogre's head glared from another jar. Nailed to a board was a glittering scaly skin in the shape of a man. In another jar was a pile of strange white round things. Rhiannon could not bring herself to examine them closely. She stood before the fire and warmed herself, wondering what kind of man would surround himself with such things.

The hands of the clock on the mantelpiece were moving towards twelve o'clock, the only time Rhiannon could tell. She held her icy hands to the fire, watching the smaller hand tick round, wondering why the room was all lit up and the fire burning, when no-one was there. When the front of her body was so hot she had to hold the cotton of her nightgown away from her, she turned and basked her backside.

A huge woolly bear stood in the corner of the room, muzzle

snarling, claws raised. Rhiannon bit back a shriek. Wildly she
looked round for a weapon. Her daggers were back in her room.
She cursed herself for leaving them there, even as she seized a
heavy silver ornament from the mantelpiece. As she swung
back round to face the bear, her impromptu weapon raised, she
wondered in amazement what a woolly bear could be doing
here, in the lord's own library. Lewen's parents had kept one as
a pet, though, so she supposed it was not as uncommon as she
would have imagined.

Breathing fast, she stared at the bear, who stared back at her
with glassy eyes. For a long moment they eyed each other, then
Rhiannon slowly lowered the ornament and took a tentative
step forward. The bear did not move. She took another step
forward. Still the bear did not move. She crossed the room warily, and reached up a hand to its stiff, cold snout. The stuffed
bear stood frozen, yellow teeth exposed, huge claws curved.
Rhiannon shook her head in wonderment.

Then she saw something that made her eyes widen and her
breath catch. One section of the bookshelves had swung sideways, revealing a narrow doorway. She would never have seen
it if she had not gone to examine the stuffed bear. Rhiannon tiptoed to the secret door and looked inside. All was black and
chill. It smelt like a grave.

Rhiannon stared at the secret passage for a long time, her
breath coming short. Every instinct in her body bade her flee
back to the warmth and safety of her own bed. Her brain, however, told her that the gaping hole in the wall must hold some
clue to all that was wrong and malevolent in this castle.

Rhiannon was not deceived by the affability of their host, or
the sweet face of their hostess. From the moment she had ridden in under the portcullis, Rhiannon's skin had been prickling
with an awful sense of dread and horror that had only grown
with every moment spent inside the massive walls. Terrible
things had happened here, she knew that as surely as if blood
oozed from every stone. Everyone who lived within these walls
felt the weight of disquietude and fear. She had seen it in the
nervous mannerisms of the maid Wilma, in the belligerent
stance of the castle guards, the surly sideways glances of the
grooms, the nervous obsequiousness of the gatekeeper, the

awkward deference of the dinner guests to their short-tempered lord. The sight of that dreadful playroom, haunted by the ghosts of dozens of murdered little boys, had only confirmed what she had already feared.

And whatever secret was hidden behind the lord of Fettercairn's smiling face threatened Rhiannon and her companions, she was sure of it. The satyricorn girl had lived all her life in the Broken Ring of Dubhslain. She knew this foul weather was unnatural. She knew gales of such ferocity did not last day after day after day, at a time when the skies were normally fair and the winds warm. She had watched the eyes of the lord and lady follow young Roden about, and she had seen the anxiety on the nursemaid's face as she begged them to take the boy and get away. She had come to recognise the white dents that appeared beside the lord's mouth when something was said to displease him, and knew that all about him dreaded that tightening of his jaw.

On the desk were a decanter of whisky and a glass. Rhiannon put down the silver ornament and swigged half a dram for courage. She knew she could not go back to her bed without finding out what secret Lord Malvern had behind his smooth manner. If danger was threatening them, Rhiannon wanted to know from which direction it would come, and when. Though she coughed and spluttered, the whisky did give her both warmth in the pit of her belly and the nerve to go into the hidden passage. Remembering Lilanthe's words, she turned her cloak inside out, so that the grey camouflage was on the outside. Then she took one of the branches of candles and the tinderbox off the mantelpiece, for she was more frightened now of the dark than anything, and went through the narrow portal.

Freezing cold, musty air flowed over her. She walked quickly, trying to warm herself. The passage was only narrow, but high enough for her not to have to worry about hitting her head. The walls and floor and ceiling were all made of the same massive grey stone blocks as the castle. She thought she must be passing through the middle of the thick walls, and wondered where the passage was taking her. The floor began to angle downwards, and then she noticed the walls were now rock, damp and slimy to the touch.

Then the passage opened out into a sizable cavern. Passages

and antechambers ran off on different sides, and Rhiannon could hear the roar of running water. She thought she must be coming close to the waterfall. She hesitated, not knowing which way to go, and unable to see very well because of the violent flickering of the candle-flames. A cold draught breathed on her neck, lifting her long tendrils of hair.

Suddenly the candles were snuffed out. She scrabbled to light one again. As the flame ignited, illuminating the cavern more fully than before, she saw, crudely etched on the far wall, the shape of a raven. Breathing quickly, she hurried that way and found another passage built by human hands, leading up at a slight angle. Rhiannon followed the passage and soon found herself climbing broad, even steps that rose steeply ahead of her. On and on she climbed, panting a little, the backs of her legs aching.

Fresh air blew coldly against her cheek. She came to another swivel door, standing sideways on its pivot. Shielding her candle with one hand, she crept out into the ruins of the Tower of Ravens. It could be nothing else, this edifice of crumbling stone with grass and brambles growing through cobblestones, and crooked walls rising like broken teeth high into the sky. It was very dark and her candle made only a small circle of light, but she held it high and examined the ancient marks of fire on the walls, the tree growing out of a crevice twenty feet above her head, the untidy ravens' nests high in the tower.

Rhiannon could hear the sound of chanting and she crept towards it, blowing out her candle and putting it down on the ground so the light would not reveal her. In the numb arc of frozen sky above her, the stars blazed whitely.

She came to a broken archway and looked through, her heart pounding.

Standing in a circle in the central courtyard of the ruined tower were nine people, all dressed in long red hooded robes. Holding hands, they were chanting in a low, monotonous tone. Rhiannon was not close enough to hear the words. A sullen fire burnt in a clay dish in the centre, reeking of strange incense. Nine enormous black candles in iron cages cast a flickering, uncertain light. As Rhiannon leant forward, trying to hear, the nine people stopped their chanting and stood in silence for a moment, all looking up at the sky, and then they broke apart. One man turned and knelt to the north, laying his forehead on the ground, his arms outstretched. Another figure came up behind up him and bent to unfasten his robe, stripping it down so his back was laid bare. The red-robed figure then drew a whip with nine knotted lashes out of its sleeve. After a moment spent in ritual prayer, the figure began to whip the half-naked man, slowly, rhythmically. Nine times the nine-lashed whip rose and fell, and when at last it was laid down, the victim's back was running with blood.

He lay still for a moment, shoulders heaving, then struggled to his feet, drawing his robe up to cover his abused flesh. Then he turned to face the others. Eager to see who it was, Rhiannon leant right forward, but all she could see under the hood were glittering eyes, a mouth clamped shut with pain, and a clean-shaven chin. The man gestured imperiously and one of the other anonymous figures came forward, carrying a sack. The man who had been whipped took the sack, plunged his hand inside, and withdrew a rooster by its spurred feet. Its raucous protests were loud enough for Rhiannon to hear, and she watched as it struggled to break free, pecking at the hand that held it hanging. The other hand came up, there was a flash of silver, and then blood sprayed from the rooster's neck. Immediately everyone began to chant again, in high, hysterical voices. Desperate to hear more, Rhiannon lay down on her stomach and wriggled slowly across the cold, muddy ground until she reached a broken colonnade of arches closer to the circle of chanters.

". . . By the power o' the dark moon, by the power o' spilled blood, by the power o' darkness and the unknown, by the mysteries o' the deep, I summon and evoke thee, spirit o' Falkner MacFerris, long dead brother and laird o' Fettercairn. Arise, arise from the grave, I charge and command thee . . ."

Three times they repeated the charm. To Rhiannon's horror, by the end of the third repetition she saw a frail shape lift out of the ground in the centre of the circle, its head bowed, its arms folded about its chest. It lifted a haunted, cavernous face and said: "Why will ye no' let me rest?"

"Falkner!" cried the leader, the man who had been whipped.

"Falkner, we come close to finding the secret. I beg o' ye, do no' despair yet. I ken it has been a long and weary time, but I swear to ye, we come close."

"A long and weary time, aye, that it has. Why do ye hold me to this world? I want only to rest now. Let me be."

"Do ye no' want vengeance?" the leader cried. Rhiannon was almost certain it was Lord Malvern, but she could not be sure, for this man's voice was high and shrill and desperate.

"Vengeance?" the ghost asked in mild curiosity. "It is all dust and ashes to me now. What do I care?"

"But do ye no' wish to live again? Do ye no' wish to embrace your loving wife, do ye no' wish to hold your son in your arms? What would ye no' give to feel the sun hot on your skin and fill your lungs with sweet air, to drink cool water and eat your fill o' the fruits o' the earth? Falkner, once ye raved for these things, ye begged me . . ."

"They are all good things," the ghost said slowly. "Indeed, I had almost forgotten."

"Falkner, Falkner, how could ye forget!" one of the others cried, stretching out trembling, age-spotted hands. The ghost turned his face towards her.

"Evaline," he whispered.

"Falkner, my love!"

"It has been so long. I had begun to let go, to drift away, to forget."

"It has only been five months, Falkner," Malvern said impatiently. "We last raised ye on All Hallows' Eve, as we have done every year since ye died. Tonight is the spring equinox, the night when the hours of darkness equal the hours o' light, and tonight the moon is dark. It seemed too good a chance to waste. We canna raise ye too often, ye ken that. It is too dangerous . . ."

As if his words were a key to unlock a door, the candle-flames suddenly wavered and were snuffed out as a bitter-cold wind swept round the courtyard. The fire whirled away in a blast of sparks and ashes, plunging the courtyard into darkness. There were a few terrified screams.

"Hold fast!" Lord Malvern shouted. "Hold the circle o' protection!"

All Rhiannon could hear were the shrieks of panic and fear,

and then every hair on her body stood erect and quivering. She could sense something new in the courtyard, something huge and cold and malevolent. She shrank down, hiding herself, as afraid as she had been when lost in the castle.

Suddenly nine tall pillars of pale greenish fire shot up from the candles. Mist was roiling everywhere, dank and foul-smelling. The ghost of a woman stood in the centre of the circle, regarding the cowering figures with amusement. In the one glance Rhiannon took before she pressed her face back down again, she saw only that the woman seemed richly dressed, and that her skin was white and her hair dark.

"Ye seek to raise the dead, ye fools?" the ghost said. "With a slaughtered cock-a-doodle-doo and a handful o' powdered nightshade? Amateurs!"

Lord Malvern struggled to his feet. "Begone, foul spirit!" he cried. "Ye were no' invited here. By the power o' the sacred circle, I command ye to return to the world o' the dead."

She laughed, and raised her hand. The bitter-cold, uncanny wind blew up again, strewing the salt and charcoal of the circle they had drawn across the stone.

"If ye open a portal to the spirit world, ye must expect some uninvited guests," she said. "Look out into the darkness. Can ye no' see the ghosts that swarm about your pitiful circle o' protection like a hive o' angry hornets? Ye stand here upon a Heart o' Stars and call upon the dead, and think ye can open and close the door at will?"

The nine hooded figures looked fearfully out into the darkness, cringing in their fear. Rhiannon looked also and had to bite her knuckle to stop from crying out, for a host of dead were indeed crowding close round the circle of candles with their strange, green flames. The ghosts seemed made of starlight and shadow and bone, only barely visible in the darkness, yet as they pressed forward eagerly, Rhiannon could see their faces, some grave and terrible, others cruel and greedy, others distorted with grief or rage. The longer she looked, the more she saw, hundreds of phantasms melting into each other like pallid marsh-flames.

"They are angry," the woman said. "I wonder why? So many spirits o' the dead, eager to kick open this door ye have opened and swarm upon ye like maddened bees. Do no' tell me. I can guess. Ye have been experimenting, haven't ye? Ye've been trying to discover the secret o' resurrecting the dead. Ye have dug up corpses and tried to reanimate them, ye have killed others in order to study the moment o' death, to understand how and when the spirit is severed, to find out how long it lingers, to study the psychic memory o' bones, to use them as objects o' power for your rituals, to seek to know death. Were ye never taught that it is no' for us to decide the time o' a man's death, but for she who cuts the thread?"

"Who are ye?" Malvern said in a high, desperate voice. "What do ye want o' us?"

"For ye to bring me back to life, o' course," she answered. "That is what all these ghosts want, crowding round your door. I am the only one who kens the secret though. I am the only one who can help ye."

"Who are ye?" he asked again.

"Never mind who. All ye need to ken is that I can help ye raise your beloved ones from the dead."

"Ye can help us?" Lady Evaline asked in a quavery voice.

"Aye, I can. I have waited long for this chance, I have clung to life with tenacious hands, I have refused to go on to the final dissolution o' self, in the hope that somewhere, somehow, I would find someone with the will, the wit, to evoke the spell o' resurrection. I will tell ye where to find this spell, if ye promise that ye will raise me first."

The hooded figures were irresolute. Some looked out at the darkness with terrified eyes, others huddled together, muttering.

Lord Malvern was not hesitant. He stood up straight, looking the ghost in the eye. "I have waited twenty-five years for this chance!" he cried, exultant. "Twenty-five years I have sought to find the secret o' bringing the dead back to life, and always I have failed. We have done such terrible things—we have dug up corpses in all stages o' putrefaction and cast all manner o' spells upon them. We have tortured men to watch how many times they can be killed and revived afore the spirit flees forever. We have tried every way imaginable, and always we have failed. O' course we will help ye, my lady, whoever ye are. We will be glad to help ye!"

"Excellent," the ghost said in her low, rich, purring voice. "First let us drive away some o' these listeners, and then I shall tell ye where ye may find the spell."

Rhiannon was suddenly convinced that the ghost knew there was a quick soul listening as well as a host of dead ones. She felt an overwhelming need to escape before she was discovered. She began to slowly creep away, keeping as low and quiet as she could, until at last she reached the shelter of the wall. She was trembling in every limb, but at last she managed to light her candle and find her way back through the secret passage and into the library.

She dared not warm herself before the fire, but hurried back up the stairs and through the maze of corridors and galleries till she at last reached her own room. By now Rhiannon was so cold and weary she could hardly put one foot before the other. Her legs threatened to buckle beneath her, every limb trembled, and black specks danced before her eyes. She came into the bedroom at last, and stripped off her cloak and boots so she could creep under the warmth of the eiderdown, shaking and prodding the sleeping Fèlice until at last the other girl yawned and half-woke.

"Fèlice! We must get away from here. Fèlice! Wake up! Fèlice!"

"What is it? What's wrong?" Fèlice said sleepily.

"We must get away from here. They mean us evil, I ken it. We must wake up Nina and Iven, and the others, and get out, somehow, I dinna ken how, we must get away as fast and as quiet as we can . . ."

"Rhiannon, ye're gabbling! What's the matter with ye?"

As Rhiannon tried to explain, Fèlice sat up and laid a hand on her forehead and then on her cheek. "Rhiannon, your hands and feet are like ice! And your head is boiling hot. Look at ye, ye're shivering."

"Cold, so cold," Rhiannon muttered, and shuddered as she realised she had echoed the refrain of the ghostly boy.

"Let me put some more wood on the fire, get ye warm."

"Never mind about that," Rhiannon said impatiently, though she gratefully huddled under the counterpane Fèlice pulled close around her. "We have to get away. There are ghosts, Fèlice, hundreds o' them . . ."

"Ye and your ghosts," Fèlice said, suppressing a yawn. She dragged her dressing-gown around her and got out of bed. "This is the second time tonight ye've woken me gabbling about ghosts. I wish I'd slept with Edithe, ye're a most unrestful bed partner." She threw some wood on the ashes of the fire, stirred it once or twice with the poker, and then caused the logs to burst into flame with a wave of her hand. She yawned again, so widely that Rhiannon could not help yawning also, and climbed back into bed.

"Nay, nay, we have to get up, we have to go," Rhiannon said feverishly.

"It's the middle o' the bloody night, for Eà's sake! We canna go anywhere. Now go back to sleep and in the morning I'll get ye some o' that wine Cameron kept raving about. I think ye must've caught the boys' cold."

"I do no' want wine," Rhiannon said, sitting up in bed, clutching the bedclothes to her chin. "Are ye no' listening? They're murderers, the lot o' them."

"Who? Who are murderers?"

"Everyone! Everyone in the castle."

"Oh, Rhiannon! Go back to sleep, please."

"Sleep? How can I sleep? Did ye no' hear me? I saw ghosts, the ghosts o' murdered boys, and then I saw them, the laird and lady, working some kind o' evil to bring back the dead . . ."

"Ye were just dreaming, Rhiannon. Come, ye're not well, and this place is enough to give anyone nightmares. Lie down, and let me tuck ye up, ye're shivering. In the morning ye'll feel better, I promise."

"I must tell Nina . . ."

"Ye can tell her in the morning. There's naught ye can do now. Ow, your feet are freezing! Let me warm the bedpan for ye. There, that's better. Go to sleep now."

"No! I must tell Nina now. Do ye no' understand? They mean us evil!"

Fèlice hesitated. "Happen I'd better wake Nina. I think ye're really ill."

"Aye, aye, wake her," Rhiannon said desperately.

Fèlice nodded and went quickly out the door. Rhiannon sighed and let her head sink down onto her pillow. Her bones felt as heavy as stone. In a few minutes, Nina came hurrying into the room with Fèlice close behind.

"Rhiannon! What's wrong?"

Rhiannon dragged herself away from the pillow. "We must get away from here," she said, clutching at Nina's hand. "Oh, Nina, it was awful." She did her best to describe what she had seen that night, but her tongue seemed more wooden than ever and she was so very weary she could hardly keep her head from drooping back down to the pillow. It was like talking through mud. Nina took her wrist in one hand, and felt her forehead with the other.

"Your pulse is tumultuous," she said. "Lie back, Rhiannon. Here, have a sip o' water."

Rhiannon drank gratefully, for she was indeed parched, then she tried again to describe all she had seen to Nina, plucking at her sleeve with nervy fingers. Nina seemed not to understand the dreadful urgency of Rhiannon's news, patting her soothingly and telling her not to fret, to lie down and rest.

"Nay, nay," Rhiannon cried, resisting all attempts to push her down on the pillow. "We must flee, now!"

"How can we?" Nina said reasonably. "It is dark, and raining still, and Maisie is very sick. The road is blocked by that fallen tree, remember, and even if it wasn't, how could we get away without rousing the whole castle? It would be unpardonably rude."

Rhiannon laughed wildly. "Rude! She worries about being rude!"

"Rest now, my dear, and we'll make ready to leave as soon as we possibly can. As long as ye're well enough."

"Me fine!" Rhiannon felt hot tears of frustration scald her cheeks. A sudden paroxysm of coughing shook her. When at last it passed she could not speak for exhaustion.

"Lie back, my dear. I'll just be a moment." Nina pushed her back onto the pillows gently and went out of the room, telling Fèlice to stay with a quick gesture. Rhiannon scrubbed her cheeks dry and laid her arm across her face, hiding her hot tender eyes. She felt Fèlice stroking back her tumbled hair and was obscurely comforted. For a long while there was silence, and Rhiannon felt herself sliding towards sleep. She tried to cling to consciousness, but the gentle stroking hand on her forehead and the irresistible softness of her pillows dragged at her. She let herself drift for a moment.

The sound of quick footsteps roused her. She felt peculiar, as if she had fallen into a dark well of time where minutes, perhaps even hours, had passed without her knowing. She struggled to sit up, opening her bleary eyes.

Dedrie was leaning over her. At once Rhiannon cried out and cowered away.

"I'm sorry, I startled ye," the nursemaid said. "Ye have a fever. Here, have a sip o' this."

Rhiannon clamped her mouth shut and shook her head. The motion caused pain to shoot through her temples.

"It will make ye feel better."

Rhiannon put one hand to her throbbing head, and shook it again, more gently this time. Her head felt strangely large, and her feet seemed a long way away. Her arms were so limp it took a great effort to move them.

"My lady? Would ye mind? Our wee patient willna take her medicine from me. Happen she will from ye."

Nina came into Rhiannon's field of vision, leaning over the bed. She held the cup for Rhiannon to sip, but Rhiannon still refused. She would have liked to have pointed at Dedrie and accused her, but she dared not. Had Dedrie been one of those red-cloaked figures in the ruined tower? Rhiannon did not know, but she viewed any intimate of Lord Malvern's with great suspicion now. She did her best to communicate her distress with nothing but her eyes and facial muscles, but Nina only looked puzzled and alarmed, saying in her beautiful voice, "Do no' fear, Rhiannon, it is only something to ease the cough and the fever. It'll make ye feel better."

When Rhiannon persisted in her refusal, Nina stepped back, looking troubled. Dedrie stepped up to the bed briskly, saying, "She's delirious, look at her! See how much her head aches, the way she turns her face on the pillow. We must bring down her fever." Then, so suddenly Rhiannon had no time to react, the nursemaid clamped her hand over Rhiannon's nose, the heel of her palm pressing Rhiannon's head back into the pillow. Rhiannon tried to heave herself away but the nursemaid was surprisingly strong. Rhiannon opened her mouth to protest, and immediately Dedrie tipped in the medicine, then grabbed Rhiannon's chin, forcing her mouth shut so she could not turn her head and spit the mixture out. It tasted foul. Rhiannon choked and spluttered, but the hands on her forehead and chin were inexorable, and the weight of the nurse's upper arms pressed so heavily upon her body that she could hardly move.

Rhiannon heaved her body upright, sending the nursemaid sprawling, and spewed the medicine into her face. She gasped for breath, the inside of her mouth and throat feeling as if they had been blistered raw.

Dedrie cried out and groped for the damp face cloth, urgently wiping her face clean.

"She's trying to poison me," Rhiannon cried.

"Rhiannon!" Nina said in gentle reproof.

"Nay, nay, that's no poison, though I'll warrant it tastes foul enough," Dedrie said. "It's my borage syrup. It has thyme in it as well, and various other things, but no poison, I promise ye. Och, ye're burning up, my lass. No wonder ye're so wild."

Rhiannon swatted away the nurse's hand, scowling ferociously. Her mouth tasted disgusting.

"Here, have some o' my elderflower wine, to wash the taste away," Dedrie said soothingly. "It'll ease that cough too."

"No!"

"It's your choice but I promise ye it'll help."

"Nina!"

"There, there, Rhiannon, ye're ill. Have a sip o' the wine; then lie back and try to get some sleep."

"Get that cursehag away from me. She's trying to kill me!"

Dedrie shook her head sorrowfully. "Completely delirious. The fever can take ye like this sometimes. It makes them very hard to nurse. She really needs to swallow some o' the syrup, my lady. Such high fevers are dangerous. Will ye help me hold her down?"

"Is that really necessary?" Nina asked.

"Aye, it is. Fever o' the brain is very dangerous. Ye do no' want it to kill her, do ye?"

"Kill her? O' course no'!"

"Then help me get some o' the medicine into her. I canna break her fever without it."

Nina looked at the small dark bottle in Dedrie's hand in perturbation. "Is she really that ill?"

"Look at her, she's raving!"

"I no' raving!" Rhiannon said desperately. "Nina, ye must believe me. Do no' listen to this cursehag! She's one o' them. She's trying to kill me. She kens what I saw . . ."

The nursemaid suddenly stepped forward and deftly tipped another measure of medicine into Rhiannon's mouth. Taken by surprise Rhiannon choked and spluttered, involuntarily swallowing a mouthful. It tasted like slime. Incoherent with anger, she swung at the nursemaid, punching her so hard Dedrie went flying back and crashed to the floor. The medicine bottle flew out of her hand and smashed in the hearth, the fire leaping up like hissing green adders.

Dedrie sat on the floor in a welter of skirts, one hand to her temple, the other bracing her on the floor. For a moment her face was white as paper, her eyes looking like hard brown pebbles, her lips drawn back and stiff with rage. She took a deep gasping breath as Nina flew to her assistance. Dedrie's eyes bored into Rhiannon's with such unmistakable enmity that Rhiannon could not believe Nina was helping her up and stammering apologies. The very next instant the colour came back to her cheeks and the rigidity of her features relaxed.

"Obh obh!" she said reassuringly. "Never ye mind, my lady. It's no' the first time a delirious patient has struck out at me. Never ye mind about me, I'll be fine. I'll rub in some arnica cream later and the bruise'll soon fade, never ye worry. But she's gone and broken the bottle and all the borage syrup is spilt. Luckily I have some more. It may take me some time to find it, though. Ye go and get yourself ready for breakfast, and leave the poor lass to me."

"I am so very sorry," Nina said again. "I do hope ye are no' hurt."

Dedrie rubbed at the purpling bruise. "I must admit she took me by surprise. Never ye mind. What she needs now is sleep.

I'll bring up some more medicine later, and one o' the maids to help me, and she'll be fit as a fiddle in no time."

"Tell her to go away, Nina! I need to talk to ye."

"No talking," Dedrie said firmly to Nina. "Hear how hoarse her voice is? She needs peace and quiet. She'll feel much better after some rest."

"Dinna need rest!" Rhiannon said forcefully and tried to sit up. The movement made the pounding in her head come back, but she ignored it, reaching out her hands to Nina. "Nina, please, listen to me." Her throat was so sore it was hard to speak.

Nina hesitated.

"Later," Dedrie said firmly. "She's delirious, canna ye see that? Let her sleep, and she can tell ye about her nightmares later."

"Very well then," Nina nodded, and allowed Dedrie to usher her and Fèlice from the room. Rhiannon moved her head restlessly on the pillow, tears choking her so she could not, for a moment, cry out or protest. By the time she had swallowed her tears, Dedrie had gathered up the dirty washing, taken the spent lantern, and gone quietly away, leaving the room dim and quiet.

Tears spilled over. Rhiannon scrubbed them away furiously, and cautiously heaved herself upright. She did feel very odd indeed. Her chest hurt, her head ached, and she felt utterly exhausted. When she swung her legs out of bed, a wave of dizziness washed over her and she clutched at the bedpost to steady herself. She sat for a moment, waiting for her vision to recover. Then she looked for her boots, but they were gone from the side of the bed. Her cloak was gone too. This frightened her. She was trembling all over with the cold, despite the fire glowing in the hearth. Slowly Rhiannon made her way to the cupboard where she had hidden her saddlebags, holding on to the furniture to steady herself, and found her shawl and wrapped it tightly round her grubby, mud-streaked nightgown. Then she made her way to the door, opening it a crack and listening. There was a low murmur of voices from Iven and Nina's room.

When she felt certain she could not hear Dedrie's voice, Rhiannon went down the hallway, one hand on the wall, and opened the door.

Nina and Fèlice were there, and all of the others too, even Maisie with her head swathed in bandages. The shutters were open, showing a clear sky just brightening with dawn. Outside the windows, ravens hovered in the wind, calling sadly. Roden sat up in bed, drinking a cup of milk. Nina, looking distressed, was telling everyone what had happened. Everyone was talking excitedly. As Rhiannon came in, they turned in surprise. Nina got at once to her feet and came forward swiftly, remonstrating with her. Lewen stood up also, looking worried.

"Ye should be resting," Nina scolded.

Rhiannon took a deep breath. "Canna rest. Nina, can ye no' see what's going on? We canna stay here, we must get away just as fast as we can. They're evil, every one o' them. I heard them . . . what the word? Say true?"

"Confess?" Lewen said.

"Aye, confess. I heard them confess to murdering people, lots o' people. And I saw their ghosts."

Cameron shook his head. "That was some nightmare."

"No nightmare! I saw truly. Boys, lots o' dead boys. And in the Tower, more ghosts, hundreds o' them, thousands o' them. Too many to count."

"Rhiannon, my dear, indeed ye are no' well," Nina said, putting her arm about her. "Please, ye must get back to bed."

Rhiannon broke free. "No! We must get away. Canna ye feel how evil this place is? Why do ye no' believe me?"

"It's no' that I do no' believe ye, dear," Nina replied, her voice as troubled as her face. "It is just . . . well, we canna get away now. Ye are unwell, and Maisie too, and the road is blocked . . ."

"It is a trap," Rhiannon said with conviction. "They want to kill us too. He said . . . the laird said . . . they like to see how many times they can kill a man and bring him back to life."

A shocked murmur rose.

"When?" Edithe said skeptically. "When did the laird say this? To ye? He confessed all this to ye last night? Oh, please!"

"No' to me," Rhiannon answered. "He did no' ken I was there. I was listening, watching."

"Spying?" Edithe said nastily.

"Och, aye, spying," Rhiannon said impatiently. "They were there in the Tower, nine o' them . . ."

"Nine?" Nina asked sharply.

"Aye, nine, all dressed in long red robes with hoods. I could no' see their faces."

"But ye ken it was the laird and lady," Edithe said.

"Aye, o' course. They raised a ghost, a man, the laird's dead brother. They said it was too good an opportunity to miss, it being a dark moon. But then, another ghost came. A lady."

"I thought ye said there were hundreds o' ghosts," Cameron said, nudging Rafferty and smirking.

"Aye, there were." A fit of coughing came over Rhiannon, so fierce she thought she would cough up her heart. Nina supported her, rubbing her back. When at last it subsided, Rhiannon was too exhausted to speak. She leant on Nina and listened to the others' scepticism.

"Loss o' blood will do that to ye," Cameron was saying, grinning. "She's been cutting herself every night, Fèlice says. Seeing ghosts everywhere. Barmy." And he rotated one finger round and round near his ear.

Fèlice cast Rhiannon an apologetic glance. "She's sick," she said defensively.

"No wonder," Cameron replied.

"It was just a nightmare," Edithe said. "Ye slept with her, Fèlice. She was there all night, wasn't she?"

Fèlice shrugged, looking uncomfortable. "I think so. I mean, I was asleep. She woke me a few times, thrashing round and calling out. She thought she saw a ghost standing over us."

"Delirious," Edithe said.

"People have rotten dreams when they're sick," Landon said defensively. "And we've heard so many terrible stories since we came here. I dreamt o' ghostly boys too, last night."

"Dreams can seem very real sometimes," Iven said comfortingly. "Especially when ye've got a fever."

"No' a dream," Rhiannon said angrily. She unwrapped her shawl. "Look at my nightgown! Would it be this dirty if I had no' been crawling around in the mud in it?"

Cameron sniggered, and Rhiannon felt blood surge up her face.

"Walking in her sleep?" Edithe hazarded.

"No, walking awake! The laddie came and took me to his

room, and showed me all the dead boys. He wants me to help them."

"Och, sure, indeed," Cameron said. "He came to ye. Why no' Nina, or Iven, I wonder?"

"Because I can see him, I think," Rhiannon said flatly, and sat down abruptly. She clenched her hands together to hide their trembling.

There was a well of silence, and Rhiannon spoke into it, trying to choose her words with care. "I was frightened. I ran away. I saw light coming from the laird's library. I went down. There's some kind o' hidden doorway in the bookcase. It leads to a hall between the walls. I followed it. It goes to the auld Tower. They were there, the nine people in hoods. Chanting. They killed a rooster."

"Indeed?" Nina said, exchanging glances with Iven.

Rhiannon was encouraged. She tried to remember more details to tell. "One o' them whipped the laird all bloody. The whip has nine . . . what would you call them? Strings?"

"A cat o' nine tails," Lewen exclaimed.

Rhiannon was puzzled. "Nay, no cat. A whip."

"A whip with nine thongs is called a cat o' nine tails. I dinna ken why. Happen because it makes the victim yowl like a cat."

"The laird did no' yowl. He dinna make a noise. It must've hurt, though, for his back was all bloody."

"Ye are sure it was the laird?" Edithe asked, scandalised.

"I did no' see his face, he had his back to me. But he had no beard, and when he spoke it sounded like the laird. And I'm sure he called the ghost 'brother'."

"Which ghost?" Edithe said. "Ye've seen so many it's hard to keep track."

Rhiannon stared at her in cold, white anger. "The first ghost to come, the one they seek to bring back from the dead. He called him 'Falkner', and then 'brother and laird o' Fettercairn.' He is the same ghost as I saw in the great hall last night, the one that was killed by the young, rough-looking man. They chanted these words, I dinna remember what, and then he just sort o' . . . floated out o' the shadows."

"Laird Malvern wants to resurrect his brother? But he died so long ago," Nina said.

"Twenty-five years they've been trying to bring him back to life. I heard them say so."

"Twenty-five years?" Iven repeated thoughtfully. Cameron went to say something and the jongleur shushed him with an upraised hand. Rhiannon went on wearily.

"They are the ones that have been messing with all the dead people, digging them up and trying to learn how to make them come alive again. He said so, I heard him. And killing people, experimenting with them."

"How awful," Landon said, whey-faced. Maisie gave a little moan and raised one hand to her bandaged head.

"Then the other ghost came, the woman. She mocked them for standing on a heart o' stars and calling the dead. They were all frightened o' her. She said she would tell them the secret o' raising the dead if they promised to raise her first."

"Indeed?" Nina said again, exchanging an incredulous glance with Lewen.

"Gracious, ye canna believe her?" Edithe burst out. "Look at her, she's sick as a dog. She canna even stand. How can ye believe such things o' our host? He was a most charming and cultured man, and she's accusing him o' necromancy, and torture, and murder most foul. She must be mad!"

"She's been seeing ghosts everywhere," Cameron said, and Rafferty gave an unhappy murmur of agreement.

"There are ghosts everywhere," Rhiannon said thickly.

There was silence. She saw Edithe roll up her eyes and gritted her teeth together, her eyes burning with tears. She looked defiantly at Nina. "Do ye believe me? Or do ye think it's just a dream too?"

Nina chose her words with care. "I do no' ken, Rhiannon. It's true ye are sick and shaking with fever, and dreams are often more vivid when ye're feverish, but even so, dreams can be true sendings at times. And though I do no' see the ghosts ye've seen, that does no' mean they are no' there. I have felt troubled and uneasy since I came into this castle, and have fancied I've seen curtains lift when there is no breeze, or heard voices crying in the night. Happen ye have the gift o' clear-seeing, more strongly than any o' us. I do no' ken what to do, though. This needs investigation. Edithe is right. These are serious allegations. I would no' like to accuse a man o' necromancy and murder without strong evidence. And my heart misgives me greatly, for if your dream be true . . ."

"It was no' a dream," Rhiannon said stubbornly.

Nina went on as if she had not spoken. ". . . then we may be in grave danger. I wish we had never come this way, but since we did, and we are here in Fettercairn Castle, I think we should do our best to leave as quickly as we can. This is a matter for the Rìgh's men to investigate. We must try to send him a message now, just as soon as we can, for if Rhiannon is right then we are in a trap and may have trouble getting out o' it. Iven, why do ye no' take the boys and go and inspect this damage to the road? See if we canna make our way past it, even if it means leaving the caravans."

Iven nodded. "Good idea."

"Rhiannon, my dear, go back to bed, please. The sooner ye are well again, the sooner we can go. Lassies, I think we should go and see what we can find out. If Rhiannon is right, then the castle is the source o' all the evil and trouble in this valley and the Rìgh will need to ken o' it."

Nina's voice was coming in waves, loud, soft, then strangely loud again. Rhiannon felt warm hands on her arms and looked up, her head feeling heavy and large on a thin, weak neck. Lewen bent over her. She looked up into his face and, to her surprise, tears sprang from her eyes.

"Come on, *leannan*," he said softly. "Ye should be in bed."

"Do ye believe me?" she whispered urgently, fixing her eyes on his.

He nodded, and gently wiped away her tears with his thumb. "O' course I do. Come, let me get ye to bed."

He bent and gathered her up into his arms. Rhiannon was too tired to argue. She put her arms about his neck, rested her head on his shoulder, and let him carry her from the room.

Cold Comfort

When Lewen came out of Rhiannon's room, it was to find the maid Wilma hovering in the corridor, her ear bent to the door into Nina and Iven's suite. She started at the sound of his step and moved hurriedly away.

"I'm sorry, sir," she gasped, twisting her apron in her hands. "I've been sent to wake ye all and bring ye down to breakfast. I dinna ken if Master Irving warned ye . . . I ken it is early . . . I dinna want to intrude . . ."

"It is early," Lewen agreed. "It's barely cockcrow."

"My laird likes to rise early," she said. "I was worried . . . I ken it is no' what is done at court, dining so early, I mean, but my laird does hate anyone being late."

"Does he?" Lewen said genially. "I imagine no-one dares ever keep him waiting then."

"Oh, no, sir," she breathed.

"Well, witches rise early too," Lewen said cheerfully, "so we are all awake."

"Och, so it's true then!" she blurted and then turned crimson. "About ye all being witches, I mean. I didna believe it. I mean, ye all seem so nice, and my laird has let ye all stay and . . ." Her words trailed away.

"No' all o' us are witches," Lewen said. "Most o' us are mere apprentices. Why, does my laird no' care for the Coven?"

"Oh, no, sir," she said in surprise. "Why, he used to hunt witches down and burn them, my da told me!"

"Is that so?" Lewen said, turning his head to stare at her.

Immediately Wilma was thrown into confusion. "'Twas a long time ago . . . times change, they say . . . I dinna ken if it be true . . ."

"Times do change, and we must change with them," Lewen said, with no change to his affable manner. His veins were swelling with rage, though, and it took an effort to keep his voice steady.

Wilma looked at him doubtfully. "Yes, sir."

"Is that tea I see there on your tray?" Lewen gestured to the laden tray on the hall table. "Ye'll be welcome at any hour if ye bring Nina tea. Come, bring it in, and tell us where we are to go for breakfast and when."

"I'll show ye all down," Wilma said. "Master Irving said I was no' to let any o' ye go wandering off by yourselves. In case ye get lost, I mean."

"O' course," Lewen said, opening the door for her. She picked up the heavy tray with a visible effort and carried it in, staring at Nina with apprehensive eyes as if suddenly expecting her to have sprouted horns and a tail.

Nina was sitting wearily by the fire, Roden on her lap, while the other apprentices were still all heatedly discussing Rhiannon's news. Nina was not listening to them, but was staring into the flames as if their ephemeral, many-tongued shapes could speak to her. She was so entranced she did not notice Wilma at first, but as silence fell, she glanced round and smiled and thanked her.

Wilma poured the tea, Lewen and Landon helping pass the cups around, and then she said diffidently that she would be back in an hour to take them down to the breakfast hall.

"Is that a different hall to where we ate last night? Thank Eà! I do no' think I could manage to eat a mouthful if I had to do so under the gaze o' all those poor slaughtered animals," Nina said.

Wilma gave a shy smile of sympathy. "I do no' like them much either," she admitted. "Us maids hate having to clean the dining hall late at night. Their eyes gleam so, it looks like they're still alive."

"Does the laird eat there every night? I wonder he does no' suffer indigestion!"

"My laird likes such things," Wilma said. "He has a whole stuffed bear in his library, and drawers and cabinets full o' strange things—a webbed hand and the head o' an ogre, and a braid o' witch's hair, and the jaw o' a dragon, and the skin o' one o' the sea-folk, and a pickled baby—"

"Urrk!" Fèlice cried.

"A pickled baby?" Rafferty and Landon both echoed.

"Surely no'!" Edithe said.

"Wilma nodded. "Aye. He collects such things. Folk here-abouts are always on the look-out for curiosities, for he pays well for them. He has drawers and drawers o' old bones and stones and skulls, and lots o' dead paws and hands. I seen them once. Normally us maids do no' clean his library, his gillie does that for him, but I was sent to fetch something for him and I saw the bear, it's near twice as tall as me and looks like it's alive! And some o' the drawers o' the cabinet were open, and so I couldna resist having a quick peek. I had nightmares after, though, I tell ye what! O' dead hands creeping after me—"

"Wilma, have ye naught better to do than stand here gossip-ing?" Dedrie spoke sharply from the doorway.

Wilma jumped as if she had been stuck with a pin, and made a hasty curtsy. "Sorry, ma'am, o' course, ma'am, I'll go now, ma'am," she squeaked, and hurriedly clattered everything onto the tray and made a hasty exit, almost tipping the whole lot to the floor in her discomfiture.

Dedrie shook her head indulgently. "Lasses! They are all the same. Will stand around all morn repeating idle gossip instead o' getting their work done."

"Is there something I can do for ye?" Nina asked in a cool voice. "We were just about to get ready for breakfast."

"Och, naught. I've just brought yon lassie some more borage syrup." Dedrie lifted her basket of medicines, but did not come in. "I would no' have disturbed ye, but I heard young Wilma chattering on, and did no' want her bothering ye. It is so hard to get reliable servants nowadays!"

"Rhiannon is sleeping peacefully," Nina said, her brows drawing together. "I do no' think she should be disturbed."

"I'll only be a moment," Dedrie said with a warm smile, and turned to go.

"Nay!" Nina cried, getting to her feet.

Dedrie looked round in surprise. As the light of the room fell upon her face, Lewen saw in surprise that, as well as the nasty bruise blooming on her temple, the nursemaid's skin was badly blistered and raw all down one side, as if she had been burnt.

"I do no' want her woken," Nina said, with a fair attempt at a smile. "Sleep is the best thing for her. Leave the medicine with me and I'll offer it to her when she wakes."

Lewen smothered a grin. He knew that witches all took an oath of truth-telling when they joined the Coven, a restriction that often irked those who worked in secret on the Rìgh's behalf, like Nina and Iven, or Finn the Cat and Jay the Fiddler. He recognised an evasion of the truth when he heard it. Nina may offer Rhiannon the medicine, but both she and Lewen knew that Rhiannon would most certainly refuse it.

By the look on Dedrie's face, she knew it too.

"Och, my lady, no need to trouble yourself," she said. "Ye go on down to breakfast and I'll look after the lass. That's my job, after all."

"No need," Nina said pleasantly. "Ye have done enough for us all. I'm sure a morning in bed will work wonders for Rhiannon, and we will hopefully all be out o' your hair by this afternoon."

Dedrie's smile was unnaturally rigid. "But my laird . . . I mean, what about the fallen tree? It has proved difficult to move with the weather so rough."

"Today looks set to be fair," Nina said, glancing out the window. The sky was crystal-sharp and azure-blue, and the windblown leaves of the trees glittered as if they had been polished. "I am sure the laird's men will have no trouble moving the tree now that the storm has blown over."

"The ground is still very wet and slippery," Dedrie said sharply.

"Och, we will go and lend a hand or two," Iven said cheerfully. "I'm sure we'll manage. We have trespassed long enough on your laird's hospitality."

"But the lass with the dog bites . . . ye canna mean to move her so soon. In those rough, jolting caravans!" Dedrie sounded scandalised.

"Maisie is much better," Nina said firmly. "Aren't ye, dearling?"

"Aye," Maisie said uncertainly.

"She shall spend the morning resting too, and then when the tree is gone and the road clear again, we'll be on our way. We'll make sure Maisie is as comfortable as possible."

"I canna agree to ye moving the lass with the fever," Dedrie said. "I dinna think ye realise just how sick she is. I've seen fevers like that afore. Expose her to a nasty wind like that, and all the jolting o' those caravans, and ye could kill her, I warn ye."

"I think ye underestimate Rhiannon," Nina said. "She's very strong and her fever really does no' seem that bad. I think she's just caught a chill."

"Well, on your own head be it," Dedrie said angrily. She turned to go.

"Happen ye had best leave the medicine with me," Nina said, holding out her hand.

Dedrie grasped her basket tightly to her. "Och, no need," she answered. "If the lass is sleeping I'll leave her be. I'll look in on her later. Ye had best all be getting ready for breakfast, my laird does no' like to be kept waiting."

"So we've gathered," Nina said dryly. Dedrie gave a curt nod of her head, a quick fake smile, and left.

Nina went and shut the door behind her. "Did ye see her face?" she said quietly to Iven. "I told ye that Rhiannon spat her medicine out all over her. Do ye think . . . ?"

"Surely no'! Imagine what such medicine would do to your insides if . . . Eà's green blood! I see what ye mean. Do ye really think so?"

Nina stood for a long moment, pondering, then turned to the apprentices, milling uncertainly near the fire.

"Maisie, my dear, I do no' think ye should go down to breakfast, ye're still rather unsteady on your poor auld pins. Do ye want to go back to bed for a while, and I'll arrange to have some food sent up to ye?" Maisie nodded and got up stiffly from her chair. One heavily bandaged arm was in a sling and she limped painfully. "Rafferty, help Maisie back to her room, will ye?"

As Rafferty offered the injured girl his arm, Nina rubbed her forehead as if it pained her.

"I do no' feel happy about leaving Rhiannon all by herself,

or Maisie either," she said abruptly. "Rhiannon did not seem delirious to me. Landon, would ye mind staying with them? Ye still have a bit o' a cough and shouldna be out in that cold wind. I'll leave Lulu with ye too. Send her to me if aught happens to worry ye."

"Ye think Rhiannon's wild tale is true then?" Cameron asked in some surprise. "Ye suspect we truly may be in danger?"

"I have a very bad feeling," Nina said. "I want to get us all away from here just as fast as I can."

Iven put his arm about her. "Your wish is my command, dearling," he said cheerfully. "Besides, I have a strong suspicion that whey-faced seneschal o' the laird's waters the wine. That stuff he inflicted on us last night was undrinkable!"

"Well, I never thought I'd say this but personally I'll be glad to ride on," Fèlice said. "This castle gives me the creeps."

"I think ye are all absurd," Edithe said with an angry titter. "The MacFerris clan is one o' the oldest and most respected families in Ravenshaw, and Laird Malvern was perfectly charming. Rhiannon is obviously a hysteric who canna bear no' being the centre o' attention. Personally I find her behaviour absolutely appalling. From the moment she joined our party she has done naught but cause one scene after another. It is all an act, I'm surprised ye canna see that, Nina. She is nothing but a scheming, conniving little cat . . ."

"Thank ye for your opinion, Edithe," Nina said wearily. "I think we ken your position on the subject. Shall we all go and dress for breakfast now? I would no' like to be late."

Iven grinned at her. "I wonder what the penalty is for being late to both dinner and breakfast? The dungeons?"

"Do no' joke about it," Nina said with an involuntary shiver. "Happen it's because I'm a jongleur born and bred and have no liking for high stone walls, but I really do no' like this place. I feel most uneasy. Let's just get through breakfast as pleasantly as possible, and get on the road again! Bairns, can we no' talk about what Rhiannon thinks she saw last night? Let's all pretend everything is fine. If by horrible chance any o' it is true, I do no' want to rouse their suspicions."

The apprentice-witches nodded their heads solemnly, all except Edithe, who sighed and rolled her eyes.

While the others went to wash and dress for the day, Nina
beckoned Lewen to come and help her. "I am worried about
that stuff Dedrie gave Rhiannon," she said to him quietly. "Did
ye see the blistering on Dedrie's face? She forced some o' that
stuff down Rhiannon's throat. I fear it's some kind o' poison. I
may no' be a healer but I ken something about the art, as all
witches must. I'm going to mix up an emetic and give it to Rhiannon. I'll make her very sick but at least it'll get that stuff out
o' her stomach. The thing is, I'll need your help to get it down
her. She trusts ye more than anyone. Will ye help me?"

"O' course," Lewen answered, feeling light-headed with the
rush of instant anxiety. "Will it have done her any harm already?"

"I dinna ken," Nina answered. "I do no' ken what was in the
potion. I hope no'. I think it would no' work too quickly, they'd
want her death to look natural."

Lewen's skin crept with horror. He hurried to Rhiannon's
room as quickly as he could, while Nina made up her emetic.
The satyricorn lay in her bed, her black hair spread out all over
the pillow, damp with perspiration. Her face was damp too, and
flushed crimson, and he saw in dismay that her lips were badly
blistered. She moaned and turned her head restlessly on her pillow, her hands clutching at the counterpane. Suddenly she
jerked upright and said something in a loud, guttural voice, in a
language he did not recognise. Her eyes stared straight at him
but did not recognise him.

Lewen soothed her, laying her back on her pillows, then
wrung out a cloth in cold water and laid it on her forehead. She
flung it from her irritably. He picked it up again and gently
dabbed her face and neck with it. Within seconds it was warm
to the touch.

"She's feverish," he said shortly to Nina, as she came hurrying in with her hands full of bottles.

Nina felt her forehead and then her pulse. "Aye. I hope I
willna be doing her more harm than good by giving her the
stonecrop. It's hard to ken what's best to do. Am I maligning
that nursemaid, suspecting her o' trying to poison Rhiannon?
Happen she saw the coming o' the fever better than me."

Rhiannon moaned and twisted in the bed, uttering more un-
intelligible gibberish.

"Her mouth is blistered," Lewen said.

Nina looked closely, then gently slid her fingers into Rhiannon's mouth so she could open it and inspect her tongue and gums. Rhiannon grimaced and tried instinctively to bite. Nina withdrew her fingers quickly.

"Aye, and so are her gums. Poor lass. Here, lift her up and hold her still, Lewen. I'm going to give her the stonecrop, and then I'll try to dab on something to ease those ulcers."

Lewen did as he was told. Rhiannon shrieked and flung herself back when she felt his hands on her, but he spoke softly in her ear and she calmed, seeming to rouse a little.

"Here, Rhiannon, swallow this for me, sweetling," Nina coaxed, holding a beaker of some thick, green liquid to her lips. Rhiannon moaned and moved her head away. Lewen shifted his grasp so he cupped the back of her head in his hand. The nape of her neck was damp and hot. He slid his other hand round to cup her chin and swiftly Nina tipped the beaker up.

Rhiannon went mad with fear, and Lewen had to hold her tightly to keep her still. He pushed her mouth shut and she swallowed instinctively, though her body twisted and flailed like a trout on the river bank. One hand caught him a glancing blow on his face, but grimly he held her firm until she had swallowed every drop. Then he relaxed his grip and tenderly laid her down. She opened her eyes, staring at him with such a look of terror that his heart lurched.

"I'm sorry, I'm sorry, it had to be done," he said.

She gazed at him with a blank, wild-eyed look, then suddenly began to vomit. Nina and Lewen flinched back, then hurried to support her, Lewen holding her upright while Nina thrust the bowl she had brought under the satyricorn's face.

For almost ten minutes Rhiannon retched, until there was nothing left in her to lose. As each paroxysm passed, she would stare up at Lewen with such a heart-wrenching look of hurt and betrayal that he felt quite miserable and choked in the throat. At last the vomiting eased, and Nina was able to give her something to help her sleep, and soothe some balm onto her blistered lips and gums. Rhiannon was so exhausted by then that she barely resisted. Lewen was able to lay her down, and wash her

face and hands while Nina quickly tore off the soiled counterpane and covered her up with the cover from her own bed.

"I'll wash this out and hang it to dry afore the fire," Nina
said. "We do no' want Dedrie to guess what we have done.
Hurry and get dressed, Lewen, and make sure ye wash well. We
both stink o' vomit."

Lewen quickly did as he was told, but even so, by the time
he had cleaned himself up and dressed, Wilma was already
waiting anxiously at the end of the corridor. Nina came out of
her room, looking ruffled, buttoning up one sleeve as she came.

"Are we late?" she asked. Wilma just bit her lip, cast them a
scared look, and hurried them down the stairs. She had drawn
her cap down low over her forehead but, walking close behind
her, Lewen could not help but notice that one ear was red and
swollen as if it had been soundly boxed.

The breakfast room was another long, gloomy room with
dark panelling and a massive fireplace with an ornately carved
mantelpiece. No stuffed animal heads stared down from the
walls, but an enormous trout was mounted above the fire and
ancient fishing lines and nets were hung all around the rails,
above a number of dark paintings depicting limp pheasants
with wrung necks, or dead fish with palely gleaming eyes.
Lewen and Nina exchanged wry glances.

Lord Malvern sat stiff-backed at the head of the table. He
was pale, with deep lines graven from his nose to his mouth,
and heavy pouches under his eyes. He looked like a man who
had not slept well.

Lady Evaline, her companion Miss Prunella, the librarian,
the harper and his son were also sitting silently in their customary places round the table. They too looked strained and
tired. As Irving the seneschal bowed and led Nina and the apprentices to their places, the clock on the mantelpiece struck the
hour. Without volition they all quickened their step, and Fèlice
gave a nervous giggle as she collapsed into her seat. As soon as
the last chime died away, the doors swung open and a procession of silent servants came in carrying covered plates and
tureens. Once again meat dominated the menu. There was
bacon and eggs, smoked haddock, a side of beef, a plate of kip-
pers, a very pink ham, and eggs scrambled with salmon.

"Just some toast and honey for me, thank ye," Nina said quietly. "Or happen some porridge, if ye have any?"

Lord Malvern nodded at Irving who bowed and jerked his head at one of the servants.

"Oh, please, do no' make it just for me," Nina said.

"I'm sure the cook will have made porridge for the servants," Lord Malvern said coldly. "It is no trouble."

Fèlice giggled again, then bit her lip and looked down at her plate.

"I believe ye are anxious to deprive us o' our company," the lord said to Iven, signalling to his gillie to fill his plate with beef. "I am sorry for it. I was hoping to persuade ye to bide a wee longer."

"We would love to stay, but indeed, we have been delayed far too long already," Iven said. "I was wondering what progress has been made on clearing the road?"

Lord Malvern made an expansive gesture. "The weather has been most inclement," he explained.

"Aye, indeed, it has," Iven agreed. "But today has dawned fair, thank heavens."

"Aye. I have ordered some men to get to work clearing the tree but indeed, we have all suffered a lot o' damage from the storm, the people o' the valley as much as we here at the castle. I fear my men will be kept busy all day mending roofs and fixing fences."

"Aye, o' course," Iven said. "And the weather is so chancy here in the highlands, I imagine ye must all be anxious to do what must be done afore another storm blows up."

"I'm so glad ye understand," Lord Malvern said.

"We must no' sit idle while all around us work, though, must we, lads?" Iven said, turning with a grin to Lewen, Cameron and Rafferty. "Happen we can relieve my laird o' having to clear the road for us? Why do we no' walk down and have a look at this pesky tree after breakfast?"

Lord Malvern looked annoyed. "There is no need, I assure ye."

"Oh, no trouble," Iven assured him airily. "In fact, I'm sure we'd leap at the chance to stretch our legs, wouldn't we, lads!"

"Aye, indeed," they chorused.

"But what kind o' host would I be, allowing my guests to undertake such hard manual labour?"

"Och, we are no' afraid o' work," Iven said. "These are big, doughty lads, my laird. The exercise will do them good."

"But I fear it may be dangerous," Lord Malvern said. "It is a very big auld tree and it has fallen awkwardly across the road, bringing down a pile o' rocks and mud with it. Indeed I think ye had best leave it to my men, who are experienced in such things."

"Och, no need to fear for us," Iven said cheerfully. "Yeomen o' the Guard are used to turning their hands to all sorts o' work, and Lewen here is the grandson o' a woodcutter and probably kens more about how to move the tree than any o' your men. We'll take a look at it, and I promise if I think it's dangerous, I'll no' lay a finger upon it."

Lord Malvern inclined his head. "Very well. I thank ye for your offer o' help. Durward, will ye accompany my guests down to examine the tree?"

The gillie-coise inclined his head. "Aye, my laird."

While Iven and Lord Malvern had been talking, a footman had brought in a big tureen of porridge and had ladled some into everyone but Edithe's bowl, the blonde girl obviously taking Lord Malvern's jibe about it being food fit only for servants to heart. She was daintily eating toast with honey, and sipping at a cup of lukewarm tea. Everything was somewhat cold, the kitchen being a long way away from the breakfast hall.

An awkward silence fell while everyone ate. Lord Malvern did not seem aware of it, frowning down at his plate with a preoccupied air, while Lady Evaline seemed even vaguer than before. Miss Prunella cleared her throat nervously and hurried into speech.

"Perhaps, while your husband rides out to look at this tree, ye and the lasses would like to have a turn about the garden? It is Lady Evaline's habit to sit there most fine days, and I am sure she would enjoy some company this morning. It is so pleasant to see the sun again, is it no'?"

"Thank ye, I am sure we would enjoy that," Nina replied politely.

"I want to explore the castle," Roden said. "I want to find that room with all the toys."

Nina's eyes flashed up from her bowl. "Ye need some fresh air, my lad," she said. "Why do ye no' go with your father to look at this tree?"

"I could do with some help, laddie," Iven said solemnly.

Roden looked pleased. "Och, aye, that sounds like fun. Can I have a go at the saw?"

"Maybe," Iven replied.

"I'll go and look for that boy's room later then," Roden said, causing Nina to flush a little and bite her lip. Lord Malvern stared at him coldly, and Lady Evaline looked up from the scrambled eggs she was pushing round and round her plate.

"Do ye mean my boy Rory's room?" she said into the silence. "Do ye want to play with his toys? I've been saving them, ye ken, for when he comes back. I do no' think he would mind ye playing with them."

"Oh goody!" Roden said.

"I hope ye are no' scared o' ghosts," she said. "He's still there, ye see, he plays there still sometimes and all the other boys too."

"Evaline," Lord Malvern said forbiddingly.

"What, Malvern?"

"Ye must no' frighten the lad with your ghost stories," he said. "He's at an impressionable age and I'm sure his mother would no' thank ye for telling him scary tales."

"I like ghost stories," Roden said. "And I'm no' scared o' anything."

"No' even ghosts?" Lord Malvern said with such heavy meaning in his voice that Nina looked up the table at him, startled.

"Nay," Roden said scornfully. "Ghosts canna hurt ye, Mam says."

"Are ye sure o' that?" Lord Malvern said, still staring at him from under beetling brows.

Roden looked troubled. "I guess so."

"Then ye canna have heard any true ghost stories," Lord Malvern said, with such a strange note in his voice that Nina looked alarmed. "Believe me, I could tell ye a few tales that would have ye whimpering in your bed at night and begging your mother no' to take the candle away. I could tell ye tales that would freeze your blood in your veins—"

"My laird!" Nina cried.

He turned his fixed, intent gaze towards her.

"Ye are right! He is but a lad and I would no' thank ye for scaring him."

Lord Malvern laughed. "No, that I warrant."

Lady Evaline said kindly, "Ye need no' be scared o' Rory, laddie. He would no' hurt ye. He was just a boy when he died, no' much aulder than ye."

"How did he die?" Roden asked curiously.

"It was cold," Lady Evaline said in a whisper. "Och, it was so very cold and we could no' get out . . ." Tears filled her eyes.

"Fettercairn was attacked by some very bad men," Lord Malvern said harshly. "They used foul sorceries to trick and overwhelm us, and my brother Falkner paid for it with his life, and with the life o' his little boy. They will pay, though. Och aye, they will pay, and one day soon too!" He laughed and Lewen felt an uncomfortable tightening of his scalp. Everyone sitting round the table was staring at the lord in fascination, all except Lady Evaline, who was nodding her head in placid agreement.

"I do hope ye will come and see us afore ye leave," the harper said suddenly to Iven. "I did so enjoy hearing some o' the new songs and stories last night. I wish ye had time to teach us more."

"Why do ye and the lassies no' take morning tea with us in the north tower?" Miss Prunella said just as hurriedly to Nina. "I'm sure Lady Evaline would like to show ye her embroidery."

As Nina and Iven both turned to answer politely, Lord Malvern laughed on. His face was white, the dents beside his mouth very deep. "They say revenge is a dish best eaten cold," he said to Lady Evaline. "Well, we are used to cold comfort, aren't we, my dear?"

She nodded her cloudy white head in sad agreement. Lord Malvern laughed, so strangely that no-one could pretend all was well. "Soon," he said. "Soon we shall have—"

The harper's son said sharply, "My laird!"

Lord Malvern whipped round to stare at him, his face suddenly transformed with rage. "Ye dare interrupt me!"

"My pardon, my laird," he said with lowered head.

"Never interrupt me again," Lord Malvern hissed, "else I'll have your entrails fed to the ravens."

There was a long silence. Iven stood up. "Well, thank ye for breakfast but I hope ye'll excuse us. The day's running away with us and I'd like to get to work. Come on, lads!"

Lewen, Cameron and Rafferty all stood up immediately. Lord Malvern turned to stare blankly at them, almost as if he had forgotten who they were. Then suddenly his brows snapped together and he cast a quick look around the room, as if realising he had revealed something he meant to keep hidden.

"I beg your pardon," he said. "An auld family joke."

"No' at all," Iven said just as politely.

After a long, frowning moment Lord Malvern stood. Lewen noticed he moved slowly and stiffly, and kept his shoulders very still. He wondered if the back under the black velvet coat was whipped raw and bloody.

"Durward will take ye to the fallen tree," he said heavily, and jerked his head at his bodyguard. Immediately the big, quiet man moved to stand at Iven's shoulder. "Take care, won't ye?" the lord then said to Iven. "I would hate any accident to occur while ye were guests in my home."

Nina threw an anxious look at her husband and stood up too, pushing her plate away from her. She had eaten very little. Iven smiled at her. "Och, thank ye for your concern," he said to Lord Malvern. "But there is no need to worry. We'll take very great care indeed."

"What about the other lad?" Lord Malvern asked suddenly. "Was there no' four o' ye? Where is he?"

He cast a piercing look at Irving, who bowed and said expressionlessly, "The other young man is resting in his rooms, my laird. Apparently his cough worsened overnight. I ordered a tray to be taken up to him, and to the two young ladies who were both still sleeping."

"Aye," the lord said thoughtfully. "The air o' Fettercairn does seem rather unhealthy to those o' your party, does it no'? It is very damp here, it is true, so close to the Findhorn Falls, and cold too, at nights." He flashed a look at Nina. "I understand one o' your young charges went sleepwalking about the castle last night and has caught a bad chill. I am sorry. I do hope she will feel better soon."

"I'm sure she shall," Nina replied.

"My nurse Dedrie will take excellent care o' her, I assure ye. She kens better than anyone what harm the damp night air can do."

"Thank ye, my laird," Nina said flatly.

He inclined his head. "No' at all."

Nina nodded to him, glanced round at the other inhabitants of the castle, who all sat as if frozen, and then went swiftly from the room. Iven and the apprentice-witches followed, the soft-footed bodyguard close behind.

"I will just go up and check on Rhiannon and Maisie," Nina said. "Have a care for yourself, won't ye, Iven? And for Roden. Do no' let him do anything reckless."

"I'll do my best," Iven said cheerfully. "Though he's as much o' a madcap as I was at his age."

Nina smiled wanly.

"Try to have a rest, my love," Iven said tenderly. "Ye're all worn out. We'll come back for lunch, and I hope to see some roses in your cheeks by then."

"Aye, dearling," Nina said submissively and turned towards the stairs. Before she had taken more than a few steps, Irving had moved smoothly ahead of her, bowing and showing the way with a fluid motion of one of those large, white hands.

As Nina and the girls went up the stairs, Iven turned to the gillie and said, "Now, let's have a look at that tree, shall we?"

Durward bowed his head and led them down the hall.

The Haunted Room

It was very quiet up on their floor of the castle. Maisie and Rhiannon were both asleep, the first peacefully, the other tossing and turning and muttering incoherently. Landon had been doing his best to soothe and comfort her, but was very glad to leave Rhiannon alone for a moment and come and join them in the main suite.

Nina moved restlessly about the room, standing at the window for a while, and then coming across to pet her sunbird, who sat on the top rung of the chair-back, head cocked.

"I just wish we could get out o' here," the journeywitch said unhappily. "I hate being confined within four walls all the time."

"Personally I'm enjoying being back in civilisation," Edithe said, smoothing the velvet of her skirt over her knees. "I canna understand why ye wish to spend all day riding through the rain in preference to being here, in the lap o' luxury."

"I canna help feeling we're caught in a trap," Nina said. "I canna even call a bird to my hand to take a message to the Rìgh! I've been trying since we arrived, but the ravens just chase any bird that comes away. I'd feel happier if someone kent where we are!"

The sunbird gave a long, melodious trill.

Landon looked up. "She's a brave bird, volunteering to fly to the Rìgh for ye. It's a long way for such a wee bird."

"Is that what she said?" Fèlice exclaimed. "Ye're good, understanding her. I just canna get my head around the language o' birds. It sounds awfully pretty but working out what it means!" She shook her head ruefully.

"It's too dangerous," Nina said. "I couldna bear to lose her. She

kens the way, o' course, she has been to Lucescere hundreds o'
times, but never alone and never across the mountains."

The sunbird trilled again, derisively.

"Could ye really give her a message to take?" Edithe was incredulous. "She's naught but a silly little parrot. How would
she ken where to go?"

Nina said angrily, "She may be small but she's smart as anything, and she kens the Rìgh well. *He* speaks the language o'
birds, and has always taken the time to converse with her."

"Then should ye no' send her?" Landon asked. "I mean, if
that's our only chance o' getting a message to the Rìgh?"

Nina stroked the bird's iridescent cheek. "She's no' strong
enough to fly across the mountains."

The sunbird squawked indignantly.

Nina smiled faintly. "I ken ye are a mountain bird, my pretty,
but ye canna tell me a sunbird is strong enough to cross the
ranges here, they're very high."

The sunbird shook out her brilliant tail-feathers and puffed
up her wings, looking cross.

"Are ye sure?" Nina said. "For indeed I am anxious to tell the
Rìgh o' our suspicions. Though we will be able to tell him ourselves, o' course, once we get to Lucescere. But just in
case . . ." Her voice died away.

There was a long silence. Fèlice looked rather scared. "We're
no' in any danger, are we, Nina?" she asked at last. "Ye do no'
suspect . . ."

Nina got up, shaking out her skirts determinedly. "I'm sorry,
my bairns," she said with a return of her usual manner. "I'm all
on edge from being kept cooped up in here. A jongleur to the
bone, I am, I'm afraid. We like the rolling road and the open air.
Do no' mind me. I'll send the Rìgh a message, just to put my
mind at peace, and then I'm going to go out and get some fresh
air!"

She sat down at the desk and tore a thin scroll of parchment
from the writing paper stacked there. She quickly wrote a brief
message on it, and then rolled it up, inserting it into a message-
tube that Lulu brought her from her bag.

"Is it safe, to just send a message like that?" Fèlice asked,
wide-eyed.

"I wrote in code," Nina said. "Believe me, Lachlan and Dide and I have been sending each other messages by bird since we were bairns. He will understand."

She held out her hand to the sunbird, who flew across to her with a flash of its brightly coloured wings. Nina crooned to it lovingly as she attached the little steel tube to the sunbird's leg. "Fly swift and safe, my pretty," she said, opening the casements wide and throwing the sunbird out. Higher and higher the little bird flew, up towards the sun, carolling joyfully to be out riding the winds again.

Suddenly there was a loud, harsh cry. A raven dropped down from the castle's northern tower, its wings so black and glossy in the sunshine they seemed to flash silver. Nina cried out in alarm. The sunbird ducked and dived, but the raven was too fast for it. It seized the little green bird in its claws and pecked it cruelly, once, twice, thrice. Then it let go, calmly circling back up to its tower. The sunbird fell in a welter of bright feathers.

Nina cried out, then turned and ran from the room. They all hurried after her, distressed. It was a long way down to the courtyard below, and they brushed past countless surprised servants and a very displeased seneschal on the way, almost toppling him over. When they finally reached the courtyard, with its green oblong of garden set in the centre, it was to find Nina on her knees, cradling her dead bird, weeping. None of the apprentices had ever seen the sorceress break down before and, appalled, they crowded round her, trying to comfort her.

Nina got to her feet, wiping away her tears with an impatient hand. "I should have kent better," she said grimly. "O' course the ravens would no' let her pass."

She kissed the dead bird's limp head and then turned to Landon. "Will ye help me bury her?"

He nodded, looking white and shocked.

"Edithe, I do no' want Rhiannon and Maisie left alone. Can ye go and sit with them, please?"

Edithe was displeased, but she nodded reluctantly and went back into the castle, while Fèlice slid one arm about Nina's waist. "I'm so very sorry."

"Me too," Nina answered. She turned her face up to the sky, where ravens wheeled ceaselessly around the two looming towers, cawing loudly as if in mockery. "I hate this place," she whispered. "Oh, when can we get away from here?"

The road down to the lowlands was enclosed on both sides by high stone walls so Lewen felt as if they walked along a tunnel. Although the sun shone and the wind blew briskly, it was cold as ice inside the walls and the stones wept water.

Gradually the wall on their right grew lower, until Lewen was able to see glimpses of the valley below if he stood on his toes. It looked impossibly benign in the sunshine, a rolling landscape of freshly tilled fields, green meadows and fluffy white sheep.

At last they came to the edge of the castle, and the high stone wall turned at a sharp right angle, continuing up a steep, rugged cliff. Only a few steps past the end of the wall, a massive tree lay right across the road. It had smashed the low wall on the right-hand side, its branches hanging out above the precipice. Its bulk completely filled the road.

"It'll take forever to saw through that," Cameron groaned.

Durward glanced at him and the heavy muscles beside his mouth moved infinitesimally. Lewen wondered if that was what passed for a smile on the gillie's face, and wondered why the man should be pleased.

Iven raised an eyebrow at Lewen, who shrugged and stepped forward to lay his hand on the thick, mossy trunk. It was an oak tree and immensely old. In the innumerable rings of years the tree carried within its core, he could still sense the slow song of growing, of wind and rain and sunshine and birds singing, the deliberate groping down of root and groping out of branch and twig, the swelling of life in countless acorns then lost to the immutable laws of gravity. That solemn song, that could have been intoned for another century or more, had been broken in a shriek of metal, shuddering branches, and then the slow inevitable topple and crash of the living giant.

Lewen stepped away from the tree, glanced at Durward's impassive countenance, and then at Iven. Then he went to the smashed wall and swung himself up into the branches, making his way out past the wall and leaning perilously above the abyss. It was a fall of several hundred feet to the river below, the steep cliff broken only by the regular lines of the road switchbacking its way down the cliff-face.

"Be careful!" Iven called. Roden jumped up and down, saying, "Can I climb out there too, *Dai*, please? I want to see!"

Even hanging as he was so dangerously above that dreadful drop, Lewen did not climb back at once, transfixed by the sight of the Findhorn Falls roaring down the cliff so close by. It was truly a magnificent sight. The waterfall looked as wide as an ocean, all foaming white and bursting in cataracts around outcrops of rock that broke the seamless curtains of water. The spray was so thick he could barely see the towering shape of Ravenscraig, built high on its crag of rock, on the far side of the river.

"Lewen!" Iven cried imperatively.

"Coming," he called back, and began to carefully make his way back to the road, clinging tightly to the massive branches. The tree rocked a little with his weight, causing Cameron and Rafferty to cry out in alarm. Lewen shifted his weight, leapt down lightly onto the trunk of the tree and ran up its length towards its roots.

"Ye should get down, lad," Durward suddenly called. "That tree's no' safe."

It was the first time they had heard the gillie-coise speak. He had an oddly light, shrill voice for such a large man. Lewen ignored him. He caught hold of the massive roots and pulled himself up so he could look down into the muddy pit where the tree had once clung to the cliffside. Then he thoughtfully made his way back down the slippery trunk and jumped down to land with a heavy thump in the ditch of the road.

"Well?" Iven said.

"Cameron's right, it's a big job to cut through the trunk," Lewen said. "That oak will be as hard as iron. I reckon we can lever it over the edge, though."

The muscles in Durward's forehead contracted slightly.

"Will it no' just crash down on the road below?" Iven asked.

"No' if we get enough momentum up. We'll use Sure and Steady to help us drag the tree forward, and weight the branches, and lever up the trunk. It should flip right over, with all that weight, and fall down into the river. We may need to help drag it out o' the river once we get down there, in case it causes an obstruction, but that willna be too hard a job."

"Excellent," Iven said. "Let us go and get Sure and Steady, and some tools, and get to work. I'd like to be on our way by this afternoon, if we can."

Durward's brows inched closer together.

As the men began the walk back up to the castle, Lewen fell back behind the others with Iven and Roden. The little boy was engaged in jumping in all the puddles, splashing mud and water high into the air, and it was not hard to let the others hurry on ahead with exclamations of annoyance as their boots and breeches were wet through.

"The tree was felled," he said to Iven in a low voice. "It didna fall naturally."

"Ye mean it was cut down? On purpose?"

"No' cut down, as such. The ground beneath the tree was loosened, with picks and shovels, it looks like, and some of the tap-roots severed. Then the tree was hauled down with a rope. The scars o' it are clear on the trunk."

"Are ye sure?"

"Sure I'm sure. Working with wood is my Talent, remember. This tree did not fall down and block the road naturally, that I'm sure o'."

"So happen the laird did mean to keep us at Fettercairn," Iven said slowly. "But why?"

"For his experiments in death, o' course," Lewen said. "Ye heard what Rhiannon said."

"So ye really think Rhiannon is telling the truth?" Iven said curiously. "It's a lot to swallow, dinna ye think?"

Lewen dropped his voice even lower as he noticed Durward turn to stare at them. "She kens nothing about witches or the Coven. How could she ken necromancers use a circle o' nine? Or sacrifice a cock? She didna ken what a cat o' nine tails was, remember?"

"I suppose that's true. Though it would be easy enough to pretend no' to ken details like that."

"She kent the name o' the laird's dead brother," Lewen pointed out. "How could she possibly have kent that without overhearing it?"

"True."

"And she said something about the tower being built on a Heart o' Stars. How on earth could she ken what that was? A satyricorn lass that has never left the mountains afore?"

Iven quirked his eyebrow. "Lewen, we only have Rhiannon's word for it that she is a wild satyricorn girl from the mountains."

Lewen stared at him in surprise. "But . . ."

"Och, I agree that it would be an elaborate deception and I can see little reason for it, but ye must no' always be taking things at face value. One thing ye learn in the business I am in is that people very rarely tell the truth. That's one reason Connor will be so sorely missed. He had an uncanny ability to convince people to tell true."

Lewen was silent.

Iven grinned at him. "I'm no' saying I think Rhiannon has been lying to ye every step o' the way, my lad, I'm just saying no' to believe everything ye hear, from anyone. No' even me."

Lewen took a deep breath. "Fine, happen that's so, but still, what Rhiannon says she saw last night explains an awful lot, dinna ye think? About what's been happening in the Fetterness Valley?"

Iven nodded. "Aye, it does. Enough to make me wary o' shadows. But Lewen, why would the laird o' Fettercairn try to keep us prisoner here? Do ye really think he plans to murder us? All o' us?"

Lewen was troubled and unsure. "After twenty-five years, it must be hard finding people to kill and then try to raise again. The people o' Fetterness Valley are frightened now, and do no' go out alone anymore. He must've thought a caravan o' wandering jongleurs a gift from Gearradh."

"Ye're right. No-one would've kent what happened to us. We would've just disappeared. So why then has he no' killed us?"

"Happen he did no' ken who ye were when he had the tree felled," Lewen answered. "It's one thing to waylay any auld traveller, but the sister o' the Earl o' Caerlaverock, the Rìgh's best friend? And a former Yeoman? Escorting a group o' witch-apprentices, some o' them nobly born? He would nu' dare. We would be missed and eventually tracked here to the castle. Nay,

I reckon once he found out who we really were, he decided it would be too dangerous to just murder us out o' hand."

"But still he does no' want us to clear away the tree," Iven said, pretending to smile as the gillie once more turned to stare at them.

"No. I wonder why?"

"Ye'd think he'd want to get rid o' us fast, once he decided it was too dangerous to kill us."

"Happen he realises that we have begun to suspect him," Lewen said. "Certainly they must ken Rhiannon saw something last night. They canna ken how much, surely."

"We will need to be very careful. If he realises how much we already ken . . ."

"*Dai! Dai!* Look!" Roden called, and jumped with both feet into such an enormous puddle that brown water flew up everywhere, splattering them from head to toe.

"Roden!" Iven said in exasperation. "Look at ye, ye're soaked! Your mama will be furious. Come here!"

He bent and brushed off the worst of the mud, then took Roden's wet hand. Lewen took the boy's other hand and between them they swung Roden back and forth, moving up the last stretch of road to where Cameron, Rafferty and the gillie waited for them, the gillie's face hard with suspicion. Roden squealed with excitement.

"We must act as if we ken naught, suspect naught," Iven said rapidly over Roden's head. "And we must get a message to the Rìgh, just in case something happens . . ."

"But how?"

"The Scrying Pool at the Tower o' Ravens," Iven said decisively. "The MacBrann used it during the Bright Wars. If the pool worked then, happen it still works now. Lewen, ye must go and see. We must think o' some excuse. Take Roden, go tell Nina what we ken. Tell her to do whatever she must to soothe their suspicions. If the laird thinks we ken, we'll never get out o' here alive."

"Again! Again!" Roden cried, and they swung him high into the air.

"Ye are nothing but trouble," Iven said to him as they came up beside the others. "Look at ye! Your boots are wet through. Your mother will have my head."

Roden looked down at his boots in surprise.

"Lewen, will ye take this wicked laddie back to his mam? The last thing we need is Roden coming down with a chill."

"Sure," Lewen answered.

Roden was furious. "No! I dinna want to go back. I want to see the tree crash down."

"No, laddie. It's too dangerous, and I do no' want ye getting underfoot. Go on back to your mam."

"No! I won't!"

"Och, aye, ye will, my lad," Iven said sternly. "Ye're soaked through and it's cold. Now do as I say."

Roden began to cry. "No! I dinna want to! Please, *Dai,* I want to stay, please, please?"

"Nay, laddie. Go on back with Lewen now."

"Come on, Roden," Lewen said winningly, but Roden dragged his hand away and sat down obstinately in the middle of the road.

"I'm no' going!"

Iven jerked his head at Lewen, who bent and picked Roden up. "Never mind," he said consolingly. "Let's go and see what we can find for morning tea. I bet I can rustle up some hot chocolate for ye. That'll warm ye up again."

Roden wept noisily, squirming like an eel. Lewen carried him swiftly through the gatehouse towards the castle. As he went he heard Iven say to the gillie, "Bairns! Have ye any yourself?"

By the time they reached the inner ward, Roden had insisted on being put down so he could walk. "I'm no' a babe," he said furiously.

"Then stop acting like one," Lewen said, and Roden thrust out his bottom lip and stalked ahead with a great air of injury.

Looking white and unhappy, Nina was sitting with Lady Evaline under the apple tree, while Fèlice and Landon wandered along the lawn. Miss Prunella sat a short distance away, working on some embroidery. Nina rose at the sight of Lewen and her mud-splattered and highly indignant son.

"Roden!" she cried. "What's wrong?"

"*Dai* willna lct me stay and watch the tree crash down," Roden said with a quivering lip and flung himself in his mother's arms.

"Iven thinks it's too dangerous," Lewen explained, "and he was worried about Roden catching a chill. He was jumping in puddles."

Nina looked rather puzzled. "Och, Iven doesna normally even notice things like that."

"He doesna want Roden to catch a fever," Lewen answered. "It does seem as if Laird Malvern is right when he says the air here is unhealthy."

Nina glanced up at him, her brows twitching together. "Well, let's go get ye dry and changed," she said to her son, then cast a rueful glance down at her own gown. "And me too, now. Look at my skirt! I've got mud all over it."

Lady Evaline had been gazing at Roden with a look of longing and now she reached out a frail, blue-veined hand to ruffle his curls. "Och, he's such a bonny lad."

Roden gave her a look of disgust. "I'm no' bonny, that's for girls!" he retorted. "I'm doughty!"

"Indeed ye are," Nina said with an apologetic smile at Lady Evaline. The old woman smiled back wistfully, her gaze returning to Roden's face.

"A big doughty lad like ye must be hungry," she said. "Would ye like to come and have tea with me when ye're changed? My cook makes some very nice honey cakes."

"Lewen said I could have hot chocolate," Roden said winningly.

"O' course, the very thing to drive out the chill. Miss Prunella, could ye ask the kitchen to heat up some chocolate milk for Rory?"

"My name's Roden," he said crossly, the scowl returning.

"O' course. I'm sorry. I get muddled sometimes. For Roden."

"O' course, my lady," Miss Prunella said, folding up her embroidery and rising. She looked as if she had been sucking on a lemon, her face was so sour.

"I'll come up with ye," Lewen said to Nina. "As ye can see, I got rather wet too." He cast a rueful hand down his mudsplattered clothes.

Fèlice and Landon had both drawn near and waylaid Lewen a few moments with questions about the fallen tree and what the others were doing. He escaped them as quickly as he could and hurried after Nina, who was climbing up the stairs hand-in-hand with her son, who was still very cross at being made to come back inside the castle. Thankfully there was no sign of the ubiquitous Irving, who was normally so careful to make sure they were escorted anywhere in the castle. He was able to tell Nina about the deliberately felled tree, and what conclusions he and Iven had drawn. She agreed that he must try to escape the castle and find the Scrying Pool at the Tower of Ravens.

"I tried to send my sunbird with a message but one o' the ravens killed her," she told him unhappily. Lewen exclaimed, and she pressed her hands to her eyes.

"Aye, I ken. I loved my wee bird, I canna believe it happened. I should no' have tried to send her." She let out her breath in a great sigh and blotted away another tear. "Anyway, what canna be changed must be endured. We must focus now on getting all o' us out o' this blaygird castle alive. Lewen, I think Iven is right. We must get a message to the Rìgh and the Scrying Pool is the only way. Though how we are to do so without arousing any more suspicion, I do no' ken," she said. "They must no' guess what ye are about."

"I'll think o' something," Lewen said. "How is Rhiannon doing?"

"She's sleeping still. The fever does seem to have eased. Landon says Dedrie came to look in on her but went away again once she saw him sitting there. Edithe is there now. I thought poor Landon needed a break."

But when Lewen opened the door into Rhiannon's dim, fire-lit room, it was not Edithe he found leaning over her bed, but Irving. The seneschal swung round abruptly at the sound of the door and Lewen saw with horror that he held a pillow in his hands.

"What are ye doing?" he cried sharply.

"Just adjusting the young lady's pillows," Irving answered suavely, turning back to the bed.

"Get away from me!" Rhiannon cried, her voice rough and breathless. "Lewen, Lewen, he try . . . he put pillow on me . . . I couldna breathe . . . Lewen!"

Lewen came swiftly to the bed. Rhiannon gazed up at him, her eyes so dilated with terror they seemed black. Her cheeks were red and had faint creases pressed into them. Her breath came harshly.

"Get away from her," Lewen hissed.

Irving looked surprised and stepped away from the bed. "I assure ye, the young lady is mistaken. She has been most fever-ish and I merely sought to make her more comfortable."

"He try kill me," Rhiannon gasped.

"Where's Lady Edithe?" Lewen demanded, sitting beside Rhiannon and pulling her into his arms, stroking the damp tan-gled hair away from her face.

"The young lady was rather bored when I came to bring her some morning tea and I suggested she go down to the library to find herself a book to read. My laird has a very extensive library."

Lewen was so furious he could not speak for a moment. Irv-ing moved away, fluffing up the pillow and placing it on a chair nearby, looking as suave as ever.

Just then, Nina came in. "What on earth is the matter?"

"He try kill me," Rhiannon said, her breath still coming short. "He put pillow on me, held me down so I couldna breathe."

"That's ridiculous," Irving said, his colour altering just a lit-tle. "The young lady is delirious."

"Oh no, has her fever got worse?" Nina asked in concern, coming across the room quickly. "She was quite incoherent this morning, but I had hoped . . . och, ye poor man! Ye must no' mind her."

"No, he try kill me!" Rhiannon protested.

"Oh, dear, she really is quite crazy with this fever! What are we to do? She hit poor Dedrie, did ye hear? And Lewen too."

Rhiannon shrank away from Lewen. "That's right," she said in a horrified voice. "I had forgotten . . . I thought it but a dream. Ye poison me too."

"No, no," Lewen said in distress, trying to draw her back into his arms. "We were trying to help."

"Ye all try kill me!" Rhiannon stared from one face to an-other with huge, terrified eyes.

Nina shook her head sorrowfully. "Dedrie said the fever can take one like this sometimes, but it's very distressing, isn't it? Look at her, the poor deluded lass!"

Rhiannon clutched the sheet to her. "Why ye want kill me? Why?"

"Nay, nay, *leannan*. Ye're safe, I promise ye," Lewen soothed her, torn between his desire to comfort her and his dismay at having forgotten they were meant to be damping down the suspicions of any of the lord's minions.

Rhiannon did not believe him. She sat very still, her breath coming fast, her eyes darting from one face to another. Lewen could see a pulse leaping in her throat.

"I am so very sorry," Nina was saying to Irving, drawing him away from the bed. "I do feel dreadful. First Dedrie hit in the face, and accused so wildly, and now ye. I hate to think what the laird must think o' us. I do hope ye will forgive us. Rhiannon is . . . well, she's difficult, there's no gainsaying that. The best thing for her now is peace and quiet."

Nina's voice faded as she escorted Irving from the room. Lewen tried to draw Rhiannon back into his arms. She resisted violently.

"*Leannan*, no, do no' be afraid," he said in distress. "Indeed, I ken what ye must think but it's no' like that. Ye must ken I would never hurt ye."

"Ye made me sick," she accused. "Ye poison me!"

"'Twas no' poison," he protested. "We . . . we were trying to make ye better."

She made a disgusted noise. "Go away," she said, pushing him with her hot, damp palms.

"Rhiannon, indeed ye are sick. Please, lie back, let me sponge your face. I ken . . . he's a bad man, that Irving, I ken that. It's just we need to pretend for now . . . until we can get away from here . . ."

She listened to him, and after a while let him lay her back down, and smooth back her hair, and dab her face with the cool cloth. After a while her eyes closed and she fell asleep again. He sat watching her, feeling such a hot painful feeling round his heart it was as if the organ was actually bruised.

Nina came quietly back into the room. "Is she sleeping? Poor lass! I could strangle Edithe. What was she thinking, leaving Rhiannon alone like that?"

"Nina, he had a pillow over her face, I'd swear it!"

"I do no' doubt it," Nina said. "We canna leave her alone. Maisie says she will come and sit with her a while now, she's feeling much better after a sleep, well enough to sit up for a while anyway. I'm going to go and find Edithe and rip shreds off her!"

"I'll sit with Rhiannon," Lewen said.

"Ye canna," Nina replied. "Ye must find some way to slip out and get to the Tower o' Ravens. Noon and midnight is the best time to use the Scrying Pool, or dawn and sunset, and I do no' want ye there at night. I'm beginning to believe all those tales about malevolent ghosts that haunt the tower! So it'd be best if ye went now, and got there afore noon."

Lewen nodded and got reluctantly to his feet, casting one last look at Rhiannon's flushed and sleeping face. She looked soft and vulnerable. He marvelled how this had the power to hurt him. He would have liked to have lain down with her, and curved his body to hers, pressing his mouth to the arch of her neck. He did not want to wake her, though. He did not want to watch her flinch away.

The door opened and Edithe came in, absorbed in a thin, vellum-bound book she held in her hand.

"Where have ye been?" Nina at once exclaimed furiously.

Edithe looked up in surprise and chagrin. "I was only gone a minute!"

"A minute is more than enough," Nina snapped. "And it was much longer than that. We've been here for close on ten."

"Well, I'm sorry, but I got chatting with Laird Malvern. He really is a very interesting man, so cultivated and so learned. His library is absolutely fascinating. I would have liked to have stayed and let him show me his collection, but I came hurrying back here because I kent ye wanted someone to sit with the satyricorn girl." Her voice was filled with self-righteous indignation. "Really, I canna think why, ye all seem to have got infected with her hysterical nonsense . . ."

"Edithe, until we arrive at the Tower o' Two Moons, I am your teacher and mentor. If I tell ye to stand on your head in a graveyard all night ye do as I tell ye, without question and without hesitation." Though she spoke softly, Nina's voice had an edge to it like a whip. "I have never kent an apprentice with less o' the qualities the Coven thinks necessary in a witch. Ye do no' listen, ye do no' watch, and ye do no' learn. Sit down in that chair and do no' move until I say ye may. And be glad your stupidity has no' had more dire consequences."

Edithe's colour was high and her eyes glittered with angry tears, but she swept to the chair and sat down as ordered, disposing her skirts about her feet with exaggerated care. She then opened her book and began to read with an air of great interest.

"I'll just tell Maisie she can bide a wee longer in bed, I want her as strong and well as possible for the journey ahead," Nina said as she led the way out of the room.

Lewen nodded, his mind already busy with plans for getting away from the castle without arousing suspicion. He took one last look at Rhiannon, sleeping restlessly in her bed, then followed Nina across the hall and into Maisie's room. She was out of bed and limping about, but it was obvious her deep festering wounds still troubled her. She was glad to get back into bed and have Nina give her another draught of pain-killing poppy syrup and tuck her up in her eiderdown. Lewen stoked up the fire for her, and moved the cup of water closer to her hand.

"Call out to Edithe if ye need anything," Nina said gently, "and try to get some sleep."

Maisie nodded gratefully and shifted onto her side, trying to find a comfortable position to lie in.

"I wonder where Lulu is," Nina said anxiously, as they went out into the hall again. "I would've thought she would have been quite happy playing with the doll I made her and no' gone wandering off. She doesna like Edithe, though. Happen I left her too long and she went looking for Roden. We'd better go find her, Eà kens the trouble she could be causing!"

She put her head in the door of the big suite. "Roden? Roden?"

There was no answer.

Nina went in, and hurriedly searched the room, her face growing whiter by the second. "He's gone!" she cried. "I left him only a moment, just while I looked in on Rhiannon. Och, the wicked boy! Where has he gone?"

Lewen came in too and searched in the cupboards and under the bed. There was no sign of Roden.

Nina was so white he thought she might faint. He supported
her with one hand and went to pour her some water but she refused it impatiently. "We must find him!" she cried. "Och, this
is no' the place for a wee laddie to be wandering round by himself. Oh, Lewen! Do ye think someone took him? That sly-
faced Irving!"

"We'll find him," Lewen reassured him. "Nina, can ye sense
where he is? Close your eyes, concentrate. Ye ken him better
than anyone. Canna ye sense him?"

Nina tried to calm herself. She sank down on one of the cushioned chairs, sipped at the glass of water Lewen passed her, and
closed her eyes, resting her face in her hands. The only sound was
the cry of ravens outside. Lewen saw one had come down to perch
on the windowsill. He went to the casement, threw open the window and violently shooed the bird away. It cawed mockingly and
flew off with slow flaps of its enormous black wings.

"I think . . . he's over that way somewhere," Nina said, waving her hand to the north. "Oh, Lewen!"

"We'll go and find him now," he said, leaning down to help
her up. "Do no' fear, Nina. He's bored and restless, and angry
he wasna allowed to watch them move the tree. He's gone off
exploring, that's all."

"Happen he's gone to find that room with all the toys," Nina
said. "I'll skin him alive!"

Together they went quickly along the hall and down the
stairs, keeping a wary look-out for any servants. They heard
voices from one room and passed it silently, then hid for a moment in an antechamber as some footmen went past, carrying
some silver down to the kitchens to be cleaned. Otherwise all
was quiet.

"I wonder where the laird is?" Lewen whispered.

"Still in his library, I'd say."

"I hope Edithe kept her mouth shut!"

"Unlikely, but I do no' think it'll matter. She dislikes Rhiannon so intensely she would've done a better job than any o' us
in discrediting her. I'm sure she told the laird that Rhiannon is
half-satyricorn and quite wild and a constant trouble to us all.
By the time she would have finished, the laird would be sure we
suspected no ill o' him!"

"I hope so," Lewen said grimly.

They came to a thick oak door that stood ajar. They could hear nothing beyond so eased it open a little further and slipped through. They tiptoed down a stone-floored corridor that led to a spiral staircase, winding upwards into gloom.

"He's here somewhere," Nina whispered. "Upstairs, I think. It's so hard to be sure. These thick stone walls confuse my witch-sense."

Then they heard the low murmur of voices from a room to their right. Moving very carefully they pressed themselves close to the door to listen.

"Someone has been sneaking about and spying," Lord Malvern said angrily. "Irving found a smashed lantern on the steps near Rory's room, and I swear someone has been in my library! Ye ken I canna bear to have things out o' place, and things have definitely been moved. None o' the circle would've done it, they all ken better!"

Lady Evaline murmured something about sleepwalking.

"Sleepwalkers do no' take lanterns with them," Lord Malvern cried. "Nay, that girl knew what she was doing. The question is, how much did she see?"

Another low murmur from Lady Evaline.

"Dedrie says her boots and cloak were all muddy. She must have gone outside at some point, and I canna help thinking she may have found the secret way to the tower. If so, who kens what she may have seen and heard! We canna risk her telling a soul. Thank the Truth the witch suspects naught."

Lady Evaline made some kind of protest.

"It's a little late to get cold feet now, Evaline. We're so close! Do ye no' want Falkner and Rory back? After all these years, all this trouble, ye canna get squeamish now!"

"There've been too many deaths," Lady Evaline said unhappily.

"But the things we have learnt! And now we are so close, ye canna say it has no' been worth it. The secrets o' resurrecting the dead! That is a prize worth sacrificing for."

Lord Malvern's voice came closer, as if he were striding around the room. Nina and Lewen flattened themselves on either side of the door, but were too eager to hear more to retreat.

"If we can just stop her from telling them all she saw! I'm sure they do no' suspect anything. Lady Edithe says she's some half-breed faery girl that is quite wild and hysterical, so happen they will no' believe her, no matter what she says. We canna take that risk though. We must stop her mouth somehow."

Lewen gritted his teeth together in rage and Nina cast him a warning glance.

"What about the lad?" Lady Evaline said pitifully.

"Och, he's just too perfect," Lord Malvern said with a strange note of longing in his voice. "It canna be coincidence that a boy just the same age and height and colouring as Rory comes riding through our gate the very day we finally get the secret o' resurrecting the dead into our hands!"

"But they'll take him away! Once they ride out o' here we may never see him again."

"Aye, o' course we will. We'll find him again when the time is right."

"How can ye be sure?" she asked. "Oh, Malvern, he's so like Rory, so bright and bonny! I wish I could take him into my lap and hold him, but that witch keeps him so close I have hardly been able to touch him. I wish we could keep him here a while longer."

"Aye, aye, I ken, but we canna take the risk, Evaline. Surely ye see that?"

She said something low and he sighed in exasperation. "Our first priority is getting hold o' the spell. I do no' ken how long that will take, Evaline."

Again they heard the soft pleading murmur of her voice and then Lord Malvern's voice, as loud as if he was standing next to them, "Och, very well, Evaline! Anything to keep ye happy! I must go now and find out what is happening. Do no' weep, now. We are closer than we have ever been."

They heard his quick impatient stride, and both Nina and Lewen whisked themselves away from the door, making it into the shelter of the staircase scant seconds before the door opened and Lord Malvern came out. He went away down the hall, as tall and stiff and black as a pillar of obsidian, and Lewen heaved a sigh of relief.

Nina's face was pinched and angry. "We have to find Roden

and get away from here! What do they have planned for him? Oh, it canna be good, Lewen!"

Lewen nodded in agreement, and pressed her hand in comfort. "Where is he? Can ye sense him?"

Nina pressed her hands to her temples. "I'm so afraid I canna think straight."

"Lord Malvern mentioned something about a broken lantern on the stairs. Let's go up and have a look around."

Nina nodded and led the way up the spiral staircase. "Why, oh, why did I ever come this way?" she murmured. "Again and again we were warned, and I did no' listen!"

The staircase wound up to a narrow wooden door, hal-hidden behind a faded tapestry curtain. They heard the sound of a boy's voice and quickened their step, though both felt a sudden superstitious chill that raised the hairs on their arms. "Let it be Roden and no' that poor wee ghost," Nina whispered, then pushed open the door.

Roden and Lulu were sitting together on the floor, playing happily with some toy soldiers. He looked up at the sound of the door opening and smiled. "Hi, Mam," he said.

"Ye naughty, naughty boy!" Nina cried and flew across the room, dragging him to his feet. "What are ye doing here! Don't ye ken ye scared me half to death?" She gave him a good hard smack across his bottom, then pulled him into her arms, hugging him tightly.

Roden looked sulky, and Lulu jumped up and down, gibbering in distress. "And as for ye!" Nina cried, turning on the arak. "I told ye to stay! What are ye doing wandering all over the castle?"

The arak hid her face in her hands, peered round in abashment, then covered her eyes again.

"Lulu was bored," Roden said defensively. "She wanted to find that little boy's room too. She came and got me when she'd found it. O' course I had to come and have a look. See, Mam? There's a castle and everything."

"I told ye to stay in your room!" Nina's wrath had not abated.

"Ye're just mean," Roden burst out. "Why canna I play with the toys? We've been stuck in this boring auld castle for days and days, and I wasna even allowed to watch the trcc go crashing down. I just wanted to look at the toys."

Nina took a deep breath. "Thank Eà ye're safe," she said. "Please, please, do no' do that again, Roden. No' here, in this castle."

"All right, Mam," he said in long-suffering tones.

She drew him close to her and caressed his dark red curls. "I ken ye're bored, dearling. Let's go and see how *dai-dein* is doing moving that tree, all right?"

He brightened at once, and Lulu skipped about joyfully.

"Leave the toys here," Nina said sternly, and reluctantly the boy and the arak put the toy soldiers back into the castle.

"It's certainly just as Rhiannon described it," Nina said, glancing round the room.

"Except for the ghosts," Lewen replied with a slight grin.

"Och, the ghost is here," Roden said unexpectedly. "Canna ye see him?"

Nina and Lewen stared at him, their flesh creeping. Roden pointed at the rocking horse. "He's there. He doesna want me to go. He's so sad and lonely."

They stared at the rocking horse. There was nothing to see.

Roden lifted a hand. "I got to go now, but happen I'll come back later. Bye!" Then he took Nina's hand and went out of the room with her, Lulu scampering on ahead. Lewen followed, the nape of his neck prickling as if someone had blown on it with icy breath. He could not help looking back over his shoulder. The wooden hose had begun to rock backwards and forwards, creaking gently. Lewen shivered and shut the door firmly behind him.

Rhiannon woke and lay for a while, staring about her room. Everything was quiet. On the hearth the fire had fallen into coals that gleamed dully. Somewhere ravens were crying. Edithe sat in the cushioned chair, one foot swinging, reading a book and sighing every now and again as if bored to distraction.

Rhiannon gently put back the bedclothes and slid her legs out. A wave of dizziness overcame her as she stood up. She leant her hands on the bed and let her head hang forward till it passed.

Edithe turned her head. "Oh, ye're awake. I thought ye were going to sleep all day!"

Rhiannon said nothing, just stared at her with suspicious eyes.

"They brought ye food if ye want it." Edithe jerked her head at a small pot of soup set in the hearth to keep warm.

"I eat naught they bring me," Rhiannon said sullenly.

Edithe rolled her eyes. "I suppose ye mean ye are afraid it's poisoned? Really, I think ye are quite mad. What do ye intend to do? Starve yourself to death? I'd expect anything from a girl who cuts herself for amusement."

"Dinna do it for amusement," Rhiannon growled.

"Well, it certainly doesna amuse any o' us! I'm quite embarrassed to be one o' your party. What the laird o' Fettercairn must think, I canna imagine."

"He bad man," Rhiannon said sullenly.

"He's a perfectly charming gentleman, and the laird o' one o' the auldest and most respected clans in Ravenshaw," Edithe said sharply. "And if ye think anyone will believe your wild accusations and slanders ahead o' his word, ye are very much mistaken."

Rhiannon lost her temper and rushed at Edithe, knocking her down with a great shove. Edithe went down with a scream, knocking over the fire-irons and bashing her head hard against the wall.

"How dare ye!" Edithe cried, pressing her hand to her head. "Ye're naught but a wild animal! Ye should be locked up in a cage like a snow-lion. Wait till I tell what ye've done. My father shall make sure ye pay!"

She scrambled to her feet and ran from the room, her face red with rage.

Rhiannon's eyes smarted with tears. Her legs were so wobbly she had to grip the back of the chair to stop them giving way. She waited a moment, breathing deeply, then made her way across the room, leaning on the furniture for support. She dressed, her fingers fumbling over the buttons and ties, and drew on her boots, which she found clean and freshly polished in her cupboard. Her cloak hung there too, and she slipped it about her shoulders, the camouflaging grey side outwards. Then she picked up her saddlebags and slipped them over her shoulder.

The morning had been one long, horrible blur to Rhiannon. She remembered most of it in weird disconnected flashes, mostly red-hued and throbbing. Her sleep had been tormented by strange visions and nightmares, and she found it hard to remember how much of it was true. Had Lewen really held her down while a grim-faced Nina forced poison down her throat? She knew it had made her sicker than she had ever been before in her life. She did not want to believe Lewen and Nina could do such a thing, but the vomiting had been no nightmare, the stink of it was still in her hair and she tasted it still upon her tongue. And she knew Lewen had seen Irving with the pillow in his hands, and yet he had done nothing to defend her. Rhiannon had to escape from this place.

It was easy enough to make her way through the castle without being seen. The sun was high and everyone was at lunch. Rhiannon did not go out into the inner ward, but found the back way to the stables. They too were empty, except for the horses that drowsily lipped at the straw or put their heads over their stalls to greet her.

Blackthorn whickered eagerly. Rhiannon felt a rush of tears to her eyes at the sight of her, but brushed them resolutely away, stroking her muzzle and murmuring love nonsense to her till the ache around her heart eased a little.

Then she opened the stall and let Blackthorn out. The winged horse came out prancing, restless after so much time confined. Rhiannon buckled on the soft pad and the saddlebags, then led Blackthorn over to the mounting-block. She was still feeling so very weak and dizzy she did not think she could mount without assistance.

Once she was astride the mare's back, she looked about her one more time and noticed that Sure and Steady were both missing, although the caravans were still drawn up to one side of the big barn. Then she realised Argent was gone too. She felt a jolt of disappointment and rage. "He left me here," she murmured. "He doesna care one little bit."

The thought spurred her on. She pressed her heels into Blackthorn's sides and the mare went daintily out into the courtyard. A groom was there, lazily forking manure into the muck heap. He straightened at the sight of her and said, "Oy!"

Blackthorn danced sideways, then broke into a trot. The groom ran towards them, arms spread wide, shouting, "What ye think ye're doing? Where ye going?"

Rhiannon urged the mare into a canter, then lifted her weight from Blackthorn's back. Obediently the mare spread her wings and soared up into the air.

Canna keep a thigearn trapped inside walls, Rhiannon thought with satisfaction.

The groom leapt out of the way hurriedly, landing face first in the muck heap. Rhiannon gave him a mocking salute as he sat up, furiously spitting and wiping clean his face. Then he was on his feet and running to raise the alarm.

Blackthorn wheeled in the air, tilting her wings, then rose higher, leaving the grim grey castle behind her. Rhiannon leant forward, enjoying the view. She could see the vast expanse of lake, whipped into shining waves by the breeze. The wind was very strong today, dragging her hair all over her face, sending her cloak whipping and Blackthorn's mane swirling. The mare had to fight to keep her course steady against its rough buffeting.

As they came over the ridge, Rhiannon saw the distant grey bulk of Ravenscraig on its pinnacle of stone, and the broken arch of the old bridge across the lake, and the great clouds of spray flung up where the water bent its great weight over the lip of the cliff. She watched it in fascination, never having seen such a magnificent sight.

A distant cry caught her attention. She looked down. Below her was the gatehouse. On the far side of it, Rhiannon saw the massive old tree across the road, and men swarming over it with ropes and tools, and the carthorses dragging at the ropes patiently. Someone had seen her and was pointing up at her. She brought Blackthorn about, heading back towards the mountains, away from all those faces turning up to stare at her. The mare's black wings beat steadily.

Below her were the broken spires of the Tower of Ravens. Beyond she could see the small walled town of Fetterness built at the foot of the hill, and the green of the forest curving all round, and the brown of the untilled fields running down to the water.

The mare was tiring in her battle against the wind, and so
Rhiannon looked for a place to land. She brought Blackthorn
down near the road, and then saw, under the shadows of the
trees, another horse and rider cantering along. At once she
urged Blackthorn up into the air again.

Someone called "Rhiannon!" behind her.

She glanced back and saw the rider was Lewen, standing up
in his stirrups, calling to her. Rhiannon's heart was filled with
anger and bitterness. She leant forward, urging Blackthorn to
fly faster. But the wind was simply too wild and turbulent.
Blackthorn whickered in distress, and Rhiannon brought her
down the ridge to land lightly on the lower curve of the switchbacking road. She thought she had left Lewen far behind her
but then she heard the thunder of Argent's hooves as he galloped round the bend. Rhiannon bit her lip and kicked Blackthorn into a gallop.

Down the steep winding road the two horses raced, the
trees tossing wildly overhead. Every now and again Rhiannon
glanced back over her shoulder and saw to her dismay that
Lewen was gaining upon her. She urged the mare on, even
though the mare skidded at one of the hairpin turns and almost
fell, the road still being very wet and muddy. Here and there
branches lay across the road, blown down in the wind, and
Blackthorn leapt them nimbly. The wind was so cold it
brought tears to Rhiannon's eyes. She had to hold back her
hair with one hand. At last the road began to level out, leading past the walled town and along the lake shore.

A girl was herding geese along the road. Blackthorn plunged
into the flock, sending indignant birds honking up into the air.
They had just settled back to the road when Argent came thundering past, sending them all up into the air again.

Rhiannon leant lower over Blackthorn's mane, murmuring
encouragements, then she glanced back one more time. Lewen
was close enough for her to see his face. It was set and grim and
angry, and her heart gave a strange little lurch. She urged the
mare to run faster but slowly, inexorably, Lewen gained upon
them.

Faster and faster the two horses galloped, moving fluidly,
silver and black together, like one horse and its shadow. Really

frightened now, Rhiannon tried to bring Blackthorn swerving away, to find room to rise into the air again, but with a curt command, Lewen brought Argent round, cutting the mare off and forcing her to slow. They came to a shuddering halt in the shade of a giant hemlock.

Lewen threw himself down from the stallion's back and seized Rhiannon round the waist, dragging her down from the mare's back.

"What in blazes do ye think ye're doing!"

Rhiannon leant her head against his chest, trembling in every limb.

He shook her, none too gently. "Ye should be in bed! Ye're ill!"

"Me need escape," she said. "They try kill me."

He had her up hard against his body, holding her so she could not escape. Now he twisted his hand in her hair and pulled her head up so he could see her eyes. "O' course they tried to kill ye," he yelled. "Ye idiot, if ye die o' pneumonia they'll have succeeded! Ye should be in bed, no' out in this freezing wind."

"Ye kent they tried to kill me? And ye still left me?" The hurt of his betrayal was bitter in her voice.

"Ye were safe. The others were watching over ye. I had to go . . ." His voice trailed away. "Did ye think I was no' coming back? Rhiannon, I would no' leave ye. I promise." He bent his head and kissed her.

Tears sprang to her eyes. She wound her arm about his neck and kissed him back.

When he spoke again, his voice was unsteady. "Rhiannon . . ."

"Why ye go?" she demanded. "Why ye leave me?"

"I have to find the Scrying Pool, at the Tower o' Ravens. I meant to find it by noon but we're too late now. I was going to tell the Rìgh what we have learnt . . . in case the laird tries something . . . in case we all disappeared." His voice was grim.

"So ye did believe me?"

"O' course I believe ye!"

"And Nina? Iven? All the others?"

"Nina does, I'm sure. Iven . . . I do no' ken. It does no' matter. Once the Rìgh kens what we ken, he will send men to investigate and they will find the truth o' it all. For now, we just

have to get away from here safely. Oh, Rhiannon, why did ye
run away? The laird will be suspicious now, and happen we
have lost our chance to talk our way out o' here. Ye should've
trusted me."

She moved away from him, her face set in its old wary, sulky
lines. "How was I to ken?"

He drew her close to him again, tipping up her face so he
could kiss her again. "I ken. I'm sorry."

The wind whipped her hair across his face, and he smoothed
it down, cradling her face in his hands. He felt as if he were
falling down a deep hole, from which there was no way of
climbing back to the life he had imagined for himself. She was
stiff in his hands, her face sullen. He bent his head again, determined to kiss her into pliancy, but she leant away from him,
her eyes suddenly widening. "Look at that storm!"

Lewen turned and immediately gaped in surprise. To the
north immense black clouds were building over the distant peak
of Ben Eyrie. Lightning played eerily along its belly, then
Lewen heard a low rumble of thunder.

"Mighty Eà!" Lewen cried. "It was such a beautiful day!
Where has that storm come from?"

"It's those necromancers," Rhiannon said in a low, husky
whisper. "They've called the storm up. They want to keep us
trapped here."

"Och, surely no'," Lewen said, even though he half-believed
her. "They are no' witches there, what would they ken o'
weather magic?"

"They can raise ghosts," Rhiannon said flatly.

"We'd better start back," Lewen said. "We dinna want to be
caught in that."

Rhiannon nodded. She seized Blackthorn's mane and let
Lewen lift her up onto the mare's back. "It's cold," she said.
"I'm shivering. That storm is no' natural, I swear to ye."

"Nina said storms can blow up fast around here," Lewen
said, bringing Argent round so he could mount.

"Aye, that's true. I lived all my life in these mountains, remember. But this cold, that makes all the hairs on my body
stand up, and makes my ears ache, that's no' natural. It happens
whenever magic is worked. I ken. I have felt it every time."

Lewen turned to stare at her. "Ye can feel a chill in the air when magic is worked?" he said slowly. "Ye must be very sensitive to it."

"Lucky me," Rhiannon answered, and wrapped her cloak tightly about her.

The horses broke into a restive trot, the wind blowing their manes and tails into banners. Thunder grumbled through the valley. The clouds chased them all the long ride home, along the shore of the loch and up the road towards Fetterness. The labourers were coming in from the field, looking anxiously up at the sky, and shop-keepers were pulling closed their shutters. By now the clouds had raced to cover the whole sky, and the trees were bending over in the wind, which crackled and roared with lightning.

"Should we stop here?" Lewen called. "I do no' want ye to get caught in the rain, when ye've been so sick. There'll be an inn where we can take shelter."

Rhiannon frowned. "Nay, let's get back. We could be stuck here all night, if the storm is as wild as the last one."

"Let's hurry then," Lewen shouted back, the wind catching at his words, and kicked Argent into a canter.

It was tiring fighting against the wind, and the horses reared and whinnied as blown branches whipped against them. Rhiannon was soon so weary she could barely keep her balance. Lewen lifted her from Blackthorn's back, holding her before him. For once Rhiannon made no protest, huddling under the cloak against the bitter cold that struck into the very marrow of her bones.

As they reached the top of the ridge, they saw the rain sweeping across the valley below like advancing ranks of grey-clad soldiers. Lightning flashed, making the horses rear in terror, and seconds later there was an enormous clap of thunder that seemed to make the ground shake.

"We'll never make it to the castle," Lewen cried, as the first scud of rain spat into their faces. "We're going to get soaked to the skin! Let us go to the tower. Ye can rest while I try to find the Scrying Pool. Sunset is a time o' power—I can try to reach His Highness then."

"There'll be no sunset tonight," Rhiannon said through chattering teeth. "Only storm."

The Tower of Ravens

Ahead of them loomed tall stone gateposts, with iron gates lying broken and open. The wind tore the hood from Rhiannon's head, and sleet lashed her face. She coughed, the paroxysm so severe she could not catch her breath.

Lewen kicked Argent forward into a gallop. "Come on then."

They rode helter-skelter through the gateposts, head bent against the vicious wind that seemed filled with thousands of little needles of ice. Within was a rising avenue of dark yew trees, growing so close overhead it gave them some protection from the storm, though they could barely see to avoid the ruts and potholes. The driveway led straight as an arrow up the hill and through a great arched gateway in a wall. As they passed through the archway, the rain hit them again like a hammer and Lewen spurred Argent on, Blackthorn cantering close behind, through courtyards and broken colonnades and blackened ruins, until at last they burst through a doorway and found themselves in a dry, dark place.

Lewen dismounted, trying to catch his breath, and wiped his face dry with his sleeve. A sudden sphere of light suddenly winked into existence above his head, making Rhiannon gasp with alarm. "It's all right, it's just me," Lewen said. "I wanted to see."

He looked about him. They were in a long low building, very grimy and filled with old, cobwebbed contraptions that once would have been carts and carriages. A row of stalls stood empty, but Lewen saw with interest that one near the door was filled with fresh straw and had been cleared of the worst of the spiderwebs. The trough was clean and half-filled with water, and against the wall was a row of clean, shiny bins that must be filled with grain.

"So someone keeps a horse here," Lewen said. "Let us hope he doesna return soon. There's no muck heap, so I'd say it's only an occasional visitor."

Rhiannon lifted a tired hand and pushed back her hood. Her cloak was dripping wet.

"Here, let me help ye," Lewen said, lifting Rhiannon down. She was shivering with cold, and so he led her to sit down on one of the bins, and unfastened her cloak. Lewen shook it out and spread it to dry over one of the low walls between the stalls. He did the same with his own cloak, then turned his attention to the horses. Rhiannon's saddlebags and her precious bow and quiver hung from the pommel of her soft saddlepad. He unbuckled these from Blackthorn's back, and hung them on the wall, then gave the mare a quick rubdown with a wisp of straw. He unsaddled Argent and rubbed him down too, then put the horses together in the stall. He gave them a bucket of oats to share, and then turned his attention back to Rhiannon. She looked pale and hollow-eyed, and coughed every now and again.

"Let's try and get ye warm," he said. "Wait here, I'll just have a little scout around."

He looked out the doorway, where the rain was still teeming down, then went through the stables into the next building, which seemed to have been some kind of quarters for the stablehands. There was a kitchen with a big hearth, and a table and some old broken chairs, a few old pots, filthy with dust and spiderwebs, and a scullery with a sink and pump. After a few energetic jerks, there was a spurt of filthy water that then ran pure. Lewen rinsed out the sink, washing away myriad dead spiders, then tasted the water, which was sweet. He explored a little further, finding a couple of dark, smelly rooms above and what once would have been a kitchen garden beyond, but was now just weeds. The best find was a pile of firewood outside the kitchen door, protected from the rain by the eaves. It was filled with all sorts of creepy-crawlies, but Lewen banged it all together and built a fire in the old hearth, which he lit with a snap of his fingers. With firelight dancing over the walls, the old kitchen began to look almost hospitable.

He went back to the stable and gathered together armfuls of straw, cheerfully telling Rhiannon what he had found. She followed him through to the kitchen and he made her a bed on the floor before the fire, then hung their cloaks out over the back of the chairs to dry.

"Are ye still damp?" he asked. "Happen ye should take off your coat and stockings, and let me hang them afore the fire to dry."

Rhiannon did as she was told then, dressed only in a loose white shirt and breeches, huddled closer to the fire, her hands held out. The wind moaned and sighed all round the ruins, and they could hear the occasional growl of thunder. An early dusk was falling.

"Happen we're stuck here for the night," Lewen said. Rhiannon looked back over her shoulder at him and smiled.

He smiled back at her and stripped off his own coat and boots, arranging them over the back of old chairs so they could both stop the draughts and receive some of the warmth of the fire. His shirt was damp as well, but he was too shy to take it off in front of Rhiannon so he simply undid the collar and sleeves, and ruffled his damp hair, and looked about for the cleanest pot. "I dinna think to bring any food," he said. "But I can make us some sort o' porridge from the oats, and I saw some herbs out in the garden, I'll go and pick some to make us some tea when the rain dies down a wee."

Rhiannon lay back in the straw, looking dreamy. "It does no' sound as if it's ever going to stop."

Lewen looked down at her, and felt an absurd desire to say that he wished it never would. He bit the words back, and busied himself with practical matters. He scrubbed out a pot, then went into the stable to scoop a couple of handfuls of oats out of one of the bins. While it cooked, he quickly whittled them a rough spoon from a piece of firewood, porridge being difficult to eat with the fingers. He and Rhiannon then put the pot of porridge between them and took turns to eat. It was rather tasteless, but it was warm and filling, and both felt much better after eating.

"I hope there are no ghosts here," Rhiannon said. "I never want to see a ghost again."

"I doubt whether anyone died in this room," Lewen said. "The Red Guards did no' kill the servants o' the witches, only the witches themselves. Most o' the battle would have taken place in the actual Tower, no' here in the stables." He reached out a lazy hand and threw another log on the fire. A small lump of wood fell down from the pile and rolled across the floor and he picked it up, and examined it in the fitful light.

"I think this is rowan," he said in surprise, and scratched at it with his nail, then lifted it to his nose and sniffed. "Ye do no' usually burn rowan," he explained to Rhiannon, taking his knife and beginning to whittle. "Rowan is one o' the sacred woods. It is thought to be particularly powerful protecting against evil spirits."

"Why?" she asked.

He shrugged. "I dinna ken. It just is. They plant it in grave-yards, along with yew, to stop the spirits o' the dead from wandering, and countryfolk often hang it above their door to keep the house safe. In the Other World, they often used it to beat suspected witches, or make crosses out o' it to try to repel the devil. All nonsense, o' course, naught but auld-fashioned superstition, but still it is a powerful tree. I'll make ye something from it, a charm against evil."

"All right," she answered, pleased. "What will ye make?"

"I dinna ken yet. Something to hang about your neck, I think. That is the best way to wear a charm." He lifted the knot of wood, and turned it first one way, then another. "A star," he said softly. "A star for my starry-eyed lass."

She smiled at him.

In companionable silence, they sat together before the fire, listening to the constant wash of the rain, as curl after curl of white wood fell to the floor. It did not take him long to make. As large as Lewen's hands were, they were deft and nimble, and he wielded the knife with great confidence. A five-pointed star set within a small hoop soon emerged. His focus grew more intent, his movements more careful and studied. Soon the amulet was smooth and silvery-pale.

"I wish I had some beeswax to polish it with," he said at last, passing the amulet to Rhiannon. "I'll polish it for ye when we get to Lucescere."

"It's bonny," she said, turning it in her fingers. The hoop was about as large as the circle made by thumb and forefinger, the star within as delicate as thorns. "Will it really protect me against ghosts?"

"Ghosts and sprites and things that go bump in the night," he answered with a grin. "Ye should wear it against your skin, just here, above your breast bone." He touched her gently with one finger, and felt her take a startled breath. "See, I've drilled a little hole here for ye to thread a ribbon through." He reached behind his head and pulled loose the black cord that bound back his unruly hair. It fell loose about his face as he threaded the cord through the aperture and knotted it together. "There you are," he said, pleased. "I'd like to see ye wear it. I've noticed ye have no necklace like the other girls."

Her face suddenly darkened.

"What's wrong?" he asked.

"Naught," she said, but he saw how she shivered and at once built up the fire so sparks flew up the chimney. "Ye're cold," he said. "Come warm yourself by the fire, and I'll make ye some tea."

She obeyed, huddling her arms about her knees, the pentagram hanging about her neck.

Lewen pulled his cloak over his head and ran through the storm to grab a few handfuls of weeds. He saw peppermint, thyme, and chamomile, and a woody old lavender. There may have been more, but the rain was coming down so thickly he did not wait to see. He came back into the warm peace of the kitchen, and saw Rhiannon sitting staring down at the star charm in her hands. She gave him a radiant smile as he shook off the rain, and Lewen felt warm happiness well up through his body.

He sat next to her, poking at the fire and throwing the herbs into the water. "I wish we had some honey," he said.

"Canna have everything," Rhiannon said. "I think we doing well, all things considering."

He nodded and smiled. "Warm enough?"

"Lovely and warm now, thanks," she said and rested her head on her hand. "Will they be worried about us?"

Lewen nodded. "If I find the Scrying Pool I'll try to scry to Nina," he said. "The storm may make it hard, and I am no' very skilled at scrying. I do no' ken if it'll work." .

"What is scrying?"

"Talking mind to mind," Lewen said.

Rhiannon stared at him in amazement. "Ye can talk to Nina, when she is there in the castle and we are here?"

"Maybe," Lewen said. "I ken Nina well, and she'll be listening for word from me. True witches can scry at distance, but I canna, no' yet. I'm still learning."

"I'm amazed," Rhiannon said. "Is there aught ye canna do?"

Lewen flushed. "O' course."

"I've yet to see it," Rhiannon said. "Ye can make a spoon out o' a lump o' wood, or a charm against ghosts, ye can light a fire with a snap o' your fingers, ye can talk to birds and dogs and horses and faeries, ye can make us a meal out o' weeds and horse food, and ye can outride and outfight any man." Her voice was full of pride.

Lewen leant on his elbow. "I've only managed to outride ye once."

"Aye, that's true," Rhiannon said complacently.

He smiled. "Well, at least I beat ye at archery."

"Aye, I ken," she said and flashed her dimple. "Ye strong." She lifted one hand and felt his arm muscles approvingly.

Lewen shifted his weight, flushing. "The water's boiling, let's have some tea," he said. "Oh, no! We have naught to drink out o'. Dinna say I have to whittle us a cup as well!"

"I have a cup in my bag," Rhiannon said. "We could use that."

"I'll go and get it," he said and sat up.

She frowned. "I'll get it," she said.

"I tell ye what, I'll get your saddlebags and ye can find the cup," Lewen said, grinning at her. "I ken how ye feel about people looking through your things."

Her frown did not lift. "No looking," she warned him.

"No looking," he promised. He got up and went out of the circle of light, into the chilly darkness beyond. When he came back, a few minutes later, he had Rhiannon's saddlebags in his hands. He tossed them to her, and warmed himself by the fire as she surreptitiously looked through her things. By the time he had swung the pot off the fire and thrown on a few more logs, she had drawn a silver goblet out of the bag. Simply made, it had a wide cup set on a smooth, slender stem. In the centre of the stem was a large crystal that caught the light of the fire and glittered with rainbow prisms.

"It's lovely," Lewen said. "Where on earth did ye get it?" She said nothing and he looked at her sharply. "Was it Connor's?"

She nodded, looking anxious and guilty.

"I thought ye gave my mam all o' Connor's things, to give to his family."

"She asked me for his *clothes,*" Rhiannon explained.

He could not help laughing, though the admission troubled him. "What else did ye keep?"

She drew out a pretty music box that played an ethereal tune when she opened the lid, and the small golden medal with the device of a haloed hand. Lewen touched it with one finger. "The League o' the Healing Hand," he said, sounding sad. "Ye canna tell a story about the Bright Wars without hearing tales o' the League. They are almost all dead now." He lifted his gaze. "Ye canna keep these things, Rhiannon. Truly ye canna. They belong to Johanna now. If Connor carried them in his travel-pack, it means they meant a lot to him, and they will to her too. Do ye understand?"

"I suppose so," Rhiannon answered crossly.

He took the goblet. "We may as well drink out o' it now, though, although it's far too precious for thyme tea!"

Very carefully he managed to pour some of the fragrant tea into the goblet. "This will help warm ye, and will ease that cough," he said. "Drink up."

She took the goblet between her hands and sipped at the hot liquid within. After a few mouthfuls she passed the goblet back to him. "Ye now."

He drank deeply, though the draught was quite bitter without honey, then passed it back to her, watching as she lifted the cup to her mouth and drank again. Her black hair was kindled with gold and bronze light where the fire struck through it, and her eyes were shadowed. He thought she was the most beautiful woman he had ever seen. As if sensing his thought, she looked up and smiled at him.

"Thank ye," she said. "I am warm all through now."

Unable to help himself, Lewen bent over and kissed her. She caught her breath in surprise, then drew his head closer, one arm sliding up round his shoulder. Lewen lost himself in sensation. Her skin was just as satiny-smooth as he had imagined, and warm from the fire. Her mouth was soft and sweet, and she kissed with an intoxicating combination of ardour and inexperience. When Lewen entwined his tongue with hers, he felt her shudder and sigh and creep closer, and he felt such a desperate eagerness he surprised even himself. He tried to draw back, but she would not let him, raising herself to follow him.

He sighed and folded her under him, feeling their bodies shift and curve to each other's shape. One of her hands slipped down under his collar and caressed the skin of his throat. He closed his eyes and let his own hand slide under her shirt, finding the naked skin of her back, slipping round to caress her slender waist, and then finding at last her breast. She moved in sudden surprise and he heard her breath catch and sigh. He had to draw away then, to look down into her face, to watch as he undid her buttons with shaking fingers. Her eyes were closed, her face as soft and vulnerable as he could ever wish for, and a smile curved her lips. As he drew away her shirt, cupping her breasts with both hands, the smile deepened and her elusive dimple flashed in her cheek. He drew a deep, shaking breath and brought his mouth down to the creamy curve of her breast. She arched her back.

"Rhiannon, Rhiannon," he whispered at last, managing to lift his mouth away. He felt drunk.

"Lewen," she whispered back, and kissed his ear.

"Rhiannon, I canna . . ."

"What?"

"Rhiannon, if we go on, I willna be able to stop. I dinna think I can stop now."

"Stop? Why?" she asked in surprise.

He kissed her again, drew back to look at her, swooped down

to kiss her again. The feel of her half-naked body beneath him was drugging all his sense.

"Rhiannon . . . are ye sure? Is this what ye want?"

She turned her head blindly, seeking his mouth. He took her head in both his hands, his fingers tangled in the silkiness of her hair, and pressed her to him. They lost themselves in each other's mouths for what seemed a very long time. Then Lewen managed to disentangle them from their clothes, each discarding revealing a new source of joyous sensation. Rhiannon's body was just as beautiful as he had imagined, slim and lithe and milk-white, with a flowing curve from breast to hip that he marvelled over with mouth and hand. She was as eager to touch and explore his body as he was hers, and Lewen's urgency was so great he feared the mere touch of her hand would be enough to undo him. So he captured both her hands in his, stretching them out above her head and holding her still with the weight of his body.

"Please, dearling, *leannan*, please, lie still," he begged.

She smiled up at him and obeyed. Cautiously he let go of her hands, but she did not try to move. Very slowly he put his hand down between their bodies and pried her legs apart. She was wet and warm and slick. He bit his lip, then drove into her. She cried out in shock, but Lewen was beyond hearing her. Again and again he thrust into her, crying aloud in pleasure, and she raised her hips, thrusting against him, so that he felt a great roar of blood race through him, deafening him. He raised himself high on his hands, his groin fused with hers, his head flung back, groaning. They were still a moment or two, Lewen slowly moving in and out of her again, then he bent his arms, laying his weight upon her again, utterly relaxed and replete.

"That was beautiful," he said at last. "Ye're beautiful, Rhiannon."

She sighed. He said her name again and turned her face with both hands so they could kiss again.

"I love ye," he said. "I love ye so much."

She looked up at him curiously, the firelight playing over the planes of her face. Her eyes looked very blue, and her lips were red and swollen.

"Ye're so beautiful," he said again, kissing her very gently.

Still she was silent. He shifted his weight to the side, so he was not crushing her, and felt himself slide out of her. He sighed with disappointment and pressed himself as close to her as he could get. She cuddled against him, and that gave him the courage to ask, against all his better judgement, "Rhiannon? Do ye love me too?"

She looked him in the eyes. "I do no' ken what love is. Is this love I feel?"

"What do ye feel?" he asked, threading his fingers through hers and holding their entwined hands up against the golden glow of the fire. He was so afraid he dared not meet her eyes.

"Happy," she said wonderingly.

"Me too," he answered gladly and kissed her. She wrapped both her arms about his neck, her breasts spreading against his chest. At once he felt his body stir and smiled ruefully, lowering one hand to caress her inner thigh, then stroking his hand up towards her breast. To his surprise he left rust-coloured streaks on the warm creaminess of her skin. He looked down, and saw blood trickling down her thigh.

"Rhiannon!" he cried.

"Aye?"

He leant up on his elbow, winding her hair around one finger. "Have ye never lain with a man afore?"

"Me? O' course no'. Who would I have lain with?"

He was taken aback. "But I thought . . . ye said . . ."

"I No-Horn," she said. "The favours o' the men were kept only for the leaders o' the herd. I saw them mate often. It was no' like this, I think."

Lewen sighed. He lay quietly, thinking. "I'm sorry," he said after a moment. "I should've stopped."

"Why?" she asked again.

He could not explain to her. She wriggled a little closer, and traced a circle on his hard belly with her finger. "It worries ye, this blood?"

He sighed. "Aye. Though I must admit, it pleases me too, that I was the one to deflower ye. I dinna ken why I tell ye so."

"Deflower?" Rhiannon was puzzled. "I girl, no' plant."

Lewen laughed and traced round and round her nipple, watching it harden. "Indeed, ye are, my dearling." He closed his mouth over her nipple and the sound of her sigh went into him like a sword. He slid his hand down between her legs and felt the hot stickiness of her, and then, his own desire quickening fast, slid down and tasted it. He had himself well in hand this time, determined to take his time over the loving of her, but her own desire was so swift, and her expression of it so honest and free, that once again it was a quick, hard, passionate coupling they had in the straw before the fire. Afterwards, he lay with his head on her stomach, feeling her hand twirling his hair, feeling exhausted, replete, and very happy.

"Ye mine now," Rhiannon whispered. "Do ye hear me? Mine."

He rolled over, reaching out one lazy hand to trace down her brow, her nose, across the soft pads of her lips, down her chin and throat and the bare cleft of her breasts to her belly-button. "Aye, I hear ye," he said softly, and kissed her. "I'm yours."

"Always," she said.

"Always," he repeated.

"So is this love, what I'm feeling?"

"Aye," he said and kissed her again. "This is love." They kissed lingeringly. "Say it," he commanded. "Say, 'I love ye, Lewen'."

"I love ye, Lewen."

"I love ye too, Rhiannon."

They smiled, and then, for no reason, laughed. The fire was dying down, and outside the storm still howled. Rhiannon gave a little shiver.

"Ye're getting cold," Lewen said remorsefully and sat up, looking for something to cover her with. "Look, it's dark. We've missed sunset. Oh well, it's teeming down out there. I doubt I could have found the pool anyway. I'll have to try again at dawn." He got up and felt the edge of her cloak but it was still damp, so he threw some more wood on the fire and then poured her some more tea, warming the goblet between his hands until steam wisped up. "Drink this, my love, and I'll find something to wrap ye in."

She took the goblet from him, smiling, and he was compelled to kiss her again, quickly, before getting to his feet. "My shawl is in my bag," she said, and drank the hot tea gratefully.

Lewen went over to the saddlebag and pulled out the

embroidered shawl with a flourish. Something came rattling out of the bag with it, and he bent and picked it up from the floor. His entrails knotted. In his hand was a necklace made of bones and teeth. Even in the subtle, changeable light of the fire he could see most of the teeth were human. He stood still, frozen with shock, while his mind neatly put all the pieces of the puzzle together and made a whole. Even while he tried to deny and make excuses, his analytical brain turned the puzzle over and examined it from every angle. There was no mistake.

He turned and went back to the fire. Rhiannon sat in the straw, her arms about her knees, her hair streaming down her naked back, looking more bewitching than ever. He tossed her the shawl, and she caught it and smiled, wrapping it about her shoulders. When he did not smile back, her expression turned grave. She looked up at him questioningly.

He held out the necklace. "Is this yours?"

All the soft, warm, living flesh of her turned slowly to stone. She lifted eyes that had gone huge and dark. "Aye," she answered reluctantly.

"Are those Connor's teeth, his finger?"

"Aye."

"So ye killed him? Ye lied to me?"

"Aye," she answered again.

He suddenly become conscious of his nakedness. He dropped the necklace on the table with as much horror as if it had been a snake, then came back to the fire pulling on his shirt and his breeches, which were still unpleasantly damp. He then sat down on the floor to pull on his stockings and boots. "Why?" he asked, not looking at her.

Her voice shook. "He would've told them I'd helped him to escape. They would have torn me to pieces."

"So ye killed him."

"He had my mother, he was going to kill her!"

"But ye hated your mother."

She nodded, tears welling up in her eyes. He thrust his hands into his pockets. She looked at him pleadingly but he would not look at her, and the tears overflowed. She buried her face in her arms.

"Why dinna ye tell me afore?" The words burst out of him.

She raised her miserable face. "They said whoever had killed him would hang. I do no' want to hang."

"Nay, I guess no'," he said bitterly and got to his feet. He did not know where to go, or what to do, so after a moment he prodded the fire, saying over his shoulder, "Ye'd better get dressed, your clothes are dry now. Ye should try and get some sleep, it's late."

She did not move. "Lewen?"

He did not answer.

"Lewen?" she said desperately.

"What?" he said harshly.

"I sorry. I didna want to hurt him. I had to, canna ye see that? Please, dinna be angry. I couldna help it, truly I couldna. I didna ken!" The words came tumbling over each other and she held up both hands to him imploringly.

He did not reply.

She tried again. "Lewen, dinna be angry. Please, please."

"Ye should have told me," he replied, prodding at the fire even harder.

"I couldna tell ye. Do ye no' understand? Lewen?"

He turned on her, his face twisted with pain. "Ye are a murderess! A liar and a traitor! Ye killed my friend!"

She tried to speak, but could not. Weeping, she pulled on her clothes and huddled herself into the shawl. Lewen got to his feet. "I'll sleep in the stable," he said. "Hopefully the storm will have blown over by morning."

Catching up his cloak, he went away from the dim, warm room into bitter cold and darkness.

The Scrying Pool

He passed in and out of uneasy sleep all the long, unhappy night. The sound of the wind in the broken stone worried him like icy teeth, so that only the imprecise memory of nightmares showed he had slept at all. Yet when he finally woke, feeling a great weight of misery, it was to find a clear, cold dawn and the winged horse gone from the stall. Argent stood there alone, his head sunk, eyes shut, one hoof relaxed.

Lewen stared in stupefaction, then turned and ran into the kitchen. It was grey and empty, smelling of smoke. On the table were the silver goblet, the music box, the golden medal, and a gruesome necklace of teeth and bones. There was no sign of Rhiannon.

Lewen could not believe she had gone. How had she managed to get Blackthorn out of the stall, when he had slept in the straw right next to the horses? He imagined her creeping out into the dark and the storm, and felt such a pit of loss open up inside him he came the closest to weeping since his roan pony Aurora had died when he was still a lad. Anger and grief together make a bitter brew, and Lewen was so angry he was blind and deaf with it. He did not know what to do. He sank to his knees and covered his face with his hands, trying to hold back the howl that seemed to be gathering inside him. At last the howl knotted itself into a hard lump in his chest, and he was able to get up. He filled the goblet with water and drank deeply, trying to wash the knot away, and then splashed his face again and again. A longing to speak to his mother came over him. He imagined her distress and felt his stomach quiver. Hurriedly he gathered up Connor's treasures and shoved them in his own saddlebags. Then he led the big grey stallion out into the courtyard.

It was almost dawn and the sky was clear. Puddles gleamed everywhere, and the courtyard was littered with broken branches and torn leaves. High overhead ravens wheeled in the wind, hundreds of them, calling harshly. They looked like ashes blown from a bonfire. Lewen moved slowly through the ruin, the stallion following. Much of the main body of the building had been destroyed by fire, leaving nothing but blackened stones all overgrown with brambles and nettles. He found the gate that had once led out to the bridge across the waterfall, and looked out over the dizzying chasm, able to see nothing of the castle on the far side of the river for the great gusts of spray that dashed him in the face. He left Argent lipping at weeds in what once would have been a pleasure garden, and climbed an old stone staircase to explore the wreck of a vaulted gallery where once great sorcerers and prionnsachan would have walked together. He came down again carefully, feeling desolate and alone. Nowhere was there any sign of Rhiannon.

Then he and the stallion came to the central courtyard and found there a round pool of water, shimmering with reflections of the dawn sky. Despite the wrack of the storm that littered the cracked paving-stones, not a single leaf spoiled the sparkling perfection of the silver-lined pool. It was enclosed inside stone arches fretted with entwining lines and knots, and guarded by large stone ravens.

Lewen sighed and sat down heavily on the curved bench encircling the pool. He had half-hoped, half-dreaded finding the Scrying Pool.

He remembered hearing Dughall MacBrann tell the story of how he had crept here to the Tower of Ravens one bitter winter's night so he could scry to Lachlan and tell him news of the war against the Bright Soldiers. "It's a wonder my hair and beard are no' as white as my father's," he had said. "For the tower was thick with ghosts and evil memories, and all I could remember was that old story about Brann the Raven and how he swore he would outwit Gearradh in the end and live again. I swear I felt him breathing down my neck the whole time!"

If the MacBrann had been able to use the Scrying Pool twenty-five years ago, the chances are the pool would be useable now. The fact that it was still brimming with crystal-clear water, untarnished after fifty years of neglect, indicated the magic of the pool was unbroken. Lewen badly wanted to speak to someone. He felt as if his inner compass, that had led him true all his life, was now spinning out of control. He did not know what was right and true anymore. Rhiannon had lied to him, she had tricked and deceived him, she had made a fool of him. The thoughts spilled through his mind like acid. He looked back over the past few weeks and writhed in internal torment, seeing how easily he had been seduced by her air of wild and innocent beauty. Had it all been a lie? He could not tell anymore. He longed to be able to tell someone, and have them set him straight again. He longed for comfort and reassurance, for someone to say to him, "But she is naught but a wild child, she did no' ken what she did, how could she? O' course she loves ye, o' course her heart is pure and true, o' course she is no' a cold-blooded murderess, how can ye think such things o' her?"

So he sat cross-legged before the pool, staring into its silvery depths, calling to Nina in his mind. It took only a few seconds for her image to appear to him in the pool. She looked white and anxious and he heard her voice in his mind.

"Lewen, where are you? What happened to ye?"

"We were caught in the storm. We took shelter in the auld tower."

"Are ye all right?"

"Aye, we're grand. At least, I am . . ."

"What do ye mean? Where's Rhiannon? Is she with ye? She's disappeared!"

"Nay. I mean, I do no' ken. She's gone."

"Gone? Do you mean she *was* with you? Where has she gone?"

"I dinna ken. She crept away last night, while I was sleeping . . . she's run away."

"But why?"

"I found out . . . something." He took a shaking breath, then the words burst out of him. "Oh Nina, it was Rhiannon who murdered Connor. She confessed it all to me last night, and now she's gone. I dinna ken where, she disappeared during the night."

Nina was silent for a long moment, then she said steadily,

"We all kent it may have been her, Lewen, we've suspected it from the beginning. Even Lilanthe feared so, and ye ken your mother always thinks the best o' everyone. We will have to find her, we need to take her to Lucescere to be tried and judged."

"But, Nina, they will hang her!"

"Maybe no'. If it was an accident . . ."

"It was no accident," Lewen said harshly.

"That will be for the court to decide," Nina answered. "Lewen, come back to the castle. We will find her, dinna ye worry."

"I am no' sure I want to find her," Lewen said, his voice breaking.

Nina looked troubled. "I canna just let her fly away, Lewen, no' if she is responsible for Connor's death. The Rìgh would want us to make every effort to find her."

He said nothing, and she said again, with deep concern in her voice, "Come back to the castle, Lewen. We've all been very worried about ye. Ye must be cold and hungry indeed. Come back, and we'll talk about it then."

"But what about Rhiannon?" Lewen said. "I do no' want to just leave her. She went out into the storm, and she's been so sick, and Blackthorn is so nervy . . ."

"The laird sent out search parties for the two o' ye, happen they will have had sight o' her. We'll talk about it when ye are here."

Lewen sighed. "All right."

"Are ye using the Scrying Pool? For indeed your face and voice are clear as if ye were standing afore me."

Lewen nodded, feeling sick at heart.

"Thank Eà! Have ye spoken to the Rìgh? What did he say?"

"I havena contacted him yet." Lewen's voice was dull and a trifle defensive. "I have only just found the Pool."

"Then will ye scry to the Rìgh now? I think he should ken everything we do, just in case we fail to make it back to Lucescere. My heart troubles me . . . the laird is angry and suspicious indeed about ye and Rhiannon going missing." She paused, then went on more strongly, "Tell His Highness all ye can, Lewen, he needs to ken."

"But it is so far . . . I do no' ken if I'll be able to reach him. I am no good at scrying." Lewen knew he was making excuses. He did not want to have to face his Rìgh and tell him he had fallen in love with a murderess.

"The Scrying Pool will help ye, Lewen, that's what it's for. Remember your scrying exercises. Empty your mind, control your breath, and imagine his face. Reach out to him. Ye will reach him if ye focus strongly enough."

Lewen nodded reluctantly and closed his eyes, emptying his thoughts. He waited a few minutes, then stared once more into the pool, imagining the dark, stern face of Lachlan MacCuinn, the Rìgh of Eileanan. "My laird," he called in his mind, "can ye hear me? Can ye hear me, my laird?"

The shadows in the pool gradually shifted into the shape of a man, black-haired and black-bearded, with the curve of black wings rising from his shoulders. Lewen heard the startled mind-voice of the Rìgh.

"Lewen, my lad?"

"Aye, my laird, it is me."

"What on earth is the matter? Why are ye calling me?"

"I have news, my laird, I thought ye should ken."

"If it is the news o' Connor's death, we received word o' it, thanks to a very tired and bad-tempered golden eagle. It is unhappy news indeed, we are all most distressed."

"Aye, my laird. I'm glad the eagle made it, we were no' sure he could cross the mountains, the weather has been foul indeed."

"Has it? I'm sorry for that. Are ye delayed?"

"Aye, my laird, we are." Lewen took a deep, shaking breath and forced himself to go on. He felt quite sick with the conflict of emotions inside him. "There's more news than that, though, my laird. We have found out who killed him, Your Highness. It was a girl we found in the mountains, dressed in his clothes, a satyricorn girl."

"A Horned One killed him?"

"She's no' horned, my laird, but a satyricorn nonetheless." Lewen heard the bitterness in his own voice. "She was travelling with us but when I discovered the truth . . . she fled, my laird."

"Ye must find her, and bring her here," the Rìgh commanded.

"The satyricorns have signed the Pact o' Peace, they are subject to the laws o' this land. The murder o' a Blue Guard is a heinous crime indeed, and Connor the Just was one o' my best and most faithful men."

"I ken, my laird," Lewen said unhappily.

"Ye must capture the murderess and bring her here to face trial, do ye hear me, Lewen? The whole city grieves his death. Where are ye? Are there men ye can call upon to help lay this murderess by the heels?"

"I think so, my laird. I am at the Tower o' Ravens."

"Ye are using the Scrying Pool? Good lad! No wonder your face just popped up in my wash-bowl. I was wondering how ye managed to scry across the mountains so clearly, I thought ye must have found some way to fly across like the eagle. I could wish ye were closer, we are all keen indeed to charge the murderess and deal with her afore the wedding. We want no unpleasantness to mar the festivities."

"No, my laird."

"Well, fare ye well, then, my lad, and good work."

"Your Highness, there is more. I think ye should ken it all, just in case something happens to us . . ."

"Happens to ye? What in Eà's green blood do ye mean? Are ye in some kind o' danger there? Is it that satyricorn girl?"

"Nay, my laird. It's just . . . my laird, in our effort to return to ye quickly, we came down the eastern bank of the Findhorn River, through the Fetterness Valley."

"Aye, o' course, ye must've, if ye're at the Tower o' Ravens. A bare, bleak place, if I remember rightly. We fought a battle there, at Fettercairn Castle, many years ago."

"That is where we are now, my laird. We've been trapped here for some days . . ."

"Trapped? Held against your will, do ye mean?" The Rìgh spoke urgently.

"Nay, no' entirely. The road was blocked. Things are no' right here, though, my laird. There is much talk o' murders, and children missing, and corpses that will no' rest, and there seems to be necromancers using the auld tower . . ."

"Necromancers!"

"Aye. Trying to raise the dead. Rhiannon saw them invoke a

circle, my laird, and sacrifice a cock, and speak with the spirits
o' the dead."

"Who is Rhiannon?"

Lewen's heart sank. "The satyricorn, Your Highness."

"The murderess?"

"Aye, my laird."

"Did anyone else see this so-called necromancy?"

"No, my laird, but—"

"She could be seeking to deceive, to throw suspicion for her
nefarious deeds onto others."

"I do no' think so, my laird." Lewen saw the Rìgh's frowning eyebrows shoot up and went on quickly, "Please, I havena
much time. Your Highness, there has been much evil done in
this valley, evil much greater than Rhiannon is responsible for.
She killed Connor high in the mountains, my laird, up under
Ben Eyrie, no' here in Fetterness. She has never been here
afore. The murders and the necromancy, that is the work o' others, and I fear it means some danger to ye, my laird. The laird
here talks o' seeking revenge for the death o' his brother—I
think ye may have killed him, sir. Or one o' your men. A little
boy died too."

"I do no' remember a boy," the Rìgh said.

"I think Connor heard something, knew something o' the
laird o' Fettercairn's plans, though I do no' ken how or what.
Connor was just across the loch, at Ravenscraig, when the auld
MacBrann died. We were there too, for my mother to help ease
him. The MacBrann was very ill, raving o' ghosts and auld
prophecies and evil deeds. We all thought him mad. All except
Connor. My laird, the very night the MacBrann died Connor
took his horse and rode out for the Razor's Edge. That is a pass
through to Rionnagan, Your Highness . . ."

"I ken the Razor's Edge, I walked it myself once, long ago,"
the Rìgh said gruffly 'It is no' a road one would take lightly."

"Nay, my laird. I think Connor must've had heard something
that made him fear for ye, or for your kingdom. Why else would
he ride that way? He died afore he could tell ye his news . . ."

"Fettercairn Castle," the Rìgh said broodingly. "That is a
name I have no' heard for many years, but I remember it well.
A place o' blood and treachery."

Lewen nodded.

"Ye have done well," the Rìgh said abruptly. "Ye must go. If there are sorcerers there strong enough to raise the dead, they will be strong enough to eavesdrop on your scrying. Get out o' there, Lewen, as fast as ye can, and come here to me. I will hear all your news and judge then what is best done."

"Aye, my laird," said Lewen and sat back on his heels. A wave of dizziness washed over him, and he felt tired enough to weep. He had not realised what a great effort of will and focus it took to scry so far, for so long. He ground the heels of his hands into his eyes and then got to his feet. Only then did he realise he was not alone.

The tall, quiet man who guarded Lord Malvern's back was leaning on his claymore only a few feet away, with a handful of men that Lewen recognised from the castle. There was Shannley, the old groom who had tended the horses, and his assistant, Jem, and a few of the footmen. They all looked surly and uncomfortable.

"Glad we are indeed to have found ye, young sir," the laird's bodyguard said in his oddly feminine voice. "We've been searching since dawn. My laird has been most anxious about ye."

"I'm sorry," Lewen stammered. "We took refuge from the rain."

"And ye so close to the castle," he marvelled.

"Rhiannon has been sick," Lewen said defensively. "I did no' want her to get wet through. It was sleeting down."

"And where is the young lady now?"

"I dinna ken," Lewen said sullenly. "We quarreled and she ran off."

There was a little rumble of laughter from the men, and a quick nudging of each other's ribs. Lewen went crimson.

"We need to find her," he said. "I was just about to head back to the castle to ask for some help."

"Is that so?" Jem sneered. "It looked like ye were mooning about, staring at yourself in the water."

There were a few more sniggers. Lewen cast him an angry look, but said nothing. He could only hope that none of them there had any witch-skills, to eavesdrop on his silent conversation with the Rìgh. It seemed a futile hope. Some at least of these men must be part of the necromancers' circle of nine.

They all rode back to the castle, Lewen feeling like a prisoner in the midst of the other men. He was escorted silently through the gatehouse and the garden to the entrance hall, where Nina and Iven were both waiting with Lord Malvern. Nina flung her arms about his neck.

"Thank heavens ye are safe! We've been so worried about ye."

"I'm sorry," Lewen said defensively. "Indeed I could no' help it."

"O' course no', laddie," she said. "It was a wild storm! It seemed to blow up out o' nowhere. I'm just glad ye could find somewhere to shelter."

"Where is the lass?" Lord Malvern demanded.

"I dinna ken," Lewen said. "We quarreled, and she ran off while I was sleeping." He turned to Nina anxiously. "We need to find her," he said.

"A lover's quarrel, eh?" Lord Malvern said with a stiff, unnatural smile. "I see, I see."

Lewen ground his teeth. As his anger and hurt cooled, he was increasingly anxious about Rhiannon and sick with fear at the possible consequences of his telling Nina and the Rìgh about her confession. He wished he had not told anyone. He could not understand why he had. Now the Rìgh demanded Rhiannon be found, and brought to Lucescere to face trial. Lewen could not bear the thought that she might be found guilty and hanged, but then neither could he bear the thought that she had flown out of his life, never to be seen again.

Surely the court would understand? Surely they would not condemn such a young and beautiful woman to hang? Lewen moved restlessly. He wished he had never found the necklace. He wished he had slept all night with Rhiannon nestled into the curve of his body, and woken in the dawn to marvel at the peace of her sleeping face. He wished he had never met her.

But he had met her, and fallen in love with her, and promised himself to her, and then betrayed her. He could not ignore that. Though he still felt gutted with pain at her deceit, he could not bear to be instrumental in bringing her to the hangman's noose. Rhiannon may have killed Lewen's friend, and hacked out his teeth and chopped off his finger, and stolen his clothes and his treasures, and lied to Lewen, but he still loved her, Eà save his soul. He thought he always would.

Lewen turned to Nina desperately. "Where is everyone?"

"Lewen . . ."

"Where's Iven?"

"He's gone to bring her back," Nina said softly. "Ye must've kent he would have to do so, Lewen."

"She'll be long gone by now," Lewen said defiantly.

Nina shook her head. "She's no'. I scryed her out. She's up on the ridge behind the castle, watching. I do no' ken why she did no' fly further away. It would no' have made any difference in the end, though. Iven would still have ridden out after her, it just would've taken longer to find her."

"Nina," he said pleadingly. "Canna we just let her go? She's only a lass. I should not have told ye."

She rose and came to him, taking both his hands in hers. "I ken how ye must feel, Lewen, but Rhiannon killed a Yeoman. She must face the consequences o' her actions. Ye ken she must."

He saw Lord Malvern's eyes narrow and wrenched his hands away from Nina so he could press them against his eyes. "She didna ken!" he cried. "She was just protecting herself."

"Then she must tell the court so, and they will judge the right o' it," Nina said with inexorable calm. "Come, Lewen, ye are worn out. Do no' be fretting so. The men have found her and will soon be bringing her back. Ye can speak to her then."

Lewen stared at her incredulously. Did she not realise the danger Rhiannon was in? He could say nothing with the lord of Fettercairn standing just there and listening, and the hall full of footmen, and Irving the seneschal, hovering nearby with his stiff, white, unpleasant face set as usual in an unctuous smile. Lewen felt as if he had strayed into a nightmare, the sort where you tried and tried to run but found your body would not move.

He turned and strode away down the hall, leaving Lord Malvern frowning after him.

Nina picked up her skirts and ran to follow him. "Lewen, where do ye go? Lewen, ye're worn out, and starving hungry! Do no' be silly. Lewen!"

He was tired and kept having to stop to rub his filthy hand across his eyes, which smarted with angry tears. She caught up with him in the inner ward. "Lewen, ye must leave it be," she said softly. "It is out o' our hands now."

"It's all my fault. If I hadna told ye . . . if I hadna . . ." He broke off, unable to speak another word.

Nina stepped closer, holding his arm with both her hands. "I'm so sorry," she said inadequately. "Indeed, I see how hard this must be. But she did kill Connor, Lewen. She shot him through the back, and hacked out all his teeth and mutilated his hand, and then tossed him into the river like a load o' garbage. She is no' the lass ye thought she was."

Lewen took a deep breath. "But she is," he said gruffly. "I always kent what sort o' a lass she was. She's wild and fierce, I ken that, but oh, Nina, she is brave and loyal and loving too, I swear to ye, and she's been treated cruelly all her life. She kent no other way to be."

"Then we'll tell the judges so," Nina said, and lifted her hand to wipe her eyes. "Oh, Lewen, I wish . . . but it's too late. The men have ridden out to find her and bring her back, and they will, ye ken they will."

"She'll no' come easily," Lewen said sombrely. "She'll fight for her freedom, and she fights dirty, Nina. Someone else may die."

"I hope no'," Nina said.

"I do no' want it to be her," Lewen said and tore his arm out of her grasp, striding away across the courtyard.

"Where are ye going?"

"To find her, o' course," he said grimly over his shoulder. "Ye think the laird's men will let us take her to Lucescere, to tell her story and throw suspicion upon them? O' course they willna! They mean to kill her!"

"But Lewen, Iven is there, he willna let—"

"What can Iven do? Besides, he is still a Yeoman himself at heart, ye ken that, and he loved Connor well. He willna save her."

Nina protested again but Lewen did not wait to listen. He broke into a run, sprinting towards the stables. Argent had been unsaddled and put into a stall. Ignoring the curious groom who sought to waylay him, Lewen seized his bow and quiver of arrows and then grabbed Argent's bridle off its hook.

"Which way did they go?" he said through his teeth.

"Durward, ye mean?" the young groom said nervously.

Lewen dragged the bridle over Argent's head. "Which way?"

"Out the back gate."

"Open it for me." Lewen vaulted onto Argent's bare back, kicking the stallion into motion.

"But . . ."

In a single swift motion Lewen had pulled an arrow from his quiver and had it aimed directly at the groom's heart, the bow's string quivering with the strain.

"Open it for me else I'll shoot ye!"

The groom ran to open the gate.

Argent galloped through before it was fully opened. It was easy enough to follow the other men. They had left a wide trail of hoof prints churning up the mud. The path was steep and slippery, and Argent almost fell once. Lewen dragged his head up and spurred him on. They reached the top of the ridge and came out on a wide, windswept moor. Rhiannon was struggling against four men. One was Cameron, the others were men from the castle. Her nose was bleeding. Blackthorn reared and plunged nearby, while Rafferty and a few other men sought to throw a rope around her neck. Iven was seeking to intervene, calling, "Rhiannon, do no' resist! They'll only hurt ye. Rhiannon!"

Durward stood watching, a bow and arrow raised high. Rhiannon sent Cameron sprawling with a well-aimed kick between the legs, then wrenched herself free of the hands that sought to constrain her. For a moment she stood, struggling to regain her breath, then she whirled and ran a few steps towards Blackthorn. Durward released the arrow.

It raced through the air towards her, swift and merciless. The spin of the world on its axis seemed to slow about Lewen. He put back his hand, seized an arrow and cocked it to his bow. He bent the bow and raised it. He released the arrow. It sprang from his bow like a bird, soaring up, up, up into the sky. It reached the apex of its flight and began to descend, singing a little in the wind. Then his arrow smashed into Durward's, snapping it in two. Both arrows fell harmlessly to the ground.

Amazed faces turned towards him, mouths hanging open. Lewen felt the world lurch back into motion again. He ran forward a few steps, his hand outstretched to Rhiannon. She had seen him knock the arrow out of the sky and her step had faltered as her eyes flew to his. The moment's hesitation cost her dearly. One of the castle men threw the noose of rope over her, and dragged her off her feet. In a minute they were all upon her, punching her with clenched fists and kicking her with their boots. One drew his dagger.

"Stop! Stop!" Iven cried, and threw himself into the fray, dragging the laird's men away. "We do no' want to kill her! Stop, ye fools."

Reluctantly they all stood back. Rhiannon lay still on the ground. A few feet away, Blackthorn neighed and pawed the ground in agitation. As the men turned towards her again, she spread her wings and soared away, the sound of her unhappy whinnies ringing in the wind.

Lewen fell to his knees by Rhiannon's body. He turned her over, lifting her into his arms. Her face was smeared with blood and mud. He could see bruises springing up on her pale skin. With shaking fingers, Lewen opened her shirt. The charm he had whittled for her fell out, so that he almost cried out in his pain. He put his hand on her chest and felt beneath his fingers the rapid beating of her heart. For a moment he could not speak, his relief was so great, then he looked up at Iven. "She lives," he said.

Iven nodded, looking very grave. "Well done," he said. He stared round at the castle men with anger sparkling in his blue eyes. "If ye had killed her, I would've had ye all arrested," he said. "This is a matter for the Crown!"

"My laird would never have let ye," Shannley sneered.

"He has no' the power to stop me," Iven replied. "Come, let us take her back to the castle. We shall ride for Lucescere immediately!"

Lewen saw how all the castle men bit their lips and muttered among themselves, but they did not try to interfere as Iven lifted Rhiannon and trussed her to the broad back of the grey carthorse. Rafferty bent and picked up Rhiannon's saddlebags, and her bow and arrows. She had not even had time to try to defend herself.

Silently they made their way back to the castle, Durward

striding ahead and looking very grim. All the men were muddy
and dishevelled, and Cameron, who sported a nasty black eye,
was limping painfully.

"Is she badly hurt?" Nina asked quietly, coming to Iven's
stirrup and looking up into his set face as they rode back
through the gate.

"I do no' ken," he said. "She would be dead if it was no' for
Lewen. The laird's gillie tried to shoot her down."

Nina's gaze flew to Lewen's face and then to the gillie's.
"I'm glad ye got there in time," she said to Lewen.

Iven dismounted with a sigh and drew Nina to him and
kissed her hair. "She's unconscious. I'd say she'll be out for
some time, *leannan.* Will ye help me put her to bed in the caravan? We'll have to shackle her to the bunk, I dinna want to risk
her escaping."

Nina nodded and beckoned to Cameron and Rafferty to help
carry the unconscious girl to the caravans. Lewen watched as
the two boys carried Rhiannon's limp form up the steps and
into the red caravan, Nina following close behind. He felt pow-
erless to move. It was as if all the will and desire in his body
had been drained away, and he was left just a husk of man, unable to even lift a finger.

The stableyard was crowded with people. Landon, Maisie
and Fèlice looked shocked and unhappy, while Edithe looked
very smug and self-righteous. Lord Malvern had been congratulating his men and hearing their account of the capture, made
Lewen grind his jaw together and clench his fists. Now the lord
turned back to Iven, saying affably, "Well, now your miscreant
is caught and the road is clear, ye will no doubt wish to be on
your way. I've arranged the kitchens to pack up some supplies
for ye, including some bottles of Dedrie's elderflower wine,
which I believe was very popular with your young folk. I do
hope ye have enjoyed your stay with us."

"Ye have been most hospitable, thank ye," Iven answered.
"We are indeed eager to be on our way."

"So I understand."

"I thank ye again for your hospitality and your help," Iven
said rather shortly. "If ye would be so kind as to arrange for all
our luggage to be brought down?"

"O' course," Lord Malvern answered, waving one hand at
Irving, who was as always hovering in the background. Irving
bowed and went silently away.

"I'm sure ye willna mind if I pack up my own belongings?"
Nina said, coming down the caravan steps and shutting the door
behind her. "I do like to make sure I have everything in place.
Lewen, happen ye could accompany me, while the other lads
get the horses ready?"

"Shannley, Jem, ye will o' course assist?"

"O' course, my laird," the old groom said with an obsequious
bob of his head.

"Cameron, ye stay here and guard the prisoner," Iven said.
"Maisie, my dear, happen ye had best go and lie down, ye are
looking very pale."

"I dinna want to go in there with *her.*" Maisie shrank back.

"She'll sleep a while yet," Iven said wearily, "and even when
she wakes, she's tightly secured. She canna hurt ye."

"Still," Maisie said.

"Very well, ye may rest in our caravan, if ye like. I do no'
want ye trying to ride yet."

Maisie nodded and limped over to the blue caravan and
hauled herself up the stairs with great difficulty. The door shut
behind her.

Lord Malvern smiled and inclined his head, and Nina gathered up her skirts and followed him. Just as she passed through
the doorway, she turned her head and said sternly, "Roden, stay
with your *dai-dein,* do ye hear? No more running off!"

"Aye, Mam," Roden answered in long-suffering tones and,
hand-in-hand with Lulu, he dawdled along behind his father.

Nina was obviously eager to cross-examine Lewen but she
could not speak because Lord Malvern had turned to them and
asked them a polite question about their plans. As Nina answered, just as politely, they came up the side of the central garden and Lewen saw Lady Evaline sitting under the apple tree.
She looked at him and raised one lace-mittened hand to beckon
him. Reluctantly Lewen approached her, the scent of sun-
warmed lavender rising around him.

"Ye are all leaving now?" Lady Evaline asked wistfully.

"Aye, the road is clear and we must be on our way."

"The laddie too?"

"Aye, o' course Roden is coming too," Lewen said.

"Aye, best get him away quickly," she said. "Too many ghosts here already."

"Aye," Lewen agreed, not knowing what else to say.

"Such a bonny lad he is," she said sadly. "Such a shame."

"What's such a shame?" Lewen asked, confused and un-nerved by this peculiar old lady with her crumpled, vacant face.

"That he must die," she answered. "They all die, ye ken."

"Do ye mean, everyone? Everyone must die?"

"Aye, everyone must die in the end," she said with a sigh. "I hope they let me rest when I die."

"Evaline!" Lord Malvern called. "Ye must no' keep the lad gossiping. Lady Nina wishes to be away."

"Away," Lady Evaline murmured. "I wish I could be away also."

"Why do ye no' go then?" Lewen asked, his sympathy stirred.

She raised her soft eyes to his. "Where would I go?" she asked simply. "At least here I have my ghosts."

"Evaline!" Lord Malvern called impatiently.

She patted Lewen's cheek. "Goodbye, lad. Have a care for yourself."

"And ye yourself," he answered and broke away so he could rejoin Nina and Lord Malvern by the steps. He felt shaken and unnerved by his conversation with the old lady. She was indeed quite mad, he thought.

"I must apologise for my sister-in-law," Lord Malvern said, smiling. "She is very auld now, and quite vague."

Lewen nodded, smiling perfunctorily. He had a sudden over-whelming desire to be away from this cold, vast pile of stones and out in the fresh, clean air. It took a strong effort of will for him to force himself to follow Nina up the stairs and into its front hall, and he glanced over his shoulder as he went in, for a last glimpse of sunlit green. He thought he understood why Lady Evaline spent so much time sitting under the apple tree.

It did not take long to pack up all their belongings and help the footmen carry them out to the gatehouse. All the horses had been saddled and bridled, and were eager to be off. Irving had supervised the loading of sacks and barrels of fresh supplies, and Dedrie had come down to say farewell to her patients. She looked rather pale and tired, and did not have her usual brisk manner as she pressed a basket of herbal remedies upon Nina, as well as a fresh tussie-mussie of lavender and herbs.

"Lady Evaline picked them for ye," she said. "She wants . . . she wishes . . ."

"Aye?"

Dedrie cast a quick glance at Lord Malvern, who was chatting with Iven some distance away. "She says to have a care for yourselves and for the lad," she said then, in a fierce, low voice. "Get him away from here, my lady! This place is no good for laddies."

Nina opened her mouth and then shut it. "Never fear, we are out o' your hair now," she said lightly. "Thank ye for your help."

"I'm glad I could do something to help. Have a good journey now," Dedrie said.

Nina quirked her mouth in sudden ironic amusement. "Let us hope it is a quick one," she answered and then turned to give her hand to Lord Malvern as she thanked him again. Then the apprentices all mounted, Nina was handed up to the driving seat of the red caravan with Roden beside her, and Iven leapt up to the seat of the blue, clicking his tongue at Steady. The massive gates groaned open, and the cavalcade rode out from the shadowy gloom of Fettercairn Castle and into the quick bright windy day.

TO THROW A PRINCE

*"They say princes learn no art truly
but the art of horsemanship. The
reason is, the brave beast is no
flatterer. He will throw a prince as
soon as his groom."*

Ben Jonson (1573–1637)

Tales of the Past

The road went down at a steep angle, so they had to go carefully, Nina and Iven both leaning on their brakes. For quite a long way they were enclosed within high walls, then gradually the wall dropped away and they were able to see down into the lowlands, which spread before them, the river winding away like a broad silver ribbon.

"Look, was that the tree that fell? Isn't it enormous? No wonder it took so long for ye all to clear the road!" Fèlice called, pointing down the hillside. An immense oak tree lay tumbled to one side of the road, smashed and broken. They could see where it had fallen through the undergrowth, tearing up bushes and scarring the ground.

"Ye ken, I wronged the laird," Rafferty called back. "I really had begun to suspect him o' making up the fallen tree to try to keep us at Fettercairn."

"Me too!" Fèlice said.

"What rubbish," Edithe said. "Ye people have such imaginations. Laird Malvern is far too noble and upright a man to stoop to such a subterfuge. Why on earth would he want to do such a thing?"

"Why indeed?" Landon said.

"Next ye'll be telling me ye believed all those terrible lies that satyricorn girl made up!"

"I do believe her," Landon said defiantly.

Cameron snorted. "Ye would."

"Well, I believe her too," Fèlice said. "Even if she did kill that Yeoman, doesna mean she wasna telling the truth about other things."

"My dear Fèlice, what an innocent ye are," Edithe said.

"That's enough, Edithe," Nina said sharply. "I think we should leave any discussion o' Rhiannon's guilt or innocence to the judges in Lucescere. Let us just concentrate on getting her there safely."

Lewen said nothing. He was very tired.

They came to a sharp corner, the road doubling back on itself, and now they rode back towards Fettercairn Castle, which loomed high overhead, ravens wheeling above its two grim towers. The vast expanse of white, falling water dominated the view. The shadow of the cliff fell over them, cold fingers of spray stroking their faces and hair. At last the road turned again, the cobblestones dangerously slippery with the damp, and they faced out into the sunlit valley again, feeling an immediate sense of relief. Six more times the road switchbacked, and then they came down a long, low decline that led them gradually out into rolling meadows where goats grazed by the river. They were able to quicken their pace until the great brooding cliff was lost to sight behind them, and on all sides there was only open pastures, small copses of trees and tilled fields, with the broad river winding through the middle. The air smelt sweetly of apple blossom.

Rhiannon woke during the afternoon. Lewen had been riding close to the red caravan, straining his ears for any sound from her, but for hours everything had remained quiet. Then he heard a cry of pain and alarm, then a sudden banging noise, and knew she had woken. Nina heard it too, and compressed her lips. Lewen made a move as if to go to her, and Nina shook her head at him sternly. For a while, they listened as Rhiannon fought to free herself, then Nina handed the reins to Landon and swung round to the steps, opening the door and going inside. Riding as close as he could, Lewen could hear nothing more than a rising and falling murmur of voices. Argent sensed his unhappiness and danced restively, but Lewen hardly noticed. After a few minutes Nina came out again, her face expressionless, and swung herself back to the driving seat. Everything was quiet.

The sun was getting low in the sky when Argent suddenly pricked his ears forward, whickering loudly. Lewen was roused from his miserable abstraction to look about him. He felt a sudden jolt of excitement as he saw a familiar black winged shape flying behind them, keeping close to the dark line of the woods. At once he glanced about but no-one else has noticed. After that he saw Blackthorn often, though the winged mare was taking care to keep herself hidden. It cheered him immensely, knowing Blackthorn had not abandoned her rider, and he wished he could let Rhiannon know.

They soon came to a village, and Nina and Iven decided to make camp for the night near the safety of its lights. Nina was eager to buy fresh supplies, being determined not to touch a single mouthful of the food given to them by Lord Fetterness. The apprentices were all glad to dismount, looking towards the village lights eagerly. None of them had been fully able to shake the unease they had felt while staying at Fettercairn Castle, and the idea of having a few drams in the village inn and talking with ordinary people cheered them all. All, that is, except for Lewen, who was racked with misery and guilt. He would have liked to stay with the caravans and try for a chance to speak with Rhiannon, but Nina would not let him.

"Let her be, lad," she said, as she poured away every drop of the soup and wine and medicines that the castle servants had packed for them.

"But I need to try and explain to her . . ."

"I'd rather ye left her alone, Lewen," Nina said, a stern note hardening her voice. "To be honest, I'm no' sure I can trust ye no' to help her escape. As sympathetic as I am to your distress, she is an accused murderess and the Rìgh has trusted us to bring her to the courts."

"Please, Nina . . ."

She shook her head. "Nay, Lewen. I want ye to stay away. Come with us to the village, and drown your sorrows with the other lads. There are times it can do ye good. Besides, this is the closest lowland village to the castle. They must've heard tales o' Fetterness. I want to hear them."

So Lewen found himself accompanying Nina and the others to the village, while a rather cross Rafferty was left behind with Iven and Lulu to guard the camp and their prisoner.

It was a clear, cold evening, with the wind shaking the black branches about and the sky over the mountains very red as the setting sun stained the clouds. Everyone was full of talk and

conjecture, for nobody had felt free to talk freely while under
Fettercairn Castle's roof. Only Lewen did not speak, even when
Edithe said she had always thought Rhiannon a sly hoar-weasel
or when Maisie wondered if it hurt to be hanged.

Linlithgorn's inn was rather small and rough, but it was
crowded with farm labourers, milkmaids, eel-fishers and plump
crofter's wives with red hands and cheerful faces. The talk was
all of the weather and the spring sowing, and despite himself,
Lewen found his mood eased as he drank his dram of whiskey,
ate a solid vegetable stew with dumplings, and listened. The
strangers were all greeted with jovial good spirits, and Nina
told them a much edited version of their adventures.

The news they had come from Fettercairn Castle was met
with great interest. "Och, they're an odd people, up there in the
highlands," the innkeeper's wife said as she ladled them a second serve of stew. "Keep themselves to themselves, they do.
Every now and again we get a family coming through, heading
for the ports and hoping for work. Terrible stories they tell. We
dinna believe most o' them, o' course, those highlanders are all
a wee touched in the head, but still . . . enough to make ye
check your doors are locked twice over. Ye can never be too
careful."

Under Nina's gentle questioning, the innkeeper's wife ex-
panded like dough in the warmth. She had nothing much new
to tell them, except that a few travellers had gone missing in recent years, along with one lazy farmer's boy, who was prone to
leaving his goats to wander as they pleased while he went fishing or fell asleep in a hayrick.

"If it's stories o' Fettercairn ye want, ye should ask auld Martin. He came down from the castle nigh on twenty-five years
ago, and married a local girl. He's full o' stories, like all those
highland dreamers."

"I'd like to hear his stories, if we have time," Nina answered.
"Where can I find him?"

The innkeeper's wife jerked her head towards the fire. "He'll
be entertaining the drinkers," she said dryly. "I'd ask him now,
afore the whiskey muddles him more than usual."

"Thank ye, I will," Nina replied and rose and made her way
towards the fire, Roden swinging off her hand, Lewen and Lan-

don following close behind. The others stayed where they were, Cameron calling for more whisky, though Fèlice turned to watch them with curious eyes.

A group of men sat before the fire, some playing trictrac, others gambling on the roll of the dice. A tall, thin man sat folded up on a chair, staring into the flames. He had a crinkled brown face and melancholy grey eyes, and was dressed in a rough smock and leather gaiters. He was telling some tale, which he illustrated with dramatic gestures of his hands. As Nina approached there was a sudden roar of laughter, and one of the men cried, "Och, pull the other one, Martin! Ye and your auld tales."

"I've heard ye're a grand storyteller," Nina said gently, pulling a stool towards her and sitting down at the thin man's gangly knee. "Will ye tell us a tale?"

"Give me a dram o' whisky and I'll tell ye two, and happen throw in a song as well," Martin said, lifting his dreamy eyes to Nina's face. "Ye're a witch, ye are. I like witches."

"That's good," she answered. "We've just come from a place where witches were hated, and I dinna like that at all."

"Och, ye've been at Fetterness, have ye? Bad place. Very bad place."

"Why? Why is it such a bad place?"

He stared down at his empty cup and ruminated. Nina glanced at Lewen, who went back and took the whisky decanter from Cameron, despite his howl of protest, and brought it to top up the old man's clay mug. Martin tasted it thoughtfully, swirled it round his mouth, swallowed, then sipped again. When his cup was empty, Lewen filled it up again.

"I was born in Fetterness, ye ken. More than fifty years ago. They were the good auld days, indeed they were. The Tower o' Ravens still stood and the town was filled with laughing students who bet on which cockroach would scuttle away the fastest, or which raindrop would reach the bottom o' the pane first. Lairds and prionnsachan came to the valley to consult the witches' wisdom, and the MacBrann could often be seen crossing his silver bridge, his cloak flying in the wind, his guards and servants trying to keep up. He was no' mad then, nay, he was sane as ye or I. But then that was afore the Day o' Betrayal, when the whole world went mad."

Martin stopped and drank some more, then looked round the little circle of rapt faces. He was indeed a master storyteller.

"Jaspar, who was the Rìgh then, he had married for love, like all young men, and like all young men, he found love can be a cruel joke." His grey eyes came to rest on Lewen's face. "His pretty wife Maya had her own plans, and one cold winter's day the whole world found out what they were. Jaspar had given her a legion o' soldiers for her own, and she dressed them in red, like she wore herself, and smiled at them and young men came flocking to serve her. That cold winter day her soldiers struck at every witches' tower in the land, and threw them down, and Maya declared the witches were traitors and should be killed, every one o' them."

He looked back at Nina. "Ye are too young to remember, but I, I remember it well. My family worked at the tower and so I was there, a lad o' only five. I remember the screaming, and the black smoke everywhere, and the way the soldiers went through every room and hall, killing every witch they found, and any who dared to defy them. Most were put to the sword, or were crushed under the falling masonry as the soldiers used their machines to drag down the walls. Some they dragged to the garth, and tied upon a great pile o' firewood and burnt them to death, feeding the flames with the books from the library. I hid down the well, and so they didna find me. My parents both died, though neither were witches. So, ye see, it is no' a day I'd forget easily."

Nina nodded, her mouth twisting.

"When at last I crept out, I didna ken where to go or what to do. At last I went to the laird. Where else would I go? They gave me a job scrubbing pots in the kitchen. I was grateful. At least I was warm there, and had food. It was there that I heard what had happened. For the Tower o' Ravens was very strong, ye ken. No pretty red soldiers should've been able to throw it down, no' with those high walls and lookout towers and all those witches with their far-seeing and clear-seeing skills inside. And then there was Fettercairn Castle itself, built to guard the road. How had the soldiers got through? I myself did no' much care, being too young and full o' misery to wonder, but the servants at the castle wondered very much, and I listened as they talked, like young boys do."

He rested his gaze now on Roden's mop of bright, curly hair, nestled in against his mother's side as he sat at the floor at her feet. Then he looked back at Lewen and suddenly his gaze seemed very clear and intent.

"The laird's younger brother was then staying in the castle, and I heard many mutters against him. He had been an apprentice once, just like ye, my lad. A witch's apprentice at the Tower o' Ravens, but he had been disgraced somehow. Cheating at exams, I think, though it was so long ago, I canna be sure. Happen it was trouble over a lass. There's always trouble over lasses. Anyways, he'd left the tower and gone to the capital, and by all accounts he was very sore at the witches who had been his teachers and fellow students and swore revenge on them. When he came back, he wore a long red robe and said he was in the Banrìgh's pay now."

"A Seeker?" Nina breathed. "Laird Malvern was once a Seeker?"

The old man flashed her a glance. "We called them witch-sniffers, for they sniffed out magic, but I've heard them called Seekers too."

Nina nodded, her dark eyes burning bright. "So he was a Seeker! Och, that explains a lot."

"The red soldiers were his friends," the old man continued. "He had brought them to visit Fettercairn, and they had gradually filled up every spare room, till the laird was very impatient and told his brother they must go. But they did no' go, they attacked the Tower o' Ravens instead, and though I dinna ken whether it be true or no', it was said Malvern, who's laird now, showed the redcloaks the secret way to the tower, so they could come in darkness and stealth, and attack from within."

Nina and Lewen exchanged quick glances.

"Later, after the laird and his son died, Malvern put aside his red robes and became laird himself. For a while all went well, for he was a favourite o' the Banrìgh. But once the Banrìgh was thrown down, well, he retreated inside his castle and I hear he hardly ever comes out now. That was when things in Fetterness went from bad to evil, I heard, though I had left by then, hoping to leave evil things behind me."

"How did the laird and his son die?" Nina asked persuasively, and Lewen topped up the old man's cup.

He drank deeply, then sighed and wiped his mouth on his sleeve.

"Another sad tale that one. Would ye no' rather I told ye the tale o' Bessie and the runaway pig?"

Nina shook her head. "Nay, please, we really do want to ken."

He held out his cup again. "To tell a sad tale like that I need to wet my whistle again," he said. "It's a tale to make ye weep."

Lewen obligingly filled up his cup, and put the empty decanter down. Martin was quiet for a moment, staring dreamily into the flames. Nina was about to prompt him again when he stirred and began again to speak.

"Your wee laddie there has a look o' the laird's young son about him. It's the ruddy hair and black eyes, ye dinna see that very often. He was born about ten years after the fall o' the Tower o' Ravens. The laird had taken a young girl for his wife, a pretty wee thing, half his age. They loved that laddie, and spoilt him half to death. Now, at the time Maya the Blessed ruled the whole country with an iron hand concealed in a velvet glove. But no' everyone loved her, and rebels worked to bring the witches back. I must admit I loved to hear the tales o' those rebels, and often used to dream o' running away and joining them. The rebels were led by a man they called the Cripple, for he had a hunch to his shoulder and a twist to his spine, and could scarce walk a step. The things that Cripple did! He must've had magic o' his own, for they never managed to catch him, even when he rescued a cartload o' witches from right under the Banrìgh's nose."

Nina and Lewen exchanged a smiling glance. They knew better than most the many stories about the days when Lachlan the Winged had hidden himself in the guise of a hunchback, working to overthrow Maya the Ensorcellor and bring back the Coven of Wtiches. It had been Nina's grandmother Enit who had masterminded many of those daring rescues and many a witch or a faery had, like Lachlan, been hidden in the jongleurs' caravan as they roamed around Eileanan. Lewen's mother Lilanthe had herself travelled that way, the jongleurs keeping her safe from Maya's Seekers, who would have burnt her to death if they had found her.

"Now the witch-sniffer Malvern hated witches and rebels, and he hunted them down far and wide. Every village skeelie and cunning man on this side o' the river was burnt alive, and anyone who had auld books, or who swore by Eà, or even protested that the witch-hunts were too brutal. And he seemed to have an uncanny way o' kenning what ye thought, so none o' us dared ever look him in the eye, or mutter under our breath. He had us under his fist, from Barbreck-by-the-Bridge down to Tullimuir and right round to Rhyssmadill itself. It was a sad day for us all when Laird Falkner let his brother come home to stay.

"One day he had his soldiers bring in a lass who was accused o' witch-talent. Her mother had been burnt as a witch and her grandfather too, but she had been taken in by neighbours and brought up as one o' their own. Her name was Oonagh and she hated the witch-sniffers for what they had done to her family. She saw one in the marketplace one day and had some kind o' fit, and thunder and lightning came out o' nowhere, and hail. She was sick as a dog after, and they arrested her and took her to the castle for questioning, which we all kent meant torture. They were dark days at Fettercairn." He sighed and shook his head.

"Somehow the Cripple found about this poor lass and that very afternoon they came to the castle, some hidden inside the dung-cart, some disguised as labourers or farmers bringing produce. There were only a dozen or so o' them but somehow they managed to lock up the castle garrison and rescue the girl. They could no' get out again, though, for Laird Malvern sniffed them out and attacked them with his own men. There was vicious fighting, all through the castle. Me and some o' the other pot-boys helped the rebels, for we hated the witch-sniffer and his cruel ways. We took the Red Guards by surprise, and locked them in one o' the halls, and then the Cripple caught the sniffer and held him hostage.

"It must've been about then that Laird Falkner took his lady and son, who was about five, I think, and hid them for safety. But then he was captured too and taken to the great hall, where the Cripple accused the witch-sniffer o' murder and torture and treason and all sorts o' other things, and held a trial. Truly it was amazing. The rebels had won the castle with only a handful o' men! We all kent we were in the presence o' greatness, even the fat auld cook felt it. Those rebels, though they were all filthy and stunk to high heaven, they were brave and bold and laughed as they fought, and they made no move to hurt us or molest any o' the maids, or even steal the laird's gold. The Cripple himself was only a few years aulder then me, and I must admit I admired him, for doing what I could only dream o' doing."

Lewen was enraptured. He wondered if his father had been one of those men. Niall the Bear had turned rebel as a young man, and had worked with Lachlan the Winged to rescue witches and undermine Maya for many years before they at last succeeded in overthrowing her and regaining the throne. Swiftly he did the arithmetic in his head. If the Tower of Ravens had been thrown down by the Red Guards forty-odd years ago, and the rebels had attacked the castle fifteen years later, then it was highly likely his father would have been fighting with Lachlan, for he had not yet been twenty when he joined the rebels.

Martin had paused only long enough to drain his cup. His eyes were unfocused now, and his words slurred, but his voice still had power to cast a spell. "The laird was furious and called the rebels cowards and cheats and traitors, but the Cripple only mocked him, and told him that he was the coward and traitor, to kidnap and torture a young lass near to death. The laird had no' kent about the witch-lass, he tried his best to turn a blind eye to the things Malvern did, and he was horrified, ye could see it on his face. Laird Falkner shouted that it was no' true, it was all lies, and attacked him with his sword. The Cripple was clumsy on his feet, being a hunchback, and no' the best fighter, but the laird was mad and blind with rage. They fought and the Cripple killed him, though I dinna think he meant to.

"It was all confusion after that, and the battle broke out again, for the laird's bodyguard went mad and attacked the rebels with naught but his bare hands. Somehow, in all the fighting, the laird's brother slipped away, I do no' ken how though I was there, watching it all with my own eyes. We found his red robe in the library.

"It was only then that we discovered the lady and her son were missing. The boy's nurse set up a great screech and the castle was searched from top to bottom, but no sign o' them was found. We all thought they must've escaped with the witch-sniffer. Half o' us joined the rebels, and the others were allowed to leave, which they did right gladly, for everyone had expected the rebels would kill anyone who disagreed with them. But they didna. There was a great feast instead, and singing and dancing, and the Cripple opened up the laird's treasury and gave it all to the poor folk. It was like a mad dream. A week or so later, the witch-sniffer returned with a big army to take the castle back, but the rebels saw them coming and went in the night, for after all, there was only a dozen or so o' them, and thousands o' the Red Guards.

"I went with them, so I wasna there when they discovered the lady and the young boy had no' fled with Malvern but had been hidden in a secret room by the laird. More than a week they were locked in that room, in the dead o' winter, with no food or water. By the time Malvern opened up the secret panel, it was too late. The boy was dead and his mother was quite mad. They say Malvern was stricken with grief and guilt, and indeed he quit the Banrìgh's service after that, and stopped his witch-hunts. I never went back to Fetterness, but I've heard the shadow o' those dark days still stretches across the whole valley and that the ghost o' the wee lad haunts the castle, crying aloud from the cold."

There was a short silence, then Roden lifted his sleepy head and said, "It's true, there is a ghost o' a little boy there, I saw him. He has the bonniest rocking horse. There are lots o' boys there, and all o' them cry 'cause they want to go home."

"Is that so, laddie?" Martin said slowly. "Obh obh, it's an evil place, Fettercairn. I'm glad I got away from there."

"So are we," Nina answered, cuddling Roden close. "I canna tell ye how much."

In the Night

Rhiannon lay in the darkness, slowly rubbing her cloth-muffled chain back and forth against the timber post of the bunk-bed. She had to control her desperate impatience, for if she jerked the chain too hard it rattled, and she did not want to alert anyone to her wakefulness. She had only these quiet hours of the night to wear away the wood till it was weak enough to snap, setting her free. If anyone discovered what she was doing, her chance would be lost.

A muted sound outside made her pause and turn her head. Then she felt the caravan shift as someone put their weight on the steps. Rhiannon found it hard to breathe. With all her muscles tense, she listened as someone very gingerly turned the door handle first one way, then another. There was a pause, and then she heard the furtive sound of someone fumbling with the lock. Rhiannon tested the chain between her hands. It was not long enough to wrap around a throat and garrotte someone, but perhaps, if she pinned them to the bed with it, she could hold them down long enough to choke them. She raised herself onto one elbow, holding the chain rigid so it would not rattle, then managed to get up onto her knees, pressing herself back against the wall.

The tiny sounds from the doorway continued, then she heard a click as the lock sprang free. The door swung open, and someone slipped inside and closed the door behind them. Rhiannon listened as they took a step or two towards her, her heart hammering so loud she thought they must hear it. A dark, faceless shape loomed over her, and she tensed, ready to strike.

"Rhiannon?" a deep voice whispered.

She launched herself at him, burying her head into his shoulder, jerking her wrists painfully as she tried instinctively to throw her arms about his neck. "Lewen!" she gasped, and then, as his arms closed about her, felt the painful swelling in her chest burst as tears gushed from her eyes.

"Hush, hush, my dearling, my sweet, they must no' hear," he whispered, stroking her hair. She buried her head deeper into his shoulder, trying to control her shuddering sobs. Murmuring endearments, he pressed her back so he could lie beside her on the bed, his arm cradling her close. He felt something hard between them, and realised, with a little jerk of his pulse, that she wore the amulet he had carved for her hanging between her breasts. Eagerly he sought her mouth, cradling her head in both his hands, desperate to tell her how sorry he was for betraying her.

She tore her mouth away. "Ye told them! Ye helped them hunt me down!"

"I'm so sorry, my dearling, I'm so sorry, I didna mean for this to happen, I didna want this." He kissed her wet face and she recoiled away from him.

"Ye told."

"It just happened, I didna mean to."

"What do ye mean, it just happened?"

Lewen buried his face in her hair. "I'm so sorry, Rhiannon. Really, I didna mean for them to hunt ye down or cage ye up like this. I just . . ." Words failed him. He could not explain. After a moment he said again lamely, "It just happened."

She was silent for a moment, then he felt her lay her head down on his chest again. "Like me and the soldier," she whispered. "I never meant him harm. It just happened. I wish it never had."

They lay in silence for a while.

"Will they hang me?" she whispered.

"I willna let them," Lewen burst out, the desperation in his voice telling her more than he meant to. She shivered and clung to him.

"I have to escape," she told him. She heard him sigh and shift his weight. "I canna stand it in here," she went on wildly. "I feel like I canna breathe! The air presses down on me and chokes me. I canna stand it! I canna! Help me get out o' here!"

"But how?" he said at last. "I only managed to get in here to see ye by putting a sleeping spell on Rafferty, but I am no' strong yet in such Skills, there's no way I could ensorcel Nina or Iven, I daren't even try. And even if ye managed to get away from the camp without anyone seeing ye, Nina has only to call out to the birds for help and she'd find ye in minutes."

"I want my horse," Rhiannon said passionately. "If I had Blackthorn, I could escape!"

Lewen hesitated, then said, "Blackthorn is near, she follows the caravans. But oh! Rhiannon!"

She pushed herself away from him, her chain rattling. "Blackthorn follows?"

"Aye, she follows, but Rhiannon, I do no' think . . ."

"Lewen, unchain me! Please!"

"I canna," he said unhappily.

"Why no'? Are ye afraid?" Her voice was thin with contempt.

"Aye, o' course I'm afraid," he answered crossly. "I risk being charged with treason just by being here with ye, do ye no' ken that! But I canna unchain ye just because I'm scared, Rhiannon. I havena got the key, and these chains are too thick for me to break, no matter how much I want to. And Iven is asleep just outside, and he'll wake at the slightest noise. So please, stop rattling those chains and hissing at me! I've been thinking and thinking what's the best thing for us to do, and I canna think that running away is it. Sssh! Please, just listen. Rhiannon, if I managed to free ye now, what would ye do?"

"Find my horse and fly away," she answered promptly.

"Where?"

"Anywhere," she answered impatiently.

"Back to the mountains?"

She hesitated. "I dinna ken. Maybe. I'd find somewhere."

"And what about me?" Lewen asked.

"Ye could come with me," she said, seizing one of his hands.

"How? Blackthorn canna carry us both, I'm much too heavy."

"Ye could come and meet me."

"If I kent where ye were, and if I was no' arrested for setting ye free."

She sighed. "They wouldna arrest ye, though, would they? No' ye."

Lewen shrugged. "I dinna ken. If the Rìgh was angry enough . . . it doesna matter. I'd be ruined anyway. There's no way I'd be allowed to join the Blue Guards or be the Rìgh's squire if I had helped an accused murderer escape, and happen they'd throw me out o' the Theurgia as well. That doesna matter. I'd do it if I thought it'd help. But I do no'. All it would mean is that ye'd be on the run for ever after. There'd be bounty hunters galore eager to catch ye if the reward was big enough, and I'm pretty sure the Rìgh would set Finn the Cat on your trail and she *always* finds what she hunts. It's her Talent."

He took a deep breath and drew her close to him again. "It's no life, *leannan,* always on the move, starting at shadows, waiting for someone to bring ye in. And there'd be no chance o' mercy if ye made the Rìgh hunt ye down. Nay, I think it would be best to go willingly to court and try and explain to the Rìgh what happened. I'd stand behind ye, and I'm sure Nina and Iven would vouch for ye too."

"But they hunted me down!" Rhiannon cried.

"Sssh!" He put his hand gently across her mouth. "No' so loud, *leannan,* ye'll wake Iven and then I'll really be in the soup. I ken they caught ye, my love, and chained ye up in here, but they were following orders. Iven was once a Blue Guard, remember, and he still works in the Rìgh's service. He could no' let ye go, but I swear he feels bad about it, and Nina too. I'm sure they'll speak up on your behalf, and they are good friends o' the Rìgh's and will have influence over him, I'm sure. And I ken His Highness would no' want to hang such a bonny young lass." He bent and kissed her mouth. She sighed and kissed him back, tasting the salt of her tears on his skin.

At last they drew apart. "So ye will no' help me escape?" she said in a very low voice.

He shook his head. "Rhiannon, I love ye. I love ye so much. I want a life with ye. I do no' want to be a fugitive the rest o' our days, sick at heart 'cause I betrayed my Rìgh's trust. I do no' want ye just to fly away into the blue yonder, never to be seen again, either. This is the only way I can think o' to make sure we can be together. If ye swore service to the Rìgh, as penance, perhaps? There must be something we can do."

"What if there's no'? What if he says I must hang?"

"Then I will free ye then, and we'll run away somewhere together, I promise. I will no' let ye hang."

Rhiannon nestled her head on his chest. She was so tired, it was a relief to murmur an agreement and let her muscles sag and her eyelids close. She felt like she had been running and fighting for so long, and all to no avail.

Lewen kissed her forehead. "*Leannan,* I must go. My sleeping spell willna last forever."

"Do no' go," she murmured, not opening her eyes. "Please, do no' leave me."

His chest rose and fell under her cheek as he took and released a deep breath. His arm came tightly round her, holding her close, and Rhiannon sighed and slipped into sleep.

She woke drowsily some hours later, as Lewen stiffened and tried to sit up. Rhiannon would have rolled over but the shackle on her wrist prevented her. The painful tug of the chain jerked her to wakefulness, and she opened her eyes and levered herself up on one elbow.

Iven stood in the doorway of the caravan, regarding them thoughtfully. Behind him stood a tousled and indignant Rafferty.

"I thought Nina told ye to leave Rhiannon be?" Iven said.

Lewen nodded jerkily. "Aye, she did, but I needed to talk to Rhiannon, I needed to explain."

"I see," Iven replied. "I suppose Nina and I have no real authority over ye, Lewen, but ye were placed in our care and so I would expect ye to listen to us and obey us."

"I had to see Rhiannon," Lewen repeated. "Nobody could have stopped me."

Iven stroked his beard.

"I didna help her escape," Lewen said defiantly. "We are both still here."

"Aye, I can see that."

"Rhiannon's promised she willna try to escape," Lewen said, with a quick glance at her. "Ye do no' need to leave her locked up in this stinking caravan anymore. It's no' right. She hates being confined. Will ye no' let her come out and breathe the fresh air and sit in the sunshine? It's cruel to lock her up like this."

Iven's brows drew together. He looked consideringly at Rhiannon. "I hope ye will no' take this the wrong way, Rhiannon, but I canna feel sure that a promise from ye is to be trusted."

Rhiannon did not reply.

"I will stand warranty for her," Lewen said.

"I ken how ye must feel, Lewen," the jongleur said after a long pause. "But ye must remember Rhiannon's crime is a serious one, and she has lied to us and tried to flee afore. I canna allow ye to take such a responsibility. If she fled, ye would hang in her place, do ye understand that?"

Lewen swallowed convulsively.

"What if ye shackled her to me?" he said after a moment. "She can ride with me, she can lie with me. I will keep her close, I promise."

"I'm sure ye will," Iven said, with a faint smile. He scratched his cheek, regarding them with thoughtful eyes. "How am I to be sure that she will no' hurt ye to try to escape?" he asked, half under his breath. "We have seen how ruthless she can be. It takes a cold head and heart to hack out a man's teeth and his finger."

"I had to do that!" Rhiannon cried indignantly. "If I had no' claimed blood-right, I would have lost everything, and I'd have been scorned by the herd. Worse, they would've been suspicious and watched me, and I could never have escaped. Ye think I enjoyed doing it? It made me sick to my stomach, and I shook all over. I could no' bear to wear the necklace afterwards. I had to do it, though. Have ye never done things ye wished ye did no' have to do?"

Iven nodded. "I'm a soldier," he said wryly. "O' course I have."

"Well then," Rhiannon answered, her voice losing none of its passion. "Why judge me so hard? Ye do no' ken what it was like in the herd. Any sign o' weakness, and they would have killed me. I was fighting for my life."

"It is no' for me to judge ye at all," Iven said rather coolly. "That will be the court's job. Mine is to bring ye to them safely."

Rhiannon lay back, covering her face with her arm. "I canna bear it in here," she whispered. "I canna."

Lewen drew her closer.

"Lewen, truly I do no' think this wise," Iven said warningly.

"If ye willna let her out, I will stay in here with her," Lewen

said. "We may no' have much time together, I willna be parted
from her."

"Lewen . . ."

"Please, Iven."

Iven sighed. "Rhiannon, ye must give me your solemn oath
that ye will no' try and escape. And do no' think I willna be
watching ye."

"I will swear a blood-oath, if ye will give me a knife to cut
myself with."

"No need for that," Iven replied, wincing a little. "Ye have
wounded yourself enough, I feel. Very well then, if ye
promise."

"I will no' try to escape while I am in your care," Rhiannon
said. "After that, I will no' promise."

"Fair enough," Iven replied. He put his hand in his pocket
and pulled out a key. "I will shackle ye together, though," he
warned. "I'm not taking any unnecessary risks."

"All right," Rhiannon said, so thrilled at the idea she might
be allowed out of the caravan that she would have accepted far
stricter preventative measures.

Lewen slid away from Rhiannon and stood up. As Iven
stepped past him, Lewen touched his arm briefly. "Thank ye,"
he said.

Iven nodded and unshackled Rhiannon. As she rubbed her
bruised and chafed wrists, he unwound the chain from the bedpost, pausing to examine the damage she had done to the wood,
then quickly and deftly snapped one of the shackles around
Rhiannon's wrist and the other around Lewen's. "I hope I'm
no' being played for a fool," he said to no-one in particular and
stood back to let Lewen lead Rhiannon out into the dawn.

The other apprentices lay in their sleeping rolls around the
fire, which had sunk into grey ashes. Although it was light
enough to see, the sun was not yet up and no birds called. The
horses stood with sunken heads and relaxed forelegs in their
hobbles. Even Lulu slept in a little round huddle.

"That was some sleeping spell ye cast, Lewen," Iven said
wryly. "I felt like I'd been hammered over the head when I
woke. Your teachers at the Theurgia must be pleased with your
progress if ye can cast a spell as strong as that already."

"Me?" Lewen asked in amazement. "I canna cast sleeping spells that strong. Most o' my power lies in wood-working, ye ken that. My spell should have kept Rafferty sleepy for half an hour at most."

Iven raised one eyebrow. "Look at the horses," he said. "Look, even the bird in that tree is asleep. Happen ye're stronger than ye thought."

"I ken my strengths and weaknesses well," Lewen argued. He glanced at Rhiannon. "Happen it was Rhiannon," he said, frowning. "She has Talent, we ken that, but she's never been tested. We have no idea what she can or canna do."

"A sleeping spell is no' the easiest o' Skills," Iven said. "Ye have to be very subtle if it is to work, and no wild talent is ever that subtle, no matter how powerful they may be."

Lewen shrugged. "It seems very odd," he began.

Just then the door of the blue caravan opened and Nina stood with her shawl wrapped tight about her nightgown, her dishevelled hair hanging almost to her knees. "Roden!" she cried, in a voice made shrill with anxiety. "Roden! Where are ye?"

Iven started forward. "Nina! What's wrong?"

"Where's Roden?"

"Is he no' with ye?"

"No, no, he's no'. I canna believe I did no' feel him getting out o' bed." She put her hand to her head, swaying. "I feel so sick, so heavy-headed. I slept so very deeply. Maisie is still sleeping, I couldna wake her. Oh, that naughty lad! Where can he be?"

Nina called her son's name again and again, and began to search through the bushes, though her feet were bare and the grass icy with dew. Iven and the others began to search too, everyone feeling a creeping sense of dread. There was no sign of the little boy. Nina became increasingly distressed.

"He was sleeping right beside me, I had my arms about him, and Maisie slept on the other side. No-one could've stolen him, it's impossible."

"Unless a very strong spell was cast indeed," Iven said grimly. "We all slept heavily, every one o' us. I could no' believe it when I woke and it was dawn. I was meant to wake and relieve Rafferty o' guard-duty in the dark hours. I have never no' woken afore."

"I slept too," Rafferty admitted shamefacedly. "I could no' help it."

"Me too," Lewen said. "I dinna think I'd sleep a wink, I had so much on my mind, but I slept like the dead."

They all looked at each other, ashen-faced, then Nina began a strange, low keening. "Nay, nay, no' my baby, no' my laddie, nay, nay, I canna believe it. They canna have got my baby."

"If they have, they'll be sorry for it," Iven said grimly. "They must have left a trail o' sorts. Do no' worry, my love, we'll find him."

"The birds!" Nina said wildly. "The birds may have seen something."

Iven pointed to a nearby tree, where two small birds slept still, their heads tucked under their wings. "A strong and subtle spell," Nina said, unnaturally calmly, when the implications of the sight had sunk in. "There's a sorcerer at work here."

"Laird Malvern?"

"I fear so," she answered. "Remember, he was an apprentice at the Tower o' Ravens once, and they said his witch-sniffing powers were uncanny. Oh, Iven! Please, we must hurry! I fear for my Roden."

Rhiannon had been standing still, the chain between her and Lewen drawn taut, looking intently at the ground. "I see a footmark here," she said then. They all crowded round her, but could see nothing but a faint smudge in the damp soil. Rhiannon ignored their questions and exclamations, walking slowly away towards the wood. Lewen followed her, tugged along by the chain between them. "He went through here," she said, examining a broken twig, then bending to look at the leaf litter.

"Are ye sure?" Nina asked helplessly, unable to see any marks on the ground.

Rhiannon glanced back at her. "One thing a satyricorn kens is how to hunt," she answered, her voice warm with compassion. Nina's eyes filled with tears.

"Rafferty, rouse the others," Iven cried. "Get the horses saddled up, get my sword."

"And my bow and arrows too, please," Lewen added.

"And mine," Rhiannon said, giving Rafferty a very clear, direct look out of her blue-grey eyes. Rafferty hesitated and looked at Iven, who waved him on impatiently.

"Rhiannon, where now?" he cried.

She led them deep into the wood, through a maze of trees and thorny bushes. At last she came to a small clearing. "Horses tethered here," she said. A mound of fresh horse droppings galvanised them all into excitement. "Three horses," Rhiannon said. She suddenly bent and picked up something from the ground. It was a small wooden soldier.

Nina's face crumpled. "He took it to bed with him last night. Oh, my laddie! Where are ye?"

"Fettercairn Castle," Iven said in a murderous voice. "I will raze the place to the ground if I have to, to get my son back."

"Aye, with a handful o' lads and your sword," Nina said in a voice blank with despair.

"We may be able to catch them afore they get back to the castle," Lewen cried.

"We must be quick!" Iven said, gripping his hands into fists. "Rhiannon, which way did they ride?"

Breaking into a run, Rhiannon led them through the trees to the other side of the wood. Beyond was a long meadow stretching back to the north. They could all see the deep indentations the horses' hooves had made in the damp soil. "They were galloping hard," she said bending to touch one hoofprint. "At least half an hour ago."

Nina was white and trembling.

"I bet they canna run as fast as Argent," Lewen cried.

"Or Blackthorn," said Rhiannon. She put her fingers in her mouth and whistled piercingly.

"Ye'll have to unshackle us," Lewen said. "Argent canna run if he is carrying both o' us."

Iven did not hesitate. He put his hand in his pocket and pulled out the key. "I'll be right behind ye. I'm sure the boys willna mind me taking one of their horses. My auld Steady is too big and slow for this task." He unlocked the shackles and the chain fell at their feet.

A shrill whinnying rent the air, and Blackthorn came galloping out of the wood, her tail held high, her mane rippling like a black satin banner. Rhiannon flung open her arms, her face ra-

diant, and the mare came to a plunging halt before her, to blow
grass-stained slobber all over her shirt. Her wings were unfurled, flashing blue as a kingfisher, and her horns cut through
the air like rapiers as she tossed her head, pawing the ground.
Rhiannon embraced her passionately.

Then Rafferty came up at a run, Cameron close behind him.
They led their two geldings, and the girls' two mares. Argent
cantered close behind, neighing in excitement, unsaddled, un-
bridled and untethered.

"He would no' let me saddle him," Rafferty panted. "I'm
sorry."

"That's all right, I'll ride bareback," Lewen said and vaulted
up onto the stallion's back. Rafferty handed up Lewen's longbow and quiver of arrows, which he slung over his shoulder.
Then the boy turned to Rhiannon and, without a word, passed
over her bow and arrows, and her beloved silver and black daggers. Rhiannon took them with a quick shining smile and a nod
of thanks, and quickly hid them about her person.

"Rafferty, I want ye and the girls to ride to Linlithgorn and
raise the reeve. Tell him to get as many men as he can on short
notice and ride for Fettercairn Castle. We canna allow the laird
to escape the Rìgh's justice any longer. Take my courier's
badge from my caravan, and show the reeve. It gives me His
Highness's authority."

Rafferty nodded, though it was clear he would rather be riding to the rescue with the others.

"May I borrow your horse?" Iven asked him. "I'm too heavy
for the mares, over such a distance."

Rafferty nodded. Iven mounted with the easy grace of a one-
time cavalier, taking his sword from Cameron with a nod of
thanks. Then he and Lewen were off, galloping across the
meadow. Rhiannon swung herself up onto the black mare's
back with a wild whoop, then the mare bounded after them, her
wings half-unfurled.

Nina seized the bridle of the brown mare, then she was up
into the saddle too and galloping away, her unbound hair whipping behind her. Cameron grimaced at Rafferty, and then swung
himself up onto Basta's back and kicked him into motion. As
the gelding broke into a run, Lulu came scampering out of the

forest, whimpering in distress. She leapt up Basta's tail and onto the back of Cameron's saddle, clasping his belt. Cameron cried out in shock and almost fell off.

"Get off!" he cried, but Lulu clung on, gibbering loudly. He scowled but did not try to shake her off, bending low as he tried to catch up with the others.

The horses were fresh after their long stay in the laird's stables and the easy ride of the day before. Their heavy hooves seemed to eat up the miles. Rhiannon rode ahead, following the trail left by the kidnappers. There was no doubt the trail led towards Fettercairn Castle.

By midmorning the castle was in sight, frowning down from the great height of its cliff. They had been alternating between a trot and a canter for the last few hours, so as not to exhaust the horses too much. Argent and Blackthorn were some distance in front, the others trailing behind.

Suddenly Rhiannon shouted and waved her arm. She could see three horses riding up the long green slope towards the road. One of the riders carried something before him. Everyone kicked their horses on to a new spurt of speed. There was a flash of a face as someone looked back at them, then the three horses broke into a gallop again. The race was on.

Up the steep, cobbled road the horses thundered, striking sparks from their steel-shod feet. Stride by stride Argent and Blackthorn closed the gap between them. The kidnappers reached the first switchback corner and took it fast, one of the horses almost slipping on the damp stones. Rhiannon dragged up Blackthorn's head, urging her into the air. With a whinny, the mare spread out her wings, tucked up her legs and rose swiftly off the ground. She landed in the middle of the road above, turning to face the three riders galloping towards her. Rhiannon saw Lord Malvern, his face twisted into a grimace of fury and hate, the seneschal Irving, and the laird's bodyguard, who cradled a small, cloak-wrapped figure in his arms.

Rhiannon unslung her bow and pulled an arrow from her quiver, setting it to her string and raising the bow high. She did not know who to aim for. If she shot the bodyguard, Roden might be severely injured in the fall. Yet she wanted desperately to save the boy for Nina. She had only a few seconds. In a mo-

ment the horses would be upon her. Rhiannon took a deep
breath, aimed for Lord Malvern, and let the arrow go.

It sang out into the air. Lord Malvern cringed back, his horse
faltering in its headlong gallop. Scant seconds before the arrow
found its mark in his shoulder, his seneschal Irving brought his
horse plunging across the road, throwing himself before his
lord. The arrow caught him in the throat, and he went down
under the horses' thundering hooves.

Lord Malvern managed to heave himself back in the saddle,
and spurred his horse on, tumbling the seneschal's body aside.
Blackthorn reared, then with a great thrust of her hindquarters,
managed to leap into the air just as the bodyguard's huge charger
galloped past underneath her. Rhiannon leant down and made a
grab for Roden, but the bodyguard had the little boy in too tight a
grip. All she managed to do was drag the cloak from his head so
she could see his bright curls, and the pale curve of a cheek. His
eyes were closed and he breathed stertorously. The wind from
Blackthorn's steadily beating wings caused the bodyguard's cloak
to toss and twist wildly. Only this saved Rhiannon, for the bodyguard had his sword in his other hand and as she reached down
for Roden, he brought it up in a great whistling swipe that would
have taken off Rhiannon's head if the sword had not got caught in
his cloak. As it was the sword nicked her arm, causing her to cry
out in pain. She dragged Blackthorn's head up, and the mare rose
higher, her wings beating strongly. The bodyguard galloped on,
Lord Malvern close behind, and Blackthorn came down to land
lightly on the road again.

Rhiannon grasped her arm, trying to stop the blood. Argent
came galloping up and she shouted, "Go! Go! They have
Roden, I saw him."

"Ye all right?" Lewen shouted as the grey stallion raced past.

"Aye, aye, just go!" Rhiannon looked down at her injured
arm and saw she had taken a nasty swipe. Cursing under her
breath, she took her shirt between her teeth and tore away a
strip, which she clumsily wound round and round the gash. She
had to bend her arm to tie the ends into a knot and this caused
her such intense pain she almost swooned. For a moment she
leant forward, resting her head on Blackthorn's mane, trying to
fight off the dizziness. Blackthorn stood steady, though her

chest heaved and her legs trembled. The dizziness passed, and Rhiannon tucked her injured arm against her body and urged Blackthorn on. At first the mare baulked, exhausted by the effort of her flight, but Rhiannon insisted and so the tired mare broke into a canter, following Lewen and Argent.

She heard hooves behind her, and then Iven was beside her, astride the brown gelding. "Are ye badly hurt?" he said. She shook her head. "I hate this slug! I wish I had my auld warcharger. Then Lord Malvern would ken what a real horse can do."

"Saw Roden," Rhiannon panted. "Tried to shoot . . . the laird down . . . Irving took the arrow."

"Aye, I saw. It was a brave try. Come on! We must get them afore they reach the gatehouse."

Iven spurred his horse on, and Blackthorn leapt to match the gelding's stride. Rhiannon was too weak and dizzy to direct her. She just hung on grimly, trying to protect her wounded arm from the worst of the jolts.

Back and forth the road climbed up the cliff, like a great stony snake. Often the sound of the kidnappers' hooves was so tantalisingly close, it felt as if they could reach up their hand and topple their horses by seizing their hock. Iven drew ahead, and Nina rode up behind, barefoot and clad only in a nightgown, her hair wild. She shouted a question to Rhiannon, who was too winded to reply. Nina shot her a look of deep concern but did not stop, racing on to catch up with her husband. Rhiannon's impromptu bandage was now red with blood, and her hands were slick with it. Suddenly Blackthorn's withers rose up and hit Rhiannon in the face. Blackness overwhelmed her, and she fell. She hit the cobblestones hard, rolled over and over, and came to a rest against the wall.

Rhiannon lay still for a moment, trying to get her breath. Her arm throbbed unbearably. A dark whiskery face bent down to nudge her and blow a worried query. Rhiannon laughed shakily, wiped her eyes, and, clinging to Blackthorn's mane, hauled herself upright again. This time she sat for a moment, waiting for the red waves of pain to recede. *Ye're no' thinking,* she told herself. *Ye have a winged horse. Use her!*

Behind her she could hear Cameron approaching fast. She clambered up the wall and remounted Blackthorn, being too weak to vault up onto her back the way she usually did. Then she set Blackthorn at the wall. The winged mare took a few strides, leapt over the obstacle and spread her wings. They soared into the air, right above Cameron's startled head. Lulu, clinging still to Cameron's belt, gibbered and cringed. The valley tilted away below them, sunlit and golden. Blackthorn veered, beat her wings rhythmically, and began to rise.

Up, up, they went, passing one level of the road after another. They passed Iven and Nina, who were both whipping their foundering horses on mercilessly. They passed Lewen, crouched on Argent's neck, the stallion galloping on tirelessly. Then, just round the next corner, they passed the foam-flecked, blowing mounts of Lord Malvern and his bodyguard. The lord drew his sword and slashed at them as they flew past, but Blackthorn swerved nimbly so he missed. Rhiannon could only hope the lord had not seen how very nearly she had been unseated by the sudden move.

They landed on the road just outside the gatehouse. The gates were wide open, yawning blackly, but there was no sign of the gatekeeper. Rhiannon slid off Blackthorn's back, and leant against her for a moment, taking strength from her warm, sweaty flank. Then she straightened herself, turning to look at the road. At the far end, Lord Malvern and his bodyguard were just turning the corner and coming towards her. Both their horses were badly winded, barely managing a canter. It was cruel to whip them on, and Rhiannon told the horses so, as they came wild-eyed and foam-flecked towards her. *Ye deserve better masters than this,* she said silently. *How dare they whip ye and spur ye and drive ye to gallop up such a cruel, steep hill as this. Ye are Horse. Ye are not their slave. Stand still. Refuse to run anymore.*

For a moment she thought she had failed, for the horses came on at the same headlong pace, their nostrils flaring red, their eyes rimmed with white. Then the bodyguard's horse suddenly came to a juddering halt, legs splayed, head hanging. Though the big, grey-bearded man whipped it with his reins and slapped it with the flat of his sword, it refused to budge. Suddenly its legs folded and it sank down in the middle of the road. The bodyguard jumped off, the unconscious child lolling in his arms, and dragged at the bridle, trying to force it on. Meanwhile, Lord Malvern's horse was rearing and plunging, refusing to go forwards. He slashed at it with his sword, and it reared so precipitately the lord was thrown from its back. Rhiannon whooped with joy, and so did Lewen, who had turned the corner and was galloping up the cobbled hill towards the foundered horses. Nina and Iven were close behind him.

The bodyguard glanced back at him, then dropped the reins and began to run up the road towards the gatehouse, Roden's arms and legs flopping wildly. Lord Malvern rolled, got to his feet and began to run too. Both men had naked swords in their hands, and murder in their eyes. Rhiannon set an arrow to her bow with shaking fingers. Again her aim wavered between them. She did not want to risk shooting Roden, but if she shot down Lord Malvern, the bodyguard would be upon her, with the open gate only a few strides past her. She tried to steady her breathing, and shot the bodyguard in the thigh. He cried out in agony, but although his stride faltered and broke, he did not stop, lurching forward with the feathered haft of the arrow sticking out of his leg. Rhiannon shot him again in the same spot, and then, in desperation, in the other leg. He fell, Roden rolling out of his arms. Lord Malvern bent, caught up the little boy, and ran on. He was too close now for Rhiannon to shoot him down. She drew her slim black dagger from her boot and flung it at him. To her horror he simply raised one hand and the dagger spun away harmlessly. Then he raised his sword and swiped at her. Blackthorn reared and he shrank back instinctively, allowing Rhiannon to roll away under his sword. Then the winged horse bent her head and charged him. One of her long, sharp horns slashed him across the face. He screamed and dropped his sword, putting his hand up to cover the gash. Rhiannon reached out a hand to try to trip him, but he stumbled past her and through the gates, Roden still clasped against his chest. The massive gates clanged shut behind him.

Storming the Castle

R hiannon sat up slowly, sick with disappointment.
Argent came to a blowing halt a few feet away, and
Lewen jumped down and came to help her up.

"He got past," Rhiannon said, her voice thick.

"Ye almost had him," Lewen said. "It was so close."

"Now what?" she asked, tears stinging her eyes.

"We go in and get him out," Lewen said, looking up at the
immense wall towering over their heads. Rhiannon heaved a
sigh that came from the very pit of her chest cavity.

"First, we question the bodyguard," Lewen said, letting go
of Rhiannon's arm as she leant against the wall. He drew his
knife and walked back down the road towards the bodyguard.
The man was clutching his shattered leg, his face twisted in
pain. He looked at Lewen's set, determined face, then back
down the road, to where Nina and Iven were cantering up towards them, Cameron close behind. With a great effort he
staggered to his feet, and then, before Lewen could stop him,
dragged himself up onto the wall and launched himself into
the dizzying space on the far side. They heard a thin wail, and
then a sickening bone-crunching thud. Soon after, there came
another, more distant thud, and then another. Then there was
only silence.

Grey with horror, Lewen ran and looked over the wall. Then
he turned back and sank to his haunches, his dagger dropping
from his hand. Iven and Nina flung themselves off their horses
and ran to look too. Nina was weeping.

"I guess he didna want to be questioned," Rhiannon said
through the roaring in her head, then she slid down the wall till
she too was sitting. Nina ran to her side.

"Rhiannon, Rhiannon," she sobbed. "Och, ye were so close! I really thought ye'd saved him."

"I tried," Rhiannon said. "I'm sorry."

"Nay, nay, ye did so well, ye were so brave, so clever," Nina wept. "Och, my laddie, my babe. We were so close!"

Rhiannon dropped her head onto her arms.

"Ye're sorely hurt," Nina said, dashing the tears from her face. "Let me look at your arm. Och, I have naught here, naught to ease the pain or stop the bleeding. What a hare-brained, mad-cap rescue this is, me barefoot and in my nightgown, and only a sword and a few daggers between the lot o' us. How are we meant to storm the castle like this?" Her tears began to flow again, but she unwrapped Rhiannon's arm deftly, examined the ugly wound with compressed brows, and then bound it up again with clean cloth torn from her nightgown. Her bandage was far more effective than Rhiannon's.

"I shall have to fly over the wall," Rhiannon said slowly, cradling her arm against her. "It's the only way to get in."

"But ye're injured," Nina pointed out, taking her shawl off and fashioning Rhiannon a gorgeous, many-coloured sling. "And Roden could be hidden anywhere inside that castle."

"It's too dangerous," Iven said reluctantly. "Unless . . ."

"Blackthorn is mine," Rhiannon said. "She willna carry anyone else."

"No' even me?" Lewen said.

"Ye're too heavy for her," Rhiannon said.

Lewen acknowledged the truth of this. It was a rare horse that could carry his weight.

Nina sat back on her heels. "It's the only way," she said. "But can I let ye do it? What if they shoot ye down? I'd never forgive myself."

"Better I die here, flying on my horse's back, trying to save Roden, than at the end of the hangman's rope," Rhiannon said wryly. She managed to stand up.

Cameron was hanging back, wide-eyed and pale-faced. Lulu, who had ridden the whole way clinging to Cameron's belt, darted forward and seized Rhiannon's blood-slick hand in her tiny, leathery paw. She jumped up and down, gibbering, waving up at the castle with her other paw.

"She wants to go with ye," Nina said. "She wants to help ye find Roden."

Rhiannon looked at the little arak doubtfully.

"She has a very precise sense o' smell," Nina said. "And she can climb anything. Happen she can help ye find Roden? For ye may be able to fly over the walls, Rhiannon, but how are ye to find my lad once ye're inside?"

"I do no' think Blackthorn will like it," Rhiannon said. "Lulu's awfully smelly."

"She willna mind," Nina said eagerly. "Oh, please, Rhiannon. Ye do no' ken Lulu. She's very clever, and quick, and nimble, and she adores Roden. She'll help ye, I ken she will."

"All right," Rhiannon said. She looked up at the stone bulwark again and could not help a little shiver.

"I dinna even have water for ye and Blackthorn to drink," Nina said remorsefully. "No' a crumb to eat. After such a hard ride too!"

"That's all right," Rhiannon said absently. "I am used to being hungry."

She whickered to Blackthorn, who whickered back, and led the mare over to the wall so she could mount. Before she could clamber up on to the wall, Lewen was beside her, lifting her in his strong arms and throwing her up onto the mare's back. She smiled at him, and he held up his hand to her. When she took it he drew her down so he could kiss her.

"Be careful, my love," he said. "Come back safely."

"O' course I will," she replied with an attempt at her usual jaunty manner.

He unslung his quiver of arrows and passed it up to her. It was full of arrows, fletched with shining, iridescent-green feathers. "I have a Talent with wood, ye ken. I made all these arrows with my own hand, and they will always fly true. Take them."

"I will, but no' because I need enchanted arrows to shoot true," she said with a flash of her dimple.

"I ken, its just . . ."

She nodded and passed him her own quiver with its handful of clumsily whittled arrows. "Yours are much bonnier, I'll be glad to take them," she said cheekily. "Thank ye."

Iven stepped up to give her his hand. "Thank ye, Rhiannon," he said gravely. "Bring Roden back to us."

"I will," she said gamely. "What will ye do now? Where shall I meet ye?"

"We will go now and bang on that door until someone lets us in," Iven said. "It's all I can think o' doing. In the meantime, let us hope the reeve from Linlithgorn is on his way. If he refuses us permission to search the castle, surely he canna refuse the reeve?"

"Laird Malvern rules this land as if he were a prionnsa and this were his kingdom," Nina said unhappily. "I'm sure he will have no hesitation in refusing the reeve, and I doubt the reeve will have the courage to insist. After all, he does no' ken who we are and he would ken and respect the laird all too well, I think. All the laird has to do is deny everything."

"He'll have trouble explaining the gash across his face," Rhiannon said grimly. "I think Blackthorn put out his eye."

"We can but hope," Iven said and stepped back, so Nina could come and embrace Rhiannon.

"Ye have power, lassie," the witch said to her intently. "I have sensed it in ye, and ye used it here, to bring the laird's horses to their knees. Trust in yourself, and draw upon it in need. It shallna let ye down."

Rhiannon nodded sceptically, then waved her hand to Cameron. "Bye, laddie!" she said. "See ye soon."

"Good luck!" Cameron replied. "I hope ye find Roden." He hesitated a moment, then said in a rush, "that was amazing what ye did afore, with the horses and all, I mean." As Rhiannon shrugged and smiled, he continued, "I'm sorry I punched ye. Ye ken, yesterday."

Rhiannon touched the yellowing bruise on her temple. "Well, I'm sorry I kneed ye in the balls," she replied.

Cameron grinned, though his brown cheek coloured. "So am I," he said.

Nina passed up Lulu, who clung to Rhiannon's waist with her skinny, hairy arms, gibbering a little and bouncing up and down with excitement. Blackthorn shied and spread her wings, dancing sideways.

"Ssssh," Rhiannon said sternly to the little arak. "Thigearns do no' bounce."

Lulu immediately stopped bouncing, though Rhiannon could feel her quivering, whether with fear or excitement it was impossible to tell. She took a deep breath. She was trembling herself, and very definitely from fear. She smiled at the circle of upturned faces, determined they would not know how very scared she was, and then wheeled Blackthorn round and set her into a canter. After a few quick strides, the mare unfurled her blue-tipped wings and leapt into the air. The circle of faces fell behind.

Blackthorn was weary and the wall was high, so Rhiannon took the ascent slowly. They flew along the wall, away from the gatehouse, gradually gaining height, then at last they breached it near the end. All was quiet. Too quiet. Rhiannon could not see a single soldier or servant. The castle could have been deserted.

Rhiannon directed Blackthorn towards the northern tower. Roden would have been taken to Lady Evaline, she guessed, who had her quarters in that wing. Rhiannon was not entirely sure she understood the madness behind Roden's kidnap, but she felt sure Lord Malvern had done it for his sister-in-law. He had called Lady Evaline old and mad, but Rhiannon felt that it was the lord who was truly the mad one, the one obsessed with bringing his brother and his son back to life, and expiating the guilt he felt at their deaths.

Blackthorn was beginning to tire, and so Rhiannon brought her in close to the tower. The castle had been built for defence and so the only windows were high up under the roof, and heavily barred. The length of the tower was broken regularly with narrow arrow-slits, however. Blackthorn hovered as close to one of these as she could get, while Rhiannon lifted Lulu and thrust her towards the tiny aperture.

"Find Roden, Lulu," she whispered. "And be quick!"

Lulu nodded, whimpering a little with fear, and leapt across to the arrow-slit. She crept through the gap and disappeared from view. Blackthorn then flew up and landed gratefully on the roof of the tower. This was steeply peaked, but there was a little flat edge just before the battlements where Blackthorn was able to stand, and Rhiannon could stretch out in the warm sunshine and rest.

She shut her eyes, feeling very tired after the long, hard ride.

She almost fell asleep there, resting in the sun, the pain in her arm dying down to a dull throbbing. But then Blackthorn nudged her with her nose, blowing on her and nibbling at her shoulder. Rhiannon sat up rather groggily.

"What is it?" she asked.

Blackthorn looked towards the battlements curiously. Rhiannon looked too, and saw to her horror a small brown wrinkled hand reaching over the stone. She thought of all the dead severed hands she had seen in the lord's library and a cold shudder went down her spine. It was all she could do not to scream. Surely the lord could not animate those embalmed hands and send them creeping down corridors and climbing tall towers, hunting down his enemies and strangling them to death?

Another hand reached up and grasped the stone, then Lulu's anxious face, so like an old, old woman's, suddenly appeared. Rhiannon's relief was so profound she almost fainted.

The arak crept over the battlement and leapt to Rhiannon's side, seizing her hand urgently. She gibbered, dancing up and down.

"Roden? Ye've found Roden?"

The arak dragged her to the side and pointed down. Rhiannon leant over the battlements, clinging tight to the stone with her uninjured hand. The tower fell away to the courtyard so far below, the vast drop making her feel dizzy. Lulu gibbered again, pointing, then swung herself down. Rhiannon watched in amazement as she clambered down the sheer drop, clinging to the stones with hands and feet and tail-tip. She came to a deep window embrasure and hung above it, looking up at Rhiannon.

Rhiannon nodded her head and climbed up onto the battlements so that she could more readily reach Blackthorn's back. Her arm throbbed painfully and her head swam, but she ignored it and managed to slide her leg across the mare's back. Blackthorn leapt out into the air, Rhiannon shutting her eyes against the sudden spin of space. She wondered how long it took most thigearns to get over the involuntary spurt of terror that came from flying on a winged horse's back.

Blackthorn flew down so that she was hovering just below the window where Lulu hung upside down. Rhiannon could hear the sound of low, murmuring voices. She felt sure one of

them was Lord Malvern. Her pulse quickened and she signalled
to Blackthorn to fly closer.

She could just make out the words.

"Do ye no' care what I've been through to bring him back to
ye?" Lord Malvern was shouting. "Irving is dead and Durward
too, and I was slashed across the face by that great horned
beast. Look, I bleed! Does the spilling o' my blood mean
naught to ye?"

"There has been too much spilling o' blood," Lady Evaline
answered in a wavering voice.

"But ye said ye wanted him! I've risked much to get him for
ye, no' to mention losing two o' my most faithful men. It
would've been much better to have let them ride away, suspecting nothing, and then to have stolen him later, when I had
the spell in my hands and was ready to resurrect Rory's soul.
Now we have to hide him and keep him safe from prying eyes
for weeks, months even, until I find the spell. Why on earth did
ye weep and wring your hands at the thought o' losing him if ye
did no' want me to take him for ye?"

"Ye do such mad, strange things," the old woman said in a
broken voice. "I canna understand ye sometimes, Malvern.
Och, I ken ye felt for me in my grief when I lost both Falkner
and Rory so cruelly, I ken ye felt ye were to blame. But so much
time has passed, and I grow auld. Such fury o' emotion seems
odd to me now."

"But ye wept!" Lord Malvern was furious.

"Aye, I wept, aye, I was sorry the laddie had to go, aye, I
wished he could stay here with me and brighten my days,"
Lady Evaline said just as angrily. "I did no' mean for ye to go
and steal him! Why do ye do these things? So many boys!
Ye've stolen so many boys for me and in the end killed them
all, for ye could no' stand the way they wept for their mothers,
or shrank away from ye, frightened. This lad is no' Rory, he can
never be Rory, canna ye see that?"

"Oh yes, he will," Lord Malvern said in a cold, malevolent
voice. "We will kill him and Rory will take over his body, and
then ye will thank me."

"But will it really be Rory?" Lady Evaline asked unhappily.
"His body rotted away long ago, and Falkner's too. We have

their bones, it's true, but we ken we canna reanimate them, we have tried and tried."

"The body is but a sack to keep the spirit in," Lord Malvern said impatiently. "It is the soul that matters, and we have tied their souls here to us. All we need do is find appropriate vessels to pour their souls back into. And ye canna tell me ye do no' think this lad a good vessel for Rory. I have seen the way ye look at him and long to caress him. Soon, soon, ye shall have him again, your own darling son, back in a living, breathing body, as ye have longed for so long."

"I just wish we dinna have to hurt this lad," Lady Evaline murmured.

"We shallna hurt him. We do no' want Rory to wake to pain or a marred body. We will kill him very gently, I promise ye."

Lady Evaline sighed. "Sometimes ye make my flesh creep on my bones, Malvern, even after all these years."

"Do no' dare stand there and stare at me with those wide, innocent eyes, Evaline," he hissed. "Ye may no' have wielded the knife yourself but ye have been complicit in each and every death! Ye think me mad? Ye think me evil? Everyone I have killed was killed to make ye happy!"

There was a cry from Lady Evaline. "Look, he wakes! Sssh! Do no' frighten him."

Then Rhiannon heard a high, treble voice, wavering with tears. "Where am I? Where's my mam? I want my mam!"

"I am to be your mama now," Lady Evaline said. "Do no' cry, my love."

"Ye're no' my mam! Ye're auld! I want my own mam!"

"I am your mama, Rory."

"My name's no' Rory! I'm Roden. Go away!"

"Rory, do no' speak to your mother like that," Lord Malvern said in a chilling voice.

"She's no' my mam! My mam is young and bonny. She's a witch, and she'll turn ye into a slug for this. And my da's a soldier and he'll step on ye and squash ye flat. They'll be coming for me, just ye wait and see!" The little boy's voice wavered and broke.

"No-one will come for ye, Rory. No-one kens where ye are. Ye would be best to keep a quiet tongue in your head, and be

loving and respectful to your new mama else I'll squash *ye* as
flat as a slug. Do ye understand me?"

There was a short, fraught silence and then Roden began to
wail, "I want my mam, I want my mam. Mam! Mam!"

"Shhh, no, sweetling, do no' cry. Ye will forget her soon, and
we'll be so happy together. Come, will ye no' sit here on my lap
and I shall read ye a story? Come, come, my darling, do no'
weep. Uncle Malvern will go now and leave ye here with me,
and we'll have a lovely cuddle and I'll play with ye. Malvern,
go and leave me with my son."

Rhiannon heard the faint sound of a door shutting, and then
there was no sound except for Roden's sobbing and the anxious
attempts of Lady Evaline to soothe him. As she kept telling him
that he would soon forget his real mama and she would forget
him, all she managed to do was drive Roden deeper into despair.

Rhiannon shifted her weight, wondering what she could do
to rescue Roden. There seemed to be no way in to the little
tower room except through the window above her head, which
was heavily barred. Blackthorn was tiring quickly, her wings
not built for hovering. Whatever Rhiannon was to do had to be
done quickly.

Lulu turned her small, wizened face to Rhiannon anxiously,
gestured broadly, and then swung herself down and into the
windowsill. For a moment the arak clung to the bars, then she
put her hand through and tapped gently on the glass. A moment
later, Roden's chubby face appeared at the window. He saw the
winged horse and rider, and shouted with excitement, jumping
up and down and waving. Then he unlatched the window and
flung it open. Lulu squeezed through the bars and flung herself
upon him, dancing up and down on his shoulder with joy.

Rhiannon stared at the bars in consternation. She flew closer
and reached out one hand to test them. They were stout and
strong. Roden reached through the deep aperture and grasped
her fingers. Behind him there was sudden movement.

Rhiannon took a deep breath. She had nothing on her that
could wrench the bars from the stone. No rope. No chain. All
she had was her desperate desire to free Roden, and her will.
Rhiannon had listened to the apprentices at their lessons often

enough to know the keystones to witchcraft were will and desire. Both of hers were strong. She grasped the bars with both hands, focused her mind with all the fierce determination she was capable of, and jerked them hard. To her surprise and wild joy, the bars wrenched free. They flew out of the window-frame at great speed, almost whacking her over the head, and tumbled down to smash into the courtyard below. Rhiannon almost followed them, jerked off balance. Only Blackthorn's speedy manoeuvre kept her on the mare's back.

Roden did not hesitate. In a second he was scrambling up onto the windowsill. Then he climbed through the window. Rhiannon grasped his wrists and swung him onto Blackthorn's back, behind her. The little boy whooped with joy and excitement. The next second Lulu was leaping after him, landing on the winged horse's mane. Blackthorn wheeled and soared away.

A despairing scream came from the window behind him. "Rory, no!"

Rhiannon looked back. Lady Evaline leant out of the window, her arms outstretched. "My son! Ye're stealing my son!" the old lady cried, tears streaming down her face. Suddenly she climbed up onto the sill and launched herself after them, calling Rory's name. Rhiannon and Roden could only watch in numb horror as she fell over and over, tumbling down the great length of the tower to the ground. She hit the paving stones and bounced once, then sprawled still like a broken doll. Slowly a tide of red crept out from her skull.

Roden hid his face. Tears started to Rhiannon's eyes. She wiped them away, then bent to stroke Blackthorn's sweat-lathered neck.

"Take us home," she whispered. "Find Lewen for me."

Blackthorn wheeled and flew to the south.

The Chain Between Them

Rhiannon lay in Lewen's arms, feeling warm and comfortable and at peace, despite the iron chain that weighed down her wrist and rattled whenever she moved.

Firelight flickered over the trees, which seemed to lean over the camp like protective guardians. Nina sat on the far side of the flames, Roden leaning against her, her arms about him as she whispered silly jokes in his ear to make him giggle. Lulu was curled against him, one paw nestled in his hand. Both looked as if they never wanted to let him go again. At the sound of Roden's laughter, Iven looked up from the guitar he was gently strumming and smiled.

The other apprentices were playing cards by the light of a lantern propped on a box. All except Edithe. She sat by herself, reading a spell book and looking very sour. She felt the arrest of the lord of Fettercairn to be a slur on her perception, and was adamant that it was all a dreadful mistake and the lord would be cleared as soon as they reached the royal court.

More than a week had passed since Rhiannon had snatched Roden from Fettercairn Castle. She had managed to stay on Blackthorn's back long enough to see Nina clasp her son in her arms. Then she had fallen.

The next seven days were nothing but a hideous blur. Strange nightmarish visions stalked her imagination. She was first burning with fire, then tossed in an icy waterfall, then dried out with merciless heat like a lizard on a rock. Her limbs seemed to grow like tentacles, reaching for miles across the countryside, and then she was very tiny, a pale crustacean pried from her shell and held dangling above an open mouth. Dark walkers

haunted her dreams and bent over her waking hours, pinned to
the heels of those who tended her.

They had tried to put her to bed at the Linlithgorn inn but she
had fought so viciously against being taken inside stone walls
that Nina had had to care for her in the open, with no more shelter than the leaves of the trees and a canopy of oilskins strung
up with rope. In her rare moments of lucidity, Rhiannon was
able to stare up at the shifting green pattern of sunshine through
the leaves, or the great vault of the night sky starred with familiar constellations. Gradually, her soaring temperature
cooled, the crippling headache faded, and the dark walkers
stepped back into the shadows, leaving Rhiannon weak and
useless as a newborn kitten but aware of who she was and
where she was.

Nina said she had suffered from sorcery sickness, a very
dangerous illness that could overcome anyone who drew too
deeply upon the One Power. It was a wonder, she said, that
Rhiannon had survived it. Many wild Talents, who had not
been taught how to use their powers properly, died after such
a display of magical strength, or at the least were left broken
in mind and body. Rhiannon must have great inner reserves of
strength, Nina said, for she had wielded powerful magic by
wresting the iron bars out of the stone. Rhiannon had already
been weakened by the poison Dedrie the nursemaid had
forced down her throat, and worn out by the desperate chase
after Roden, and the loss of blood from her injured arm. "Indeed I think Eà was watching out for ye, my dear," Nina had
said, "and I am so glad. I could no' have forgiven myself if ye
had died rescuing my laddie, after all ye've been through this
past week."

Nina had insisted that the whole company wait until Rhiannon was strong enough to ride again before they left Linlithgorn, and she had not allowed anyone to talk to her about what
had happened at Fettercairn Castle. At first Rhiannon had been
grateful for this, for her dreams were still disturbed with visions
of creeping hands, pickled babies, bloody puddles, the unhappy
ghosts of murdered children and the dreadful scream of an old
lady as she fell to her death. She was content to spend a few
days sitting in the leafy glade, enjoying the tender ministrations

of Nina, who could not do enough for the rescuer of her son, and watching the sorceress as she called birds and small animals to her hands, and sang quiet songs of peace and healing over Rhiannon's head.

Once Rhiannon had been strong enough to walk about the clearing, or to ask after the others, her peaceful time was over, though. Iven had come with the chain and shackles in his hands, and a most apologetic look, to fetter her limbs again. Nina had protested angrily, and Iven had said, "I'm sorry, my dearling, I'm sorry, Rhiannon, but naught has changed. I still must take ye to Lucescere to face the Rìgh's justice. Ye ken I wish I could just leave ye be, and pretend I do no' ken ye were the one who killed Connor, but I do ken and so does the Rìgh. I canna take the risk that ye will decide to fly off once more."

"But Iven!" Nina cried, almost in tears. "If it were no' for Rhiannon, we would no' have our own boy back again. We are in her debt!"

"I ken, dearling, and believe me I shall make sure the Rìgh kens it. He is a fair man, and fond o' ye and Roden. I am sure he willna let the courts hang Rhiannon when he understands—"

Nina was aghast. "Iven! Surely there can be no question o' . . . Iven, ye canna allow . . ."

Iven's face was troubled and unhappy, but still he clasped the shackles around Rhiannon's wrists and fastened the chain to the tree. "I'm sorry. Believe me when I say I will do all in my power to make sure the courts deal fairly with ye, my dear. Your help in rescuing Roden and your testimony against the laird o' Fettercairn—these will no' mean naught, I promise ye."

Rhiannon had not fought him, or protested in any way, but she had felt a heavy mantle settle over her shoulders, a sort of weariness and fatalism she had not previously felt. Nina was worried about her, she could tell, and had tried to argue that they must stay a few more days until Rhiannon was stronger. Iven had shook his head, though. "We must ride on, my love, ye ken that. We have been delayed far too long already."

So Lewen and the other witch-apprentices had at last been allowed to join them, and the obvious affection in the faces of most of them had bolstered Rhiannon's spirits, and made it easier to bear the heavy chain that rattled every time she moved. Lewen had brought Blackthorn with the other horses, and the sight of the mare had given her fresh strength and courage.

The apprentices had spent the afternoon fussing over her, giving her little gifts of flowers and honeyed cakes, and telling her how brave and clever she was. This had been sweet. Sweeter still was the sight of Lewen's steadfast brown eyes and the warmth and strength of his hands, which he found impossible to keep away from her. She was able to lean against his broad shoulder, and rest her head on his chest, and feel his fingers entwined in hers, and felt a warm glow of happiness she would have thought impossible earlier that day. Lewen had, without the need to speak, unshackled the chain from the tree and clasped it round his own wrist and Rhiannon had understood this gesture as it was meant—he would stand by her, and support her, and help her bear her fate.

The company planned to ride on again the next day and Nina had prepared a feast to celebrate. The village of Linlithgorn had provided them with fresh fruits and vegetables and ripe cheeses and newly baked bread, which everyone had enjoyed very much, and now Rhiannon was replete and drowsy, and ready to hear at last what had happened while she had been lost in nightmares.

"So what did ye do then?" Rhiannon asked Lewen.

"Well, it was just as Iven predicted. The gatekeeper opened the gate and was surprised to see us. He told us there must be some mistake, no-one had been in or out of the gatehouse all day, but he sent his lad to fetch the laird when Iven insisted. The laird made us wait for ages, which made Nina furious, and she marched into the castle. When the gatekeeper tried to stop her, she sang a spell o' sleep, which was rather funny, particularly since Cameron did no' heed her warning to cover his ears and so he fell asleep too. She ensorcelled half the castle garrison and quite a few servants too, and at last found the laird in his library, much to his dismay. Ye should've seen his face when he called and called for his servants, and then found them all snoozing!"

"What did he do?" Rhiannon asked, grinning.

"He was all honey and poison, looking Nina up and down as if she was a madwoman and speaking to her very soothingly. I must admit she looked rather wild, being barefoot and dressed in a torn and bloody nightgown, with her hair looking like she'd ridden through a whirlwind. Nina didna care, though, she looked and acted like the countess she is. I do no' ken what would've happened, if the auld lady's servant had no' come bursting in, sobbing and raving about Lady Evaline. That must've been so horrible, seeing her fall like that."

"It was," Rhiannon admitted. "I wish she had no' done it. I canna help feeling it was my fault. If only I'd been quicker, happen I could've caught her or something."

"Ye probably all would've fallen then, Blackthorn's no' strong enough to carry such a load."

"Aye, happen so . . . still, I wish she hadna done it." Rhiannon pressed Lewen's arms about her more firmly, the star amulet pressing into the tender flesh between her breasts.

Lewen kissed her temple and went on. "Anyway, after that, the laird had to change his tune. He acted all shocked and distressed and pretended he kent naught about it all. He put the whole thing onto Lady Evaline and her companion. Miss Prunella confessed to helping the seneschal kidnap thirty-four boys over the past twenty-five years, and to helping him dispose o' them when they failed to make Lady Evaline happy. That was why they did it, she says. To make the auld lady happy."

"And the laird is trying to pretend he's innocent in all this?"

"Very persuasively," Lewen replied grimly. "He has the reeve o' Linlithgorn more than half-convinced."

"But I saw him!" Rhiannon said indignantly.

"Aye, but ye're no' the most credible witness, my love," Lewen said. "The laird has argued most compellingly that ye are trying to deflect suspicion away from yourself. Nina and Iven have had to admit, most unwillingly, that they never actually saw the laird's face. Ye were the only one."

"What about his eye?" Rhiannon cried. "How does he explain Blackthorn putting out his eye?"

"He says the seneschal did it. He said he'd been worried and suspicious about Irving for some time, since he was often no' there when the laird wanted him, and so he had lain in wait for him that night, wanting to see where he went and what he got up to. Except Irving pulled a sword on him and slashed him, and the laird was so sorely wounded he was unable to pursue him. The laird says Irving had been his brother's servant and was faithful to Lady Evaline, no' to him."

"It's unbelievable!" Rhiannon was so angry and upset she sat up, and Lewen had to draw her down into his arms again.

"Unfortunately, it's all believable. For every accusation we've made, the laird has been able to come up with a most plausible explanation. And the fact that he has placed himself so willingly in the reeve's hands has worked in his favour too. All he asks for, he says, is a chance to go to the Rìgh's court and plead his case. He has offered to pay restitution to the grieving families for their loss, on behalf o' his sister-in-law, who he says was quite mad. He has offered to give any assistance he can to the Rìgh's officers in their investigation. All he asks for is a chance to clear his name."

"It's very odd," Rhiannon said after a moment. "What about the necromancy?"

"Again, ye are the only one who saw that," Lewen said unwillingly. "Basically, he's put his word against yours. The reeve did find a chest full of red cloaks, and black candles and so on, but that was hidden under the seneschal's bed, and so Laird Malvern has been able to deny any knowledge o' it. A few o' the footmen have fled, and the auld groom, and a few others, making it seem as if they were the ones involved."

"But I saw him! Laird Malvern! He called the ghost his brother."

Lewen said nothing.

"But I'm a half-satyricorn accused o' murder and treason," Rhiannon said glumly. "And he's a laird."

"The worst thing is, Miss Prunella, the auld lady's servant, canna be questioned about her role in all this anymore."

"Why no'?"

"She's dead," Lewen said shortly. "She took poison . . . or someone gave it to her, we do no' ken which. We never thought . . . if we had only guessed what she planned, happen we could have stopped her somehow."

Rhiannon was appalled. "Ye mean, she just died? And now she canna tell anyone the truth o' it all?"

Lewen nodded. "That's right. I canna help wondering how she got the poison. I swear the nursemaid Dedrie kens more than she's saying, but she's shut up tight as a clam and willna say a word, and neither will any o' the other servants. They have all been arrested too and face trial with the laird in Lucescere, but they do naught but swear their innocence most convincingly."

"I guess they all fear the hangman's noose too," Rhiannon said in a very unhappy voice.

Lewen kissed her. "They willna hang ye now, Rhiannon, surely? No' after ye saved Roden. He's heir to the Earl of Caerlaverock, after all, the Rìgh's dearest friend. Nina will testify on your behalf, and His Highness has a real soft spot for her, he's known her since she was a babe. I'm sure he'll pardon ye."

"I hope so." Rhiannon shivered.

"We ride for Lucescere tomorrow. We'll be there in a few weeks, and then we'll ken. Do no' fear, Rhiannon. With Nina and Iven and me all vouching for ye, the Rìgh canna condemn ye."

"Well, we'll find out all too soon," Rhiannon said. She looked up at the star-strung sky and the sliver of new moon hanging over the mountain. By the time the two moons were full, she would be in the Shining City, facing her fate. Despite Lewen's confidence, Rhiannon could not feel the same optimism. Satyricorns believed in dark walkers and fearsome gods. Happy endings were not part of their mythology. She had the space of one moon, though, to grasp what happiness she could. She slipped her hand under Lewen's shirt and caressed his bare back, her chain rattling.

"Since we are so tightly shackled together, do ye think Iven would notice if we slipped away to the forest? I have had enough o' ghosts and death. I want some warmth and loving."

Lewen's breath caught and he bent his head and kissed her. "I think he may turn a blind eye . . . for a wee while."

"Let's go then," she said and stood up, tugging him up by the chain fastened to his wrist. "Though I think we'll need more than just a wee while."

"Ye're a forward lass," he said approvingly, getting up with alacrity. Hand-in-hand they went away from the flames and into the darkness of the wood, the chain swinging between them.

Glossary

acolytes: students of witchcraft who have not yet passed their Second Test of Powers; usually aged between eight and sixteen.
ahdayeh: a series of exercises used as meditation in motion. Derived from the Khan'cohban art of fighting.
Annis: apprentice to Ashelma, the witch of Ardarchy.
apprentice-witch: a student of witchcraft who has passed the Second Test of Powers, usually undertaken at the age of sixteen.
arak: a small, monkey-like creature.
Arran: south-east land of Eileanan, ruled by the MacFóghnan clan.
Ashelma: the witch of Ardarchy.
Aslinn: deeply forested land, ruled by the MacAislin clan.

banprionnsa: princess or duchess.
banrìgh: queen.
Beltane: May Day; the first day of summer.
Ben Eyrie: third highest mountain in Eileanan; part of the Broken Ring of Dubhslain.
blaygird: evil, awful.
Blèssem: rich farmland south of Rionnagan, ruled by the MacThanach clan.
Blue Guards: the Yeomen of the Guard, the Rìgh's own elite company of soldiers. They act as his personal bodyguard, both on the battlefield and in peacetime.
Brann the Raven: one of the First Coven of Witches. Known for probing the darker mysteries of magic, and for fascination with machinery and technology.

Broken Ring of Dubhslain: mountains which curve in a crescent around the highlands of Ravenshaw.
Bronwen NicCuinn: daughter of former Rìgh Jaspar MacCuinn and Maya the Ensorcellor; she was named Banrìgh of Eileanan by her father on his deathbed but ruled for just six hours as a newborn baby, before Lachlan the Winged wrested the throne from her.

Candlemas: the end of winter and beginning of spring.
Carraig: land of the sea-witches, the northernmost land of Eileanan, ruled by the MacSeinn clan.
Celestines: race of faery creatures, renowned for empathic abilities and knowledge of stars and prophecy.
Clachan: southernmost land of Eileanan, a province of Rionnagan ruled by the MacCuinn clan.
claymore: a heavy, two-edged sword, often as tall as a man.
cluricaun: small woodland faery.
Connor: a Yeoman of the Guard. Was once a beggar-boy in Lucescere and member of the League of the Healing Hand.
corrigan: mountain faery with the power of assuming the look of a boulder. The most powerful can cast other illusions.
Coven of Witches: the central ruling body for witches in Eileanan, led by the Keybearer and a council of twelve other sorcerers and sorceresses called the Circle. The Coven administers all rites and rituals in the worship of the universal life-force witches call Eà, runs schools and hospitals, and advises the Crown.
Craft: applications of the One Power through spells, incantations and magical objects.
The Cripple: leader of the rebellion against the rule of Jaspar and Maya.
Cuinn Lionheart: leader of the First Coven of Witches; his descendants are called MacCuinn.
Cunning: applications of the One Power through will and desire.
cunning man: village wise man or warlock.
cursehags: wicked faery race, prone to curses and evil spells. Known for their filthy personal habits.

dai-dein: father.

Day of Betrayal: the day Jaspar the Ensorcelled turned on the witches, exiling or executing them, and burning the Witch Towers.

Dedrie: healer at Fettercairn Castle; was formerly nursemaid to Rory, the young son of Lord Falkner MacFerris.

Dide the Juggler: a jongleur who was rewarded for his part in Lachlan the Winged's successful rebellion by being made Didier Laverock, Earl of Caerlaverock. Is often called the Rìgh's minstrel.

Dillon of the Joyous Sword: captain of the Yeomen of the Guard. Was once a beggar-boy and captain of the League of the Healing Hand.

Donncan Feargus MacCuinn: eldest son of Lachlan MacCuinn and Iseult NicFaghan. Has wings like a bird and can fly. Was named for Lachlan's two brothers, who were transformed into blackbirds by Maya the Ensorcellor.

Dughall MacBrann: the Prionnsa of Ravenshaw and cousin to the Rìgh.

Durward: Lord Malvern's bodyguard.

Eà: the Great Life Spirit, mother and father of all.

Eileanan: largest island in the archipelago called the Far Islands.

Elemental Powers: the forces of air, earth, fire, water and spirit which together make up the One Power.

Enit Silverthroat: grandmother of Dide and Nina; died at the Battle of Bonnyblair.

equinox: a time when day and night are of equal length, occurring twice a year.

Evaline NicKinney: widow of Lord Falkner MacFerris, former lord of Fettercairn Castle.

Fairge; Fairgean: faery creatures who need both sea and land to live.

Falkner MacFerris: former lord of Fettercairn Castle.

Fettercairn Castle: a fortress guarding the pass into the highlands of Ravenshaw, and the Tower of Ravens. Owned by the MacFerris clan.

Finn the Cat: nickname of Fionnghal NicRuraich.

Fionnghal NicRuraich: eldest daughter of Anghus MacRuraich of Rurach; was once a beggar-girl in Lucescere and lieutenant of the League of the Healing Hand.

First Coven of Witches: thirteen witches who fled persecution in their own land, invoking an ancient spell that folded the fabric of the universe and brought them and all their followers to Eileanan in a journey called the Great Crossing. The eleven great clans of Eileanan are all descended from the First Coven, with the MacCuinn clan being the greatest of the eleven. The thirteen witches were Cuinn Lionheart, his son Owein of the Longbow, Ahearn Horse-laird, Aislinna the Dreamer, Berhtilde the Bright Warrior-Maid, Fóghnan the Thistle, Rùraich the Searcher, Seinneadair the Singer, Sian the Storm-Rider, Tuathanach the Farmer, Brann the Raven, Faodhagan the Red and his twin sister Sorcha the Bright (now called the Murderess).

Gearradh: goddess of death; of the Three Spinners, Gearradh is she who cuts the thread.

gillie: personal servant.

gillie-coise: bodyguard.

Gladrielle the Blue: the smaller of the two moons, lavender-blue in colour.

gravenings: ravenous creatures that nest and swarm together, steal lambs and chickens from farmers, and have been known to steal babies and young children. Will eat anything they can carry away in their claws. Collective noun is 'screech'.

Greycloaks: the Rìgh's army, so called because of their camouflaging cloaks.

Harriet: servant to Lady Evaline.

Hogmanay: New Year's Eve; an important celebration in the culture of Eileanan.

Horned Ones: another name for the satyricorns, a race of fierce horned faeries.

Irving: seneschal at Fettercairn Castle.

Isabeau the Shapechanger: Keybearer of the Coven; twin sister of the Banrìgh Iseult NicFaghan.
Iseult of the Snows: twin sister of Isabeau NicFaghan; Banrìgh of Eileanan by marriage to Lachlan the Winged.
Iven Yellowbeard: a jongleur and courier in the service of Lachlan the Winged; was formerly a Yeoman of the Guard; married to Nina the Nightingale and father to Roden.

Jaspar MacCuinn: former Rìgh of Eileanan, often called Jaspar the Ensorcelled. Was married to Maya the Ensorcellor.
Jay the Fiddler: a minstrel in the service of Lachlan the Winged. Was once a beggar-lad in Lucescere and member of the League of the Healing Hand.
Johanna: a healer. Was once a beggar-girl in Lucescere and member of the League of the Healing Hand.
jongleur: a travelling minstrel, juggler, conjurer.
journeywitch: a travelling witch who performs rites for villages that do not have a witch, and seeks out children with magical powers who can be taken on as acolytes.

Kalea: a nisse.
Keybearer: the leader of the Coven of Witches.
Khan'cohbans: a faery race of war-like, snow-skimming nomads who live on the high mountains of the Spine of the World.

Lachlan the Winged: Rìgh of Eileanan.
The League of the Healing Hand: a band of beggar children who were instrumental in helping Lachlan the Winged win his throne.
leannan: sweetheart.
Lewen: an apprentice-witch and squire to Lachlan; son of Lilanthe of the Forest and Niall the Bear.
Lilanthe of the Forest: a tree-shifter; married to Niall the Bear; and mother to Lewen and Meriel.
loch; lochan (pl): lake.
Lucescere: ancient city built on an island above the Shining Waters; the traditional home of the MacCuinns and the Tower of Two Moons.

Mac: son of

MacAhern: one of the eleven great clans; descendants of Ahearn the Horsle-laird.

MacBrann: one of the eleven great clans; descendants of Brann the Raven.

MacCuinn: one of the eleven great clans, descendants of Cuinn Lionheart.

Magnysson the Red: the larger of the two moons, crimson-red in colour, commonly thought of as a symbol of war and conflict. Old tales describe him as a thwarted lover, chasing his lost love, Gladrielle, across the sky.

Malvern MacFerris: lord of Fettercairn Castle; brother of former lord Falkner MacFerris.

Maya the Ensorcellor: former Banrìgh of Eileanan, wife of Jaspar and mother of Bronwen; now known as Maya the Mute.

moonbane: a hallucinogenic drug distilled from the moonflower plant.

necromancy: the forbidden art of resurrecting the dead.

Niall the Bear: formerly a Yeoman of the Guard; now married to Lilanthe of the Forest, and father to Lewen and Meriel.

Nic: daughter of.

Nila: King of the Fairgean; half-brother of Maya the Ensorcellor.

Nina the Nightingale: jongleur and sorceress of the Coven; sister to Didier Laverock, earl of Caerlaverock, and granddaughter of Enit Silverthroat.

nisse: small woodland faery.

Olwynne NicCuinn: daughter of Lachlan MacCuinn and Iseult NicFaghan; twin sister of Owein.

One Power: the life-energy that is contained in all things. Witches draw upon the One Power to perform their acts of magic. The One Power contains all the elemental forces of air, earth, water, fire and spirit, and witches are usually more powerful in one force than others.

Owein MacCuinn: second son of Lachlan MacCuinn and Iseult NicFaghan; twin brother of Olwynne. Has wings like a bird.

prionnsa; prionnsachan (pl): prince, duke.

Ravenscraig: estate of the MacBrann clan. Once their hunting castle, but they moved their home there after Rhyssmadill fell into ruin.

Ravenshaw: deeply forested land west of Rionnagan, ruled by the MacBrann clan, descendants of Brann, one of the First Coven of Witches.

Razor's Edge: dangerous path through the mountains of the Broken Ring of Dubhslain, only used in times of great need.

Red Guards: soldiers in service to Maya the Ensorcellor during her reign as Banrìgh.

Rhiannon: a half-satyricorn; daughter of One-Horn and a captured human.

Rhyssmadill: the Rìgh's castle by the sea, once owned by the MacBrann clan.

rìgh; rìghrean (pl): king.

Rionnagan: together with Clachan and Blèssem, the richest lands in Eileanan. Ruled by MacCuinns, descendants of Cuinn Lionheart, leader of the First Coven of Witches.

Roden: son of Nina the Nightingale and Iven Yellow-beard; Viscount Laverock of Caerlaverock.

Rory: deceased son of Lord Falkner MacFerris of Fettercairn and Lady Evaline NicKinney.

Rurach: wild mountainous land lying between Tìreich and Siantan, and ruled by the MacRuraich clan.

sabre-leopard: savage feline with curved fangs that lives in the remote mountain areas.

sacred woods: ash, hazel, oak, rowan, fir, hawthorn, and yew.

Samhain: first day of winter; festival for the souls of the dead. Best time of year to see the future.

satyricorn: a race of fierce horned faeries.

scrying: to perceive through crystal gazing or other focus. Most witches can scry if the object to be perceived is well known to them.

Seekers: a force created by former Rìgh Jaspar the Ensorcelled to find those with magical abilities so they could be tried and executed.

seelie: a tall, shy race of faeries known for their physical beauty and magical skills.

seneschal: steward.

sennachie: genealogist and record-keeper of the clan chief's house.

sgian dubh: small knife worn in the boot.

Siantan: north-west land of Eileanan, famous for its weather witches. Ruled by the MacSian clan.

skeelie: a village witch or wise woman.

Skill: a common application of magic, such as lighting a candle or dowsing for water.

Spinners: goddesses of fate. Include the spinner Sniomhar, the goddess of birth; the weaver Breabadair, goddess of life; and she who cuts the thread, Gearradh, goddess of death.

Talent: the combination of a witch's strengths in the different forces often manifest as a particularly powerful Talent; for example, Lewen's Talent is in working with wood and Nina's is in singing.

Test of Elements: once a witch is fully accepted into the coven at the age of twenty-four, they learn Skills in the element in which they are strongest, i.e. air, earth, fire, water, or spirit. The First Test of any element wins them a ring which is worn on the right hand. If they pass the Third Test in any one element, the witch is called a sorcerer or sorceress, and wears a ring on their left hand. It is very rare for any witch to win a sorceress ring in more than one element.

Test of Powers: a witch is first tested on his or her eighth birthday, and if any magical powers are detected, he or she becomes an acolyte. On their sixteenth birthday, witches undertake the Second Test of Powers, in which they must make a moonstone ring and witch's dagger. If they pass, they are permitted to become an apprentice. On their twenty-fourth birthday, witches undertake the Third Test of Powers, in which they must remake their dagger and cut and polish a staff. If successfully completed, the apprentice is admitted into the Coven of Witches. Apprentices wear black robes; witches wear white robes.

Theurgia: a school for acolytes and apprentice-witches at the Tower of Two Moons in Lucescere.

thigearn: horse-lairds who ride flying horses.

Tìreich: land of the horse-lairds. Most westerly country of Eileanan, ruled by the MacAhern clan.

Tìrlethan: land of the Twins; ruled by the MacFaghan clan.

Tìrsoilleir: the Bright Land or the Forbidden Land. North-east land of Eileanan, ruled by the MacHilde clan.

Tòmas the Healer: boy with healing powers, who saved the lives of thousands of soldiers during the Bright Wars; died saving Lachlan's life at the Battle of Bonnyblair.

The Towers of the Witches: Thirteen towers built as centres of learning and witchcraft in the twelve lands of Eileanan. Most are now ruined, but the Tower of Two Moons in Lucescere has been restored as the home of the Coven of Witches and its school, the Theurgia. The Coven hope to rebuild the thirteen High Towers but also to encourage towns and regions to build their own towers.

tree-changer: woodland faery that can shift shape from tree to humanlike creature. A half-breed is called a *tree-shifter* and can sometimes look almost human.

trictrac: a form of backgammon.

uile-bheist; uile-bheistean (pl): monster.

Yedda: sea-witches.

Yeomen of the Guard: Also known as the Blue Guards. The Rìgh's own personal bodyguard, responsible for his safety.